M000012185

Dream of Shadows

Seressia Glass

Parker Publishing, LLC

Isis is an imprint of Parker Publishing, LLC.

Copyright © 2007 by Seressia Glass

Published by Parker Publishing, LLC
12523 Limonite Avenue, Suite #440-438
Mira Loma, California 91752
www.parker-publishing.com

All rights reserved. This book is protected under the copyright laws of the United States of America. No part of this publication may be reproduced, stored in a retrieval system, or transmitted in any form or by any means—electronic, mechanical, photocopying, recording, or otherwise—without the prior written permission of the publisher.

This book is a work of fiction. Characters, names, locations, events and incidents (in either a contemporary and/or historical setting) are products of the author's imagination and are being used in an imaginative manner as a part of this work of fiction. Any resemblance to actual events, locations, settings, or persons, living or dead, is entirely coincidental.

ISBN 978-1-60043-030-5

First Edition

Manufactured in the United States of America

Dedication

To Sidney, for her patience and whip-cracking. To my readers, thanks for daring to dream with me.

I had a dream which was not all a dream.

—Lord Byron, *Darkness*

Prologue

"Are you sure you don't want me to get someone to take you to the station?"

"No, Kathy, but thanks," she answered. "It's only a block away, and there's plenty of light. Besides, this will make Ramón feel even worse, knowing I had to walk so far."

"Well, with a husband as fine as that one, I'm sure you won't be mad at him for long."

"You got that right," she cracked back. "See ya tomorrow."

Still laughing, she stepped out into the crisp night air. A sudden wave of disorientation slammed into her, and she had to reach out for the stone wall beside her for support. For a heart-stopping moment, she forgot who she was and what she was doing.

"Hey, are you all right?"

She looked up and saw a young man in medium blue scrubs. Scrubs. He was a nurse. "I'm fine. I think my scrunchie may be too tight or something."

He smiled. "Okay. As long as you're not sick. Seeing a sick nurse might scare the patients away." He rolled his eyes as he moved to the ER entrance. "Yeah right. Like that'll happen."

A nurse. She was a nurse too. Taking a deep breath to exhale the disorientation, she pulled the scrunchie from her hair, attempting to shake the weird feelings she'd been experiencing all week. Working in the ER couldn't be called easy by any means, but she'd never left work feeling like another person before.

"Girl, it's time to seriously think about giving this up," she muttered to herself as she headed for the train station. She always managed to find energy at quitting time, because it meant going home to her husband and

daughter. Volunteering for the late shift had been a tough decision, especially since she spent so little time with little Ismelda, but she and Ramón had agreed that sacrifices now meant they'd be closer to their dream later.

Something wasn't right. The absolute stillness of the night had her pausing, the strange disorientation returning full force. The intermittent street lamps with their orange phosphorescence highlighted the distance between her and the rail station. It was the time of night between revelry and waking, a time when loneliness and danger were magnified. Where was everybody?

"You're being paranoid," she told herself sternly, drawing her jacket closer about her. "Nothing's up and about this time of night anyway." That didn't stop her from stroking her gold crucifix or making the quick gesture her grandmother had taught her as a child, to ward off the evil eye.

A sound had her glancing behind. Glimpsing the shadowy figure in dark sweats was more than enough to trigger a response of flight. She didn't wait to see if it was another nurse, or a policeman. If she was mistaken, she could laugh about it later, in the safety of her home.

Hurried footfalls told her the truth. Someone was chasing her. She broke into a run down the deserted, glistening street, her throat too clogged with fear to scream. Knowing she was being chased, feeling the adrenaline rush of fear surging through her veins. Hoping that safety was a terror-filled sprint away but knowing that it was beyond her reach.

With survival instinct seething through her, sounds became amplified. She heard rainwater dripping from a broken roof drain, the wheezing of her lungs as she pushed her body beyond its capabilities, the harsh breathing of her pursuer, coming ever closer.

Swishing split the damp, dark air as something whizzed over her head, catching about her neck like a thin, spiked rope. She felt her necklace break, the pendant falling away. Her hands clawed at the sharp spikes gouging her neck even as her attacker dragged her from her feet, even as pain sliced into her windpipe, choking off her futile attempt at a scream with a flood of blood.

Nicole jerked upright, kicking her bedcovers away and drawing air into her lungs with a half-scream. Her fingernails dug into her throat, trying to loosen the tightness that had almost suffocated her.

No. *Strangled her.*

She fumbled for the lamp on her nightstand, gasping with relief as light flooded the room. Stumbling to her feet, she fought for air, for escape, for the realization that she still lived. Because in her dream the woman had died, horribly.

She wanted it to be a dream, just a random nightmare from the shadows of her psyche. But it wasn't. No one had dreams in which they could smell, taste, experience things just as real as in the waking world. She'd felt the chill mist that clung to the ground, felt the pounding of the woman's heart and the surging of her blood, felt the sharp metal prongs dig into her neck, breaking the skin before taking her life.

"Stop," she told herself, just to hear a sound other than her ragged breathing. Shivering from more than the dream's chill, Nicole pulled her robe around her curves, then made her way to the bathroom. Flipping on the bright light helped calm her, and splashing her face with cold water drove the last remnants of the dream away from her thoughts.

Splashing away the dream couldn't wash away her feelings, though. Emotions surged through her like a revolving door of aftershocks, with fear uppermost.

The panic she'd felt had been real, absolute. Terror still danced along her nerves like drops of water on a hot griddle. The metallic taste of blood lay thick on her tongue. Her muscles hummed with the need to flee. All from a nightmare.

Except she knew it wasn't a nightmare. The dream that made her heart pound in her chest mirrored everything from the dream she'd had the previous night. One more time, one more night, and she'd know for sure that it wasn't a coincidence.

She gripped the edge of the beige marble sink, head down, sucking in deep, even breaths. It was happening. Again. The dreams had returned, but she didn't want to believe it. If she believed it, she'd have to do something about it.

"Six years," she said aloud, lifting her face to stare at her reflection. Brownish hazel eyes stared back at her out of a rounded face, angry, bitter, afraid. "Six freakin' years of peace and this is how you come back?"

Her voice cracked, and she had to swallow hard to keep the tears away. "I don't want this," she whispered. "I don't want this at all."

Nothing answered her, not that she expected it to. She toweled her face dry, then inspected the cloth, half-surprised not to find blood. Blood had filled the nurse's throat, blood instead of the air she'd desperately needed. What kind of cord had spikes that bit so deep into someone's neck that they choked on their own blood? Who would chase someone down and drag them to the ground so brutally?

"No!" Her voice echoed off the tiles. She clenched her stomach muscles and her teeth with the effort not to vomit. "I won't go back into it. I won't."

The dream still tugged at her, a psychic quicksand threatening to swallow her whole. Fear and adrenaline swirled inside her, a combustible mix. She pushed the emotions and the images away. Telling herself it was perfectly reasonable to leave the bathroom light on, she returned to her bedroom.

She glanced at the clock on the nightstand. The amber readout reminded her of the street lamps in the dream. No, don't think about the dream, think about the time. A quarter to two. Little more than four hours before she had to wake Dani to send her off to school before going to class herself. Normal, practical things that defined her life.

Up until now. She knew better than anyone that some things went beyond the practical and the logical. Some things went beyond what people considered normal.

She reached for her journal in its customary place on her nightstand, noting how her hand shook. The fear wouldn't leave her for a while, not even through purging the dream from her psyche and onto paper. No matter how her mind wanted to rationalize it away, the fact remained that she'd dreamed twice that a nurse had died by a particularly vicious form of strangulation. One more, and the pattern would be set.

She had to stop it. But what could she do?

Go to the police. She latched onto the idea. She could call the crime-stoppers tip line, be completely anonymous . . . .and have no one believe it.

Nicole sighed. If she wanted to tell the police, she'd have to tell them in person. As plans went, she didn't like it, but she didn't have another option.

She did, however, know who to talk to. She scrambled off her bed to retrieve her briefcase. Last semester they'd had a guest lecturer, a Detective Browning. The detective hadn't laughed when someone had asked her if they'd ever used psychics to solve cases. She hadn't said that psychics were kooks out to have their fifteen minutes of fame. Maybe she'd listen to Nicole's story.

Nicole found the detective's information and felt the first true rush of relief since waking from the dream. She'd tell the detective her story, convince her that she spoke the truth, then leave it in the police's hands. It would be all right. It had to be all right.

Chapter One

"Excuse me."

The voice was soft, thrumming with an exotic rhythm. Detective Carter "Jax" Jackson looked up from his perpetual stack of paperwork and found himself staring. Then staring some more.

Class. That word came to mind first as he looked at her. She was the epitome of upper-class Black America, from the cultured voice to the makeup expertly applied to her honeyed features, to the expensive cut and cloth of her clothing. She looked just shy of thirty, her round face unlined, although her cognac-colored eyes seemed aged and weighted by her thoughts.

Elegant and gorgeous, but not the pencil-thin, it's-a-sin-to-have-dessert type of woman. No, she curved the way a woman should curve, all delicious roundness under her scooped-neck burgundy sweater and tailored charcoal trousers. She was beautiful.

And way out of his league.

"Is there something I can help you with, Mrs. . . . ?" Yeah, he knew he was fishing, but damned if he was going to stop.

"Ms.," she corrected him. "Nicole Legère." She shifted her coat and purse, both made of soft, expensive black leather, before taking his hand, gripping it firmly.

"Jackson. Detective Carter Jackson." Her hand was smooth in his, though slightly damp and trembling.

"Detective Jackson." She acknowledged his introduction with a slight nod and a slighter smile that made her seem upset. "I was looking for Detective Browning, but they told me that she's not here."

"No, she's out on maternity leave. Perhaps I can help you?" He'd never used the word *perhaps* in his life, but this woman made him want to mind his manners and remember his SAT words.

Her gaze flitted about the bustling squad room. "Is there somewhere we can talk privately?"

Intrigued, Jax released her hand. "Of course. Follow me."

He led her through a sea of desks, people, and paperwork, wishing all the while that she was walking in front of him. Few things got him going like watching a sophisticated woman walk.

Cool it, Jax, he thought to himself. *You act like it's been years since you've seen a gorgeous woman. This is business.*

Choosing the first empty conference room he came to, he steered her inside, gestured her to a chair, then shut the door. She draped her coat over the back of the chair, then settled in, crossing her legs at the shins and keeping her knees firmly pressed together, with her purse clutched in both hands atop them.

The ring finger on her left hand was bare, he noted. He smiled to put her at ease. "How do you know Detective Browning?"

Her gaze rested on his, and he felt something, everything, jump deep inside. "I met her last semester, at Georgia State," she explained. "She did a talk for one of my psychology classes."

Beautiful and smart, but she seemed too mature and sophisticated to be a coed. Jax straightened his posture. "Are you a professor there?"

She smiled. "No, I'm finishing my doctorate in psychology. Almost done, thank goodness."

He enjoyed her smile for a moment, then regretfully steered the conversation back. "If you want Browning's notes or something, I can try to contact her for you."

Like throwing a switch, her smile disappeared. "Actually, I didn't come to talk to her about class."

Whatever Nicole Legère wanted to talk about, it obviously wasn't a happy subject. Jax assumed an open, friendly position. "What did you want to talk to her about, Ms. Legère? Maybe I can help."

She took a deep breath, leaving Jax hard-pressed to keep his eyes on her face instead of dropping lower. "I'd like to report a murder."

"What?" He sat forward, hoping he hadn't heard her right. Surely he hadn't heard her right. She repeated her statement with the same calm as before.

Something definitely sounded off. Her eyes swept the office, him, everything, constantly on the move. "Who was murdered? And why come to the precinct instead of calling 9-1-1?" Jax asked, already dreading the answer.

She looked down, her fingers entwining in the straps of her supple leather purse. Her shoulders bunched together as if she were a bird about to take flight. "Because it hasn't happened yet."

Jax sighed. Great. Just great. A beautiful woman glides into his precinct, asks for his help, and turns out to be off her rocker.

Except she didn't look crazy to him. She looked concerned, collected, and classy, but certainly not crazy. Not ready to throw her out, Jax decided to try a different tack.

"Have you or someone you know been threatened?"

"No," she replied, her accent softening the word. "I don't know her, but she's in trouble. Or will be."

"And this person is?"

She loosened her grip on the purse, settling it on the floor before fixing him with an earnest stare. "She's an emergency room nurse at one of the area hospitals. As she heads for the train station, someone chases her, catches her, then strangles her."

Jax resisted the urge to look around for the hand basket his day had just hopped in. Being stuck doing paperwork while his partner was off following up a lead was bad enough. Ending up in a private office with a beautiful woman who wanted to report a murder, *a murder that hadn't happened yet*, definitely didn't top the list of how he wanted to spend his day.

He allowed himself to get a little pissed and to show it. "So what, are you telling me that you've had a premonition or something?"

Something crept into her expression, a blend of wariness and pride. "That's exactly what I'm telling you, Detective Jackson."

The temperature in the room dropped several degrees, driven down by the chill in her voice. Not that Jax gave a damn, mind you. "Ms. Lejeune—"

"Legère."

"Legère," he conceded. He sat forward in his chair, piercing her with a less-than-friendly look. "I'm sure you realize that the Atlanta Police Department has a significant caseload. Wasting the department's time with frivolous charges could get you in a lot of trouble."

Irritation marred the perfection of her features as her purse landed at her feet with a thump. She rose to her feet, settling her hands to her hips in the classic pissed-off-Black-woman pose.

"Detective Jackson. I understand how valuable your time is. Mine is equally so. I am doing my duty by reporting a crime, even though it hasn't occurred yet. I certainly don't believe that what I'm doing is frivolous." She grabbed her coat off the back of the chair, then leaned over to snatch her purse off the floor.

"Wait." It must have been the flash of cleavage, full and sweet against the v-neck of her sweater. Jax couldn't think of another reason why he ignored her attitude and the urge to let her keep walking to the door.

"Why don't I take your statement now, just for the record?" His tone was reasonable, meant to soothe. He'd throw the damn file away tomorrow. "That way, we can have your information on file."

When she didn't turn, he added, "Please."

She returned to her seat, still defensive but somewhat mollified. "Believe it or not, Detective, this isn't easy for me. I know you think I'm certifiable at the very worse or hallucinating at the very best. I'm not. Someone is going to die, horribly. If I don't convince you, if I don't try to do something—"

"What?"

Her gaze shifted to the plaques on the wall behind him. "I don't want her death on my conscience."

Jax leaned back in his chair again, wanting to put a little distance between himself and the woman he suddenly couldn't pin down. She seemed so sincere. But then, most lunatics were perfectly sincere in their madness.

But Nicole Legère didn't look crazy to him. Worry creased her forehead, and she had her wavy hair, a mixture of gold, bronze and brown, gathered at the nape of her neck. Simple gold hoops graced the lobes of her ears, the only sign of jewelry. She was the picture of a successful career woman with no time or patience for flights of fancy. And her eyes, large, whiskey-colored doe eyes, the kind of eyes he was a sucker for, shone with her sincerity.

He blinked away his thoughts. Sure, he was paid to notice things about people, but paying too much attention to this woman would definitely be bad for his blood pressure. He pulled a ballpoint pen and notebook from his jacket pocket. "Let me get some contact information from you. Then you can tell me everything you know."

Without hesitation she gave him her phone number and address, a neighborhood known for its security, family atmosphere, and high prices. Either she'd married and divorced well, or her family had money. He'd bet the latter was the case in her situation. "All right, now tell me everything you know about the victim, the possible victim."

She ran her palms across her tops of her thighs as if drying sudden perspiration. Jax followed the movement, trying not to imagine what her bare thighs would look like.

"I don't know her name. Like I said before, she's a nurse at one of the downtown hospitals. Hispanic, I think. She was thinking about her husband Ramón and how they have to struggle to spend time with each other and their daughter Ismelda. Her husband and daughter are her whole world.

"When she gets off work after eleven, someone named Kathy asks her if she needs a ride to the station, but the nurse laughs and says she doesn't need one because it's not that far. The night is misty, and everything has that funky orange glow because of the streetlights. She wonders why there isn't anyone else around because it's always so busy. It's so quiet that it freaks her out.

"She looks back and sees a man—he's wearing a hooded sweatshirt and dark pants, but his face is blurry. He scares her enough to make her run, even though she feels like a fool, until she realizes he's catching up to her. Something flies over her head, a cord of some kind, with metal spikes that bite into her neck, tearing away the crucifix she always wears as she's knocked off her feet. She's suffocating and then the chain digs into her throat. There's pain, then blood, then nothing."

She stopped with a ragged breath, then covered her face with shaking hands, leaning forward to rest her elbows on her knees. Quiet filled the office, punctuated by the bustle beyond the door. Jax let the silence continue, keeping his gaze on the woman across from him as she regained her composure.

Sighing, she dropped her hands and gave him a watery look of resignation. "You don't believe me."

"Why the hell should I?" He made his voice deliberately harsh, feeling a minute twinge of guilt when she flinched. "A Hispanic nurse is going to be strangled as she goes home from work. That's all the information you have? You don't know where, you don't know who, and you don't know when?"

"It will happen in the next few days," she corrected him. "Before the week is over, she'll be dead."

Truth weighted her words. She believed the line she fed him. He refrained from rubbing at his forehead. "This is an incredible story. Even you have to admit that."

"I can. I do."

"Then why should I believe you? How can you possibly know something like this?"

She dug into her purse, coming up with a packet of tissues. Pulling one out, she dabbed at the corners of her eyes. "If you think coming down here telling this story is my idea of fun, you're mistaken," she informed him in an unsteady tone. "I have a full load at school, an internship, and a terrific daughter who is my entire world. My life is almost perfect. I don't need these premonitions. I didn't ask for them, and I sure don't want them. They come when they come, and if I don't at least try to do something about them, I pay."

"Premonitions?"

She looked at him as if he'd misunderstood her. "That's what I said."

Great. Just freaking great. He put down his pen with a precise movement. "So you're telling me you're some sort of psychic?"

Caution crept into her gaze. "Not intentionally or professionally," she answered. "I don't receive messages the way other psychics do. Psychic impressions come to me through my dreams."

Now he'd heard everything. He bit back a smile. "Through your dreams, huh?"

Ice seeped through the wariness. "Yes, through dreaming. If the same dream occurs three times, it invariably comes true."

Indulgence curved his lips into a smile. He could see the joke, even if she couldn't. "A psychic who dreams the future." He shook his head. "Somehow, you don't seem to be the type."

"The type." That pushed a button. Jax watched a flush of color sweep up her neck to her ears. "And exactly what type do I seem to be, Detective?" she asked, her voice deceptively calm.

He full on gave her the look he'd been surreptitiously using before, taking his time, measuring her. "Well, for one thing, you're solid."

"Solid." The word came out of her mouth as if she'd tasted something nasty.

Jackson gestured, sweeping her head to toe. "Yeah, you know, full of common sense. Steady, dependable."

Her jaw dropped. "Detective Jackson—"

"You don't strike me as someone who would be into weird stuff. Next you're going to tell me aliens exist."

She swallowed whatever retort she'd been about to make, leaving Jax slightly disappointed. It would have been refreshing to hear a crude word come from that lovely, cultured mouth.

The spark in her whiskey eyes held a wealth of meaning, however. "Detective Jackson. For someone who supposedly makes a career out of reading people, you couldn't be further away from the truth."

"What truth? Yours?" He climbed to his feet, leaning over the desk toward her. "Dreams and psychics and preordained murder? I don't think so."

She joined him in getting to her feet. "Just because you're too narrow-minded to believe it doesn't make a thing less true."

"You know what I believe? I believe your dinner disagreed with you, causing you to have a nightmare. And something on your conscience made you come here to report it."

He put down his pen. "I'm sorry you're having nightmares, Ms. Legère," he continued in a tone that unapologetically doubted everything about her. "I'm certainly not an expert in that department, but I'd recommend some sleep aids, maybe even a change in diet."

"You arrogant, thickheaded son-of-a—" She bit back her words with an effort. Her eyes sparked fire as her hand came up in a fist.

Blowing out a breath, she stepped back, forcing her hand back down to her side. "You don't know me. You don't know anything about me. Save your snap judgments for criminals."

She gathered her expensive belongings and whirled for the door, but speared him with a withering glance. "I've done what I came here to do, despite being insulted by some Neanderthal. What you do with the information is entirely up to you. I just hope it's not too late when you decide I'm telling the truth."

"Ms. Legère?"

She spun back to face him. "Yes?"

He smiled, though he no longer saw humor in the situation. "Trust me on one thing: If it is too late, you'll be the first to know."

Her eyes darkened. "Of course I'll be the first to know. I'm psychic, remember?"

Chapter Two

Nicole gripped the steering wheel, imagining with savage joy her fingers wrapped around the detective's neck instead. Then remembering why she'd gone to see him in the first place, she quickly abandoned the image. Yet the anger still simmered inside her.

How dare he demean her like that! Dismissing her dream as a case of acid indigestion!

The car suddenly shuddered as if it had thrown a rod, and the radio suddenly spit and hissed. Her heart hammering, Nicole wrestled the car over to the curb. She had to get her emotions under control before she destroyed the car.

She worked hard to keep her life calm; she wasn't about to let some jerk of a detective send her into a psychic temper tantrum.

Humiliation clawed up her throat but she forced it back. Detective Jackson had gotten to her. He'd had the nerve to call her solid, but she'd describe him the same way. Solid and cool like concrete, a suggestion that he was comfortable in his own skin. As nervous and unsure as she'd been when she first entered the precinct, he'd managed to put her at ease—at least, until he'd heard her story.

Checking her rearview mirror, she eased back into traffic. Remembering the way he'd looked at her brought heat to her cheeks again. Who did the man think he was, calling her solid? She'd show him solid.

She took her frustration out on the slow-moving driver in front of her, laying on the horn. Had she really expected anything other than Detective Jackson's response? She'd gone to the precinct with vague hopes and even vaguer information. She'd really wanted him to say that they'd look into it, that they'd handle it, even if he hadn't meant it. She'd wanted the responsibility taken from her hands. Instead, she'd been all but arrested or laughed right out the door.

It would have been different back home, she thought. Back home, people listened when Legère women spoke to them. Back home, people tried repeatedly to get a Legère woman to use her gifts for profit.

She wasn't back home.

She'd turned her back on her abilities and her family six years ago, essentially running away from New Orleans and the burden of being a Legère. If she herself had dismissed her heritage, how the hell could she expect someone like Detective Carter Jackson to take her seriously?

As she pulled into her driveway, her next-door neighbor, Gertie Bruce, came out her front door. "Nicole, what you doing home so early?"

"Hello, Miss Gertie." Nicole exited the car, slammed the door shut for good measure, then crossed to her neighbor's yard. Everyone on the block considered the eighty-something Gertie Bruce to be the neighborhood busybody, including Gertie herself.

It didn't bother Nicole though. Miss Gertie loved visiting with Dani while Nicole ran errands, and she knew her daughter loved the old woman. Besides, Nicole felt comforted knowing that someone on the street knew what went on, so she didn't mind Gertie being a one-woman neighborhood watch. "I'm not going to afternoon classes today."

"What's wrong?" Syrup-brown eyes, bright with concern, swept over her. Gertie, who'd outlived a husband and two sons, always reminded Nicole of a bird, especially when the older woman cocked her head to one side, as she did now. Even her arms, poised so her fists rested on her hips and draped in a pale wool shawl, brought to mind a small brown bird poised for flight.

Nicole sighed away her fanciful thoughts. "Nothing and everything."

The older woman gestured toward the steps, and Nicole stopped to scratch Perseus, Gertie's hound dog, behind the ears before following. "That sounds like a reason to break out the chamomile tea. I've got some fresh orange-banana muffins just out of the oven. Low fat, not that you need to worry about that."

Gertie laughed, showing a row of teeth she was proud to call her own. Especially since she'd paid for them.

Nicole hesitated. She enjoyed spending time with her neighbor, despite the older woman's penchant for digging into her personal life, or lack thereof. She checked up on Miss Gertie almost as often as Miss Gertie checked up on her. At that moment, however, she needed to decide what to do about her dreams, and the last person she could talk to about that was Gertie Bruce.

Still, it wouldn't hurt to have tea and conversation. It definitely wouldn't hurt putting off a decision for an hour or two. "I'd love some tea, thanks."

"Good. Have a sit-down and I'll be right back. It's a beautiful day to be outside."

Nicole made her way up the steps as her neighbor went inside for tea, then peered through the screen door. "Isn't it too chilly for you to be outside, Miss Gertie?"

What she could see of the hallway exploded with growing things from floor to ceiling, like a conservatory. Nicole knew the rest of the house was just as covered. Some older women did cats or crochet; Miss Gertie did plants. "I know it's March, but there's still a nip in the air."

Gertie's laugh floated out the door. "Child, you think I'm worried about a little chill? It just puts a pep in your step, that's all."

Nicole saw her come up the hallway bearing a loaded tray. She opened the door for the older woman.

"Besides," Gertie added, "who can stay cooped up inside, away from nature all the time?"

Nicole tried to take the tray from the elderly woman, but Gertie shooed her away. "I'm old, not decrepit," Gertie said. "The magic of an afternoon like this gives me strength."

"Magic of an afternoon?" Nicole let her gaze roam over the yard. Pollen season had started early, thanks to unseasonably warm weather two weeks ago. Yet a foggy chill packed the air, dampening the fluorescent yellow that blanketed everything and reminding her that winter could sneak back in at any time.

Gertie set the wooden tray on a weathered wicker table. Nicole cautiously lowered herself into a matching chair, afraid it would give away this time for sure if she breathed too deeply. The muffins, wrapped in a green cloth napkin nestled in a straw basket, steamed in the afternoon chill. The sunny yellow teapot and butter dish painted with multicolored tulips brightened the afternoon.

"If there's anything magic around here, it's got to be your muffins," Nicole said, retrieving one. "I swear, if more people could eat your muffins, the world would be a better place."

"Oh, I don't know about that," Gertie said, pouring them both cups of tea. "I just think nothing's better when you're feeling down than a hot cup of tea and a fresh bit of sweetness."

Nicole spread butter onto the halves of her muffin. "Are you feeling down, Miss Gertie?"

"No, child, not me." Gertie looked at her as she dolloped honey into her teacup. "I'm talking about you."

Nicole froze in mid-bite. "Me?"

The older woman gave her a stern look that reminded Nicole of her mother. "You can fool yourself all you want, Nicole Legère, but you can't fool Gertie Bruce. You're the only one looking down-in-the-mouth 'round here."

Nicole sat up straighter in the woven chair. "I guess I shouldn't have slammed the car door so loud, huh?"

"You weren't exactly skipping down the walk singing when you left this morning," Gertie recalled.

"Yeah." Nicole felt heat rise to her cheeks. She'd never before been snappish with Danielle and her friends, no matter how exuberant the six-year-olds became, but this morning definitely wouldn't have won her any brownie points with *Good Parenting*.

"Would you like to talk about it?"

"Well." Nicole hesitated. While it would be good to unload on someone, Gertie wasn't exactly her first choice. The only person she felt would really understand and help was her father, far away in New Orleans. If she contacted her father, however, her mother would catch wind of it. She wasn't sure she was ready to involve her mother in this, whatever this was. For sure, it was one more event to prove she wasn't capable of following in her mother's psychic footsteps.

Gertie reached over and touched her hand. "Listen up, child, I'm the neighborhood watch, not the neighborhood snitch. Sometimes a body needs to talk. Even if the problem doesn't get solved, you get the pressure off your chest and you can think clearly."

She poured more tea for herself, then topped off Nicole's cup. "I would never betray your confidence, I hope you know that."

"I know that, Miss Gertie." She did, somehow. Everyone knew Miss Gertie knew everything, but not everyone knew what Miss Gertie knew. If she asked the older woman to keep it in confidence, Miss Gertie certainly would.

Nicole lifted her teacup, stalling. How in the world could she tell her neighbor about her dreams and what they meant? Outside of the family and a few paranormal junkies, no one knew about her sporadic abilities. After that fiasco of a meeting with Detective Jackson, she really wanted to keep it that way.

"You talk about magic a lot, Miss Gertie," she said, not really changing the subject. "You speak as if you actually believe in magic."

"Of course I do," her neighbor replied, settling back in her chair. Her white hair, tamed into two braids wound into flat discs on either side of her head, glinted in the afternoon light.

"Magic's all around you." Miss Gertie dropped a chunk of muffin on the wooden-slat floor, and Perseus gobbled it quickly. Nicole had never seen the hound move so fast. "Take my azaleas, for instance. In a few weeks they're going to burst with color."

"That's botany, not magic," Nicole felt compelled to point out to her.

"Just because science can explain a thing doesn't reduce its magic," Gertie informed her. "A few hundred years ago, people thought the earth renewed itself in spring because the gods made it so. It wasn't too long ago that people believed spirits and their ancestors helped their crops and would leave out little offerings for them. Some parts of the world still remember."

Her voice saddened. "Sometimes I think we've lost that, the belief in magic. And that's a tragic thing."

Nicole felt worse than she had when she came home. "I didn't mean to make you sad, Miss Gertie."

Gertie reached over and covered her hand with her tiny brown one. "Ah, it's not your fault, child. It just saddens me sometimes that people nowadays are too busy living their lives to notice the magic that's around them, the magic of simple things."

"What about other kinds of magic?" Nicole asked. "Not just nature magic, but like moving things around or making things appear?"

"You mean like Siegfried and Roy?" Gertie chose another muffin with her trademark laugh. "I'm not sure I'd call what they do magic. Magical is more like it."

Her eyes twinkled. "Now those twin boys, they know how to put on a show. What are their names?"

Nicole coughed on a bite of muffin. "You mean the ones calling themselves The Brothers Mystère?"

"Oh, yes, those are the ones." Miss Gertie sat back in her chair. "Fine, fine-looking men. If I were a few years younger and they were a few years older, you know what I mean?" She laughed again. "Maybe we should see about getting you introduced when they come to town."

"Thanks all the same, Miss Gertie," Nicole said, "but I'm not interested." Especially since they were her brothers, a fact she didn't feel necessary to point out to her neighbor.

"Hhmph." The older woman made her opinion clear. "You're a good mother and a good student. When you gonna take the time to be a woman?"

Nicole sighed. Their conversations always came around the same corner eventually. "Really, Miss Gertie, I don't have the time or the inclination to get involved with anyone, especially right now."

Uninvited, an image of Detective Jackson rose in her mind. The build of a football player, tall and wide, with smooth walnut skin, dark eyes more brown than black, the hard slant of his lips softened by a moustache, and thick dark hair tamed into a brush-cut. She'd felt something when he'd taken her hand, she just wasn't sure what. Relief, hope? Something that made her think everything would be all right. Instead, Detective Jackson had let her down, hard.

She shook away her thoughts. "What about psychics, ESP and all of that? Do you believe any of that can be real?"

Gertie leaned back in her chair again, fixing Nicole with an unblinking brown-eyed stare. "Some say there's a world out there where myth and magic are real, where the energy of the Universe touches all and changes all. Folks are so busy with their lives or just too plain scared to see it, so they've lost their belief. It's a shame, though, because losing your belief can cost you your blessings and your gifts. Me, I like being blessed. It just so happens I use my gift to nurture and make things grow."

She laughed. "Though I suppose some would say my gift's in knowing what a somebody's about to do before they do." Fathomless eyes slid over Nicole's face. "How do you use your gift?"

Taken aback—way the heck aback—Nicole busied herself with drinking tea. She could deny she had a gift, but that would be lying and she'd never excelled at lies. No one in the family did—not with that many psychics running around.

A depressed smile curved her lips. "I suppose I'm one of the great unwashed masses who've squandered their gifts."

"Do you really believe that?"

A heavy sigh escaped Nicole as her gaze wandered over the yard. Early afternoon sunlight tried its best to warm the air, but winter stubbornly refused to relinquish its grip just yet. It would be time to fetch Danielle soon, time to decide what to do. "There are days when I think I'm doing all right, but now I don't know."

She returned her teacup to the table. "I've failed a lot of people, including myself. I don't want to be a failure anymore."

"You haven't taken a good look at yourself lately, have you?" Miss Gertie broke off another chunk of muffin for her dog. "Otherwise you'd know your words aren't true. If you need reminding, then I guess I'm the one to remind you, 'cause old Perseus ain't much for talking."

The old woman wiped her hands on a napkin, then shifted forward in her chair, fixing Nicole with a righteous stare. "You raise your daughter all by yourself, never asking for help from nobody, even when they offer it to you. You go to college to get a fancy psychology degree, and you work to pay for it. Somehow in the middle of all that, you got time to keep up a beautiful house."

Miss Gertie leaned back. "I don't see no failure around here."

Well, Nicole thought. She'd just been set straight. "You're right, Miss Gertie. In my mind, I know you're right. I'm doing better than I thought. But in my heart, I still have doubts."

Gertie took her hand again. Despite the thin, papery skin and fragile bone, Nicole could feel the strength in her grip. "The heart's a powerful thing," Gertie said. "You just need to use it to your advantage. I can see something weighs heavily on you, child, and I believe it's gonna get worse before it gets better. But you're a whole lot stronger than you give yourself credit. Believe in yourself. You're never given more than you're meant to handle."

Disquieted, Nicole changed the subject to one of Miss Gertie's favorites, gardening. Another twenty minutes and she excused herself with the truthful explanation of getting Danielle from kindergarten and calling her boss to explain her absence.

Talking with Miss Gertie left her full and comforted, but not any closer to solving her problems. The thought of going to bed and facing the third dream filled her stomach with icy dread. Out of options, she sent a text message to her father's mobile phone, asking him to call her privately.

She hadn't planned to pull her father into the middle of her problem, but she didn't know what else to do. Besides, her father understood what it felt like to have sporadic talent.

She'd spent her youth in awe of her powerful mother, especially since she'd gone through much of her childhood without any of the abilities a First Daughter should possess. So her father had been the one she could always talk to, the one she ran to for every scraped knee or bruised feeling. Her father had understood why she'd left home, even if he'd never approved.

Ten minutes later, her phone rang. "Daddy?"

"Is Danielle hurt?" her father answered by way of greeting. "Are you in any trouble?"

"No, Dad." *Except for a police detective who thinks I'm certifiable, things are peachy-keen.*

"Why then would you text me instead of leaving a message? Do you want to give your old man a heart attack?"

"First of all, you're healthier than most men half your age," Nicole answered, glad to hear her father's voice, and gladder that he still didn't sound upset. Yet. "Second, I didn't really want Mom to know about this."

Silence. After a moment she thought she heard her father sigh. "You know I won't keep anything from your mother, especially if it concerns our children or the Business."

He capitalized it the way people capitalize Family when talking about the mafia. Nicole supposed that placing psychic women where their talents did the most good *was* the family business. Much easier to swallow that name than the "calling," or the alliterative Legère Legacy.

"I know, Dad." Nicole felt tired already. "I just—I just need your expertise."

Another thick silence, then, "Have your dreams returned?"

"I'm not really sure," she answered honestly. "It feels different somehow. But just in case, I thought I'd get your advice." If anyone could help her, her father could. Stefan Antonescu had led the parapsychology community for her entire lifetime. His work in cataloguing psychic phenomena had led him to her mother in the first place.

"Are you still keeping your journal?" her father asked, slipping into a scientific tone. His tone made her dreams seem more like an everyday occurrence instead of a paranormal experience, reassuring her.

"Yes, but not diligently," she admitted. "I've got a heavy load at school."

"Don't think about what you're writing down," her father cautioned. "If you do, you'll automatically edit yourself and the dreams. It's about getting the raw data down on paper, not writing a best seller."

Nicole laughed in spite of herself, feeling some of the tension ease from her shoulders. "Okay, Dad."

"Just let your mind relax while you're getting the dream down," he continued. "You might even do some automatic writing during the process. Once you've done all you can without thinking about it, you can write down a detailed analysis. I suppose if you weren't diligent with the journal, then you haven't been filming your sleep?"

"I haven't slept with a camera on since college," Nicole said, wondering if she'd disappointed her father by abandoning the process. The dreams had begun in her fourteenth year, after she and the family had given up on her displaying any of the abilities that her brothers and sisters had been born with. Once they'd discovered that some of her dreams were extraordinary, a camera had been installed in her room.

It had been strange at first, but she'd eventually adjusted so well to it that it had been even stranger when she'd stopped filming her sleep while married to Randall.

"If you don't have a camera now, you'll need another," her father said with his customary briskness. "Do you have enough money to buy one?"

"Dad!"

"How am I to know if I do not ask?" her father retorted, his accent becoming pronounced. "I'm not so old that I do not remember what it's like to be a starving college student. You've barely used any of your savings."

Savings. A euphemistic word for the trust fund she'd received on her twenty-fifth birthday. At several million dollars, it had served as the engine of her escape, the machine that made her life in Atlanta possible.

"I'm fine, Dad," she said, feeling like a teen instead of a thirty-one-year-old mother. "I use enough for school and to maintain the house. I'm not going to let Dani starve. Just because I ran away from home doesn't mean I'm irresponsible."

Regret hit her as soon as the words left her mouth. "I'm sorry, Dad. You didn't deserve that."

"No, I didn't." He cleared his throat. "These dreams, are they serious? I ask because your mother has been restless for several days, and I wonder if there is a connection."

Nicole felt a stab of concern. "Is she all right?"

"You know your mother," Stefan said with obvious affection and exasperation. "If she doesn't want you to know something, you won't know something. But truly, she doesn't have a definite sense of anything happening."

"I've only had two of these dreams, and they haven't been about the family," Nicole said, reaching for the journal she took everywhere. "I don't even know the woman I've seen. I'd hoped you could tell me how to pick up on anything so that I can find out who she is."

"You know I will do anything I can for you," her father answered. "You will need to buy another video camera tonight if you've already had two dreams. I think you should also try to meditate. If you don't have the third dream tonight—and even if you do—I want you to meditate morning and evening. It will help clarify your mind. And Nicolette?"

"Yes, Dad?"

"No matter what, your mother and I are and always will be here for you, as parents first. Do you understand?"

"Yes." She understood. She just hadn't been able to believe, still had difficulty believing it. The Legacy had dominated all their lives. It now threatened to pull her back in whether she wanted it to or not.

"Call me if you need anything, anything at all."

"I will, Dad. I promise."

After disconnecting, she took chicken breasts out of the freezer for dinner. Realizing she had a half-hour before needing to leave to pick up Dani, she decided to try her father's suggestion and attempt a short meditation. Even if nothing happened, she'd at least soothe her frazzled nerves some.

In the living room, she lit a lavender-scented candle, then kicked back in her recliner. Folding her fingers over her stomach, she closed her eyes and focused on her breathing, grounding herself. Almost at once, she felt herself relaxing into the chair, drifting into the sound of her breathing, her heartbeat.

A fire danced in the darkness of the night. Millions of stars swirled overhead, different yet familiar. From the other side of the fire, a woman got to her feet. A clay-red robe wrapped her dark, honed body, and a gold circlet wrapped her forehead. Her eyes were ageless, mysterious, commanding. On her upturned palms she balanced an ornately carved wooden box that seemed to glow with an inner fire. She held it out.

Nicole hesitated. The box drew her like a compass pointing north, the urge to open it burning inside her. *I am what you have been seeking,* a voice whispered through her in a language known yet unknown. *I am what you have been missing.*

The woman thrust the box at her again, this time in unspoken demand. Nicole found she couldn't resist the powerful command that was more compulsion than order. She stretched one hand towards the box, her fingers warming at touching the intricate carved lid. A murmur rose around her but she ignored it. Her breath caught at the feeling of welcome that spread through her. Sure now, she lifted the lid. Golden bright light burst out, wrapping around her in blissful joy at being freed—

A sharp crack snapped Nicole out of her meditation. The crystal candleholder had shattered, sending wax and flames across the runner on the coffee table. Without thinking, she grabbed a pillow off the couch, smothering the flames. Shaking, she wadded up runner, pillow, and wax, taking the warm mess to the kitchen to douse with cold water.

It took a couple of moments to slow her down her heart. This had never happened before. She'd always made sure to buy heavyweight candleholders just so they wouldn't shatter. The timing of the break unnerved her. Nothing happened by coincidence, not where her family was concerned. But what did it mean? For that matter, what did the imagery in her meditation mean?

She ran her hands down her arms to suppress a shiver. She'd get the camcorder as her father suggested, but she doubted if she'd meditate again. She didn't need more weird occurrences.

Gathering the soaking mess into a trash bag, she headed out to pick up Dani and her friends from school, determined to put the event, and the dreams, out of her mind.

Chapter Three

The spiked cord tightened around her throat, ripping the skin, breaking through her larynx and making it impossible to scream—

"Mamma, wake up!"

Nicole broke through the surface of the dream like someone finding air after nearly drowning. "Oh God, help me!"

"Mamma, are you all right?" Hands shook her.

The obvious fright in that voice jerked Nicole firmly back into the waking world. Nicole opened her eyes to look into her daughter's tear-streaked face. "I'm fine, Dani," she managed to say, though it was far from the truth.

"You scared me."

She wrapped her daughter in her arms. "I'm sorry, sweetie. It was just a bad dream."

But it wasn't.

The third dream had come upon her, just when she'd thought she had embarrassed herself for nothing with that detective. Just when she had relaxed her guard, she had begun to hope that the second night of dreaming had been no more than her own fear imposed upon her subconscious. Now she knew better.

She set her fear aside long enough to comfort her daughter, rocking Danielle until she fell asleep. Nicole settled her against the pillows, then got out of bed to stop the camcorder. Back home, her father had catalogued each day's tape with the date, the subject, and the dream's sequential number. She'd never, not once, looked at any of the tapes. It had been bad enough reliving the dreams by recording them in her journal.

Sighing, she returned to bed and the waiting journal. She'd have to call her father, tell him about the third dream, so much stronger and different than the other two. He'd probably want the tape and she'd gladly send it to him. It would probably be a good idea to send him copies of her journal entries. First, she had to record the last dream, so different from the last two. Before, she'd been an observer. This time, however, she'd been the nurse.

She'd felt each and every panicked, pain-filled second as if it were her own, and it terrified her.

She stretched out on the bed, careful not to disturb Dani. As her father had instructed, she turned off her inner editor and let the words flow. Her pen flew across the page, scrawling details that caused fear to swarm over her again. Four pages, five, six. By the time she finished, she had to fight to prevent herself from sobbing aloud. The poor nurse was dead, leaving behind a daughter and a husband, and she hadn't had enough information to prevent it.

"I'm so sorry," she whispered into the quiet. "I'm so sorry I failed you. Please forgive me."

Jax stood in the muck and mud of a narrow alley, trying to ignore the brutal downpour beating down on him. Blue and red lights from the crush of emergency vehicles obliterated the pale orange glow of the lamps lining the street at the mouth of the alley. The lights combined with the flashbulbs of the crime scene photographer to induce a stunner of a headache.

Head pain was the least of his problems.

"What have you got?"

Murphy Murdoch, the forensic specialist, stood beside him. A large man with a shock of red hair, Murdoch always wore the expression of someone who had just finished a good long belly laugh. Today, with his hair plastered to his head, he looked more like an overweight, half-drowned leprechaun.

He passed Jax a plastic-shrouded wallet. “Name’s Ananda Gutierrez. She’s a nurse.”

She’s a nurse, at one of the downtown hospitals . . . Hispanic . . . .

The nearest hospital was less than five blocks away. The closest MARTA station, a block and a half.

“Assailant came up behind her, got her around the neck,” Murdoch continued. “Bruises on the side of the neck are consistent with rope marks, but puncture wounds to the throat suggest metal spikes of some sort. He dragged her, struggling all the way, to about here. Then he finished what the spikes started by strangling her.”

He follows her, catches her, strangles her . . . .

Jax looked down at the body, already bagged and zipped. “Did you find her before the rain started?” he asked, dreading the answer.

“Nope,” Murdoch said cheerfully, which meant he was royally pissed. “Thanks to Mother Nature, we got jack for evidence. Witness found her around six, and it was already raining then. Uniforms got here fifteen minutes after the call with paramedics right behind. They tried to preserve what they could, but it was already screwed to hell.”

“Crap.”

That eloquent comment came from Detective Cedric “Bear” Marshall as he stepped gingerly through the rust-colored muck towards them. They’d become good friends in the five years that they’d been partners, despite the fact that Jax was a UGA grad and Bear had the misfortune of being a Buckeye. They were so alike in temperament as well as their build that they’d earned the nickname “The Brothers Grim.”

“Yeah, there’s probably some of that around here too,” Murdock said in response to Bear’s comment, adding a long-suffering sigh. “Not exactly the cleanest of scenes.”

He looked down at the bodybag, trying to see something, anything else that would assist them. “The state of her clothing—no visible rips or tears—suggests an absence of sexual assault. Purse looked to be in the same position it originally fell, halfway between here and the entrance to the alley. Money and credit cards are still inside."

Bear shifted his weight. "So he either didn't have time to get the money, or robbery wasn't the motive in the first place."

"Whatever this was supposed to be, it wasn't robbery," Murdoch said. "Her eyes are gone."

"What?"

"The bastard took her eyes," Murdoch said again. "And not gouged out either—technique so neat, it was almost surgical."

Jax suppressed a groan. If it wasn't a case of robbery or rape, that left them two choices. One, that someone she knew wanted Ananda Gutierrez out of the picture. Two, that she was killed for the hell of it. He hoped it wasn't the latter. But why take the eyes? Some sort of trophy or revenge? Had Ananda Gutierrez seen something she shouldn't have?

"Who found her?" Bear asked.

"A guy named Jasper Evans, about an hour ago," Murdoch replied, pointing to a tall thin man being interviewed by a uniformed officer. Even through the slanting rain, Jax could see the horror still imprinted on the man's dark face, a horror that couldn't be faked. "He was on his way to work at the hospital. Says he doesn't know her."

"Anything else?"

Murdoch passed the wallet to Bear's gloved hands. "Nothing else I can give you here. I'll call you from the lab when I find something. If I find something. Happy freakin' Thursday."

By the end of the week, she'll be dead.

Jackson huddled in his jacket, watching the coroner load the body on a stretcher. He catalogued the scant evidence in his mind, a mind known and rewarded for its brilliance with difficult cases. Had the killer followed her from the hospital after lying in wait for her? What was the significance of removing the eyes? Had he felt so guilty about the murder that he'd tried to distance himself from his victim by disfiguring her face?

Bear manipulated the plastic covering the wallet. "Got the address. 4782 Pembroke Street. And here's a wedding picture, and a family photo. She has a little girl."

. . .All she can think about is getting home to her husband Ramón and her little girl . . . .

"You know what this looks like," Bear said, facing him.

"Yeah," Jax muttered, pissed with the rain slanting down the back of his neck. "It looks like Nicole Legère is in this up to her freakin' eyeballs." Except that his sexy psychic had failed to mention the part about the eyes being taken.

"Or she could be legit." Bear had gotten the entire story two days ago. Jax found his partner's lack of outright skepticism a little irritating.

"Sure she is," Jax retorted, sarcasm running full force. "She waltzes in, reports a murder before it happens. Now it's happened exactly the way she said, and I'm supposed to believe she had nothing to do with it? Gimme a break."

"Well, she did miss on the necklace and the eyes," Bear said. "But she hit on enough to make me wonder."

"Yeah, she makes me wonder too," Jax said. "Wonder where she was last night."

"Fine," Bear shrugged. "What do you wanna do first? The hospital, the husband, or the psychic?"

"What do you think?"

Shaking his head, Bear turned to the uniformed officer who had been first on the scene. "Get two or three officers over to the hospital. Find out which section our victim worked in, starting with the emergency room. I need to know who she worked with, even patients she helped. Have somebody find her next of kin, and let us know when you do. And nobody says squat about the eyes, all right?"

He turned back to Jax. "Why don't we take your car?"

"Does this mean you're still conducting a lab experiment in your back seat?" Jax said, growing more disgusted as they walked through the sucking mud and debris back to the street. Whatever evidence Murdoch could have found was probably washing down the sewage drain at that very moment.

"Wait." Bear fished a pen out of his pocket, then squatted carefully before digging into the mud.

"What is it?"

"It looks like we're down to one miss," Bear said. A broken gold chain with a gilded cross dangled from his pen.

"Mama, I saw an angel."

Nicole, with one part of her mind on the griddle and the other turned inward, almost missed her daughter's words. "Hhm?"

"Yeah, I was sleeping, but Tela told me to wake up. When I opened my eyes, I saw a lady at the end of your bed."

Hairs on the back of Nicole's neck rose as she focused on her daughter, forgetting about her pancakes. "What did she look like?"

Danielle made neat stacks of the pancakes Nicole had already prepared. "She was see-through, so I couldn't tell what she was wearing, but I think it was a robe like what angels wear. She had really pretty long dark hair, like Louisa's mama."

Nicole's stomach knotted. Louisa's family, who lived across the street, was from Puerto Rico. The nurse in her dreams had been Hispanic with long dark hair. This could not be a coincidence. "What else happened?"

"She talked to me. It was funny, 'cause her mouth didn't move, and I could hear her in my head." Dani took the bottle of syrup to the table, and Nicole numbly followed with their plates. "I wasn't scared, 'cause she was so nice. Maybe she wasn't really an angel though. She was really sad, and I don't think angels are sad, do you?"

Her appetite gone, Nicole poured a glass of juice with trembling hands. "Why was she sad?"

Her daughter concentrated for a moment on her breakfast, as if conversing with an angel was the most ordinary thing in the world. "She said she had to go away, and she was going to miss her family. She said she needed help."

Nicole gave up all pretense of enjoying her breakfast. The chill that had started in her veins upon waking settled in her stomach like an iron fist. "Help?"

"She said what happened to her was gonna happen again, and we have to stop it." Danielle's eyes were luminous as she regarded her. "What happened to her, Mama? Was she sick?"

Nicole had to swallow several times before she found her voice. "No, baby, she wasn't sick."

"Can we help her, Mama? She was so sad. I want to help her."

This couldn't be happening. Nicole closed her eyes against the threat of sudden and violent tears. First the dreams, and now her daughter had apparently been visited by the spirit of the woman she had envisioned. And she still didn't want to believe it.

"Mama?"

Nicole opened her eyes, focusing on her daughter. "Is this the first time that you've seen an angel?"

"No, Mama, I told you, Tela's an angel. She's got wings and everything."

Acid joined the knots in Nicole's stomach. All this time she'd blithely assumed "Tela" was her daughter's imaginary friend. Now she faced the possibility that Tela was something more. But what? An angel, a fairy?

"Sometimes other angels show up with Tela," Danielle added. "She says they just like stopping by. And sometimes when I wake up in the middle of the night, I see an old lady sitting on my bed. She likes to tell me stories."

"What kind of stories?"

"I don't 'member."

"Remember," she automatically corrected, which prompted a fight against hysterical laughter. Her carefully ordered existence was sliding off the deep end, and apparently she was taking her daughter with her.

"How long have you been seeing angels?"

"Don't 'mem-remember. Tela's always here." Danielle's face scrunched up. "She says you're mad."

Mad? Nicole swallowed another bout of hysterical laughter. No, she wasn't mad—unless you meant the off-her-rocker sense of the word. More than anything, she was scared.

Forcing a brittle smile, she reached over and gave Dani's cheek a light pinch. "I'm not mad, sweetheart, just thinking. Why don't you finish your breakfast? We don't want to be late."

After breakfast, Nicole bundled Dani and her backpack into the car as they waited for Louisa and her brother to join the carpool. "Mama, we are going to help the angel-lady, aren't we?"

She cupped her daughter's cheek, looking into eyes that reminded her more and more of Randall's each day. "Of course we're going to help her, however we can. But I need you to do me a big favor and keep this just between us for now, until we can figure out how to help her. Okay?"

" 'Kay."

Taking Dani and her friends to school forced Nicole's mind away from her fear. On the way home, however, the fear resurfaced. Dani, her sweet, innocent six-year-old, could see angels. She almost laughed aloud. *Her daughter could see dead people.*

Her memory skipped back through the last six years. Even as a baby, Danielle had seemed to see things that weren't there. Nicole would hear her laughing and chortling on the baby monitor, only to enter the nursery and find the mobile over the crib swinging even though there wasn't a draft in the room. She shivered as she remembered that Dani's first word wasn't "Mama" but "Tee."

Anger pulsed through her. Anger and, God help her, a little jealousy. Her daughter was only six, much too young for the Legacy to manifest itself. Yet Nicole's sisters and brothers had had their gifts from the time they were born. Only she had been a late bloomer, and even then, her gifts hadn't come easily or often.

Now her daughter saw beings that she shouldn't be seeing, and apparently could even communicate with them. How could she have been so blind? What was she supposed to do now?

As far as she knew, nothing dangerous had happened to Dani. But that didn't mean that only "angels" would attempt to communicate with her. A mean person didn't change their ways just because they'd passed over. What if someone like that was drawn to her daughter without her knowledge? How was she supposed to protect her daughter from something she couldn't see?

Again came the thought to get her mother involved. Her parents would want to know about Dani's gift, and Nicole felt on some level that they had a right to know. Beyond that, however, she felt very much the prodigal daughter, instantly rebelling at needing the family for anything.

The family had never stood by her. They hadn't been there when the burden of her gifts ripped her marriage apart. They hadn't been there when Randall's death had sent her into premature labor. They hadn't even supported her understandable move to the East Coast. Why should she turn to them now?

Because your daughter's life is more important than your feelings.

Nicole heard the voice inside her head; she just didn't want to listen to it. Of course her daughter's life was more important, and she would do whatever was necessary to keep her daughter safe.

At the moment, nothing threatened Danielle. They'd made a promise to help the "angel lady," and Nicole fully intended to keep that promise. If she involved her parents, they would either fly to Atlanta as soon as they could file a flight plan, or they'd demand that she and Dani return home. Either step would mean admitting that her choices were wrong, and Nicole wasn't ready to concede. Not yet.

She would come up with a solution, a solution that would hopefully not involve her parents. This way, Dani could keep her promise to the spirit that had visited her. Nicole would endure whatever she had to in order to convince the police or whoever would listen that the killer would strike again.

As she was unlocking her front door, she heard a car pull into the driveway. She turned, wondering who could be visiting so early. Her heart sank as she met the cold, assessing gaze of Detective Carter Jackson.

"Good morning, Ms. Legère. I was wondering if I could have a few words with you."

Chapter Four

Jax concentrated on surveying his surroundings. Nicolette Legère lived in a modest, tree-lined neighborhood, a throwback to the days when kids still played outside. Her house was an unpretentious two-story painted baby blue, with a huge porch complete with swing that reminded him of his childhood home. The hedges lining the drive were neatly trimmed, and a profusion of plants and flowers graced the edges of the walk and the porch itself.

A huge oak tree sat on the left side of the house, new leaves a brilliant green in the gray drizzle. The other houses along the tree-lined street were just as picturesque. It looked like something from the cover of a postcard, homey and comforting. Hardly the home of a psychic.

Or a killer.

"Detective Jackson."

She seemed neither surprised nor nervous at his presence, but resigned, as if she had been expecting him. Yet she had obviously just returned home. The dark blue Saturn sedan had still been warm when he'd passed it. Her umbrella lay open on the porch to dry. The morning paper was tucked under her arm, her hands poised in the act of unlocking the door. Her long navy jacket and matching skirt hid all but the swell of her hips and the length of her legs from him.

Angry with himself for letting his mind wander, he stepped onto the porch. "Ms. Legère. This is my partner, Detective Marshall. We want to ask you some questions about Ananda Gutierrez."

Her eyebrows lowered in confusion. "Who?"

Jackson moved deliberately along the porch until he could stare down into her eyes. "Ananda Gutierrez. She's an emergency room nurse at Memorial Hospital. At least she was until someone murdered her this morning. But you already know that, don't you?"

Her eyes flashed, not with surprise, which he didn't expect, or with guilt, which he did. Instead, a deep sadness welled behind her lashes, sadness so profound and disturbing it caused him to take an involuntary step back.

"Ananda Gutierrez," she whispered. "I didn't know her name. I had hoped with this last dream—"

She broke off, concentrating on opening the door. "Won't you come in?"

Stepping on the ivy-edged welcome mat and into the hardwood foyer, he followed her inside, knowing that Bear would have his back. Before him, a stairway with a handsomely carved banister led to the upper level. On his right was a small sitting room of burgundy and cream, and on his left a formal dining room whose gold-colored walls and crimson drapes were anchored by the mahogany dining set.

"May I take your jackets, Detectives?" she asked, her voice polite and proper.

"Why?" Jax asked. Bear was already shouldering out of his coat.

"Because you're dripping on my carpet."

Glaring at his partner, Jax shrugged out of the jacket and passed it to her. Her eyes widened as she caught sight of his shoulder holster, but she said nothing as she hung his jacket and Bear's coat on the oak hall tree. Well, this wasn't a social visit, he thought to himself. She'd better get used to that real quick.

"Where were you?"

"Excuse me?" she said, throwing her keys and the paper on a tall, skinny table beneath a gold-framed mirror.

Bear shut the door, but didn't lock it. He hadn't said anything yet, obviously having no problem with letting Jax take the lead. Fine. Jax stepped closer to her, until she had to crane her neck to look into his face. "Your car's still warm, and your umbrella was open. You just got back from somewhere, right?"

"I took my daughter and some of the neighborhood kids to school," she answered, showing no outward reaction to his closeness, which only irritated him further. "I take turns with the other parents, and this is my week."

She removed her own jacket to hang on the coat rack, revealing a short-sleeved beige blouse that clung to her generous curves like icing on cake. He wondered suddenly and completely inappropriately what it would be like to hold those curves in his hands

"Will this take long, Detective? I have to get to labs soon."

"Labs?" Bear found his voice.

"Yes. Tuesdays and Thursdays are lab days at school."

Jax shook himself out of his lecherous thoughts with an image of Ananda Gutierrez's bloodless face. "I'm sure your professors won't mind you being late for helping in a murder investigation." Jax smiled without humor. "I can write a note for you, if you like."

His attempt to get a rise out of her failed. "If you'll follow me?"

She led them past the stairway into what had to be the heart of the house. The living room looked like a tropical getaway with its profusion of bamboo, palm and fern. Cream-colored furniture with cushions of moss green, beige, and pale melon was casually arranged over the hardwood floor. Two floor-to-ceiling windows dominated the main wall, looking onto a sprawling backyard. Tucked in one corner was a larger version of one of those tabletop fountains that gurgled water like a stream. If he closed his eyes, Jax was sure he'd hear calypso music.

"Would you care for something to drink, Detectives?" she asked politely, heading for a doorway that presumably led to the kitchen.

Jax frowned. "You do realize that this isn't a social visit?"

"Of course." The cool reserve in her expression became tinged with that haunting sadness again. "I also know this will take some time, so I thought come coffee might come in handy."

Bear moved into the center of the room with precise steps, as if afraid he'd knock into something at any moment. "You don't seem surprised to see us here."

"Unfortunately, I'm not." Her voice was sad as she paused in the doorway. "I had the last dream this morning. I'd have called you if you hadn't stopped by."

"Well." Discomfited by the mention of her supposed psychic powers, Jax rocked back on his heels, studiously avoiding his partner's gaze. He really shouldn't accept her offer, but if it helped to relax her, he'd agree. He'd make sure to put her at ease first, and then he'd launch his attack. "Coffee would be great, if it's no trouble."

"No trouble at all. I'll be right back."

She disappeared through the doorway to the left. Bear leaned closer to him. "Man, you didn't tell me she was a hottie. I like a woman with meat on her bones."

"Shut up," Jax said, scrutinizing his surroundings again. Photos vied with the greenery. There were montages of pictures on the wall, pictures of women and children on a tropical beach and before a sprawling mansion.

"Nice-looking family," Bear said, crossing to the fireplace that boasted an arching candelabrum instead of logs.

Only four frames graced the mantel above the beige marble fireplace, Jax noted. One showed two women in their mid-twenties, identical in features only, one dressed as a neo-hippie, the other a biker chick. Another photo showed Nicole building a sandcastle with a little girl, both of them beaming into the camera. The third showed two identical men, in their late twenties to early thirties, dressed in top hats and tails and surrounded by showgirls.

The fourth had to be a family portrait. Twin girls sat on stools in front of a teen-aged Nicole and a thin, copper-skinned woman with short, raven curls and fathomless brown eyes. Behind them stood male twins, tall and lanky, and a white man, tanned, with dark brown hair and laughing green eyes that were reflected in the eyes of the children around him.

Despite his surprise at the man in the picture, Jax's gaze kept returning to Nicole. She seemed uncomfortable as she sat behind her sisters, as if she felt awkward in her own skin. Even then, her eyes seemed to hold an ancient sadness, as if she had witnessed things no one ever should.

"Do you think the whole family's psychic, or just her?" Bear whispered.

Jax snorted. "You know my answer to that. And why are you whispering? She's supposedly got psychic ability, not super hearing."

There was a crystalline *thunk* from the kitchen. "There is no 'supposedly' about it, Detective. But I'm not deaf, and all the women in the family have some sort of ability." Another thump. "How do you take your coffee, gentlemen?"

Ignoring Bear's amused grin, Jax followed the sound of Nicole's voice into the kitchen. The light and breezy atmosphere of the living room was manifested here in the citrus-colored accents on the white cabinets, the sunshine yellow curtains on the window over the sink, and the turquoise and white tiled bistro set in the breakfast nook. It looked like permanent summer in the room.

"I'll have mine straight," Bear called from the living room.

"Milk and sugar will be fine for me," Jax said.

She raised an eyebrow at that, pausing as she placed things on a tray. "I thought all police officers took their coffee black."

"One of many misconceptions the public has about us." He accepted the mug she offered him and nodded towards the dishes on the breakfast table. "Feeding a small army?"

Her smile froze as she looked at the table. "No, my daughter and I always have breakfast together each morning before I take her and her friends to school. Today was pancake day."

Again, a shift in her personality. "Why don't we return to the living room? I don't want your partner's coffee to get cold."

He satisfied himself with watching her walk in front of him and place the coffee tray on the bleached rattan and glass coffee table before sitting on the couch. Bear left the fireplace and took the spot beside her, leaving Jax to sit in an over-pillowed moss green chair that matched the sofa she rested on. One of the large windows stood open, and the pale ivory curtains floated upward as they caught a rainy breeze. "How old is your daughter?"

This time her smile was unforced, and lit her eyes as well as her face. "Danielle is six going on sixty. She's a great kid, but she thinks she has to take care of Mama, not the other way around."

"So it's just the two of you?" Jax took pride in the casual tone of his voice. He told himself the answer was important to the investigation, not to him personally.

"Yes." She fiddled with her cup. "My husband died just before Dani was born."

"I'm sorry." The obvious pain in her voice urged him to do something really stupid, like lift her to her feet and wrap his arms about her. He could feel the tingling in his fingers, the desire to do just that. Only the nature of the visit and his partner's presence kept him in the chair.

It had been with him for three days now, that desire, ever since she had waltzed into the precinct. Her voice and scent had lingered in his mind. So had her story.

"It's all right," she finally said, the standard response to the standard sentiment. She sat back, as if distancing herself from the memories. It was obvious that she had no intention of divulging her life story to a stranger. Which only served to make her more intriguing.

She put her cup down on the table, then sat back. "I gather you have some questions for me, Detectives?"

She was calm, real together. Jax had to admire that. She had to know she was on the short list of suspects. Hell, she was the only one on their list of suspects. Yet she sat there as if she were listening to door-to-door salesmen, her hazel eyes a mix of curiosity and reserve.

"You're real calm about this," he said aloud, "considering the woman you supposedly had a dream about is dead."

"Would you prefer that I become hysterical?" she asked. "Would you rather see me all red-eyed with runny make-up? Would that make you treat me any differently?"

They all knew the answer to that, but he said it anyway. "No."

She sat back. "I'm a single parent, Detective Jackson. Except for one sister, none of my family lives here. I don't have the luxury of being able to fall apart."

Bear sat forward and turned slightly, making an almost imperceptible invasion of her space. "Where were you between eleven-thirty last night and six A.M.?"

"Here, asleep."

"Were you alone?" Jax brusquely asked.

Nicole frowned as she looked at him, her first outward show of emotion. "If you mean in my bed, yes. In the house, no. About two, my daughter awakened me from my dream. She stayed with me the remainder of the night."

Bear's shift effectively caged her between him and the back of the couch. Jax tried not to let it bother him that his partner was that close to Nicole. "And you know the time because?"

"Because I glanced at the alarm clock on my nightstand."

Jax pulled a small notebook from his jacket pocket. Not a big window of opportunity there. "What was your day like yesterday?"

"Dani and I woke up at our regular time, six. We had breakfast, and I dropped her and some of the neighborhood kids off at school, then went on to school myself."

"How long do your classes normally last?" Bear asked.

"Until noon. After lunch I go to work. I assist Dr. Mark Rosenberg several times a week. He's a psychologist."

"Where?"

She gave him the information, which he recorded in his notebook. "What time did you leave work?"

"In barely enough time to get Dani from school." She related the rest of her day, typical for a single parent.

"Who's the last person besides your daughter who can account for your whereabouts?"

"You could probably ask my next door neighbor, Gertie Bruce," she answered. "Miss Gertie fancies herself a one-woman neighborhood watch. Other than that, my sister Malita called me around ten forty-five, and we talked for about half an hour."

Bear gave him a look, part resignation and part acceptance. The body had been discovered at five A.M. On their way to Nicole's they'd been called with the news that Ananda Gutierrez had left her shift just after midnight, and it would have taken her at least fifteen minutes to walk to the rail station. At eleven on a weeknight and breaking a few traffic rules, Nicole Legère could have gotten downtown within the window of opportunity. It wasn't much for either side, but with everything else, it had possibilities.

What everything else? He had no murder weapon, no witnesses, and a crime scene that couldn't possibly be any more fucked up than it was. In other words, he had shit.

"When was the last time that you went to Memorial?"

"I've never been there."

"Never?" Bear asked. "It's not that far from the university."

"I realize that," Nicole replied, "but I've never had a reason to go there."

"Not even to see a doctor?" Jax found that hard to believe.

"I don't get sick. The last time I was in a hospital was when Dani was born."

Crap. It was an easy enough thing to check, but she still could have gone to the hospital and scoped it out without signing in and getting medical attention. "So you didn't see Ananda Gutierrez before today?"

"I still haven't seen Ananda Gutierrez, except in those three dreams."

Jax shifted forward in the chair, effectively sandwiching her in between him and Bear. "So you're saying you don't know her?"

"That's what I'm saying."

"You do realize that we can check that out by talking to her family?" Bear reminded her in a tone way too apologetic for Jax's taste.

She swung to face Bear. "Go ahead," she all but dared him, her tone angry. "I don't know Ananda Gutierrez or her family, and they don't know me. And even if they say they do, it's because anyone can punch my name in on the Internet and think they know all about me."

"And why is that, Ms. Legère?" Jax asked.

"Because everyone remotely interested in psychic phenomena has come across the Legère name." She gave him a look that could have frozen a blowtorch. "This ping-pong questioning method may work with other people, but I will not be intimidated by the two of you breathing on me."

She sat forward, picking up her coffee. Her hand remained rock steady. Jax shot a look at Bear behind her back. His partner shrugged as if to say, I'll follow your lead.

Great. Jax had no problem playing bad cop. "We'd like to speak to your daughter."

"No."

She seemed almost happy to deny him, and that ticked him off. "You do realize that she's the best corroboration for your story?"

The coffee mug returned to the table with a sharp click. "My daughter is six. I'm not about to let her be exposed to a murder investigation, let alone be grilled by two detectives who look like defensive tackles."

She glanced from one to the other. "And if either of you believe I'd either leave my daughter at home alone or take her along while I kill someone, you're out of your everlovin' minds."

Jax did his best not to frown, especially since Bear was grinning ear-to-ear behind Nicole's back. She didn't give an inch, and he had to admit, if only to himself, that he liked that about her. 'Course, that wasn't the only thing he liked about her.

"Are you really expecting us to believe that you're psychic?" he demanded, angry for letting his mind wander.

"I don't expect you to believe anything, Detective," she responded. Coolness replaced the fire that had flared in her eyes.

Bear shifted on the couch like an excited puppy. "Can you read me, like those people on TV?"

She made a face. "Not like those people on TV. One of my sisters probably could. Or my mother. My ability is prescience—I know things before they happen. But that knowledge only comes in the forms of dreams."

Bear nodded. A simple explanation, or an easy way out? Jax had his own conclusions. Still, she remained consistent with what she'd told him when she'd come to the precinct.

Jax turned to Nicole, expecting something. What in the world should he expect? She sat back against the pillows, and for a moment she looked really tired and completely human. He didn't like to think that she wasn't normal.

"Detective?"

Dredging up a smile, Jax shoved his notebook back into his pocket and retrieved his coffee. "You have a nice home."

She smiled in self-deprecation. "Not what you imagined, I suppose?"

"It does seem at odds with what you've told me about yourself."

"Detective, if you remember, the last time we talked about your perceptions of me I became horribly insulted."

"You did?"

"I did. And if you call me 'solid' again, I'm going to have to slap you."

Bear coughed a laugh into his hand. Jax couldn't blame him, even if he did suddenly hate the man. Nicole's voice was calm, even amused, and completely at odds with the violence of her words. She sipped her coffee as if they had been discussing the weather, but the glint in her eyes was readily apparent.

"I certainly didn't mean to disrespect you," he apologized, setting his cup down. "It was actually my back-handed attempt at a compliment."

"You were complimenting me?"

Surprise raised her voice. Had no one ever complimented her before? "Of course I was. You're beautiful, smart, successful—"

He broke off, got to his feet, conscious of Bear's presence. What the hell was he doing? He was here to pump her for information, not jump her bones.

Agitated, he moved to the mantel. "This your family?"

"Yes." Nicole's voice was still limned with curiosity, but she allowed his obvious deflection to pass. "My sisters, Mala and Malita Legère, my brothers Derek and Darien Antonescu, and those are our parents, Dr. Stefan Antonescu and Arielle Legère."

"Why the different names?"

"Tradition," she said, rising to her feet. "Every woman born a Legère remains a Legère even when they marry."

She moved to a gilded frame on the closest wall, showing several dozen people. "That's us at the last family gathering in New Orleans two years ago. My father is a scientist, specializing in psychic research. In this day and age, the Legacy's not something we can keep quiet, no matter how fiercely we guard our privacy. Papa was part of an international team sent to New Orleans to document the phenomena of the women in my family. Ultimately he married my mother. It was his idea to start bringing all the Legère women together every few years."

He studied the photo. A quick glance couldn't give him an accurate count, but there were several dozen men, women, and children of all ages and hues spread on a lawn before a sprawling house that recalled *Gone With the Wind*. "My family had its semi-annual reunion last year. Uncle Jonas still hasn't lived it down."

A reserved smile, barely curving her lips, had him wanting more. "Well, our gatherings really aren't about barbecue and beer, especially when the gatherings are on Martinique where we're originally from, by way of West Africa."

That explained the lilt in her accent. "What are they about?"

"The Legacy."

He could hear the capitalization in her voice. Something about the way she said it was both prayer and epithet. It caught his curiosity, held it.

"What legacy?" Bear asked.

"The Legère Legacy. The inheritance of all the female members of my family. And now my brothers have inherited it as well."

Jax felt the hairs on the back of his neck start the Wave. Bear spoke. "There's a special fund only the women in your family get?"

As soon as he asked the question he knew it was wrong. "It's not about money, Detective Jackson, although we have plenty of that," she said with an indulgent smile. "The Legacy doesn't have a monetary value, although some have tried to gain from it. The Legacy is what it is, and the Legères are what we are."

"This Legacy you're talking about, you mean your psychic stuff."

"Yes. All the women in my family have psychic talent in one form or another," she explained calmly. She replaced the gilded frame. "Normally it bypasses the males born in the family, and they take their fathers' names but pass the Legacy to their female children. My brothers have inherited the Legacy for some reason. The talent has run through the female line of the Legère family for more than four hundred years."

Four hundred years. Jax felt his world irrevocably shift. "You're serious."

"Very." She returned to her spot on the couch, settling back against the multicolored pillows. "Our gifts manifest themselves in different ways. My strongest talent is my ability to predict future events based on my dreams."

Bear turned to face them. "And your dreams told you that this nurse was going to be killed."

She looked up at him, her honeyed gaze steady. "Yes."

Jax snorted his disbelief. "And if you dream you can fly like an eagle, I suppose you're going to jump off a building."

"That's not the way it works, Detective Jackson. Even though this hasn't happened in a while, I know the difference between ordinary, random images and the prophetic dreams." She straightened a small wooden box on the coffee table. "The psychic dreams are more real."

"And you're telling me that you dreamed about Ananda Gutierrez?"

Shadows crept across her eyes. "I had the first dream about the murder a week ago. Then I just brushed it off, even though I knew it was more than a nightmare. I had the second one on Sunday, the night before I met with you. I had the last dream this morning."

"What did you dream?"

"Before it was as if I were watching a movie unfolding with someone I didn't know starring in it." She shuddered. "This time, I became the person in the dream. It was as if it all happened to me."

"Tell me what happened."

She wrapped her arms about herself. "I had to work late, so Ramón wasn't able to pick me up before he had to go to work. We only get a couple of hours together with Izzy, but it'll be over in a couple of months. Kathy asks me if I want a ride to the station, but I laugh her off and decline her offer.

"When I leave the hospital, I feel a little strange. A guy, another nurse, asks me if I'm all right. After I pull the scrunchie from my hair, I feel better. I'm only a few blocks away from the hospital, when I realize someone is following me. Dark pants, dark, bulky sweatshirt with the hood pulled up. There's nobody else around. I touch my crucifix and make the sign against the evil eye. The quicker I get to the train station, the better I'll feel, so I start to run. Oh God, he's running too. I can hear him behind me, hear his footsteps getting closer. I want to scream, *Dios*, but I have to keep running."

Nicole's face grew anguished and flushed as her story continued, her voice taking on a different rhythm. "He's right behind me. *Madre de Dios,* I can feel him right behind me. Some kind of spiked rope flies over my head and around my neck, knocking me off my feet. I try to fight, oh God, I fight as best as I can, kicking and clawing and trying to scream."

Her hands shook in violent spasms as she reached for her throat. "My fingers curl up, trying to get the thing loose. But the points stab into my neck, and there's this incredible pain, so much pain that I can't scream and then my mouth fills with blood, and all I can hear is someone giggling. God help me, please God . . . Izzy, my baby . . . ."

She sank back against the cushions, burying her face in her hands as her shoulders shook.

Jax stared at her. The final moments of Ananda Gutierrez's life had spilled from Nicole Legère's mouth in flawless Spanish. It creeped him out, and Bear looked as if he'd just seen Elvis go by riding on a pink elephant. One part of Jax wanted to Mirandize her on the spot. The other part saw the tears in her eyes, the fear in her voice, the trembling in her hands, and knew, just *knew*, that she was a victim who had barely escaped with her life. Except that she wasn't and the nurse hadn't.

"Ms. Legère." He heard the bite in his voice and mentally cringed, but he couldn't afford to be soft with this woman. Not while she was connected—was the only connection—to this case. "You're telling me that if you dream something three times, it comes true? And it's happened more than once?"

She sighed heavily, brushing at the moisture beneath her eyes with long, slender fingers devoid of jewelry. "The future is malleable, Detective Jackson. What I see is simply one possibility. I warn people when I can if something detrimental could happen to them. Usually I tell them to do something like take another way home, make a doctor's appointment, postpone a trip to the grocery store. But I also let them know about the good things: love, a birth, promotions. Things like that."

"I don't believe in that stuff."

She shrugged, as if to say, your loss. "What *do* you believe in, Detective Jackson?"

His reply was swift. "I believe in what I can see and hear and touch and taste and smell. I don't believe in mumbo-jumbo."

"Do you believe in God?"

She had him there. No matter how he answered it, it would be wrong. He had a sudden image of himself at eight, sitting beside his mother and grandmother while a preacher exhorted them to repent of their sins. He'd been raised to believe in God, but being in homicide had a way of shaking one's faith. "That's different."

Her smile was faint. "Is it?"

"You know it is."

"Why? You just said that you only believe in things that are physical. What about things you can sense, things you can feel? Do you believe there's a wind? Do you believe there's more than the sun, moon, and stars? Do you believe in courage, hatred, love?"

"You wanna know what I believe? I believe that every person is capable of doing something wrong. What makes them different, what places them on one side of the law or the other, is the level of guilt they feel about it."

"What have you done wrong?"

"Excuse me?"

One perfectly manicured hand swept toward him. "You said everyone is capable of wrongdoing. What have you done wrong that you feel guilty about?"

Jax started, realizing that he had said too much. Even Bear was looking at him strangely. Jax fought down his temper. He was supposed to be interviewing her, not the other way around. "My supposed guilt is not the issue here."

"No, but mine is."

Her eyes dimmed, and Jax found himself missing the light in them. "I'm a cop, a damned good cop, if I may say so. I've been doing this for fifteen years, and never once, in all that time, has any so-called 'psychic' help actually helped. There are only two people who know what happened to Ananda Gutierrez, and one of them is dead."

"And the other is the killer?"

"Yes."

"And I suppose you believe that would be me?"

He hesitated, not because he was afraid to answer, but because he didn't want to hurt her feelings. And God help him, he didn't want Nicole Legère to be guilty. He didn't want her to be anything other than what she appeared: a beautiful, respectable woman with some really weird views.

"We have to follow every lead, Ms. Legère. Right now, leads are few and far between."

"And my story is too farfetched to be believed, correct?"

She was offended, he could tell. Her speech had become downright encyclopedic. "Can I tell it to you straight?"

A spark lit her eyes. "Please do."

Yep, definitely offended. It didn't matter. He had a crime to solve. "We've got one dead nurse. We've got a washed-out crime scene. We've got more than thirty people we have to question, who may or may not be helpful. And then we've got you."

She shifted slightly, as if his words had made her uncomfortable. Good. She needed to be uncomfortable. She needed to realize just how damn serious this situation was.

"You, Ms. Legère, are the most remarkable part of this whole investigation. Monday morning you came into the precinct to tell me someone was going to be murdered. You proceeded to give me the how and the when. All I didn't have was the who—until this morning. Now I want the why and the murderer. Can you tell me that? Can you give me those answers?"

"Don't think to berate me because you didn't listen to me three days ago," she retorted. "I tried to help you. I tried to tell you, but you just brushed me and my claims off as a case of indigestion!"

"Your claims? Some nurse on some night is going to be killed somewhere? What was I supposed to do with that line of crap you gave me? Shut down every hospital between here and Miami? You psychics never can get the straight story, can you?"

She folded her arms across her chest. "Yeah, like detectives can solve a crime in five minutes."

His ears burned at her words. "Maybe what I should have done was lock you up. Maybe then Ananda Gutierrez would still be alive."

She didn't blink at the implied threat. "Locking me up would have changed nothing. Except perhaps, your opinion of me."

Frustration rising, Jax strode towards her. "If you want my opinion to change, I'm gonna need a whole lot more than what you've given me. And you're not giving up anything, are you Ms. Legère?"

Nicole stood, her eyes glinting in anger. "I refuse to be treated this way in my own house. It's time for you to leave."

Royally pissed, Jax strode towards the door. "Don't even think about leaving town, Ms. Legère." He snatched his jacket off the rack.

She yanked open the door. "I have a child, a job, and a doctorate to complete. I'm not going anywhere."

Jax frowned as she handed Bear his jacket. "We're not done," he warned.

"Unless you get a warrant, we are most certainly done." She deliberately turned her back on him. "Have a good day, Detective Marshall." She slammed the door behind him.

Chapter Five

"What d'you have, Bear?"

Bear Marshall sat in the chair beside Jax's desk. Jax felt sorry for the chair. Marshall was a big man, a former defensive back for the Falcons. His intimidating size concealed a heart as big as his frame. The kids he mentored climbed over him as if he were a human jungle gym. If you were a criminal, however, God help you. Jax knew Bear's tackling skills were still sharp.

Bear slapped a folder onto the desk. "She didn't lie."

Jax stared at the folder with a sinking feeling. The name Nicolette Legère stared back at him. "What's that supposed to mean?"

"Just what I said." Bear popped three sticks of gum into his mouth. "The woman's practically got wings. She's so clean she squeaks, but the stuff around her is as freaky as she said. And she's a looker on top of that." Bear whistled around the wad of gum. "I like women I can hold on to."

Jax quickly quelled the surge in his blood at Bear's words. He didn't want anyone to talk about Nicole like that, especially if he couldn't. And even if he could. "You couldn't find anything on her?"

"Actually, I found a whole helluva lot—a lot more than what she told us." Bear paused long enough to smack a large bubble. He'd been off cigarettes for two weeks, Jax knew, and the gum was the only way he could cope in a precinct full of smokers.

"Like what?" Jax prodded

"First off, no parking tickets or other violations. Her neighbors love her, never had any complaints. She's active in the neighborhood, carpooling the kids to school, community watch, PTA. Even the neighborhood snitch, Gertie Bruce, who has dirt on everybody, didn't have dirt on your lady. Says she's never seen anyone other than her sister visit the house. And she's certain that Ms. Legère never left home after eleven Monday night. Phone records back up that statement. Last call that night ended close to eleven-thirty. So unless Ms. Legère can fly, she didn't intercept that nurse." Another smack. "Like I said, she squeaks."

"Nobody's that clean." Jax opened the file. "Did you talk to her professors?"

Bear rolled his eyes. "Of course I did. Her professors describe her as an average student, conscientious and quiet. In fact, the only thing they have a problem with is her doctoral thesis."

"Which is?"

"The effects of dreams—in particular, nightmares—on the human psyche."

Well, well. So Ms. Legère studied the effects of dreams on people, and just happened to come to him with a dream of murder—a murder that became a reality. That was a revelation.

"And what about her family?"

"Here's where it starts to get interesting. Seems Nicole Legère comes from a rich family. I'm not talking I-got-a-couple-of-ballplayers-in-the-family rich either. They're quiet-rich, very low key. People in Louisiana call them the 'Black Rockefellers.' You name a pot, they got their fingers in it. They actually have a plantation called Beau-Rêve that's been in the family since the end of the Civil War."

Black Rockefellers? Owning plantations? Jax remembered the sprawling house in one of Nicole's photographs. He couldn't conceive of how much money that represented. He felt the start of a headache, and pinched the bridge of his nose to head it off. "So why is Nicole Legère working part-time in a doctor's office here instead of being a good Black American Princess in Louisiana?"

"Don't know," Bear grunted. "Maybe she has issues with her mother, who's currently running the show. Mother's a pillar of the community when she's not bossing thousands of people around, and the father's an internationally respected scientist and professor of something called parapsychology. His last name's Antonescu."

"So the last name deal is true?"

"Yep." Bear shot him a get-this look. "The daughters use Legère, and the brothers use Antonescu. One sister lives here, an interior designer who's done jobs for the mayor, among others. The other sister has a rep as a rebel."

"I guess that's the one dressed like a biker chick in that photo. What'd she do?"

"Nothing substantiated. She got sent to Europe for college and reportedly raised all kinds of hell before becoming a paranormal investigator."

"What the hell is a paranormal investigator?"

Bear flipped through more notes. "When she's not helping the father with his research, she's traveling the country hunting ghosts and anything else that goes bump in the night, like those guys on TV."

"Interesting. I'll see if she put in an appearance here in the past few weeks. Maybe she passed some info on to her older sister." Not much to go on, but he had to look into everything. "Anything on the brothers?"

"Like I said, they've got the father's last name, but shortened it to Anton. Derek and Darien. They're those magicians calling themselves the Brothers Mystère."

Jax snapped his fingers. That's where he recognized them from. "My sister drove me crazy, thinking I could score her tickets the last time they came to town."

"You got a source now," Bear pointed out. "That is, if she's not in jail the next time they come to town." He flipped through a sheaf of papers. "That's it for immediate family. There's a whole bunch of cousins, so many they could have a reunion at Six Flags and take over the park."

A crude comment escaped Jax before he could stop it. His headache blossomed full force in his skull. Even if he could tie the nurse's death to Nicole Legère, her family probably had a stable of lawyers that would eat him for breakfast and have his balls for dinner.

A sigh seeped from him. "Instead of getting clearer, this is getting more messed up."

Bear thumped the file down on the desk. "There's something else."

Jax raised bleary eyes. "What else could there be?"

"It seems Ms. Legère was married once."

"She told us that," Jax said. "Said her husband died before her daughter was born."

"What she didn't tell us was that her husband filed for divorce before he died."

"You're shitting me." How convenient to leave that out of the conversation. Still, Jax couldn't imagine what that must have been like, pregnant and going through a divorce. His sympathy for Nicole increased. "What happened?"

"Husband's name was Randall Thibideaux, and apparently his family is almost as connected as the Legères. Cited irreconcilable differences, but he told anyone who would listen that Ms. Legère and her family were cultists."

"Cultists?"

Bear shifted on his seat in a futile effort to make his bulk more comfortable. "Yeah, and you're gonna love this. According to a private investigator he'd hired, Thibideaux claimed the women controlled the family like a mini kingdom, and the men were little more than sperm donors."

Damn, that was deep. "Did anyone investigate his claims?"

"No, and it gets stranger." He tapped the file with a thick finger. "Your girl claimed to have dreams that her soon-to-be-ex was going to die. Tried to get him to come back home. He refused, and a week later, his house was swept into the sea by a freak tropical storm. With him inside it."

The hair on Jax's arms stood on end. "What happened after that?"

"Nothing."

"Nothing?"

"The Thibideaux family never made any claims against the Legères. A formal investigation proved that Ms. Legère was nowhere near her husband at the time of his accident. She moved here a couple of months after her daughter was born."

"How long ago was this?"

"Ms. Legère was about seven months' pregnant when Randall Thibideaux died."

Bear looked down at the file. "The whole family is strange. Just for kicks, I did a search of their name on the Internet. Got a whole butt-load of hits from various psychic and paranormal web sites. There's one site that has nothing but supposed 'eye witness' accounts and synopses of psychic stuff the Legères have done for the last seventy-five years."

"Is that how they made their money?" Duping innocent people with smoke and mirrors.

"Nope. No one with the Legère name is making money directly off the paranormal stuff. No psychic network, no palm reading shops. They don't even take the reward money if they find missing people or solve crimes. In fact, they supposedly have a foundation that gives away millions every year, mainly to women and children's charities. The magic show that the brothers put on is the closest they come to cashing in, and even they don't advertise the family talent in any way."

"You're shitting me."

"Check it out yourself." Bear slid a stack of papers across the desk, smacking his gum a mile a minute. "According to various web sites, supposedly every female in the family has some sort of psychic ability, just like Ms. Legère said. The family even had a documentary done on them. People in New Orleans treat them like celebrities. You ask anyone in New Orleans about them and it's like, 'Oh yeah, isn't it great?' Like they're proud to have a family like that around. They're like the Jacksons of the underground paranormal community."

Jax stared blankly down at the file, his mind replaying the moments that he'd spent with Nicole Legère. He pushed the psychic stuff aside and concentrated on the woman and the life she'd led up to now.

Had she loved her husband? Had Thibideaux requested a divorce because he'd fallen in love with someone else? Jax knew from years as a beat cop that spouses who felt betrayed could be vicious. Had Nicole somehow killed her ex-husband, then begun to take his betrayal out on the female population at large?

That seemed like a contradiction to the demeanor she exhibited, but the alternative, the psychic stuff, was hard to swallow. He knew some police departments used psychics—swore by them, even—but he still couldn't bring himself to believe that it was more than smoke and mirrors. As far as he was concerned, they were all tricksters cheating people out of their hard-earned money for nebulous generalities disguised as messages from on high.

If Nicole's family wasn't in the business for the money, why the hell were they doing it? Just what in the hell was she?

"Interviewing Ananda Gutierrez's family came up empty," he said, filling Bear in on his day. "Her husband had never heard of Ms. Legère, and no one at the hospital, including Nurse Kathy Anderson, can remember ever seeing her. Her boss says the same thing about her as everyone else, that she's conscientious and hard-working."

Jax dropped the papers onto his desk. "So let me get this straight. Our lead suspect, the woman who came here and told me about the murder three days before it happened, is cleared?"

Bear's disbelief matched his own. "Sorry, man. We got no motive, no probable cause, no support for a search warrant, and your girl's got an alibi verified by phone records and her nosy neighbor. By all accounts, there's no way Ananda Gutierrez and Nicole Legère could have even know each other, so that's a wash. Besides, Murdoch says he found natural fibers in the bruises on the side of the neck. Murder weapon is most likely a homemade rope woven around a strip of spikes. Not exactly a woman's weapon. Besides, he says a woman wouldn't have the upper body strength necessary to lift and strangle a struggling victim."

"Crap."

"Yep," Bear agreed. "Despite some weird sideline shit, the way it looks now, Nicole Legère is just what she says she is: a bona fide, real-life psychic. And unless she's covering for somebody, she's clean."

"Damn!" Jax wanted to pound the desk in frustration. This was not what he wanted to hear. But even he had to admit, if Nicole Legère hadn't walked into his life with her crazy story, there was no way in hell he would have considered her as a suspect.

"So what're you gonna do now?"

"There's only one thing to do. Become Ms. Legère's new best friend."

Chapter Six

The dream had her.

She hiked her pleather, hot-pink mini skirt further up her thighs as she balanced on four-inch stilettos. Thank goodness it was a warm night. Business sucked—or not, depending on your point of view—when it was too cold.

Flicking her cigarette to the ground, she checked out the street. This stretch wasn't busy yet, but that was fine with her. As she ground her cigarette into the asphalt with a pointed toe, she heard a voice behind her. "Hey, babe."

She turned, saw the figure standing just outside the circle of lamplight. "Hey yourself," she answered. "What's your pleasure, sugar?"

For answer, a bill was thrust at her. Grant's taciturn expression stared up at her.

A smile split her hardened lipstick. "Fifty won't get me horizontal, sugar," she purred, stepping closer. "But people tell me I have a golden tongue."

Mr. Strong Silent Type stepped back into the shadows between two buildings. Well, she wasn't crazy about doing a trick in the alley, but fifty bucks didn't rate a drive to a motel either. Besides, ten or so minutes and she'd be back in her spot waiting for the next one to come along. There was always a next one.

The trick backed against the brick wall, opening his jacket, a nice leather number kids shot each other for. She stepped forward and took Grant off his hands, sticking the dour dead president into her cleavage. Bet you never had that much fun in real life, Mr. President.

"Not one for conversation are you, sugar?" she asked, not really expecting an answer. "That's okay, the strong silent type makes me hot."

She knelt before him, briefly mourning her stockings. They wouldn't be on long anyway, but the lace-topped stockings were the one indulgence she allowed herself, and some of the tricks liked seeing her roll them down.

His hands snaked into her hair, pulling her closer. "Like to get right to it, huh? Fine with me, sugar. It's your money."

She reached for the zipper on his trousers. Without warning a whistling noise cut the night air as a cord zipped about her throat, cutting off her air. She reached one hand to her neck, pricking her fingers on metal spikes, while the other hand fisted into his private parts. It was an ineffectual blow, and the man moved around her to tighten the cord, the sharpened metal biting into her throat. She died, kicking and cursing and bleeding.

Nicole fought the covers for air, kicking and screaming. She bolted out of bed and stumbled into the master bath, retching. When only dry heaves were left, she turned to the sink and spun on the cold water faucet, rinsing her mouth and splashing her face with the rejuvenating brisk water.

Grabbing a washcloth, Nicole wiped water from her face, then straightened. Instinctively she glanced into the mirror, then froze. The facecloth dropped forgotten to the floor as her hands rose to her neck. Bruises marred her skin, ringing the base of her throat in an angry, purplish-red band.

It looked as if someone had tried to strangle her.

"Oh God."

It was suddenly torture to take a breath. She collapsed to the floor, drawing her knees to her chest and sobbing.

Worse, it was so much worse than the previous set of dreams. She'd expected one dream, but to have the dream twice in one night? She'd felt the concrete, dirt and trash of the alley, felt her lovely stockings rip, felt the blow she'd delivered. And God, she'd felt the spiked cord tighten about her neck, severing her vocal cords so she couldn't scream—

"Mama?"

Lifting her head, Nicole stared into her daughter's tear-filled eyes. Dani's frightened face was impetus enough to gather her will and push the fear away.

"I'm fine, baby," she said, dredging up a smile. "Mama had another bad dream, that's all."

Dani looked at her with those all-knowing eyes, her lower lip trembling. "Is somebody else going to die?"

Nicole managed to raise herself to the edge of the bathtub. Oh how she wanted to lie to her daughter, wanted to pretend that they were part of a normal family and her dreams were simply a result of too much tomato sauce. But she couldn't.

"Not if I can help it, *ma petite*. I'll go see Detective Jackson after I drop you and your friends at school."

Dani's arms curved about her. "I love you, Mamma."

Nicole closed her eyes against more tears, savoring the reality of her daughter's love. "Ditto, princess. Never doubt it. Now go get dressed while I shower."

Dani scampered off and Nicole wiped her mouth again before returning to her bedroom. The camera was still going. With shaking hands she stopped it, then ejected the videotape. Her sleep had been recorded this way for years before she'd married Randall. Starting again was as second nature as leaving a night-light on.

She never looked at the tapes, preferring the catharsis of her journal. Her father had said the tapes were necessary documentation, however, and she had to agree. Especially since she planned to present one to Detective Carter Jackson. She just didn't know if it would exonerate her in his eyes or instead forever damn her.

Feeling relieved to have made the decision, she finished her morning ritual, dropped Dani and her friends off at school, and went to class. Even school couldn't distract her from her thoughts and she ended up turning on her tape recorder to capture the lecture. It was a relief to leave campus and drive to Dr. Rosenberg's office.

Transcribing the doctor's notes also proved difficult to focus on as fear and doubts wormed through her mind. Would going to Detective

Jackson be enough? The clock was ticking, meaning she had a day at the minimum to prevent another murder. She didn't dare call her father again. He'd just put her mother on the phone.

Arielle Legère was the Keeper of the Legacy, the powerful matriarch of a powerful family, whose designer shoes Nicole couldn't possibly hope to fill. Her mother had become head of the family at eighteen—eighteen, for goodness sake—and has never looked back since then.

Nicole had been aware of her mother's power even in the womb; growing up, she had never seen her mother be anything other than serene and successful and perfect. Apparently that was something she'd passed on only to Nicole's brothers and sisters.

She felt ill-equipped to handle this, but she didn't feel inclined to involve her mother. Besides, if her mother was supposed to be involved, wouldn't the warnings have gone to her instead?

She pushed back from the desk, gathering her things before heading for the door. Deep inside, she believed this was something she was meant to handle. She herself, not her mother. But how could she when she was scared to death?

"I won't fail," she said aloud, her voice sounding small in the silence of her car. "I will stop this. No matter what it takes."

"Hey Jax," an officer called. "There's a lady here to see you. Glad to see you still got it."

Jax refrained from punching the officer as Nicole Legère crossed the room. The sight of her caused his body to tighten with awareness, straining to catch the essence that was hers alone.

She was again dressed for business, this time in a tan wool dress coat over teal-colored pantsuit, a scarf tied about her throat. Dark sunglasses shielded her eyes, but the stiffness of her gait and the death-grip she had on her briefcase communicated her unease to him.

His protective instinct brought him to his feet. Bear rose to his feet behind him. Then he moved forward, his hands hovering near her, wanting to shield her.

"Ms. Legère." He kept his voice formal, though inside he seethed with questions. Something had happened. He knew it in his bones. Why else was she here? "You remember Detective Marshall."

"Ma'am." Bear nodded, deftly moving in front of the desk to block what was on the surface from Nicole's view.

"Detective Marshall." The dark shades swung back to Jax. "I need to speak with you. Please."

Urgency limned her voice, her posture. She was deathly afraid and trying hard to control it. He went on full alert. What happened?

"I'll be more than happy to speak with you, Ms. Legère. If it's about this case, though, you might want to do this with your lawyer present."

Her grip on the briefcase tightened until her fingers trembled. "I have nothing to hide. And I want to help you, if I can."

He heard Bear mutter under his breath and silently cursed with him. "All right, Ms. Legère. I'll speak with you but I want to make sure you understand your rights."

"I understand," Nicole nodded, then licked her lips. The action sent an unbidden bolt of desire though him. Why did she want to talk to him? Why did she seem so afraid? Why was he dreading this conversation?

He gestured her towards a conference room but she shook her head. "I-I would rather talk outside, Detective Jackson," she said thinly. "I need the air, as smoggy as it is."

Jax looked at Bear, who shrugged. "Okay."

He placed his hand lightly on the small of her back, just to escort her, nothing more. The undulation of her stride reverberated through his fingertips and curled into a tight knot of desire in his groin. He clenched his teeth against it. Whether or not Nicole and her family were bona fide psychics, he didn't want his feelings broadcast. But he didn't remove his hand.

They stepped outside into a day that was brilliant blue and new-growth green, dusting everything with pollen and sun. Any moment now, pollen would go surging into his lungs, causing his allergies to go haywire.

Nicole suddenly leaned into him, and his next breath was full of her scent, heady, subtle, sweet and spicy. His lungs settled.

They crossed the street to a swath of greenery that was more an angry gash made by a pissed-off Mother Nature than a park. She sat on a granite bench, her case clutched on her knees. He sat beside her, closer than he should have, but not as close as he wanted. A breeze sifted into the scant space between them, lifting her hair in a curly, brown-gold cloud. It was all he could do to keep his hands from reaching up to tuck one of the wild strands behind her ear.

"What did you want to talk about, Ms. Legère?"

An air of vulnerability hung about her shoulders and made her full lips tremble. He wondered how much of an ass Randall Thibideaux had to have been to walk away from her.

"I had another dream last night," she finally said. "Two, actually."

"Like the others?"

A jerky nod was his answer. "This time, a p-prostitute. Been around long enough to be smart, but a trick's a trick."

She started, as if shocked by her own words, but continued. "He gives her a fifty and they go deeper into a side street, an alley. He kills her, the same way he killed the nurse. Faster though, because she's on her knees in front of him."

Her hands trembled as she reached up, removed her sunglasses. She looked at him, and Jax waned to growl in anger at the desolate, wounded fear in her reddened eyes. "I felt her die, Detective Jackson," she whispered. "I felt her die twice."

One moment he was sitting beside her, the next he was closer, his arm around her. Comforting her, shielding her. What the hell was he doing?

She took a shuddering breath as she leaned into him. "Something else happened last night, something that's never happened before." Visibly trembling, her hands reached up, untying the brightly colored scarf about her neck.

"My God." Jax looked in horror and rising anger at the livid bruising and skin abrasions that bit deeply into her soft throat and curved around her neck.

Without conscious thought his hands reached up, fingertips light to the frantic pulse at the base of her throat. She moaned once, a slight sound, hopefully in reaction to the same sharp current that he felt instead of pain.

"How did this happen?" An inexplicable rage welled within him, the need to hurt whomever had hurt her. "Did somebody grab you?"

"No. I—I don't know," she whispered, her voice hoarse with the effort of control. "When I woke up this morning, my throat was unaccountably sore. I didn't think much of it until I looked in the mirror and saw this. It-it worries me."

She was more than worried. She was terrified. Fear radiated from her in palpable waves. His left hand slipped from her shoulder to stroke her back even as his right continued to rest lightly against her throat, stroking of its own volition. Such soft, beautiful skin to be marred in such an ugly way. "Have you seen a doctor?"

"I can't see a doctor, not when I can't explain how this happened. Besides, I don't need a doctor." She took a deep breath. "I need your help."

The air around them grew quiet. Jax's hand stilled on the middle of her back, where he could feel the clasp of her bra. He immediately wanted to charge into the fight, slay whatever dragons she faced. He wanted it so badly he trembled with it. He wanted her.

Then his detective instincts kicked in and he forced himself to stop touching her. No matter what, Nicole Legère was still his only link to Ananda Gutierrez and her murderer. Maybe Nicole's feared she was about to get caught.

"You don't believe me."

Nicole didn't need to say the words to know they were true. She'd felt the change in him, the sudden stiffness of his body. He'd been so protective earlier, probably reacting instinctively to the fear she'd tried to dampen. There was little sign of that protectiveness now, and she missed it. Missed the tiny zing of awareness that had flared when he'd touched her.

Her body shifted away from his, sliding further along the hard bench. He shifted too, and she was able to breathe again, think again. So he didn't believe her. Fine. She didn't need his conditional comfort. She was a Legère, a dreamer. She would be strong.

Taking another deep breath, she tied the scarf around her neck again, marveling at the blessed steadiness of her hands. "You know, I didn't have to come to you that first time. I could have just convinced myself that it wasn't my place to get involved, that the police didn't need me and my dubious help. Except for the fact that I told you about the nurse's death before it happened, you have nothing to tie me to it."

"But you are tied to it."

Nicole's lips twisted. "I was tied to Ms. Gutierrez's death when I had the first dream. I can't escape that. I know you believe I'm responsible for her death. In a way I am. I failed to convince you to believe in me, so her blood is on my hands."

Her voice shook at the last, but she forced it to steady. "The process is starting over now, Detective. I didn't have to come here today, but I did. I don't have to risk your censure and disbelief or even outright arrest, but I am."

She turned to stare at him, wanting him to acknowledge her words. "But I refuse to let another person die because you won't believe me."

He turned toward her. She could feel the heat of his body so close to hers, comforting and intimidating at the same time. She could feel his gaze, heavy on her neck, before rising to her eyes. Assessing. Condemning.

She refused to look away. "I want to make you a deal."

Surprise lifted his eyebrows. She would have smiled had she been able. "What sort of deal?" he demanded.

"I want you to have someone watch me for the rest of the day. Every day if need be, until this is done. You can camp out on my porch if you want to. I don't care. If I had two dreams last night, there's a good chance I'll have the third before the weekend is over."

He grunted over that. "What else?"

"I want you to come to my house tonight, to meet with me. To listen and not dismiss what I say out of hand because you can't see or feel or touch it."

He remained silent for a long time, studying her. "Are you setting me up?"

"No." She settled her sunglasses into place so he wouldn't see the hurt he'd caused her. Of course he would think it was a setup. "Despite what you think of me, despite what you think you know about me, I've got enough to deal with without needing to play elaborate games with the police or people's lives."

She opened her briefcase, reaching inside to extract a videocassette. "This is the first step in getting you to believe me," she informed him, thrusting the tape at him. "It's the documentary done on my family. Granted, it's probably drier than the sensational file you have on your desk, but it is unbiased."

He shuffled beside her on the bench as if mildly discomfited. Serves him right, she thought to herself. "There's other documentation I can give you, including another video and my journal, when you arrive tonight."

"If I come."

She rose, looked at him. The fear she felt as she'd walked into the precinct had left her, replaced by a heavy resolve.

"There are two things I know right now," she said into the stillness. "The first is, we have to work together to track this-this killer. The second thing is, if we don't he will kill again. So you will show up. You and I both know you have no choice. Good day, Detective Jackson."

Chapter Seven

Of course Jax showed up to her house that night.

He tried to pull the frown off his face as he pulled the car into Nicole's driveway. He felt as if Nicole Legère led him around like a dog on a leash, giving out information piecemeal. She held the key; he knew it in his bones. He wanted to show up on her doorstep with a squad of officers and turn her house upside down until he found whatever he needed to tie her to the case. He wanted to rattle her cage, shake her tree—

Jump her bones.

He shifted uncomfortably in his seat. That admission didn't sit too well with him, but he couldn't deny his reaction whenever he and Nicole were in the same room. Becoming rock-hard whenever she spoke wasn't something he could easily conceal—at least not for him.

Despite his attraction, he couldn't shake the feeling that more had gone on than Nicole shared. He knew it in his gut, with the instincts that had saved his life more than once.

Yet when he recalled the fear in those soft green eyes, the bruises on her throat, he wondered if he could ever doubt her. Maybe he was finally going off the deep end, as the department shrink wanted.

Irritated, he pulled out his phone and called his partner. "Okay, I'm here."

"Hey man, I don't know about this."

Jax shifted in the car seat again, trying to shake a nagging sense of something about to happen. Bear's doubt came through crystal clear over his earpiece. "Relax. The chief told me to sit on her. Besides, you were the one who told me this family's strictly legit."

"On paper anyway," his partner muttered. "That video had some freaky shit in it."

Jax had to agree with his partner there. Seeing all those white-coated people as they poked and prodded each Legère woman, stuck electrodes to their skin, hadn't been an easy thing to watch. It had become downright impossible when things started floating in mid air.

"Just watch your back."

"Isn't that your job?" Jax asked, eyes fastened to the house across the street. Nicole's Saturn sat in the drive. A lantern light lit the doorway, and a golden glow filtered from the windows. To Jax it looked more like the cover of a Christmas card than a meeting about murder.

"It's supposed to be," Bear groused. "But I wasn't invited to this little party, remember?"

Jax remembered all right. Bear had been less than enthusiastic about it, but they'd gotten green-lighted anyway. "I'll be fine, Bear. Besides, nothing's going to happen with her daughter present."

Bear's snort was unconvinced. "First sign of trouble, I'm there."

"Okay." Jax disconnected, then exited his car and paused, staring at the house. Something told him that when he left it again, he wouldn't be the same.

The front door opened before he could reach the top step. "Good evening, Detective Jackson." She was dressed more casually than he'd seen so far, in a multi-colored tunic and black leggings that accented the gorgeous length of her legs. He had a brief, electric image of those legs wrapped around his waist and went hard in an instant.

"Ms. Legère." He felt as if he should dip his head or something. Instead, he gave her his jacket again, hoping like hell she wouldn't notice his reaction to her. If she did, she gave no sign.

She led him into the living room again. The whitewashed armoire stood open to reveal a large television and entertainment system. Candles were lit unobtrusively about the room, including a couple of small ones on the coffee table. A stack of videotapes and a journal also lay on the table.

"How should we do this?" she asked, standing in the center of the room.

Jax shrugged. "It's your show. How do you want to do it?"

He watched her hands tangle together before she spoke. "I don't know. I've never done this before."

She seemed nervous, as jittery as an electrical current. If he got any closer to her, she'd probably zap him. Hell, he was zapped anyway.

He stepped closer to her, so close he could smell the subtle scent of her perfume, see how the light slid along the fabric of her blouse as her breasts rose and fell with each breath she took.

"Why don't we get right to it?" he asked, his voice low. "I'm not one for beating around the bush."

"A-all right." She sank onto the couch and he sat beside her, keeping a minimum amount of distance between them.

"What are these?" he asked, pointing to the stack of tapes. "More documentaries?"

She shook her head. "I have a small stand camera pointed at my bed that holds an eight-hour tape. I start the tape each night before I get into bed, and I stop it each morning when I get up. I label it with the date, and if anything out of the ordinary happened during the night, I note it on the face."

"How long have you been videotaping your sleep?"

"Almost since I first began having the dreams. But I stopped when I got married."

Silence fell, awkward and loud. "And you started up again after you were widowed?"

"My father suggested I start again, after I dreamed about the nurse."

She reached out, straightening the stack of tapes. She seemed to have a habit of straightening things when she was nervous, he noted.

"The coffee should be ready by now," she commented. "Would you like some?"

"Sure. I'll go with you."

He followed her into the kitchen, watching as she set up a tray of coffee things. "Your daughter's not here?"

"No, she's at a sleepover at my sister's." Her hands stilled. "I didn't want her here while we talked."

How convenient, Jax thought to himself. Then again, he didn't suppose he'd want his kid around while he was talking about murder either. Almost immediately on the heels of that thought came another: He was alone with Nicole Legère, the woman who had gotten under his skin in a major way.

Man, he liked the way she moved. She made him think of sunshine and fresh breezes, of lying next to her in a hammock. He could imagine running his hands over her luscious curves, enjoying the softness of her skin against the calluses on his hands.

"Detective?"

"If we're going to be working together, you should call me Jax," he said, taking the tray from her.

"All right, but you have to call me Nicole." She preceded him out of the kitchen and he once again enjoyed watching her walk.

"You know, I should probably apologize for riding you so hard the other day," he said, putting the tray down.

"Maybe, but you won't," she responded, a hint of a smile on her lips. "You were just doing your job. I must say, it was a very good version of Good Cop, Bad Cop."

Once they were seated with cups of coffee in their hands, Jax asked the question he most wanted an answer to. "Why didn't you tell me the truth about your husband?"

"What do you mean?"

"I mean how he filed for divorce before he died."

The cup trembled in her grip, forcing her to hold it with both hands. "You investigated me?" she asked, as if the revelation shocked her.

"Don't be so surprised. I always investigate suspects. It's what detectives do."

With careful, precise movements, she placed her cup on a stone coaster. "I didn't lie to you about Randall, Detective."

"Jax. Maybe you didn't, but you didn't tell the whole truth either, now did you?"

She turned to him, agitation written clearly in her expressive eyes. "So what? I'm supposed to bear my soul to you, share my tragedies and my failures with you, when you don't even know me, much less believe in me?"

He shifted closer to her, put his hand on her knee. "Then help me know you. Help me believe in you. I don't want to think of you as guilty of murder, but hiding things from me won't help me clear you."

"So you want the truth about Randall? All right, I'll give you the truth." Her voice and posture stiffened, but she didn't back away from him.

"I fell for his charms in college. He was handsome and flattering and polite, and he actually paid attention to me, said he liked that I was big-boned." She paused, swallowed. "It wasn't until after the marriage that I realized that he didn't want me, just my family connections and my money. Especially the money."

"Why did he file for divorce, especially if you were pregnant with his child?" Jax waited a beat, then added, "It was his child, right?"

He thought he heard her back pop as she straightened even further. "Danielle is his child. Despite everything he did, I was faithful to my husband. Regrettably, I can't say the same thing about him."

"He cheated on you?"

"He did more than that, Detective." Nicole looked at him, her shoulders slumping. "I never got the chance to tell him about Dani. Announcing my pregnancy would have seemed anticlimactic after he told me he'd gotten his mistress pregnant and decided he'd rather deal with the embarrassment of our divorce if it meant he could have a normal life with his wife."

Damn. Jax felt an unaccountable anger rise inside. Nicole recounted the details of her life as if it were someone else's story, all distant and unemotional "What did you do?"

"What most women do at times like that: threw him out of our house. I couldn't go back home with my tail tucked between my legs, and he preferred to leave anyway. We had a joint household account, but our main accounts were separate. It's amazing how easy it was to separate our lives. Amazing and sad."

She shook herself and continued the story. "He moved into a place near the Gulf that his family owned, and a week later I had my first dream of his death. I tried to talk to him, to convince him to leave. Lord, I even went to his parents. He actually thought I was trying to reconcile."

A bitter laugh escaped her. "Maybe I was, I don't know. Despite everything, I didn't want to deprive my child of her father. I had two more dreams, the next two nights. The night after the third dream, a storm came up, out of nowhere, and decimated that part of the coast. Randall didn't make it. With the inquest and news of the divorce, it was a painful time for me. I almost lost Danielle, and she was—still is—the most important thing in my life. I left New Orleans a couple of months after she was born."

What the hell was he supposed to say to that? Sorry? Jax didn't feel sorry. The bastard obviously didn't deserve her or his daughter.

She mistook his silence. "I don't want your pity, Detective. I've given you my truth. Now I want yours."

"What?" He backed off her. "You know my truth."

"No, I don't." Her green-gold eyes searched his face. "I know nothing about you, Detective Carter Jackson. I asked you before, about the guilt that drove you. I want to know what it is."

The defensive hairs on the back of his neck stood at attention. "And if I don't tell you, then what? You'll pick it out of my mind anyway?"

She shifted back as if he'd punched her. "I wouldn't do that, even if I could."

"Why should I tell you my story? So we can be even?"

"This isn't about being even. It's about trust. I don't trust you and you don't trust me. But if we're going to work together—"

"Which I'm having serious doubts about right now," he cut in.

"If we're going to work together," she repeated calmly, "then we're going to have to trust each other. Once this is over, you can go back to your life, and I'll go back to mine. Fair enough?"

Jax took his time answering. Yeah, he'd made her spill her history. But it was a history he'd had to go into anyway, when she was a suspect. Even if that was no longer the case officially, he still needed to know what made her tick. He had to make her comfortable enough to share with him. But mostly he'd wanted to know why her eyes always seemed to be so sad.

"All right," he said before he could change his mind. "I was married once. Felecia was a patrol officer."

Three-year-old memories swamped him. Felecia had been a decorated cop, beautiful, athletic, and friendly. She was the poster-child for police fund-raisers, and people had a tendency to flock to her like moths to a flame. The powers-that-be had wanted to take her off her beat, put her in an office, make her a spokesperson. Jax had even pleaded with her to forsake the neighborhood, but Felecia had laughed off his concerns. "My people need me," she'd said.

And one of her people had killed her.

His wife had died in a drive-by, gunned down by the brother of a gang member she had sent to jail. Gunned down while waiting for Jax, to celebrate their anniversary. Gunned down because he'd been late, he'd gotten there too late, three fucking minutes too late. Three minutes sooner and he would have been beside her, in front of her, would have seen the car coming, would have pushed her down and returned fire, would have taken the bullets that ripped her beautiful body apart.

He became aware of Nicole sitting beside him, gripping his hands strongly in hers. Her eyes were soft on his, not with pity, but with commiseration. She understood, he realized. Hell, she probably understood better than anyone the impotent anger and the debilitating guilt that never truly went away.

As if reading his mind, she said, "No matter how many times people tell you it wasn't your fault, it's hard to stop blaming yourself."

He let go abruptly, pushing away the memories and the instant bond Nicole had created. "If the psychoanalysis is over, we really should get back to the case."

"All right." Accepting his change of subject, she reached across him for one of the videotapes. "Like I said, I tape myself every night, hoping to capture something that could be of use to someone, or as a backup if I can't remember the dreams. They begin like I'm stepping into a painting or landscape. Then it slowly becomes real: sights, sounds, smells—all my senses work, just like in the waking world. Next there's this disorienting, wrenching sensation as I become the person in the dream."

He should have been spooked, listening as Nicole described her psychic dreams to him. But her straightforward, didactic style and the enjoyment of just watching her made it easy to listen, even if he didn't out-and-out believe. "Do you dream the entire time you're asleep?"

"No. From what my father tells me, I have the same sleep patterns as most people, at least at the outset: four progressively deeper levels of sleep that then reverse until the REM or heightened brain activity sleep begins. Then the process repeats itself, several times during the course of sleep.

"But my father discovered that my REM sleep is different. When I have one of the dreaming episodes, I go into deeper and deeper sleep, almost to the point of catatonia. Instead of ramping back through the lighter levels into REM, I experience dreams from the deeper end of sleep. He says it's almost like an out of body experience."

Jax remembered then that her father was a research scientist. "Your father studied you?"

"My father helped me—helped all of us—discover what our gifts were and how to manage them instead of letting them manage us. It would be so easy to let the paranormal take over. Having Papa's scientific understanding helps to keep us balanced."

"Why doesn't your family cash in on it?"

"You mean why don't we charge $2.99 the first minute, $5.99 each additional minute?" She gave him a smile that clearly said, *You poor misguided idiot.*

"That's not what our gifts are about. We help people, and by helping people, the family has prospered. Sometimes our gifts enhance our career choices. Malita, for example, is an empath—she's sensitive to people's emotions. She's also got a great talent for interior design. So why not combine the two and help people create living spaces that are emotionally and physically comfortable for them?"

"Makes sense," Jax conceded.

"So a lot of my cousins do that. A lot of them are involved in artistic endeavors, but a lot are in service and care industries too—healthcare, restaurants, things like that. The main thing is, we need to help people, to make them happy, lighter, to help them find peace. That's what the calling is for most of my family."

Jax shifted, feeling uncomfortable yet again. "You make it sound like something more than human, almost godlike."

"It's a gift of goodness, but we're definitely human." Her eyes darkened. "All too human, with the same fears and wants and frailties added to the talents we have."

"So none of you advertise your abilities?"

"Why would we do that?" she asked, crossing to the entertainment center. "I've had a good, quiet life until recently, and I prefer it that way. My daughter is in public school here. My neighbors know me to be responsible and trust me with their children. Advertising my abilities would be like hanging a neon sign on my front door. All kinds of people would come out of the woodwork, disrupting my life, accusing me of being the spawn of the devil, wanting me to tell their futures or wanting to experiment on me."

She shivered. "No, we Legères don't want the spotlight. Besides, I can't force my dreams to be about a particular person. They come when they come, and they are what they are."

She put the tape into the VCR. "This is the tape from this morning. I went to bed at my usual time, around eleven. Dani woke me up about two."

"This isn't going to be spooky, is it?" Jax asked as she returned to the couch with the remote. "No floating above the bed like *The Exorcist?*"

"I don't know. I've never watched any of the tapes."

That surprised him. "Why not?"

"First of all, I'm not all that jazzed about seeing myself on tape," she said, her tone wry. "Secondly, I record the dreams in my journal as soon as I wake up, while they're still fresh. I recount the dream straight through, then I go back and hypothesize about its meaning."

She handed him the remote. "So I don't know what you'll see or hear. Probably eight hours of nothing but me tossing and turning and snoring."

Jax sat back against the plushness of the couch, aimed the remote at the entertainment unit, and pressed the button. The television flashed on, then the VCR. The image on screen started out blurry, until it he realized it showed a close-up of Nicole's sleep shirt as she leaned in to turn on the camera.

She stepped back and straightened, giving him ample time to examine the movement of her breasts beneath the Tulane University logo. Then she turned around to head for the bed, and his mouth began to water. Good God, she was luscious, all ripe curves and warm womanhood, sugar and spice and everything nice.

The angle of the camera shot showed only the right side of the bed, a nightstand of dark wood, and a shaded lamp that could be dimmed or brightened by touch. Nicole slipped under the gold and ivory patterned bedcovers, then reached out to dim the light to its lowest setting. It still provided enough illumination for Jax to see her features clearly as she lay on her back, her hands resting demurely atop the folded down comforter.

Minutes ticked by. She shifted once, turning to face the lamp, and sighed. The sound of her breathing stole into him, weirdly giving him a sense of peace. Had he ever slept like that, as if the world was a better place than it actually was?

"How long did it take you to get used to the camera?" he whispered, pressing the fast-forward button.

"A few months," she whispered back. "At first I couldn't sleep at all, at least not normal sleep. The older cameras were noisy, but eventually I got used to it. Besides, the dreams come when they want to, whether I'm ready for them or not."

As if on cue, the onscreen Nicole moved. Jax paused the tape, then rewound a few seconds. "Hey yourself," he heard her say in a voice deeper and rougher than her normal tone. "What's your pleasure, sugar?"

She flicked her hair back over her shoulders. "Fifty won't get me horizontal, sugar, but people tell me I have a golden tongue."

Her left hand reached out, then closed, as if taking something. Jax watched in surprise as Nicole stuck her hand into the top of her nightshirt. He assumed in her dream she'd just taken money from her trick. "Not one for conversation are you, sugar? That's okay, the strong, silent type makes me hot."

She moved beneath the covers, giving a smile that heated his senses. "Like to get right to it, huh? Fine with me, sugar. It's your money."

Again her hands reached out; again she gave a smile that Jax had never seen on her face before. Without warning she emitted a short scream, a cry that was abruptly cut off. Her legs flailed beneath the bedcovers, flinging them off. One hand went to her throat while the other fisted into the air. Choking sounds were audible on the tape as she writhed on the bed. Her movements grew fainter until they finally stopped all together. She lay like the dead.

Suddenly she gasped for air, screaming as she struggled to a sitting position. She stumbled out of bed and ran to the right, out of view of the camera. After a few moments, a blur ran across the screen from the left: Nicole's daughter, calling for her. Muffled sounds, then the little girl came back, at a slower pace. After another moment Nicole came back. He could hear her sniffling, as if she'd been crying. The screen went blurry as she reached for the camera, then dark as she turned it off.

Jax sat quietly for a moment, unsure of what to say and unwilling to say anything. The cynical side of him wanted to say that she'd staged the whole thing for his benefit. If she had, she needed to take herself to Hollywood instead of getting her doctorate. But it would be a low thing to scare her daughter like that, just to make an impression on him.

Jesus, if it was real . . . .

He turned to face her. Whatever he'd been about to say died on his lips.

Nicole sat stiffly on the couch, her hands balled into fists on her clamped knees. Her eyes, wide with shock and fear, stared blindly ahead. She trembled as if she were about to fly apart.

"Nicole?"

He got no response until he shook her. Then she jerked to awareness, blinking as if to clear her head. "Now I know why I never watch these." Her attempt at lightheartedness fell flat.

Jax again felt torn between wanting to believe her and wanting to arrest her. Between wanting to hold her forever and staying as far away from her as possible. "That was some nightmare."

She put her head in her hands, not answering for a moment. He let her have the silence. If he'd been in her place, he'd want a moment too.

Lifting her head, she sighed, then sat back. "Have you ever been wounded, Detective Jackson?" she asked. Her voice was hoarse with tension. "Have you ever had to face your own mortality?"

"I've never been wounded, but I know what it's like to put my life on the line. I'm a cop—I do that every day when I go to work."

She pointed to the television, her movements slow. "That is much worse. A thousand times worse. And I experienced that twice last night. I know what it is to die, with my last thought being for my beautiful stockings. I know what it is to be rushing home to see my little girl after a long night in the emergency room, so tired I can't see straight. I know what it is to be attacked and killed, dying choking in the mud. I know what it is to choke on blood and feel the pain of having my throat ripped into. That is what my life has been. Not just nightmares, but actual pain, fear and death."

"Then tell me what you saw. Where were you? Inside or outside? Was it dark? Was there a moon? Did you see a street sign, recognize the neighborhood? Give me something here."

"Don't you think I want to?" Her voice cracked, along with her normal reserve. "Don't you think I want to be able to give you everything you need to catch this guy? God, if I could, I'd give you his name and address!"

She jerked to her feet, then moved to lift her journal off the coffee table. Her hands moved over the dark blue fabric cover, smoothing away nonexistent wrinkles as if she tried to smooth out her emotions.

"I write my dreams down as soon as I wake up," she went on, her tone struggling for normalcy. "Straight through without stopping to think about it, just to get it down on paper. Then I go back and try to analyze it. I try to recall the things I've experienced, the settings, smells, all those things. I try not to over-analyze it, or I could end up with false memories." She handed the book to him.

Jax stroked the book in the same manner she had, more to control his urge to open it right then than anything else. "Have you ever tried hypnosis?"

Her lips twisted into a semblance of a smile. "It doesn't work well on me. My father said he was able to communicate with me in my dreams a handful of times, but it's been years."

"I know a little bit about it," Jax said. When she glanced at him, he added, "I minored in psych while getting my criminology degree."

She nodded, seemingly not surprised by his admission. "I suppose communicating with me while I'm dreaming is like hypnosis in a way, except that I'd be asleep instead of in a suggestive state."

"So we could certainly give it a shot, see if it works," Jax offered, keeping his tone casual.

"You mean having you ask me questions while I'm dreaming?"

"Yeah." Jax warmed to the idea. "You're either going to respond to me or not. But we should give it a try."

Her brows dipped as she considered his words. "I suppose we could, but I'm wide awake now. I won't be able to sleep until nightfall, and even that's no guarantee that I'll dream tonight. It could happen tomorrow or Sunday."

"You're right. Thanks for the invitation."

"What invitation?"

"To spend the weekend with you."

Chapter Eight

Nicole stared at him as if he'd just pronounced himself as Emperor of the World. "I don't think so."

"No? I think it's a great idea."

"A great idea?" Nicole knew her voice had climbed into the stratosphere, but damned if she could do anything about it. "How by any sane stretch of the imagination can you think this is a great idea?"

He smiled at her. Under other circumstances she would have thought him handsome when he smiled, but now his grin only served to further unnerve her.

"You do want to prove your innocence, don't you?"

"I don't have to prove my innocence," she shot back. "You have to prove my guilt—which you can't do because I'm not guilty!"

"You're wrong," he said in a pleasantly agreeable tone that grated on her nerves. "I don't have to prove you guilty or innocent. All I have to do is present enough evidence to have a warrant issued for your arrest. And that I can do. Or, I can discover that you really are what you say you are, and that you have nothing to do with the murders."

Caught between the proverbial rock and a hard place. She swallowed. "So you want to be my alibi, is that it?"

"No. I want to catch a killer, and you're my only connection. So if that means I have to stick closer to you than your shadow, I'm gonna do it."

The hardness of his voice didn't surprise her. Really, she couldn't blame him either. If their places were reversed, she'd want the same thing. And she'd practically ordered him to have someone watch her. But to have *him* in her house, watching her while she slept?

She tried again, knowing she was attempting to stave off the inevitable. "You don't have a change of clothes."

"Sure I do. I always keep some in the car, in case my cases go beyond nine to five, which happens all the time."

"This is highly unorthodox, isn't it?" she asked, on the verge of giving in.

"Absolutely," he agreed. "This whole case is unorthodox. In fact, you could probably have my badge for this, with just one phone call. Or you could just flat-out refuse and I'll stay in my car. But I think you're just as eager to clear yourself as I am to clear you."

She couldn't conceal her surprise. "You want to clear me?"

"Yes." His gaze held hers. "I don't like thinking of you as a killer. It goes against the gut instinct I have about you. And I certainly can't get involved with a suspect."

"Get involved with a—oh." Nicole let her hands fall into her lap, feeling totally out of her depth.

Jax's expression hardened. "Nothing's been by the book on this, and I have the feeling that it's gonna get stranger before it gets better. All I can say is that you get a rise out of me—literally—like no one ever has."

No one had ever spoken to her like that in her life. Certainly Randall had never been so matter-of-fact. "That's definitely blunt."

"I can get a whole lot blunter." Jax sat next to her. "I want you. In the worst way. But I'm not going to try to jump your bones or anything, no matter how much I may want to. First and foremost, I'm gonna do my job. And I'm sure as hell not gonna force anything on you. But don't try to deny that there's something here."

"All right." She rubbed her damp palms on her thighs. What in the world had she gotten herself into? She'd asked for truth and received it in spades. "All right, there is something here. But I still don't know if I even like you. You have to admit, the time that we've spent together has been nothing short of antagonistic."

He didn't seem to mind her declaration. "All the more reason for us to spend some time working together. Isn't this what you wanted when you asked me to come here today?"

Nicole wasn't sure what she wanted anymore. But if Jax could help her get it, she had to try.

"All right," she said again. She got to her feet and began tidying up the coffee table. "How do you want to do this? I don't think I'd be comfortable with you watching me sleep in my bedroom."

"We can do it down here," he said. They both realized the suggestiveness of his words at the same moment. "What I meant to say is that we can set up your camera down here, train it on the sofa. I'll take the loveseat."

"I'll take the loveseat," she asserted. "I won't have you griping at me tomorrow because you had to fold into a pretzel to sleep."

"All right," he agreed with obvious relief.

"Is there someone you need to call, to notify of your whereabouts?"

"You mean so that you'll be safe from me?"

She restrained herself from folding her arms across her chest. "No, so you'll be safe from me."

His expression showed his lack of worry. "I think I can take you if need be, but Bear—Detective Marshall—knows I'm here. I'll call him anyway. By the way, did you eat dinner? I could order some Chinese or Thai or whatever you like."

This was quickly becoming surreal. Nicole had to remind herself that there was nothing ordinary about this night or this man. This was not a friendly get-together. And most definitely not a date. Carter Jackson was a detective investigating one murder and possibly another and she was either his prime suspect or witness.

"Nicole?"

"Either is fine. I like chicken dishes. There're some takeout menus in the drawer next to the wall phone in the kitchen. I'll, uh, go upstairs and get the camera and some extra linens."

She wasn't retreating from the absurdity of the situation, she told herself as she climbed the stairs. She was just giving Jax privacy as he made his calls.

Sure you are, she thought. Honestly, she needed time to think. Even though she'd asked for this, asked for someone to watch her, she had a sense of things moving much too fast. Jax's blunt declaration that he wanted her had surprised and pleased her. Oh yeah, and scared her senseless.

She'd been aware of him on an instinctive level from their first meeting. Now that her anger didn't flare at the sight of him, that awareness had cranked up a notch. He was a man—a broad-shouldered, protect-the-family-and-hunt-the-game kind of a man. She had a feeling that he could be intensely loyal to those he gave his trust to, and that not many people made it onto that list.

He didn't seem to mind that she wasn't built like her sisters; she'd even go so far as to believe he preferred her curves. Nothing like this had ever happened to her before; even Randall had never bluntly said he wanted her. Of course, her body wasn't what Randall had been after.

She pulled open the linen closet, removing extra pillows, sheets and blankets. She didn't believe Jax wanted her for her part of the family fortune, and if he did, the story she'd told him about how the Legacy was handled should have disabused him of that notion. But she'd seen the look in his eyes as he'd made the matter-of-fact statement. She'd believed him when he'd said he wanted her. Just as she'd believed him when he'd said he wouldn't touch her.

His expression floated in her memory. Naked need had smoldered there, a need that had stolen her breath and made her insides quiver. Beyond a shadow of a doubt, she was headed into uncharted territory. Dangerous, thrilling territory.

Jax was still on the phone when she returned to the living room. She turned to go back upstairs to give him privacy, but he waved her into the kitchen.

"There's nothing to worry about, Bear," he said into the phone. He listened for a moment, then looked at her with a grin that made her lightheaded. It was the first time he'd ever smiled at her. "No, I don't trust her, but she doesn't trust me either, so that makes us even."

It was the truth, but it still surprised her to hear him say it, especially while she stood in the room. "Bear, we both know she's connected to the case. You were the one who said we should keep an open mind and pursue every angle. Besides, Nicole is just as determined to get to the bottom of this as we are. If you don't believe me, you can ask her."

His grin widened. Nicole could hear Bear's voice coming through the receiver loud and clear, even though she couldn't make out the words. "Yes, she's been standing here the whole time. We're trying to trust each other, and we gotta start somewhere."

We gotta start somewhere. There was more than a little truth in that statement. She also had to trust him. He was either going to help or hinder her, and it all depended on what she did over the next two days.

She went back into the living room and began replacing and lighting candles. Just having the soft glow filtering through the room made her relax. *Just don't think about it,* she told herself. *Don't think about this large man with a gun being in your house. Don't think about him watching you while you sleep. Don't think about how it felt when he put his hand on your back. Just don't think at all.*

Jax entered the room. "I ordered Chinese." He made it seem as if it were a normal occurrence. "It should be here in a half hour or so."

"All right." Nicole put her lighter way. "Sounds like your partner isn't exactly thrilled with your idea."

"Nope, but I didn't expect him to be."

"What? He thinks I'm going to try to kill you in your sleep or something?"

"Something like that. Bear's not nearly as trusting as I am."

She matched his wry smile. "If you're supposed to be trusting, I'd hate to have to come up on the wrong side of your partner."

"Well, we do trade off sometimes. He was more believing toward you than I was at first."

"Are you saying that you believe me now?" she asked, one eyebrow raised.

"I'm not in the amen choir just yet. I'm in that I'll-believe-it-when-I-see-it choir."

"How can I forget?" Skeptical Jax she could handle. The considerate, human Jax was a different ball of wax. She smiled at her rhyming thoughts. "What do you want me to do? Float something across the room?"

"Can you do that?" Jax sat forward on the couch, his expression eager.

"Telekinesis isn't my strong point. That's what my brothers do best." She swallowed her laughter, sobered. "Sometimes, though, when I get really upset, things have a habit of moving."

"Moving like how?"

Her hands knotted in her lap. "Moving like violently. Vases flying off shelves and into walls. Windows rattling, cabinet doors slamming, that sort of thing."

She refused to look at him as heat crept up her cheeks. "It hasn't happened in a while. That's why I try to live as calm a life as possible."

Silence filtered through the room like the scent from the candles. Nicole's hands tightened in her lap. If Jax had thought her certifiable before, he was probably convinced of it now.

"We all need some place of serenity in the chaos of our lives," he finally said. "I think your home does that for you."

The evenness of his tone almost made her slump with relief. "It does," she said, glancing around the room with affection. "I consider this my sanctuary, no doubt about it. Coming home and spending time with my daughter is the best part of my day."

"I can understand that." He reached for the remote. "Would you mind if I turned on the television?"

"Of course not." She got up, crossing to the coffee table to pick up the stack of videocassettes. "I'm assuming you'll want these as evidence or something?"

"I'll go through them. But with the timestamp and your daughter's corroboration, they probably won't need to be admitted as evidence. The journal may be a different story, if it's as detailed as you say."

Nicole placed the stack of videos beside the VCR in the cabinet, then crossed back to retrieve her journal, clasping it to her chest. "Will you have to keep it?"

"For a little while, at least, especially if it helps us track the killer."

She stroked the soft cover. The journal was as much a part of her life as Dani was. Besides recording the dreams, she'd confided in her journal in ways she never would confide in a person. In a lot of ways, it was her best friend. The thought depressed her. "What if, what if I make photocopies for you? Would that be enough?"

Jax got to his feet in an easy movement at odds with his size. "I'll tell you what. Tomorrow we'll go and make copies together, and you'll have your journal back by nightfall." He stepped close, close enough to touch, his voice and posture offering reassurance. "All right?"

She nodded in agreement, but she couldn't make herself relax the death-grip she had on the diary. "I'm sorry." She ducked her head. "I know it's just a book."

He moved closer still, until she could feel the heat emanating from him. "But it's more than just a book to you," he said, his voice soft. His hand cupped her cheek, the calluses on his fingers deliciously rough against her skin. "It's a part of your life. A very personal part of your life that you'd just as soon keep private."

"Yes." Her body tingled with the nearness of his, making her lightheaded.

The gentle press of his thumb raised her face to his. "But we both know that sometimes we have to do things we may or may not want to do. Not because it's wrong, but because it's so very right."

She watched in fascination as his face moved closer to hers. Why was he lowering his lashes like that? Oh Lord, he was going to kiss her!

No sooner did the thought cross her mind than his lips closed the distance between them. His moustache tickled against her upper lip and then she forgot about it entirely as a rush of feeling swept through her. Her pulse jumped beneath her skin as his tongue swept her mouth, commandeering her senses.

She kissed him back with more than seven lonely years of pent-up desire, her hands circling his waist. With a grunt of what sounded like satisfaction, he pulled her closer. Her hands gripped his belt to steady herself as she leaned into him, molding herself to him.

The kiss deepened, became almost brutal, but she didn't care. All she cared about was the heat that coursed through her veins, the desire that flowed between her thighs, and the man who was making it all happen.

Her hands moved up his waist, needing to touch him. Her right hand bumped something heavy, smooth. His gun.

The spell of desire shattered. She backed away as if he'd drawn the weapon on her. "What's wrong?" he asked. "And don't tell me you didn't like it."

"Of course I liked it." It didn't cross her mind to fib. "That's what I don't like." She leveled a finger at his gun. "Do you have to keep wearing that?"

He looked at his holster. "I take it off at bedtime. Does it bother you?"

"Guns are such ugly things." She shuddered with a mixture of reactions, passion and distaste. "They make it easier for people to kill each other."

He took a step toward her. She took a step backward. He sighed and rubbed his forehead. "I've found that when people have the urge to kill, they usually find a way to do it, whether it's a gun or a butcher's knife or their car."

She touched her fingers to her lips. He zeroed in on the movement, and the gleam in his eyes made her take another step back. "Each successive advance in weaponry has made the act of killing more impersonal," she said, her words rushing over each other as she strove for some semblance of normalcy and distance. "People can distance themselves from it. It was more horrifying to have to club or stone someone to death. Guns make killing no more of a big deal than killing electronic demons in a video game."

She flushed. "We studied that last semester, violence in, and its effect on, society."

He sighed again, and she thought there was more than a little frustration in the sound. "Murder of any kind is definitely a big deal, even with guns," Jax said. "Though I have to admit, it take a certain kind of person to slice someone open with a knife. Or strangle someone almost to the point of decapitation."

"Exactly. Someone for whom evil is as natural as the sun rising in the east."

"Doesn't that counteract your psychological training?" Jax wondered. "I'd figured that you'd say no one is evil, just misguided, or mentally ill."

"That can explain some people, but not all. Unfortunately, some people are simply evil, and murder and hurt people for the enjoyment of it. We as a society have to say they're ill because that's the only way we can accept it, be comfortable with it. If we don't accept it, then we'd have to do something about it, and no one wants that responsibility."

"Except maybe psychologists."

"And police," she added.

"All right." He squared his shoulders. "Now that we've got that settled, I'd really like to get back to our original subject. Come here."

Maybe it was the tone of his voice. Maybe it was the way he held his arms out to her. Or maybe it was the heat that sparked his expression. Whatever it was, Nicole found that she couldn't ignore the summons. Even if she'd wanted to, her body mutinied, moving forward without conscious thought.

The doorbell rang. Jax muttered something that should have scorched her ears, except that it echoed her sentiments. "I'll get it," he said.

"I think I'll get it," Nicole said. "You'll probably scare the delivery guy to death if you answer the door wearing your gun."

"Too bad he's not trying to break in. I really feel the need to shoot something right now."

Chapter Nine

Jax turned on the video camera and returned to the couch. There was just enough light to read the journal without disturbing Nicole, and reading would give him something to do while he waited for her to dream.

Instead of picking up the journal, he turned to the loveseat. The piece of furniture was almost as long as the couch he occupied and Nicole stretched its full length. She faced him, her makeup-free skin glowing. She looked peaceful and beautiful.

He'd never been one to daydream, but he caught himself imagining what it would be like to watch her sleep every night, to touch that soft skin and pull her beautiful body close.

Need pulsed through him. It had been three years since he'd lost Felecia. Actually, three years, two months and twenty-six days that he'd spent questioning his life, his commitment, his duty as a cop. Grief had almost made him walk away, which would have been the second biggest mistake of his life. The first was letting his wife die.

Instead, he'd thrown himself into his work, and his work had saved him. He'd been decorated a number of times, but that wasn't why he went to work every day. It certainly wasn't for the paycheck, though he wasn't hurting in that department. No, he was still a cop because he was good at it, because he believed in right and wrong, and because people needed someone to protect them, if only from themselves.

He looked at Nicole again. She was stronger than she believed, he knew that already. He also knew that she needed help. He wanted to help her, wanted to protect her, wanted to erase that bleakness from her eyes. He wanted to find this killer, not only for the victim and her family, but also so Nicole could stop having the dreams that cost her more than anyone should have to pay.

She was an unusual woman. He didn't know anyone who washed out take-out food containers with soap and water before putting them in the trash.

He picked up the journal and settled back against the couch.

She took a final drag on her cigarette before flicking it behind her. Maybe it would catch fire, bringing some heat to the night. Sure would be better than standing here freezing her ass off waiting for a trick to come by.

She tugged on the hem of her cheap leatherette skirt that barely covered her hot pink crotchless panties. She'd been working too long to be vain about anything, but she did have one indulgence: stockings. Lace-topped stockings had been her trademark in her younger days in Vegas and even though she'd fallen far from that heyday, she couldn't bear to give them up.

She eased off the wall as a man approached her, stopping just short of the light. Tall, wearing what looked like a cowboy hat. Not a regular then. "Well hello, sugar. What's your pleasure?"

For answer, a bill was thrust at her. Grant's taciturn expression stared up at her.

A smile split her hardened lipstick. "Fifty won't get me horizontal, sugar," she purred, stepping closer. Actually it would, but he didn't need to know that. "But people tell me I have a golden tongue."

Mr. Silent Type stepped back into the shadows between two buildings. She frowned. "Why don't we go to your car, sugar, so we can be more comfortable?"

He didn't answer, just leaned against the wall. She shook her head. She should leave, pass up the fifty bucks. But she was a businesswoman, and she could grab her knife quick enough. Besides, ten or so minutes and she'd be back in her spot waiting for the next one to come along. There was always a next one.

The trick opened his jacket, a nice leather bomber-style number that kids shot each other for. She stepped forward and took Grant off his hands, sticking the dour dead president into her cleavage. Bet you never had that much fun in real life, Mr. President.

"Not one for conversation are you, sugar?" she asked, not really expecting an answer. "That's okay, the strong silent type makes me hot."

She knelt before him, sliding her hands up his jeans-clad legs. His hands snaked into her hair, pulling her closer. "Like to get right to it, huh? Fine with me, sugar. It's your money."

She reached for the zipper on his trousers. Without warning a whistling cut the night air, as something zipped about her throat, breaking the skin. One hand fisted into his private parts as she instinctively went for her knife. He cursed, then pulled tighter, pressing into her windpipe.

The knife! Get the knife! She tried to jerk away from him, jerk him off balance, but he shifted around behind her, tightening the rope about her neck, pushing the spikes in deeper. She stabbed her knife into his thigh, but it was a weak thrust. He kicked her hard, sending her flying. Before she could loosen the spiked cord, he pressed down on her, growling, ripping into her throat. Cold and warmth poured through her. Then darkness came, taking the pain away.

"Nicole!"

Jax shook Nicole again, wanting her to wake up. What had begun as an attempt to communicate with Nicole while she dreamed had quickly gone south. He'd seen the exact moment the dream descended into desperate nightmare. She'd been fighting, fighting for her life when she suddenly went completely and utterly still.

Air screamed into her lungs as her eyes opened wide with terror. He eased his grip, calling her name again, waiting for recognition to replace the fear.

"Jax." All at once her body relaxed. She put her hands to her forehead. "Oh God."

"Tell me what happened," he suggested, his grip easing further.

"I—I need to write it down before it slips away." She rubbed her hands over her face. "It helps to exorcise everything."

He found the journal and handed it to her, pleased that his hand didn't shake. She'd damn near freaked him out, and he hated being freaked out. "Can I get you something to drink? Water? Maybe tea would be better for your throat."

Her fingers fluttered about her throat like nervous butterflies. "Tea would be good," she whispered, "but tequila would be better."

"Tequila?" She didn't seem like the type to turn to hard liquor. But after what he'd just witnessed, he could use a swig himself. "Okay, where do you keep it?"

Following her instructions, he retreated to the kitchen for the liquor and a couple of shot glasses, all the while wondering what the hell he had gotten himself into.

Sure, he'd agreed to watch over her just in case she had a dream, but he hadn't really meant it. Not that way. He hadn't truly believed that Nicole would have another dream—and certainly not one that she acted out. Even now, he wanted to doubt that it had been anything more than an elaborate ruse on her part.

But his gut told him different. His gut made him remember how the hairs on his arms had stood on end, remember the tingle of something along his skin. Made him remember the heat of energy that had radiated from her when he'd attempted to wake her.

Something had happened. His mind wasn't quite ready to call it a psychic episode, but he knew without doubt that whatever Nicole had experienced went beyond the ordinary.

He pulled the cork from the expensive bottle of tequila—100% pure premium agave, thank you—and poured two generous shots. After corking and replacing the bottle, he took the two shot glasses back into the living room.

Nicole pulled her head out of her hands as Jax returned. The notebook lay beside her, open and facedown. "I wrote down as much as I could," she said, accepting the shot with an unsteady hand. She tossed the tequila down without ceremony, breathing an audible sigh as she set the glass on the coffee table.

"I figured that you'd want to ask me some questions, so I left the camera on."

With the warmth of the liquid spreading through her, Nicole answered his questions as best as she could. Jax's matter-of-fact questioning helped ease some of the horror she'd experienced. Despite her desire to continue, her voice soon gave out.

Jax muttered a soft oath as he crossed to the video camera. "I'm pushing you too hard," he said in an apologetic tone as he powered the camera off. "Maybe we should go to the hospital, let a doctor take a look at your throat."

She shook her head in denial to both statements. Her fuzzed mind couldn't think of a reasonable explanation for her bruised throat that a doctor would accept, even with a police detective to back her up. And she certainly couldn't tell the truth.

Urgency and frustration clawed through her. She understood Jax's need to get answers and didn't mind being pushed for them. She wanted answers as much as he did. The sooner the man was caught, the sooner the dreams would stop, allowing her to return to her normal life.

"Maybe you should spend the rest of the night upstairs," he suggested, his voice gentler than she'd ever heard it.

She nodded, overcome with sudden lethargy. Just the act of rising to her feet caused her to stumble. Jax caught her, a thick muscled arm snaking about her waist. She leaned against him gratefully, even though she knew mere politeness caused him to help her.

He assisted her to her bedroom. "I'll go get your journal for you, in case there's something else you want to write down. I'll be right back."

After Jax left, she shucked her leggings, then pulled her arms through the sleeves of her t-shirt to remove her bra. As she crawled beneath the comforter it all hit her. She'd had the third dream; that poor woman was going to die. She'd fight, kicking, scratching, and screaming, but she'd still die. If Nicole had been able to give Jax enough information, he would have left, calling his partner so they could stake out the location. But they couldn't, because she hadn't done enough. She hadn't seen enough.

A sob escaped her before she could stop it, followed closely by another. Her body shook with the effort to control her tears, conscious of Jax just a floor below her, but she couldn't stop them. She sat up in bed, hunched over with a pillow on her raised knees to staunch the sobs that threatened to become screams.

"Nicki."

She gasped at the nickname, lifting her head to look at Jax. He stood in her doorway, a blurred form. "Jax."

Arms went around her, cradling her against a wide, solid chest. He held her and she let him, taking comfort whether he offered it or not. With her world spiraling into the unknown, she needed to cling to something real, something warm and alive.

She turned her face into the curve of his neck, pressing her mouth against the stubble along his jaw. He stiffened against her, his hands safely against her shoulder blades. That wasn't the type of safety that she sought.

Needing, daring, she kissed him, leaning against him in unspoken demand. Desire overrode her fear of being a suspect, a psychic conduit. At that moment, assuaging need mattered more than anything else.

Just when she thought she'd have to learn how to seduce or be reduced to begging, Jax reacted. His arms tightened around her, one hand cupping the back of her neck. He turned his head to meet her lips with a heavy, bruising demand she couldn't, wouldn't refuse.

Parting her lips, she stifled a sigh as his tongue swept into her mouth like a conquering hero. Oh yeah, this was a kiss. Sensation swept through her, stealing her breath, tightening her core, curling her toes. She had to wrap her arms around his neck to keep from slipping to the floor.

Muscles flexed against her as Jax lifted her to her feet. She wondered why for a split second before his hands went to her hips, molding her curves to the hard planes of his body. She groaned aloud as his lips continued their devastating assault, blazing a trail from her lips to her throat with deadly accuracy.

Her hands plucked at his shirt, eager to feel his skin. Somehow she managed to work the buttons free without resorting to ripping them away. But she wanted to.

Lord, how she wanted to.

Desire shot through her, as potent as a swallow of premium tequila, heating her insides with a steady, delicious burn. After throwing the shirt away, pulling his t-shirt over his head, she ran her hands over the wide expanse of his shoulders, caught up in admiration of God's artistry. The mahogany of his skin felt like velvet beneath her fingers. Velvet that barely restrained the steeled power of his strength. She had to brush her lips across his skin to see if he tasted as velvety as he felt.

He did. Lord have mercy.

"Nicki." Her name on his lips was plea, demand, prayer. He had to call her again before she could pull her gaze, her touch, her lips, away from his chest. He stared at her in a way no man ever had, raging desire barely held in check.

"Tell me this is real," he demanded, catching her hands before they drifted to his zipper. "Not some damn side effect. Tell me you want this, need this, as much as I do."

She did. God help her, she did. She'd worry about the consequences later. Right now she needed to drive the horror away. She needed to reaffirm that she lived, that she was alive.

Throwing away all caution, she kissed him again. He responded by vising her to him, taking over the kiss with an insistent slant of his mouth. All at once his grip eased, the kiss gentled. His hands slid up her back to cup her neck, his thumbs brushing along her jawline as he nipped at her bottom lip.

Lord have mercy.

Nicole's moan sent a surge of satisfaction through Jax, enabling him to exert control over his desire. He wanted her, had been wanting her for forever. He wanted to pull the worn nightshirt over her head and pin her to the bed, then slam into her until they were both breathless and satisfied. And done.

He didn't want to be done. He wanted her to shiver with savor, shake with sensation, then shatter with satisfaction. Then he wanted to make her do it all over again.

He parted from her long enough to rid them of the last of their clothes, retrieving the condoms he'd stuffed into his wallet a few days ago as a vain hope. Then, because his hands burned with the need to touch her, he skimmed his fingertips up her thighs, skating over her stomach to cup her breasts. Breath shuddered between them as he caressed the tips with the pads of his thumbs, watching as they hardened further.

He looked up to see her eyes fastened on his hands, her lips parting as she breathed out desire. Her short nails dug into his shoulders. "Your mouth. Please."

Knowing what she meant, he took his time, claiming her lips before bearing her back onto the bed, one arm locked around her waist. He nipped at her full lower lip, her chin, before doing a slow slide down the column of her throat to the soft, honeyed rise of her breast. His tongue swept out, touched the tip just a moment before his mouth closed over it. Her low moan of pleasure brought an answering grunt from him. Damn, she tasted good.

He suckled her gently, building the pressure and the pleasure until he pulled strongly with his mouth, teeth, tongue. Until she whimpered. Until she shivered.

He smiled into her right breast. Two to go.

His hand stroked down her body, cupping her. She stiffened, but he murmured to her, low, as his hand smoothed across her thighs, his lips continuing their assault on her breast. He could feel her melting, relaxing, opening. His middle finger curved down, around, in.

Her whole body arched off the bed, up against his hand. A hiss of pleasure became his name. He slipped another finger inside her, the heat driving straight up his arm and right down into his groin. Ready, she was nearly ready.

Withdrawing his fingers, he concentrated on the delicate whorl of flesh, swirling his fingertips over her. Watching the passion play across her face made his body rage with the need to be inside her. Not yet, though. Not until—

With a soft cry, her entire body shook.

One more to go.

He wanted to blaze a meandering trail back up to her lips, but Nicole had other plans. She actually tugged on his ears, pulled him to her, almost desperate. He responded to her urgent demand, fitting himself to her, entering her with one determined stroke. Even sheathed, he could feel her, hot, tight, all around him. Her groan echoed his as she flexed against him.

Jax froze, holding himself rigid inside her and against her, his forearms bracketing her head. She shifted in delicious agony, and every nerve ending enflamed. It was almost too much. He shivered. "Jax?"

"Wait." Testing himself, his control, he moved against her, one long advance and retreat that left her gasping and him shaking with the urge to break down and fuck her brains out. "You're so fucking beautiful," he breathed.

He kissed her, hot and open against her mouth, her cheekbone, the sensitive place just below her ear. "Your legs. Around me. Now." She complied and they both groaned again as he settled deeper, filling her completely.

He wanted to be gentle, wanted to take his time and make the moment last. But her heat wrapped around him, her breasts pushed against his chest, and the need that had ridden him for days roared inside him, like an angry god demanding to be appeased. Settling into a relentless pace, he pushed into her over and over and over again, determined to have her shatter. When she came, clenching him within and without, something inside him snapped, made him wild. Burying his face into the crook of her neck, he pushed his arms beneath her and slammed into her like a madman, again and again, desperately racing for the peak. Another final, frantic thrust and he joined her, his entire body shattering before they collapsed against each other, spent.

Chapter Ten

The phone rang beneath his ear, wrenching Jax from barely-begun sleep. He grabbed it and flipped it open. "Yeah."

"We got another one."

"Shit." Jax sat up, instantly alert. He glanced at the readout on Nicole's alarm. Just past four. He'd had only half an hour's sleep. "Where?"

Bear gave him the location as Nicole stirred beside him. He cursed again. "Okay. I'm on my way." He flipped the phone closed.

Nicole switched on the lamp beside her as he left the bed. "She's dead, isn't she?"

"Someone is." He found his pants next to three discarded condom wrappers. Shit. He scooped them up, then went into her bathroom to retrieve the rest of the evidence. Just in case.

When he reentered the bedroom, she sat up, running a hand through her hair to smooth it down. Her eyes were soft with sleep and sex, and he remembered the last time inside her, the silent, sensitive time that hadn't been about need or comfort.

"Do you want me to make you some coffee?"

"No time. Bear's already at the scene." He pulled his shirt on, forcing his eyes away from the sheet that barely covered her breasts. He didn't want to be rude, but he didn't want to talk about Bear's discovery. Not yet, and not with her.

Besides, he knew if he looked at her again, he'd do something really stupid—like pull her into his arms and kiss her. That was what a man would do when he left his woman. *His woman.* The thought made him angry. Nicole Legère was his witness, his link to a murderer, not his woman, despite the tissue of used condoms stuffed in his pocket.

He grabbed his gun off the nightstand behind him, checked it, then put it into the shoulder holster. He could feel Nicole's stare.

"W-will you come back today?"

"I don't know," he answered, deliberately evasive as he shoved his feet into his shoes. He could feel the coldness growing inside him, distancing her. "These things kinda consume a day."

"I understand."

Jax winced at the obvious hurt in her voice, but he had no time to deal with it. He'd make it up to her later, somehow. "I'll call you."

He probably would, he thought later as he drove away. But it wouldn't be the kind of call Nicole would want.

What the hell had he thought, going to bed with her? He hadn't been thinking; that was the point. He'd just reached for her, to hell with the consequences. Three times. With a sinking feeling he realized he'd be the one damned.

Need slammed into him, hard and demanding. He gripped the steering wheel, fighting the urge to turn the car around, tires squealing, engine roaring, and head back to Nicole's as fast as he could. Back to sensuous curves and soft sounds of pleasure, back to feeling, for a few precious moments, something besides the burden of his job.

Jax brought the sedan to a stop and killed the engine. He made no move to get out. For the first time, he didn't want to go to a crime scene. Besides, he already knew what they'd find.

Dilapidated buildings and second-rate businesses dotted the neighborhood: barred and boarded-up convenience stores and check-cashing places that specialized in liquor. Even the soft morning light couldn't improve the look of the area. It was a place stalked by second- and third-tier prostitutes, those whose looks were beginning to fail, along with their health.

A uniform came up to his window. Jax flashed his badge and took that as his cue to get out. "Detective Jackson. I'm looking for Detective Marshall."

"He's back there," the man replied, jerking his thumb towards an alley. Across the street, people had already lined up to see what all the fuss was about. The red, white, and blue lights of emergency vehicles danced over them as if lighting a macabre sideshow. Jax surveyed them, but few looked more than mildly interested. Another dead body to pay attention to, so they could ignore the crap in their own lives.

"Keep them back," Jax said unnecessarily. "And see if any of the shiny, happy people want to make a statement." He stomped over to the alley.

Bear looked up as he approached, his expression grim. "Looks like our M.O. This one went down fighting though."

"There should be a knife," Jax said, feeling sick to his stomach. Not about the crime scene, but about Nicole. "She stabbed the bastard in the thigh."

Bear raised an eyebrow at his words. "And you know this because?"

"How do you think I know it?" Jax welcomed the sudden irritation he felt. "She had a dream last night. The tape's in my car."

"You could have shared that with me a few hours ago."

"Dammit, Bear, don't you think I'd have been out here if I'd had something concrete to go on?" He watched the forensic team work, fighting his temper, fighting to keep from thinking of her. "I tried to get more information about the dream, but it didn't work."

They watched the M. E. bag the body. "You sure she wasn't faking it?"

"It wasn't her, Bear." He shoved his hands in his pockets. "She didn't do it."

Bear's skepticism shone like a beacon on a foggy night. "You weren't with her every second yesterday."

"Well, I didn't shit and shower with her, if that's what you mean," Jax snapped. "But I'd have known if she'd made other phone calls besides to check on her daughter."

"Shit. You did her, didn't you?"

Jax curled his hands into fists. "I'm not going to answer that, and you shouldn't even ask about it."

Bear grunted. "Then we got two choices. We either accept her as a psychic, which makes her a material witness, or we charge her with accessory to murder."

Jax hesitated. Neither one was a feasible option in his opinion. Despite what he'd seen, he still couldn't make the leap of faith that believing in psychic ability would require. If he believed in her ability, he'd have to believe everything else she'd told him. He wouldn't, couldn't do that. "Accessory, huh?"

"You bet your ass," Bear said. "We know she had prior knowledge. Maybe she's not doing it, but she sure as hell knows who is."

"She doesn't. You weren't there, Bear. You didn't see what she went through. That wasn't acting."

Bear stared him down. "Are you losing your objectivity?"

"Hell, I lost it the first time I laid eyes on her," Jax said, fighting the urge to put his fist through something, like his partner's smile.

"Figures," Bear said after muttering a crude comment. "Not that I blame you. But she's our only link, our only source of information. And we got to get that information out of her, whatever it takes. Let's bring her in, rattle her cage a little. See what shakes loose."

"Damn." Frustration balled his fists. What the hell choice did he have? Either way, they had to bring her in, if only to get her version of the story. "All right. Let's bring her in."

Nicole sat in the dim room, her head in her hands. Sheer determination kept her from screaming, but it was a losing battle.

Jax. How gullible she'd been, trusting him, believing him when he said he wanted to help her. She must have looked like an idiot, opening her door to him with a smile. With the sour Detective Marshall shadowing him, he'd been so cold, ordering her to come with them quietly as if they were strangers. As if she were a criminal.

She'd trusted him, had opened her home and her family and her past to him. And yes, she thought bitterly, even her legs. And he'd betrayed her. He'd spent the entire weekend with her, had been with her constantly after she'd had the third dream, and still he hadn't believed her. *What did you think, you freak? That you'd become friends? Something more?*

"Ms. Legère?"

Nicole hastily swiped at her eyes, then raised her head. Jax—correction, Detective Jackson—and his partner entered the room. Both men wore blank, neutral expressions, as if they couldn't care less if she exploded before their eyes.

Detective Marshall took the initiative. "We need to ask you a few questions, ma'am."

Taking a deep breath, Nicole reined in her rampant emotions, searching for the cold resolve that had gotten her through Randall's betrayal, the end of her marriage, and the yearning to return home with her tail between her legs. "You're treating me as if I had something to do with this."

Their silence was answer enough. Detective Marshall took the chair opposite her. Jax leaned against the far wall, his arms folded across his chest, his expression hooded. Nothing remained of the warmth and concern he'd shown her yesterday. Fine. If that's the way he wanted it to be, so be it.

"Ms. Legère." Marshall's voice brought her attention back to the matter at hand. "Right now, things don't look so good. We know you were nowhere near the scene of the murder when it occurred. We know a man had to commit the crimes. But that doesn't mean you didn't set this up. You could have claimed to have a dream when actually what happened was that you picked a target for your guy."

Fear twisted in her gut, insidious and slithering, causing her stomach to roil violently. "What are you talking about?"

"Oh come on, Ms. Legère. You want to be a real psychic badly, don't you? You want people to think you've got these special abilities. You want it so badly that you picked out these women, then set your guy on them."

He leaned over, his face looming before her. "Who is he? Some lover you have tucked away? Did you promise him access to your trust fund? Is that what you did?"

"That's ridiculous!" she exclaimed, knowing she should be silent, also knowing she couldn't. Her gaze swept over Jax, who remained impassive. "You know I've been trying to help you. You know that. What will it take to convince you that I'm telling the truth?"

Marshall sat back, opening the folder in front of him. "Just be honest with us, Ms. Legère. When was the last time you spoke to or saw Connie Reid?"

"Who?"

"Constance O'Reilly Reid, of 114 Oak Street," Marshall replied. His voice was brutal, his movement abrupt as he tossed something on the table between them. "Perhaps this will jog your memory."

Despite every instinct warning her, Nicole glanced down at the photos. In brutal color they showed a woman wearing a leopard print top and an almost non-existent black leatherette skirt, her stockings ripped. Bleached orange hair framed a bloodied and swollen face. Her throat was lacerated and bloody. She'd obviously died painfully.

Bile, acidic, suffocating, rose in Nicole's throat and she cried out. She lurched to her feet, sending the chair spinning crazily away. Papers and the brutal photos flew off the table, scattering about the room as if tossed by a wind. The table shuddered, then bounced repeatedly like a bucking horse.

Fighting the urge to scream, she balled her hands over her eyes. It was useless. The horrific image was burned in her mind's eye with the permanency of forever. A low sound seeped from her, a helpless wail. *Oh God, I couldn't save her. I did everything I knew to do, and it wasn't enough. I couldn't save her.*

"What the hell?" Marshall's voice bounced off her, the bass in it rumbling with surprise and disbelief. She could hear his chair scooting back, away from her. Smart move.

"Nicole?"

Jax. Electricity danced along her arms, standing the tiny hairs on end. She couldn't let him touch her. If he did, she could hurt him. "Don't touch me," she ground out.

He ignored her warning, moving closer. "Why don't you—"

"I said, *don't touch me!*" She pressed her palms against the table. The metal groaned, then screamed as the legs bowed out. Then the table shuddered into stillness.

Silence filled the room like a living, profound thing. Nicole, trembling and full of the energy that had shortened the table by a good two inches, took a shaky breath. Dream-memories tugged at her, pulling her under as her voice dropped.

"I couldn't see his face real clear 'cause he was wearing a hat. He was tall, at least six feet, and bulky. But that could have been from the jacket and sweater he wore. Dark hair, light skinned. He coulda been a Mexican, black, or white, I didn't care.

"He wasn't a cop, he said, but I made him touch me first anyway, just to be sure, y'know? You can't be too sure and I ain't gonna be taken that easy. He had a real nice voice, kinda smooth and educated. All's I could see was the fifty he gave me. *Hello, Mr. President.* A fifty for a blow, and I knew it would be quick because he was breathing hard already, excited. It was gonna ruin my stockings and I paid good money for 'em, lace-topped 'cause some tricks like to roll them down, put them on even. But hell—fifty bucks for five, ten minutes, and I didn't have to make small talk, just go right to it.

"I reached for his zipper, then something went around my neck. What the fuck? The sumbitch was choking me! I ain't into that kinda crazy shit. I kicked, scratched, tried to scream, fisted him in the nuts, but he wouldn't let go. Goddamn. sumbitch. Where's Tony? Got my knife, stabbed him in the leg, but it just pissed him off. Ripping, tearing blood, trying to scream, wanting to scream, can't breathe can't scream, nobody will come, nobody will care, darkness, coldness and laughter—"

Her voice broke off with a cry as she dug the heels of her hands into her eyes. "My eyes," she moaned. "My eyes." She slumped down, almost missing the chair.

"Nicki?"

Jax's hand was on her shoulder, shaking her. She jerked to awareness, blinking up at him through misty lashes. "Jax?" Her voice was a hoarse whisper. She cleared her suddenly sore throat and tried again. "What happened?"

Both men were staring at her, disbelief written clearly in their faces. "You tell me. All of a sudden you changed as you started telling us what happened to Constance Reid. And you were saying 'I,' instead of 'she.'"

Nicole closed her eyes slowly, sinking completely into the chair, not wanting to see the revulsion they must surely feel. It was obvious she'd had some sort of psychic episode triggered by remembering the dream. Never before had she felt so much power. What in the world was happening to her?

She cradled her throbbing forehead in a trembling hand. "I don't feel well."

The door opened, capturing their attention. "Detectives, a moment please."

Jax suppressed a groan. When the captain became polite, he knew he was in deep shit.

Bear must have had the same thought. He sighed once before pushing up from the table, scooping some of the photographs back into their folder.

With a last look at Nicole, Jax followed his partner out the room to face his captain. A petite woman in a gray suit that cost more than his mortgage payment stood beside him. As soon as Jax recognized the woman, he knew his day had bought a one-way ticket to the toilet.

Assistant District Attorney Karen Walsh was called "Washboard" Walsh behind her back because she had a habit of putting everyone, even the pizza delivery guy, through the wringer. Her black hair was pulled so tightly back from her caramel face that Jax wondered why her eyes didn't slant.

"Detectives, you know Assistant District Attorney Walsh." The captain sounded just as thrilled as Jax felt.

The assistant district attorney pinned Jax with a baleful glare. "What the hell was that?" she asked, gesturing at the one-way mirror. Nicole slumped sideways in the stiff metal chair, her head down. Jax could hear quiet sniffles through the intercom, making him feel even more like shit.

"We followed proper procedures," Bear said, though from his expression he knew full well what the ADA meant.

"Cut the crap." ADA Walsh took a step forward and though she didn't quite come to the middle of Jax's chest, she looked taller. She must have been in the military. "You know full well what I'm talking about. The captain and I both saw papers go flying about that room. We both saw the table bounce like it was jump-roping. Like to fill me in on that little magic trick?"

"It wasn't a magic trick," Jax said, feeling his right eye begin to throb with the beginnings of a major headache. Great. Just fucking great. "We didn't even know you were out here. In the process of interviewing Ms. Legère, objects spontaneously launched into motion."

It sounded stupid to say it, but he couldn't pretend it didn't happen. Neither, apparently, could the A.D.A. She looked at him with flat courtroom eyes. "I was told you had a material witness and instead, you present me with a genuine psychic."

The district attorney's tone gave no clue as to whether she thought that was good or bad. Which made Jax think it very bad indeed.

Bear finally decided to throw his two cents in. "Look, we weren't trying to put on a show. We were just interviewing a witness." He shrugged as if to say, make of that what you want. "We had no idea something like that would happen."

He looked at Jax, a silent question in his eyes. Jax shook his head. Nicole had said something about things shaking and slamming when she became upset, but she hadn't mentioned anything like this—and if she had, he wouldn't have believed it in any case. He had no choice but to believe now.

Walsh turned back to him. "She seems to trust you."

"I doubt it." Jax had a feeling Nicole wouldn't trust him ever again.

A cell phone rang. They all reached for their pockets, but soon realized the ringing came from the conference room. "You let her keep her things?" Walsh said.

"It was just an interview," Bear said. " Didn't see a need to take them from her."

They watched Nicole fish her cell phone from her purse. "Hi, Malita," she said, her voice tired but no longer shaky.

"Who's Malita?" Walsh asked.

"Youngest sister," Jax replied. "She's taking care of Nicole's daughter for the weekend."

"I'm fine," Nicole said into the phone. "I was just upset, that's all. No, nothing's wrong. Look, I need you to keep Dani for a little while longer. I just need to take care of a few things. It's important. Let me talk to Dani, okay?"

She wiped at her eyes. "Hey, baby, I need you to stay with Auntie Lita for a little while longer while Mommy takes care of a few things, all right? I know, baby, I know. I'm trying to help. Mommy didn't mean to scare you. Mommy loves you, sweetheart, so very much. Now put Malita back on the phone, okay? Malita, I don't know how long I'll be. I'll call you when I'm on my way. Thanks."

She flipped the phone shut, drew a deep breath, then faced at the mirror, fully aware they were watching her. "I'm ready to leave now. Unless I need to call a lawyer?"

They turned to the assistant district attorney. She looked unhappy. "Anything we can hold her on?"

Bear looked at Jax, but Jax wasn't about to give up details of Nicole's life irrelevant to the case. "We're not going to get anything else out of her."

Walsh frowned. "Evidence?"

"No physical evidence linking her to the crime scene," the captain said.

The ADA stared through the glass in a way that Jax instinctively mistrusted. "That little mini-tornado was enough for me to believe she's the real thing. Cut her loose."

Jax turned. "So what do you want us to do, Captain?"

"Your job," he answered. "You can start by apologizing to her and then get her help to solve this mess before the press connects the dots. Do whatever you have to do, but stay on her good side. She's the only lead we have. Try not to blow it. You got it?"

"I got it." A shitload of trouble, that's what he got.

Chapter Eleven

Nicole fully intended to give Jax a piece of her mind. Her mind, unfortunately, wanted sleep. As soon as she buckled herself into the passenger side of Jax's car, her mind shut down.

She awakened to see Jax leaning over her. "What happened?" Her voice trailed off as she realized she lay on her couch. "I must have been dreaming."

He helped her sit up, his expression unreadable. "No. All of it happened."

"Oh God." She put her head in her hands. "How did I get here? The last thing I remember is buckling my seat belt and waiting for you to get in the car so I could tell you off."

He grimaced at her words. "You fell asleep," he said, dropping to one knee in front of her. "You pretty much sleepwalked yourself into the house. I didn't know if that was normal, so I figured I'd try to wake you up."

"Normal?" Choking back a sobbing laugh, she pushed her hands through her hair. "Oh yeah, dreaming of murder, waking up bruised, and having sex with someone I barely know is normal. And thanks to my spectacular little freak-out in your precinct, everyone you work with thinks I'm certifiable."

"I don't think so," Jax answered, his voice carefully neutral. "If anything, they think they're certifiable."

Nicole buried her face in her hands. "Oh God, they all think I'm a freak."

"Does it matter what they think?"

"Seeing as how they can throw me in jail or lock me in a mental institution, yeah, it matters what they think."

"Okay then." His voice dropped, became soft. "I'm telling you that you don't have to worry about them. And just so you know, my middle name is Emanuel, I have a brother two years older and a sister three years younger, and I'm a dog person."

She pulled her hands from her face. "You think this is funny?"

"Hell no. There's nothing funny about investigating murder, or witnessing what you did back there."

Hard edges surrounded his words, and his expression was still unreadable. She couldn't tell if he wanted to comfort her or get the hell out as soon as he could. To be honest, she didn't know which she wanted either.

Her heart sank. She'd never known anyone like him. All she'd been able to think about after he'd left was that he wasn't Randall and how happy that had made her. Jax, big and tall and gorgeous, someone she should have never met. Someone now firmly entrenched in her life, but not for the right reasons. Not because he wanted to be there. Someone who wanted to be with her wouldn't empty her wastebasket to hide what they'd done together.

Despite the hurt, she wanted to lean against that wide chest, feel the steadiness of his heartbeat, and hear the sexy rumble of his voice telling her that everything would be all right. She wanted to tell him to leave, wanted to hurt him as much as he'd hurt her. She wanted to start the weekend over. If she hadn't dreamed, if she hadn't let him comfort her, she wouldn't be this wounded. She'd still be angry, but she wouldn't feel betrayed.

He gathered her hands in his. "Tell me what happened back there."

Hesitation filled her. This was something she should share with her parents, maybe Malita. Not Jax, skeptic supreme. Besides, she didn't really know what had happened.

"I-I'm not sure," she said, pulling her hands free. "It felt like I was standing in a shower, and I could feel this energy pouring over me like warm water. It was like a conduit or something opened, letting me feel more of what happened. That energy only increased when I got upset."

She closed her eyes briefly. “I’ve never felt that kind of power before. It felt-it felt so good it was scary, like the way I felt when you—never mind. When it was over, though, I felt like I was going to pass out. The only reason I didn’t was because Malita called.”

“You did pass out, but not until we were on the way home,” he reminded her. He captured her hands again, his thumbs brushing across her skin. “Maybe you should get some rest for an hour or two before your daughter comes home.”

She felt the gentleness of his touch and wanted to kiss him and hit him at the same time. She wanted him to go away and she wanted him to stay, wanted him to give her that euphoric feeling again. She wanted him, period.

How could she still want him after he’d hurt her? Need that had been fed in the wee hours of the morning awakened again, demanding, but she shook it away. Too much still simmered inside her, making her head spin.

“Jax, please.” Her voice trembled as she pulled her hands away. She shifted, putting a little distance between them. “You don’t have to do this.”

“Do what?”

“Pretend,” she said gently, too emotionally and psychically exhausted to fight the sudden, silent tears sliding down her cheeks. “Look, I know your boss told you to become my new best friend, but you don’t have to do that. You don’t have to act like any of this is normal, or that you’re not bothered. You don’t have to pretend that you want to be here, with me. I’m still going to help you in every way that I can. I owe that much to these women.”

“Ah shit, Nicki. Don’t do this.”

“Do what?”

“Cry because of me. Get pissed. Throw something, slap me, but don’t cry.”

She looked at him then. “You don’t really want me to get upset again, Jax,” she said, tired and aching. “You saw what happened earlier when I let my emotions get the best of me. I can’t get mad at you, no matter how much I want to. Besides, I'm not going to make it easier for you to walk away than I already have. You want to walk, go ahead and walk. I know last night wasn't the same for you as it was for me. But you were very convincing. I believed you when you said you wanted me."

She wiped at her eyes. "And when you saw me naked and told me I was beautiful, I believed that too. I wanted so badly to believe that you were attracted to me and not my money or my usefulness, but you were just doing your job. I don't know if I can forgive that, but I do understand why you thought it was necessary."

"Hold up." Jax's brows lowered in abrupt anger. "You think I played you?"

"Didn't you?" she asked with her own flare of anger. "Solving this case means everything to you and you told me more than once that you'd do whatever it takes to solve it. Why else would you sleep with a freak, then remove the evidence?"

He gripped her forearms. "For a psychic, you don't know squat. What happened last night was between you and me. What happened at the precinct was business. I'm trying with everything I got to keep the two separate but you don't make it easy."

She tried to break free of his grip. As exhausted as she was, she'd have better luck moving a mountain. "So it's my fault?"

"You damn right it's your fault!" He looked ready to explode. "You're so fucking hot that I've been walking around half-cocked since I met you. I'm so deep into you I don't know how in the hell I'm gonna crawl my way out. I think about the case, I think of you. I think of you, I get sprung. I want you so much I can barely fucking breathe. I nearly turned around to come back to you this morning instead of going to meet Bear. You're already ahead of this case, so don't tell me that I played you."

He looked so sincere, kneeling before her with anger burning in his eyes. "You still want me?"

"I just said so, didn't I? You want convincing, fine. Maybe this will convince you."

He hauled her off the couch and to her knees. His hands cupped her buttocks and dragged her close. Feeling his erection pressed between them, Nicole had no doubt about him wanting her. It was the last thought she had before he crushed his mouth to hers in bruising fierceness.

The tightness around her heart shattered. This was something he couldn't fake. Despite everything that had happened, Jax still wanted her. She didn't know why he wanted her or even how he still could, but it didn't matter.

The demanding kiss eased. "I had to do my job, Nicki," he whispered as his lips traced along her jawbone to her ear. "But I had to protect you, too. I emptied the trash because I didn't want you to have to answer questions about us. Not because I'd get into trouble, but because I thought it would make you uncomfortable."

He cupped her face between his palms. "I'm trying to find the middle ground here, I swear to God I am, but it's completely new territory. Give me a chance to figure it out, that's all I'm asking."

Instead of answering, she wrapped her arms around his neck, returning his kiss with everything she had in her. "Take it away," she demanded against his lips, her hands clawing his jacket off his shoulders. "Give me something else to see, something that's good and beautiful and right."

Without a word Jax pulled her up and led her to her bedroom. Once there, she slipped out of his arms to jerk off her clothes, desperate to feel his skin against hers. She didn't care that it was broad daylight, she didn't care that she broke a nail getting her jeans unbuttoned. All that she cared about at the moment stood facing her, hard and hot and ready.

She took a step towards him, but he drew back. "Are you sure about this, Nicki?" he asked, his face hard with leashed need. "I don't want there to be any doubts. Or regrets."

For answer, she let her hand slide down the hard planes of his chest to the hot thickness of his erection. "I don't doubt this."

And she didn't, at that moment. But it was daylight, and she knew he could see every effect that gravity and giving birth had had on her body. She had freaked out in the conference room. She still didn't know what he thought about that. If he turned away now, what would she do?

"Nicki, open your eyes."

She did, not realizing that she'd closed them. He stared at her with eyes stark with hunger. "Come here."

He eased her back on the bed, then settled beside her. She was conscious of his size as she hadn't been last night. He was a large man, from the hands that glided over her skin to the mouth that teased her breasts to electric wakefulness, to the penis pressing like a hot brand against her thigh. She didn't have to worry about being too heavy for him. If anything, she'd have to worry about him being too heavy for her.

His mouth moved slowly from her lips to her neck to her breasts, leaving a path of fire behind. She gasped aloud as he took one distended nipple into his mouth, circling it with his tongue. His hand went to her other breast, the rough tips of his fingers teasing over the peak. He pinched the one while he bit down gently on the other, and the answering flash of pleasure stabbed her to the core of her sex, making her moan loudly.

He left her breast, running his tongue down the valley between them and over the rise of her belly. She clenched her stomach muscles in response, in longing, in hopeful anticipation. Randall had never wanted to touch her like this but she wanted it, wanted it so badly she was willing to beg for it. "Please Jax," she whispered, breathless.

At the first intimate touch of his tongue she froze, her body threatening to shut down at the overwhelming pleasure that rushed through her. Then she sighed, melting into his attentions, lifting her hips to offer him more.

With kisses and nibbles and fingers he pushed her to the edge again and again. She writhed on the bed in complete abandon, freer than she'd ever been, more alive than she'd ever been. His fingers curved inside her as he drew on her. All at once the orgasm slammed into her, causing her to cry and sing and scream out with pleasure.

He drank her joy from her, even the aftershocks, on and on until she had to breathlessly plead with him to stop before she died. After one final caress of her sheath, he kissed his way back up beside her. "Will you do the honors?" he asked, pointing to the condom on the nightstand.

Still breathing heavily, Nicole reached for the foil package, sitting up to tear it open. She shifted on the bed for a comfortable position, finally deciding to straddle his knees. His erection jerked once in response, and she reached out with her free hand to steady him.

Delicious heat seeped into her fingers. She curved her hand around him, then moved down the shaft slowly before reversing direction. Jax groaned in appreciation. "Yeah, baby, just like that," he murmured in encouragement.

She continued to stroke, long, sure movements that had him lifting his hips off the bed and digging his fingers into the sheets. When she leaned over to taste him, he went absolutely still. She licked him again, savoring the saltiness of him, then closed her mouth around the thick head.

"God. Nicki. Stop." She could barely understand his words.

Breath left her as she looked up and caught the heat of his gaze. "Put it on me now," he ordered in that same mangled tone, "or I'm gonna come in your mouth."

The condom. She'd forgotten she held it. After another long, slow pull that had him groaning and cursing, she released him, straightened. She eased the condom onto him, then began to move aside. He gripped her hip. "Ride me, Nicki. Please."

She froze. "I-I don't—I've never done this." She bit her lip, her cheeks burning. Need cooled in the face of insecurity. What if she couldn't do it? What if she looked like an idiot trying? What if—

"Nicki." His hand smoothed down her arm. "We'll work it out."

Decision made, she scooted forward, lifting up to guide him into place. Slowly she lowered herself onto him. Her soft folds, still tender from his kisses and last night, welcomed him back. Welcomed him home. A sigh of pure satisfaction escaped her lips as she settled against his thighs. She could feel him, deep and hot and thick, throbbing inside her.

She liked it.

Splaying her fingers across his chest, she lifted herself up, concentrating on the friction inside her. His hands settled on her hips, helping her. The last of her inhibitions fell away as sensuous sensations swept over her, melting her insides, molding to him.

Jax watched as Nicole gave herself over to passion. His heart thumped hard in his chest as she rose and fell. The pace was slow enough to kill him but he knew she needed this, needed to feel the power and the pleasure. Seeing how their bodies joined, watching as she moved on him, was enough to make him forget how to breathe. When she opened her eyes and smiled at him, that woman's smile of pure sexual bliss, he forgot his own name.

She shifted forward and he caught her breasts in his hands, savoring the fullness of them. He urged her to lean forward more even though it would make her strokes shallower. She did, and he gathered her breasts in his hands, lightly biting one nipple, then the other, soothing the bites with slow draws of his mouth. Her body shuddered, her breathing came faster as she increased her pace, short strokes that took just half of him inside.

All at once she cried out, coming down fully on him as her body shuddered with release. Jax immediately rolled her over, driving into her with enough force to cause the headboard to knock against the wall. He hooked her legs with his arms, tilting her to receive more of him, pounding into her harder, faster, deeper. Her nails dug into his back as she lifted her hips to met him, her inner walls massaging him as he felt her come again. White-hot light burst behind his eyelids as his body exploded, pouring into her like a never-ending flood.

He collapsed against her, easing her legs down, not wanting to leave her just yet. She seemed to have the same idea because she entwined her legs around his, keeping him in place. He still throbbed deep inside her, blood pounded in his ears, and his heart threatened to jump right out of his chest. What a way to go.

Lifting up slightly to allow her room to breathe, he fixed her with a glare. "Do you still have any doubts?"

She smiled up at him, "Not a one," she answered shakily.

"Good, 'cause I don't think I can do that again." He kissed her long and slow. "You were amazing."

"So were you." She yawned widely.

"Yeah, so amazing I'm putting you to sleep." He eased from her with reluctance. Her arms and legs fell away from him heavily, letting him know just how exhausted she was.

"No, it's not you." She yawned again, her lids sliding shut. "It's been a day."

"That it has." He got out of bed, not wanting to leave her, but knowing he had to.

"I think I forgave you too easily," she said, snuggling into the pillow. "I'll have to fix that."

"I'll even let you as long as you let me start taking multivitamins first," Jax said, pulling the covers up over her shoulders. "I'll call your sister, ask her to bring your daughter home. I'll stay till she gets here."

"Wait." She tried to sit up, but the effort was too much. "She'll know. She'll look at you and know."

Right. Her sister could read people. "I won't tell her anything you don't want me to," he said, promising to keep his mind as blank as possible. Difficult to do when all he could think of was the woman in front of him.

"I know. Thank you," she whispered. "For everything."

She was fast asleep when he got out of the shower, so deeply and quietly asleep that he had to check her pulse just to make sure she was still alive. Vulnerability graced her features, making her look years younger than she was. The instinct to protect rose in him hard and bitter, and he had to fight the urge to pull her into his arms and just hold her.

She'd been through a hell of a lot in the last two days, most of which he didn't understand and didn't want to, some of which he'd put her through. It humbled him how easily she'd forgiven him, simply because he wanted her so badly he could hardly see straight.

He went downstairs, retrieving clothing as he went. Remembering how she'd looked at him as she rode him caused him to break out in a sweat. How the hell was he going to get his job done without wanting to drive back over here and dive into her every chance he got?

By surrounding her with her family. He had the feeling Nicole was the kind of woman who wouldn't let her lover stay over while her daughter slept down the hall. And he had to admit he was the kind of man who didn't want to sneak out of his woman's house.

Pushing back his thoughts, he dug Nicole's cell phone out of her purse. The model was close to his and it didn't take him long to find her sister's number in the memory and place the call.

It didn't even make it to the second ring. "Nicole, what the hell is going on?" a feminine voice demanded. "And don't you dare tell me everything's fine. I know it's not."

"Ms. Legère?" Jax assumed her last name would be the same. "Malita Legère?"

"Yes?" the voice on the other end went cautious.

"I'm Detective Carter Jackson, Atlanta police. Your sister's fine," he said, cutting off any hysterical questions. "We just needed to interview her, but it was a long process. She's had a very trying day."

"I knew something was wrong," the woman said sharply. "She told me it was nothing, but I could feel it." She broke off. "Where is she? Why are you calling me instead of her? Has she been arrested?"

Jax took the questions in reverse order. "No, she hasn't been arrested. She asked me to call you to bring her daughter home. She's in her room, asleep."

"You're not telling me something," the woman said, and Jax hurriedly blanked his mind. "What's going on?"

"Do you really want to do this over the phone, Ms. Legère?"

"I'll be there in fifteen minutes," Malita Legère said. "And there'd better not be anything wrong with her or I'll have your badge." She hung up.

Apparently the high-and-mighty act was a family trait. Jax placed the cell phone on the table, then sat down to wait for the sister's arrival.

He jumped to his feet. The sister who would immediately want to go upstairs to check on Nicole, who just happened to be lying in bed stark naked.

Crap. Jax sped up the stairs to Nicole's bedroom. She probably had never slept nude in her life. He knew she'd be mortified if her sister found her naked in bed with the scent of sex still clinging to her.

He dumped her clothes on the chair by the window, then found a baggy t-shirt on the back of the bathroom door. Nicole hadn't moved since he left her. She didn't even make a sound as he pulled her upright enough to fight the shirt over her head. He threaded her pliant arms through the right places and managed to drag the hem down over her hips.

Tugging the covers back over her, he couldn't resist running his hands over her curves one more time. God Almighty, he wanted her again. He hadn't acted like this even in his twenties. Had it been like this, this overwhelming need to be inside, with Felecia? He couldn't remember, and that scared him enough to make him wrestle his emotions under control and leave Nicole's side.

Malita Legère was as good as her word, arriving fourteen minutes after he'd placed the call. She strode into the house, tall, thin, and model-beautiful, dressed in low-slung worn jeans and a yellow blouse with ethnic embroidery all over it. A gold pendant shaped like a woman hung about her neck. A little girl held tightly to her hand, drawing back when she caught sight of Jax.

Jax held out his badge and identified himself. "Where's my sister?" the woman demanded, moving around him to the stairs.

He blocked her way easily and politely. "Nicole's sleeping, and probably will be for a while," he said, not wanting the sister's hyper attitude to disturb Nicole's rest.

Malita looked at him suspiciously, but didn't try to go upstairs. Trying hard not to feel relieved, Jax turned to the little girl, a miniature of Nicole down to the fathomless green-gold eyes. "You must be Danielle. I'm Detective Jackson."

The child hugged her doll, a fairy with blue-green wings, tight to her chest. "What's a 'tective?"

"I work for the police department, but I don't have to wear the uniform."

Danielle's eyes widened. "Tela says you're gonna help my mommy help the angel lady."

Tela? "Who's Tela?" he wondered, turning to the aunt. "What angel lady?"

"Nothing," Malita Legère said, some of her anger replaced by concern. She turned to Dani. "Honey, why don't you go play in your room while I talk to the nice detective? Then we'll wake your mother up and get some dinner."

"Okay." She started up the stairs, then stopped. "Are you really gonna help my mommy?"

"I'm going to do everything I can," he promised.

Danielle smiled, and just like that, delivered an emotional sucker-punch to his heart. "Thank you for helping my mommy help the angel lady," she said very solemnly, then sped up the stairs.

Malita watched until Danielle made it all the way upstairs before turning back to Jax, her arms folded across her chest. "Now, why don't you tell me just what in the hell you did to my sister?"

Chapter Twelve

"Tela likes him," Dani said through a face covered in purple lather.

Nicole squeezed water from a bright orange washcloth and began wiping the suds from her daughter's face, aware of Malita waiting impatiently. "Tela likes who?"

Malita leaned against the bathroom sink, snorting as she folded her arms across her chest. "As if you don't know."

Nicole shot her sister a look before Dani's voice caught her attention. " 'Tective Jackson. He said I could call him Jax." Danielle looked up at her with wide, eager eyes. "Can I do that, Mama? Auntie Lita was talking to him, so he's not a stranger."

Nicole wished for all the world she had been awake when Malita arrived with Danielle, if for no other reason than to see how Dani reacted to Jax's presence. Instead, she'd slept for nearly three hours and awakened to find her daughter and her sister both leaning over her in worry. Since she hadn't taken naps since before Dani's birth, they had a right to be concerned. She'd managed to put off all their questions through dinner, a feat she still couldn't believe she'd accomplished.

"No, he's not a stranger," she answered, wondering to herself what Jax actually was. "And you can call him Mr. Jax."

"I asked Mr. Jax if he was gonna help the angel lady and he said he would. Tela said he would too. Tela knew he was coming."

Tela again. "Tela certainly knows a lot," Nicole said gently, kissing her daughter's forehead before wrapping her in a large towel. "Does she also know it's past your bedtime?"

Her daughter argued, just as Nicole expected her to. She fell asleep as soon as her head hit the pillow, also as Nicole expected. After tucking her daughter into bed, Nicole retreated downstairs to the living room, expecting Malita to begin the Grand Inquisition.

She didn't expect the sudden and violent flow of tears that hit her as soon as she sat in her favorite chair. Malita, poor, empathic Malita, rode it out with her, rubbing her back and trying to soothe her.

As she struggled to regain her composure, Malita went into the kitchen, returning minutes later with two cups of tea. "I think you could use this," Malita said, placing a tray on the coffee table. "It's a soothing blend."

"I'm sorry," Nicole said at last, pulling a tissue from a box on the side table. "I didn't mean to go off like that."

"You obviously needed it, after what happened today."

"It's not just today, it's everything that's been happening for the last two weeks. My life's been turned completely upside down."

"Calm down, Nicki," Malita urged, taking the chair opposite her. "You're bombarding me with chaos."

"I can't help it!" she exclaimed, rising to her feet to stalk the room. "That's what my perfect life has become. In the last two weeks, I've dreamed of two women being strangled, had the police thinking I'm a suspect until I flipped out in the interrogation room, my daughter's talking to dead people, and I slept with a man I barely even know."

Malita stared at her, her mouth hanging open in apparent surprise. "Tell me I didn't hear you right."

"Oh, you definitely heard me right," Nicole said, not knowing whether to laugh or cry at her sister's stunned expression.

"Would you mind starting from the beginning?" Malita asked. "And do me a favor, pause after each major revelation. I can only take so many shocks at once."

Returning to her chair, Nicole proceeded to tell her sister everything that had happened since her first psychic dream, leaving out the details of sleeping with Jax.

"And I guess the dreams and the sex are the reasons that detective was here?"

"Keep your voice down!" Nicole hissed. "The man you saw here today, Detective Jackson, was here last night, and he helped me break out of the dream. Then one thing led to another. I don't know how to explain the second time, except that I really needed to feel something besides being strangled and my eyes cut out."

Malita stared at her with wide eyes. "I can't believe that you slept with someone you barely know—twice, mind you—since you've hardly even looked at a man since you left New Orleans. This just isn't you."

Nicole spread her arms wide. "That's what I've been saying. I feel like my world is spinning out of control."

"What are you going to do?"

"I don't know." Nicole thought of how Jax looked at her, how he touched her, how he moved inside her, and shivered. After her disastrous marriage, she'd made peace with the fact that she'd spend her life alone except for raising her daughter. She'd suppressed her needs and moved on with her life.

According to family history, most Legère women didn't stay in relationships long; either their mates died early or couldn't handle the family's idiosyncrasies, or tried to use them for their own purposes. The only women besides her mother that Nicole knew of who'd been able to have lasting relationships were the few who turned their back on the family, dropped the Legère name, and blended into society. Basically choosing to be normal.

Obviously, choosing normalcy was no longer an option for her. The Legacy had come back to her with a vengeance, and she had no choice but to accept it. Which meant that now that she'd found someone who wanted her and her extra pounds, she'd have to give him up.

Or did she?

"He didn't leave." Realization widened her eyes. "He saw me dream. He saw me flip out in the interrogation room and he didn't leave. Actually, he helped me. Maybe he doesn't think of me as a freak after all. Or maybe he'd just rather not talk about the elephant in the room."

She sighed, heart-heavy. Having sex twice did not a relationship make. What had happened between them was a fluke, an opportunity that wouldn't present itself again. It had been necessary and right at the time. Time out of time. Right now she had more important things to deal with, and so did he.

"For the record, you're not a freak."

Nicole added honey to her tea. "Of course you wouldn't think so," she replied before taking a sip. "You've had your magic since before you were born, and you wear it as comfortably as those old jeans. You didn't have a whole precinct witness you flipping out, but then, you've never not had control of your abilities, have you?"

"Nicki." Malita touched her arm with concern.

"Sorry. I don't mean to lash out at you." She forced her emotions away from the surface, not wanting to overwhelm her sister with feelings she hadn't completely sorted out yet. "I'm just, I'm just trying very hard not to freak out about freaking out."

"Has anything like this happened before?"

"Once, before Randall died." She remembered how upset she'd been, how angry and hurt. How the wilding had broken out like a hot sweat, sowing destruction, and stopping only when cramps doubled her over. Nearly losing Danielle had made her swear off the magic as nothing else could have.

"It was different this time," she said, half to herself. "It was stronger, and it felt like a tangible thing. I could feel the power welling up in me, demanding that I do something, but I had no idea what."

Malita gripped her goddess pendant, meaning she was worried or thinking hard. Or both. "All I know is that I was helping Dani decorate cupcakes when this wall of agony hit me out of nowhere. I nearly passed out from it."

"Malita." Nicole didn't know what to say, pained and embarrassed that she'd hurt her sister, however unintentionally.

"You didn't mean for that to happen. I thought something had gone horribly wrong, and even though you told me different, I could still feel you, feel your pain. Then that detective called, but he wouldn't tell me what happened." Malita's composure cracked. "I just got scared."

Nicole shot to her feet to wrap her arms around her younger sister, returning the comfort she'd given earlier. "I'm all right now. After resting, I feel just fine. No harm done."

"You might change your mind." Malita's voice was muffled against her shoulder. "I didn't know what else to do, so I called Mom."

Nicole stiffened, just a fraction, but Malita felt it. Malita felt everything. "I'm not going to apologize, Nicki. I thought you were seriously hurt. Mom and Dad would want to know."

"I know that." Nicole squeezed Malita once, then let go. She couldn't help her instinctive reaction any more than she could help her display in the interview room. "If you felt it, Mom had to notice a ripple of it, even in Louisiana. I guess I'd better call her and let her know what happened. I'm going to need her help with this. Dad's too."

"Maybe this means that you're an omnipath like Mom. Maybe this means you're coming into your power."

Nicole's stomach clenched at the words. She was anything but like her mother. "You're kidding, right? Mom has unbelievable strength. And don't forget control. Except for that one incident seven years ago, nothing like this has ever happened to me. Ever."

"Do you think you'll do it again?"

"I don't even know how I did it the first time." She closed her eyes, her hands forming fists. "All I can remember is wanting those terrible images away, wanting everything to go away. It felt like my skin broke open and all this power rolled out like a flood crashing through a damn. I can still feel the current a little, but it's like pushing against a net. Maybe it was just a fluke. I mean, if I was an omnipath, Mom and Dad would have known."

"Maybe they do know. At least, maybe they know now."

"So I'm a late bloomer, making up for lost time?" Nicole rubbed at her forehead. "Only one way to find out. I just hope they don't ask me to go back to Beau-Rêve."

"You don't think the police will let you leave Atlanta?"

"No, not the police." Nicole wrapped her arms about herself. "I don't think I can go back."

Malita's sleek eyebrows scrunched. Everything about her, even those riotous natural crinkles in her hair, was sleek. "What do you mean?"

Nicole shook her head, not knowing how to explain in a way that Malita would understand. Malita who'd had her abilities from birth, who'd never doubted her place in the family or their parents' love for her.

"You don't know what it was like," she said, her throat clogged. "You guys didn't hear the whispers, how our cousins called me Plain Jane because I didn't have a gift. You didn't hear Aunt Jeanette in Mom's office, telling Mom how having me follow her as Keeper of the Legacy would destroy the family. Every night, I would pray for some sign that I belonged, that I really was a Legère, and every morning I would wake up a dud, wondering if that was the day Mom and Dad would make me leave."

"Oh, Nicki." Malita's eyes brimmed with tears.

"Don't sweat it, Malita," Nicole said gently. "It was a long time ago. Finally, I stopped caring."

That was a lie. She'd never stopped aching for her part of the Legacy, even after the intermittent dreaming began. She'd never stopped wanting to prove herself to her cousins, her siblings, their powerful mother. The more she'd wanted to belong, the less she actually did, until she'd practically run into Randall's deceitful arms.

Uncertainty clawed at her. She'd fought hard to establish normalcy in her new life, even while yearning to be as powerful as her siblings. Now that her gifts had exploded into being, she felt forced to choose between two lives, two parts of herself. No, she felt as if the choice was being made for her and it scared her more than she would ever admit to her family.

"I gotta call Mom," she said finally, reaching for the cordless, "even though she probably knows already. I talked to Dad about all this last week, before it got bad."

She punched in her mother's mobile number before she could chicken out. When she'd left New Orleans with her tail between her legs all those years ago, she'd sworn that she'd never need her mother or the family again. In truth, she didn't need her mother. She needed Arielle Legère, Keeper of the Legacy.

Her mother answered quickly, as if waiting for her call. "Nicolette? Are you all right?"

Instantly defensive, Nicole tensed, tightening her fingers on the receiver. "I'm fine, Mom."

"You know better than to fib," her mother chastised. "What happened this afternoon?"

Suddenly Nicole felt fifteen again. Awkward, ungifted, and chubby in a family full of graceful, talented, and slender people, wondering if she'd been adopted.

Her mother continued, "Malita called and said that you were sleeping it off, so it must have been something significant."

"Oh, she did, did she?" Nicole turned to shoot her sister a dirty look and received a flush of embarrassment in return. "I guess you could call twisting a metal table into a pretzel significant."

"Nicolette." Her mother's voice grew strained. "Your father told me that you've been dreaming again, but this, this is something new."

"Yes." Nicole had to swallow hard to keep the tears from flowing again. "More's been happening, stuff that I can't go into on the phone. Do you think you and Dad can come here in the morning?"

"Of course. Your father and I are in Seattle right now, settling some business. The plane's being refueled as we speak. Malita swore that you were okay, else we would have already been in the air."

"Good." Despite her worry, Nicole felt relief at her mother's words. "I don't think the police will let me leave town."

"The police?" her mother shrieked. "What do you mean, the police? Stefan, call the pilot, we're leaving for Atlanta right now."

"Mom." Nicole gripped the receiver so tight her fingers went numb. "Mom, please. I'm the one who's supposed to freak out, not you."

"You tell me that the police won't let you leave the city and you expect me not to freak out?" Arielle Legère asked. "I'm your mother, of course I'm going to freak out! Were you arrested? Why didn't you call? We could have at least sent a lawyer to you."

Her parents would ride to the rescue, stepping in, taking over the shambles of her life. They'd know exactly what to do. They'd done it before. "No, I wasn't arrested, and no, I don't need a lawyer," Nicole answered, feeling acid bubble in her stomach. "I need you and Dad to help me understand the dreams and try to control them and this wilding that's happening. You certainly don't need to fly out here in the middle of the night."

"Nicolette—"

"Mom." Nicole forced her voice lower, calmer. "It's been a long, rough day, and I need to get some sleep. Besides, I've survived here for almost seven years. I think I can handle seven more hours."

Her grip on the phone eased as she heard her mother sigh. "All right, I'll do as you wish. But we will be there first thing."

"Thanks. Mom?" Nicole hesitated, an apology stuck in her throat. "Tell Dad I said hello."

"Of course, Nicolette. We'll call you as soon as we get in." They said their good-byes, then disconnected.

"Ouch," Malita said. "Don't you think that was a little harsh?"

"And your point is?" Nicole asked, still feeling defensive. Dammit, she had survived without them, without the Legacy. Everyone needed to remember that.

"I'm going to bed. You staying or going?"

"Going. You obviously need more sleep." Malita dug her keys out of her pocket. "Call me when they get in, okay?"

"Okay." Nicole escorted her sister out the door, closed it, then leaned against it with a sigh. She regretted being harsh to her mother, her sister. But it would be too easy to slip back into old patterns, and she couldn't afford to. She wasn't as helpless as she had been seven years ago. She wasn't.

If she thought it enough, maybe she'd even believe it.

Chapter Thirteen

The chiming of the doorbell hit her like a lump of metal in her stomach. She wasn't ready. She'd been up before dawn, scouring the house from top to bottom, and still she wasn't ready to face her parents, face the Keeper of the Legacy.

Instead of her mother's serene expression, she opened the door to Jax's less than pleased features. "What are you doing here?" she asked as he shouldered his way past her.

His brows lowered. He opened his mouth to answer her, but Danielle galloped down the stairs. "Nanna's here!"

Nicole turned to her daughter as Jax shut her door, apparently thinking she'd invited him in to sit a spell. Not what she needed at the moment. "No, darling, it's just Detective Jackson." She turned to look at him. "He won't be staying long."

Jax grunted in patent disagreement. Dani beamed at him. "Hi, 'Tective Jackson. My mommy said I should call you Mr. Jax."

His expression cleared. "Is that so?" he said, squatting to her eye level. "How about just Jax?"

"Just Jax." Dani giggled. "That sounds funny, Mr. Just Jax."

He smiled—grinned was more like it—and something in Nicole melted at his expression.

"Hhm. How about we go with your mom's suggestion and try Mr. Jax for a while?"

"Okay. Are you gonna help my mommy today?"

Nicole felt Jax's gaze slide over her. "Actually, Danielle, I'm hoping your mother can help me."

"Maybe my nanna can help," Dani piped up. "She's coming to visit us today. Gran-da too. They have their own plane an' everything!"

"Really? You must be really excited about that."

"I am." Danielle bobbed her head. "I always have fun when my nanna's here. She's really pretty, and she lives in a really big house that almost a castle. But she's not a fairy princess. That's what Tela is."

Nicole turned back to her daughter. "Sweetheart, why don't you run back into the living room and watch Nickelodeon while I talk to Detective Jackson? I'll call you as soon as Nanna gets here."

" 'Kay." She turned her small face back to Jax. "Will you come back, Mr. 'Tective Jax?"

Nicole heard the plaintive note in her daughter's voice and held her breath. While Dani had never known her father, she could still miss his presence in her life. Dani's uncles visited when their touring schedule allowed, but Nicole knew in her heart it wasn't the same. Nicole had done all she could to ensure that her daughter had the best of everything, but there were some things money could never replace.

Jax, to his credit, didn't look the least bit uncomfortable. "That's up to your mother," he said, "but if she says yes, I'll be back."

He climbed to his feet as Danielle trotted off to the living room. "I suppose if your parents are coming in, I won't be able to take you and Dani out to dinner."

"You want to take us out to dinner?" Nicole asked before she could stop herself.

"Of course. Why does that surprise you?" he wondered, leaning against the banister as if he had all the time in the world.

Nicole felt her cheeks flush. "I-I thought all you wanted was—" she darted a glance to the living room—"S-E-X."

His dark molasses eyes regarded her steadily. "You don't strike me as a one night stand type of woman. Is that all you want, S-E-X?"

"Yes. No. I don't know what I want anymore." She sighed. "It used to be so simple. Finish my degree, keep Dani happy and well-adjusted. For the last few years that has been my life, and I was perfectly happy with that. Now I've got these dreams, weird manifestations of power, and you. Not to mention the fact that my parents are flying in this afternoon and I have to talk to them about things I thought were behind me. I don't think I can handle this."

"Nicki." He stepped closer to her. "If there's one thing I know about you, it's that you're a strong woman. You've handled a lot of stuff already with amazing style. You can handle this to. And I know for a fact that you handle me very well."

She blushed at his words and the sudden warmth they caused. "Jax."

He leaned in, pressing a soft kiss to her lips. Soft but so thorough that she had to rest her hands on his forearms for support.

"If it means anything, I believe you and believe in you."

She cupped his cheek. "It does. Thanks." She stepped back from him before she did something really stupid like throw him against the wall and kiss him like crazy. "Would you like a cup of coffee or something?"

"Yeah, I'd like something, all right." His heated gaze roved over her. "But I'll settle for the coffee. You make a mean cup."

They walked through the living room, past Dani singing the theme song from a Nickelodeon show, and into the kitchen. Nicole told herself she'd have to get over blushing whenever Jax made an innuendo, but she couldn't help it. Despite everything, he was here, in her house, and he'd asked to take her and Dani out to dinner. He wanted her, and he'd definitely proved that yesterday. She'd finally come to believe it herself. Maybe, just maybe, she could start to dream about something other than death.

Just the thought of her dreams dampened her mood as she set the coffee to brew. "Why did you come by, Jax?" she asked, nervous energy surging through her again. "Did something new happen on the case?"

She didn't know he was behind her until he covered her hand. "I thought we'd settled this, Nicki," he whispered against her right ear. "You'll learn soon enough that I'm not a one-night stand type of man. One night with you ain't enough. Two weren't enough. It will never be enough. Got it?"

He said it so bluntly that she had no choice but to believe him. She leaned against him, hoping the contact would be answer enough. One worry down, ten thousand to go.

Jax looked down at Nicki's profile and felt something inside him tighten. Whatever that something was, it had been building since the day he'd met her. He'd hoped he'd get over it after they had spent the night together. If anything it'd been ratcheted up a notch. Even seeing her flip out in the interrogation room hadn't changed it. Something about the bruised look in her eyes and the sweetness of her curves made him want to wrap his arms around her and never let go.

Which scared the bejesus out of him.

"You didn't call," he said, stepping away from her, all too conscious of her daughter in the next room. He couldn't very well feel up Mommy while Danielle watched cartoons ten feet away.

"What?" Nicole removed cups from an overhead cabinet. "What are you talking about?"

"I asked you to call me. Or rather, I asked your sister to have you call me today, first thing this morning to be exact. I wanted to make sure you were okay. Since you didn't call, I showed up."

"Oh." She filled both cups then replaced the carafe. "The funny thing about phones, they can make calls as well as receive them."

"I was trying to be considerate," he growled. "I figured you'd have to do a lot of explaining to your sister or Danielle or that you'd still be resting."

"Malita and I talked last night, and as a single parent, there's no such thing as lying around in bed when there's a child to take care of," she informed him. "Besides, you never gave me your number."

He nearly dropped the mug he'd just lifted. "Are you kidding me? I know I gave you my card the first time I came out here."

She gave a small smile. "It just has the precinct number on it. I got up early and figured you wouldn't be in yet and I didn't want to leave a non-business message, so I didn't." She dipped her head so he couldn't see her expression.

Damn. No wonder she'd thought he didn't want her. He pulled his wallet out of his back pocket, extracted a business card. He reached into his shirt pocket for a pen. "I'm giving you my home and cell numbers, and I'm throwing in my address for good measure. I'll be more than happy to stand right here and watch you program them into your phone."

"That won't be necessary," she said, taking the card and sliding it into her pants pocket. He had to fight the urge to follow her hand with his own.

With a bunch of her shoulders, Nicole removed the used grounds from the coffee maker. "Does this mean that you're not, you know, involved with anyone?"

Jax resisted the urge to settle his hands on her shoulders and kiss some sense into her. "Obviously, I've given you the wrong impression about me. I'll have to work on that."

"You have to admit we didn't start out on the best of terms," Nicole pointed out, dumping the grounds into the disposal. "I mean, as gorgeous as you are, I can't imagine you not being involved with someone."

"Did you just give me a compliment? I think I need to write that down."

He watched as she rinsed the used filter before putting it with the recyclables, then washed the basket. He'd known a few neat-freaks in his life, but he'd never met a compulsive cleaner before.

Actually, as he thought about it, he only recalled her cleaning up when something had her agitated. He decided to make sure he wasn't the source of her agitation.

"No, I'm not involved with anyone. My job isn't exactly conducive to dating. And honestly, before now I hadn't met anyone I wanted to go through the motions with."

"Oh, okay." She topped off his coffee with an absentminded gesture before pouring the remainder down the drain.

"Of course, now I'm thinking it's time to rethink my game plan," he said over the sound of running water as she soaped and cleaned the coffee carafe.

"Game plan?" she echoed, putting the carafe in the bright yellow dish rack to dry.

"Never mind. What do you think about my idea?"

"What idea is that?" she wondered, breaking out a sponge and a bottle of cleaner.

He hurriedly lifted his mug out of harm's way. "Letting me take you and Danielle out to dinner sometime."

She paused in mid-spray, her finger slacking on the trigger. "Ah. Oh."

"Is that French for 'yes'?" he asked, keeping a straight face behind the rim of his coffee cup.

"No. *Oui* is French for yes." She rinsed out the sponge, setting it to dry on the rack before putting the cleaner away. Only to break out the broom.

"So I can take you and Dani out to dinner?" He decided to back a safe distance away before she decided he needed sweeping.

She barely glanced at him before sweeping imaginary dirt into the long-handled dustpan. "Sure, Jax, whatever you say."

"Nicki?"

"Hhm?" She replaced the broom with a mop contraption that squirted cleaning fluid from the handle. And a bottle of ammonia.

"Is she that bad?"

Nicole turned around to face Jax, looking surprised to still see him in her kitchen. "Who?"

"Your mother," he said by way of explanation. "Is she that bad that you're cleaning a hole in your floor?"

"I'm not . . . ."she looked down at the spritzer mop in one hand, a bottle of ammonia in the other . . . .

"Cleaning a hole in the floor. Oh God."

She put the mop and ammonia away, then sank into a kitchen chair. "No, no, she's not that bad. She's just . . . ."

She lifted her hands as if pulling words from the air. "She's my mother."

Jax pulled out the chair next to her. "And what? You think you can't live up to her standards or something?"

"How can I? She's this powerful, larger-than-life figure. Not only that, but my brothers and sisters had their gifts from the time they were born. I grew up surrounded by siblings and cousins with varying degrees of ability, and I had nothing. Nothing."

She shook her head as the old pain resurfaced, urging her to confess what she'd confessed to no one. "It was hard, being untalented in a family that celebrated the gifted. Hearing the whispers of my aunts and cousins rippling like dead leaves through the halls. The heiress apparent, about as psychically powerful as a tree stump."

"But you do have psychic power," Jax pointed out. "After what happened in the precinct, even I'm convinced."

"But I don't have any control over it," Nicole exclaimed, frustration raising her voice. She balled her hands into fists. "Everything my mother's touched has been a success. Except for me."

"Nicki." His hands, large, callused and warm, covered hers. "I don't believe that, and I bet your mother doesn't either."

"It doesn't really matter," she said with a shrug, shutting away the hurt with an ease born of years of practice. "I've learned enough in my psychology classes to know I have issues and I can't solve them with a five-minute pep talk. Or scrubbing my house from the attic to the basement. But thanks for the vote of confidence."

She freed her hands, then rose to her feet. "Maybe you should come back for dinner. I'm sure my mother will be able to do more for you than I have or ever could."

"I don't think so."

She leaned against the counter, facing him. "Jax, I know you've had a difficult time believing what I've told you, but believe me when I say my mother is an extremely powerful psychic. She has a lot of different abilities, and I'm sure that once you talk to her, you'll realize that she'll be more help to you than I am."

"Does she dream like you do?"

That stopped Nicole. "No, I don't think she ever has. She always said it was a rare talent in the family."

"So that makes you even more special."

Nicole heard the softness in Jax's voice, the sincerity. She wanted to believe his words, believe him, but she'd had years to come to the realization that her place in the Legère Legacy was not following in her mother's footsteps.

Her thoughts must have showed on her face, because Jax rose to his feet. He crossed to her with power in every step, yet his hands were gentle as they settled on her shoulders.

"Nicki, I'm sure your mother is the greatest thing since sliced bread, but she didn't walk into my precinct to warn me of a murder. You did. That means, at least in my mind, that you're the key to all of this. I'll appreciate all the help I can get, and that includes your mother. But I'm convinced you're the link and nothing's going to change my mind on that. So stop selling yourself short."

"Jax." She didn't know what to say in the face of his assurance. Randall would never have calmed her fears.

He cupped her face in one rough palm. "You made a believer out of me, Nicki," he said, his voice rough and gentle at the same time. "Yeah, it took me an hour or two to get my heart back into my chest the other day, but I believe in you. Don't doubt yourself, okay?"

She looked into his eyes, finding the assurance and courage she needed. "Okay, Jax."

Chapter Fourteen

"And that's what's been happening for the last two weeks."

Nicole stood at the mantel, her mouth dry from recounting her experiences with the dreams and their aftermath. As she waited for her parents' reaction, she remembered Jax's words to her earlier. She'd tucked them into her heart, savoring the reassurance they gave her. Sometimes you just needed someone not related to you to believe in you.

She turned to face her parents and Malita, arranged on her couch like a jury. No, she told herself, like the concerned family they were. She had to stop thinking of her family as opponents and as the support group they should be. Only they could truly understand the importance of her dreams and her fear of having them.

Yet their silence began to grate on her new-found confidence. "Say something."

Arielle Legère eased from beneath her granddaughter's sleeping form and rose to her feet. Nicole was struck once again with how tiny her mother seemed. She had four inches on the woman who had given birth to her, a fact she'd never truly noticed until now. Her mother had always seemed larger than life, a psychic superwoman. Now she seemed . . . not diminished, but somehow more human, more real than Nicole remembered.

She watched her mother pace the carpet, her heeled red Prada boots sinking into the carpet. "I'm trying to talk myself out of marching down to that precinct and showing them what a psychic temper tantrum really is."

"Mom!"

"I mean it!" her mother said, settling her hands on the hips of her scarlet Donna Karan jacket. Her mother might have been knocking on fifty, but you'd never know it by looking at her or her wardrobe. "No one hurts my children. No one."

"They didn't hurt me," Nicole said, feeling the need to defend Jax even though his partner and the ADA had been her main antagonists.

"I don't care," her mother declared. "You shouldn't have been put into that situation. You handled it extremely well, but they had no right to put you through that."

"That's what I told her, but she wouldn't listen to me," Malita chimed in. "Especially after she let Detective Jackson—"

"You're not helping," Nicole cut in, glaring at her sister.

Her father eased off the couch to stand behind her mother, calming his wife down simply by resting his hands on her shoulders. "Calm down, *chèrie*," he said. "That part is over. We must concentrate on what to do next."

Then he added, "I really want to meet this Detective Jackson, though."

"Ooh, that's a good idea, Dad," Malita agreed, her spiral curls bouncing with the vigor of her nods.

Nicole speared her with another look. "Again, not helping."

She turned back to her parents, straightening defensively. "They were just doing their jobs, Mom. I understand how they thought I was responsible. For a while there, I thought I was too."

Her father frowned in reproach. "You can clear that thought from your mind right now."

"Oh come on, Dad," Nicole said, her control fraying. "Don't tell me you and Mom haven't thought that, that I've flipped out again and hurt someone else, or somehow created this guy with my mind."

The import of her words slammed into her, stealing her breath, making her heart stutter. "Oh God, do you think—"

"No, I don't," her mother said firmly. "And neither should you. One, I would have sensed that in my capacity as Keeper and taken measures to stop it. Second, you're the psychology expert. Don't you think you'd know if you'd suffered some sort of psychotic break?"

"Don't insane people always think they're sane, that it's just the rest of the world that's gone crazy?" She attempted a smile, but felt her lips tremble instead. "Maybe that's been the problem all along. Maybe I did lose my mind after Randall died and that's why all of this is happening now. I'm finally being punished because I somehow wanted him hurt—"

"Nicolette!"

Her mother's voice, shocked and angry, stopped her words. Nicole looked at her mother, surprised to see her near tears. Arielle Legère never cried. Never.

"Mama?"

Nicole watched her mother turn to look at her father. Something unspoken passed between them, communicated by his hand reaching up, gently cupping her cheek. Then her father stepped towards Danielle, mercifully still sleeping on the couch. "Come, Malita, let us put Danielle to bed."

"Why?" Malita asked, even as she got to her feet. "How come I can't hear what's going on? Just because I'm the baby doesn't mean—"

"Malita."

She stopped as their mother turned to stare at her. Even Nicole could feel the power wafting through the room. Malita had been rebuked, not by their mother, but by the Keeper of the Legacy.

Malita swallowed. "I'll go turn down the covers." She scurried ahead of their father, who'd already scooped Dani into his arms.

Nicole took a step back as her mother turned back to her. "What is it?" she asked, feeling panic swell her chest. "What do you have to say that Malita can't hear?"

Arielle's face grew solemn as she gathered Nicole's hands. "I'm sorry, *bébé*."

Nicole snatched her hands back. "You're going to tell me I'm adopted, aren't you? That's why I never fit in growing up, why the cousins picked on me. I'm not really a Legère, am I?"

"What? Nicolette, of course you're a Legère. You're my firstborn, my precious baby girl."

"Then what happened?" she cried, clenching her hands together as her throat began to burn. "Why wasn't I born with my talent?"

"I think you were, Nicolette. I just think it wasn't ready to manifest."

"And it never got ready either. You don't know what it was like, seeing everyone else exercise their abilities. For fourteen years I was less than nothing in my own house, until those damn sporadic dreams started. And they stopped completely after Danielle was born."

Arielle clasped her hands together. "That was my fault."

Nicole choked on a half-laugh. "Oh, Mom, how could my issue with the Legacy be your fault? Did you cause me to be born with a defect?"

"No." Her mother's eyes grew bright. "I blocked your talent."

Her heart dropped. "Wh-what? H-how could you—*when* did you switch me off?"

"In the hospital," Arielle whispered, "after Danielle was born."

Nicole had to sit down, her mind unable to handle the simple function of standing as she tried to comprehend her mother's words. She said the first thing she could think of. "Why?"

"You were hurting." Her mother sank into the chair opposite her. "You were in so much mental and physical pain, bébé, that Malita couldn't even come visit you. It broke my heart, and I wanted, I needed, to take that pain from you. So I did."

"You blocked my abilities," Nicole said, hoping that saying the words would make it easier to understand. To accept.

"Your father and I did," Arielle Legère nodded. "After you gave birth to Dani, you weren't able to shield yourself as you normally did around us. We found out how you suffered with your cousins. We know how you struggled growing up, what happened between you and Randall. We know how you hurt, and raged, and wept. How could I let my baby keep feeling that pain? How could I?"

Her mother looked up and Nicole could see a mother's righteous anger in her eyes, the kind of anger she herself had felt when she'd thought of nothing but protecting Dani at all costs.

"So I bound your power," her mother said, her voice shaking. "It normally takes a willing participant or two strong psychics, but your father loaned me his strength. So I did it. I locked your gift away in the deepest part of your mind to give you what you wanted most: a chance at a normal life."

"Mom." Nicole couldn't speak. What had that cost her mother, the Keeper of the Legacy blocking the talent of her First Daughter? Now she knew why her mother hadn't protested when she'd decided to leave New Orleans. Although she knew her mother loved her as all mothers loved their children, this proof—this terrible, awesome act—showed just how much.

Arielle stretched out one hand between them, then let it fall back into her lap. "More than anything else, I wanted a normal life for you, all of you," her mother murmured. "I wanted the Legacy to be secondary in your lives. I became head of the family at eighteen, not something I'd wish on any of you. And though your father came into my life two years later, the time in between was the loneliest I'd ever experienced. I had nothing but the Legacy, and I would not wish that on any of my children."

She wiped at her eyes with a fragile gesture. "We did what we thought was best for you, best for Danielle. And I would do it again, with no hesitation."

Nicole swallowed her own tears back, needing to understand. "That explains why I had all those years without dreams. But it doesn't explain why they came back."

"I have to take some of the blame for that too." Tears glittered in her mother's eyes. "Even as I did what I thought was best for you, I selfishly hoped that you would want to come back one day. I didn't block your abilities permanently, but I didn't think that they would try to break through the shield."

Tears spilled down her mother's cheeks. "I'm so sorry. I didn't think it would hurt you like this. Can you forgive me for doing this? Can you forgive a mother who can see everything but her daughter's pain?"

"Mama, don't cry." Nicole slipped to her knees and wrapped her arms around her mother's slender frame. She'd never seen her mother cry, and it frightened her more than anything else, even the reemergence of her dreams. She closed her eyes and held on tight, feeling years of resentment and supposed inadequacies falling away.

"I was afraid to tell you," she confessed. "I thought you'd be disappointed in me. I thought I'd disappointed you already."

"I'll never be disappointed in you, Nicolette," her mother whispered, curling over her. "Not about anything, especially the Legacy. Please believe that."

"I do." She did, at long last.

She felt her mother's hand caress her hair. "The meditation you told me about, in which you opened that box, apparently unleashed your abilities."

"The dreams are more intense now," Nicole confessed. "I woke up with bruises. I felt everything the victim went through. I felt like I was the one being attacked."

Hands cupped her cheek. She stared into her mother's soft eyes, seeing nothing but love and support. "Do you want me to take this from you?" Arielle asked. "I will, if that's what you want. I'll block it again. If you are willing, I could block it permanently."

Nicole hesitated. Wasn't this what she'd wanted, longed for, for most of her life? A chance to be normal? A chance to be with Jax as an ordinary woman? She'd never once realized that her mother could, and would, take the Legacy away from her. She'd be free. Free of the agony of experiencing the dreams, free of the guilt for not having enough information for Jax.

Free to be herself, not the First Daughter.

"What about this man? Can you see anything? Will you be able to find him and help Jax stop him if I stop dreaming?"

Her mother closed her eyes, and Nicole felt the prickle along her skin that let her know her mother was flexing her psychic muscles. She held herself perfectly still and open, letting her mother read her completely for the first time in years.

"No," Arielle Legère answered after a while, a frown dimpling her forehead. She opened her eyes. "I'm sorry, Nicolette, I didn't see anything. All I sense is that this isn't over. Maybe if I had something that belonged to one of the women, I'd be able to focus more."

"Then I can't be blocked yet. If this man has done this twice, he'll do it again. I want to help Jax. I want to keep the promise I made to Dani, to help these women." Nicole had to swallow against a sudden lump in her throat. "But I don't think I can keep on like this."

"I believe you can," her mother replied. "Your father believes it as well. Part of the problem, the pain you've been experiencing, could be because the flow to your ability is only partially open. If we open it fully, it could ease some of the agony you've been going through, and the lack of control."

A tremor of shock stole down her back. "You mean the incident with the paper flying and table-twisting wasn't an emotional fluke?"

Her mother gave a small, sad, smile. "You know the answer to that as well as I do."

"I do." After years of being repressed, her abilities had awakened with a vengeance.

"What if it gets worse?" Nicole shuddered, dreading the thought of waking up bruised and battered again. "I was hoping that you or Dad could guide me through my dream tonight, if I dream. But what if you completely remove the block and I'm more than bruised?"

"We would not let anything harm you, if we are there to prevent it," her mother said, her tone fierce. "I'll monitor you myself and put up the shield again if I think you're coming to harm. It will be like old times."

"Old times?"

"Your mother would sneak into your room at night and watch you sleep," her father said as he entered the room. Malita was nowhere to be seen, relieving Nicole. "She did it for years, even before you began having the dreams."

"You did?"

"Of course we did," her mother said. "You were—and still are—our miracle child, conceived in a magical moment that saved your father's life. We'd spend hours watching you sleep. Sometimes it would be just your father, or me, but it became part of our nightly ritual to sit at your bedside, watch you sleep and think of how blessed we were."

Nicole felt her throat tighten. "Why did you stop?"

"Why?" Her father sighed. "The question of the ages. Why do parents stop reading bedtime stories to their children or tucking them in at night? Why do children not want their mothers and fathers to hug them in public?"

He ruffled her hair. "Life changes and people change. You all grew up so fast. If we could, we would have wrapped you all up like priceless treasures and guarded you so that you'd never know a moment's pain. But we have to let you, each of you, find your own way. That's what parents do."

"Dad." She didn't know what to say. There were nights she spent hours sitting by Danielle's bed, praying that she'd done the right thing by leaving New Orleans, that she'd be a good mother to her only child. Had her parents' thoughts been the same?

"Let the past stay in the past." Stefan Antonescu cleared his throat. "We have other things to focus on now. I think we should contact this detective of yours."

Nicole turned to face her father. "Contact Jax? Why?"

Stefan's green eyes looked entirely too innocent. "It's possible that your mother may be able to get a hit off him if he's willing to discuss the case with her. That's what you wanted, yes?"

"Yeah," she answered, regarding her father with deep suspicion. She couldn't believe he'd put aside his anger so quickly. She'd seen her father furious only one other time, when Darien had been seriously hurt by a school bully, and it had taken her mother hours to calm him down.

He gave her an open smile. "Good. Your mother and I will go check into the hotel. Ask the detective if he will join us for dinner. Malita has volunteered to watch Dani tonight."

Nicole went into the kitchen to dial Jax's cell number. He answered on the second ring.

"Hi, Jax," she said. "Is that offer for dinner still open?"

Chapter Fifteen

"You sure you don't want to come?"

"And deprive you of the privilege of meeting the Black Rockefellers?" Bear laughed. "No, thanks. Besides, I'm not the one marrying into the family."

"Neither am I," Jax retorted.

Bear laughed again, so hard Jax thought his chair would give away under him any moment. Which would suit Jax just fine, since he really wanted to knock his partner on his ass.

"I don't see what's so funny," he said, frowning as Bear wiped at his eyes. "I'm meeting her parents to discuss our case, not to announce our engagement. I barely know Nicole and I sure as hell ain't getting married."

Bear sobered enough to open his desk drawer. "Yeah. You keep thinking that. And if you want to put money on that, you let me know." He extracted a pale blue shirt and dark patterned tie, still in the wrapper. "Here. The least you can do is make a good first impression."

"I don't give a damn what they think about me," Jax said. "Besides, if Nicole's told them everything that's happened, it's way too late to make a good first impression."

Still, he took the shirt and tie, hoping the spare suit he kept in his car wasn't too badly rumpled. Nicole's parents had managed to book themselves into the Presidential suite of the Atlanta's most exclusive hotel on one day's notice. That showed their clout with a serious pulling of strings, not to mention how much they wanted to aid their daughter. He wasn't about to get stopped in the lobby because of his appearance. Why give Nicole's parents one more reason to dislike him?

A short time later, he entered the brass and glass doors of the hotel. Jax avoided straightening his tie. His job had taken him from whorehouses to penthouses. He'd had enough dealings with the rich and famous and infamous to last him a lifetime. One thing he'd learned during his years on the force was that it didn't matter how blue the blood, everyone bled the same in the end.

Despite what he'd told Bear, he did care what Nicole's parents thought about him. As adamant as he was against the idea of marriage, he had to admit that getting on the good side of Nicole's parents would help his case. He needed their help, and more importantly, he needed Nicole's help. He didn't need or want them to think of him as future son-in-law material. Besides, he doubted they'd let some blue-collar cop marry into the family anyway.

Just business, he reminded himself as he walked into the lobby. Nothing more, nothing less.

"You're frowning," a voice said. "Is something wrong?"

Turning, Jax saw Nicole on his left. She'd been sitting in a dark leather club chair and now rose to her feet. She'd dressed for dinner in knee-high boots of chocolate suede, a knee-skimming matching skirt, and a blouse of deep rose colored silk.

"Not a thing," Jax said, when he remembered how to speak. "You look incredible."

A pleased smile poured across her features. "Thank you," she replied. "You look pretty spiffy yourself."

Jax nodded, ridiculously pleased until he remembered he wore a borrowed shirt and tie. "Are we meeting your parents in one of the restaurants?"

"No, we thought it would be best if we had dinner in their suite." She gestured towards the bank of gilded elevators on the other side of the marbled entrance. "By the way, thanks for not pushing on meeting at the precinct instead of here."

"No problem." Jax fell into step beside her. Nicole's heeled boots made a determined click as she strode across the gold tiled floor, and he took a man's moment to admire it.

"What should I expect from this?" he asked.

"I don't know." She pressed the up button to call the elevator. "I'm hoping that Mom will be able to get a hit off you while you're talking. Did you bring something tangible with you?"

"You mean evidence?" After a muted ding, the elevator door opened. He followed her in. "It took a little finagling, but I managed to bring a couple of things from each case file."

Words dried in his throat as he watched her extract a passkey from her cleavage. She gained them access to the penthouse level. "Do you need any help putting that back?"

She laughed. "No, I think I got it."

"Are you sure? 'Cause I don't mind helping a sister out."

"Why, Detective Jackson." She turned to him with a smile beaming through a southern drawl. "I do believe you're getting distracted."

"You're damn right I'm distracted." He put the briefcase down so he could reach for her. "Why haven't I seen those boots before? And I should arrest you for wearing that skirt."

"Thank you." She sidestepped him, her eyes sparkling as she returned the passkey to its hiding place. He'd never wanted to be a piece of plastic so badly in his life.

The subtle scent of her perfume wrapped around him, jabbing deep into his senses. He knew he should have been focusing on the case, but his mind suddenly filled with memories of running his hands over her beautiful behind and down those long sexy legs. "Tell me something."

"Like what?"

"Will your mother freak out if I feel her daughter up in an elevator?"

"Jax." Something went through her gaze that made his heart beat faster. "You have this amazing way of making me feel good."

"I can make you feel a whole lot better."

"You do realize that we're in an elevator?"

"What? Oh, yeah." He stepped back from her, bending down to retrieve the briefcase, wrapping both hands around the handle. Focus, focus. "I've never done it in an elevator before. I'd be willing to give it a go, if you're up for it."

Her gaze dropped. "I'd say you're up for it all by yourself. But maybe we should get through this meeting first."

"Hell." He'd forgotten the meeting. He'd forgotten where he was and what he was supposed to be doing. "You're addictive, did you know that?"

With a soft ping, the elevator opened. He hadn't even realized they'd stopped.

Nicole stepped out, then gave him a glance over her shoulder that had his blood heating again. "So are you."

He followed her out, his loafers sinking into the plush burgundy carpet. "Wait. What did you say about your mother getting a hit off me? Does that mean your mother can read minds?"

"She can, but it's not polite," Nicole replied. Only two suites occupied the top floor, and she went to the one facing east. "Kinda like eavesdropping on a conversation in another room. 'Course, if you're shouting, it makes it easier to hear what's being said."

"So you mean since I'm so focused on you right now, your mother will be able to pick up on that?" That put a damper on his need.

"Yes." She turned to look at him. "But I know that once you think about your case, it fills your entire mind. Mom will ask your permission before she reads you. When she does, you'll probably feel something like . . . well, you know how the air gets thick before a thunderstorm? It will feel something like that."

He fell into step beside her. "You seem different. I guess the reunion went better than you expected?"

"Yes." She paused, hazel eyes seeking his. "We cleared the air, and Mom removed a partial block on my abilities. I shouldn't have any problems now when I dream."

Jax sobered. If Nicole's abilities had been blocked before, what the hell would happen with full access?

They stopped before the door of the suite. Jax could feel sweat dampening the briefcase handle. Damned if he would admit to being nervous though.

Nicole surprised him by knocking. When Jax threw her a look, she explained, "My parents still act like newlyweds. I caught them once, and I never want to do that again."

Jax shuddered. "Just great. That's the thought I want to have in my head before I meet your psychic mother."

The door to the suite opened, and Jax got his first look at Nicole's father. Who didn't exactly look pleased to see him.

The lanky Romanian leaned against the doorframe, green eyes piercing beneath dark brows. "So, this is the man who arrested my daughter?"

So much for improving international relations.

"Dad." Nicole stepped closer. "This is Jax, Detective Carter Jackson. Jax, this is my father, Professor Stefan Antonescu."

"Sir." Jax loosened his hold on the briefcase long enough to grip the elder man's hand. Though Jax didn't have a clear idea of what a typical Romanian male looked like, he didn't think Nicole's father epitomized it.

Despite the stone gray dress trousers and dark green sweater, Stefan Antonescu looked more like the pirate character on the bottle of rum, with wavy dark hair tipped with silver brushing his collar and a goatee on his angular face. Jax half-expected a parrot to come winging into the room at any moment.

"Detective Jackson." Those eyes didn't give an inch as the professor stepped back to allow them into the room. "Thank you for offering my wife the courtesy you neglected to give my daughter."

Okay, Stefan Antonescu wasn't the jocular, let's-have-a-drink pirate. Jax had a sense the man, for all his lankiness, could be dangerous when needed. He admired that.

"Your wife isn't a suspect," Jax pointed out with a minimum of politeness. Obviously his chance to make a good impression had been thrown out the window. "And, I'd like to say, your daughter isn't either."

"Not now." Antonescu didn't budge.

Jax acknowledged his words with a grim nod. Yep, he was definitely on the professor's do-not-call list. "Not now."

"Stefan," a soft voice called, "stop antagonizing the man. He was simply doing his job."

A slender wisp of a woman with a dark cap of curls entered the granite foyer. Polar opposites, Jax thought. Arielle Legère looked nothing like her daughter, greyhound thin in beige skirt and designer boots, blood red tunic, and gold glittering at her neck, wrists, and ears. While Nicole's beauty was something you wanted to wrap yourself in, Arielle Legère's beauty was more of the hit-you-over-the-head type.

"Good evening, Detective," she said in a rich, lilting tone. She touched her husband's arm, and the man immediately relaxed, stepping back to give her room. "May I shake your hand?"

Jax knew enough to know it was meant as a gentle warning to prepare himself even before Nicole touched his shoulder. Prepare himself for what, he didn't know. "Yes, ma'am, it would be an honor."

Gathering himself, he extended his hand, half-afraid he'd crush her delicate bones and be in deeper trouble with Antonescu. When her fingers connected with his, Jax discovered that Nicole's mother possessed strength he hadn't guessed at. A lot more strength.

He felt something—he wasn't sure what—course up his arm, infusing him with warmth and peace. Then he looked into the molasses dark eyes and found himself falling, drifting, becoming unglued.

"Detective Jackson." That voice brought him back from wherever he'd gone. How long had it been? "So good to meet you. You have a very strong and healthy aura."

He took his hand back, resisting the urge to check it for burns or a glow or something. "Did you just read me?"

Her laugh reminded him of Nicole's, the way it danced around him. "No, that was just our energy fields saying hello. When two strong auras come together, it can be like magnets repelling—or attracting, as the case may be."

They both turned to look at Nicole. Standing next to her father, she focused completely on Jax, worry creating a little dimple in her forehead. *Are you okay?* she mouthed at him.

It surprised him to discover he was okay. He should have been freaked out, at least a little. Instead, he felt something like excited expectation.

"I suppose it's a good thing you can't bottle that," he said, turning back to Arielle Legère. "I'd suspect you of drug trafficking."

With another trilling laugh, Arielle Legère led him deeper into the large and airy main room. Dark leather couches and chairs circled a muted rug, all placed to offer a spectacular, heart-stopping view of the Atlanta skyline through huge floor-to-ceiling windows. The furniture was equally dark, some sort of mahogany wood. A table for four had been set beneath the windows and an ornate bar took up the wall opposite. Two doors led off to the right and left. Bedrooms, he supposed. Flowers arranged in crystal vases and dozens of ivory candles offset the heavy masculinity of the room.

Jax suppressed an urge to whistle. He had no idea how much the suite cost per night, but he knew he'd never be staying in it. It forcibly reminded him just how different a circle he circumnavigated compared to Nicole. These people weren't just rich, they were *understated* rich. He probably made less a year than Arielle Legère spent on shoes.

Stefan Antonescu crossed to the bar. "Would you like something to drink before dinner arrives, Detective?" he asked, pulling the stopper from a crystal decanter. "The hotel stocks a fine brandy."

He just bet it did. Jax put his battered briefcase on the overstuffed leather sofa. It looked as out of place as he felt. "No, thanks. I'm more of a beer man. Besides, I'm still on duty."

Yeah, he needed to remind himself of that. He was here for business, nothing more. Certainly not to prove himself worthy of their daughter's attention. Nicole's parents would just have to deal with him as he was.

After dinner, Nicole and her father retreated to one of the couches while Jax and her mother remained at the table to discuss the case. "You didn't have to be so hard on Jax, Dad."

Her father leaned back against the cushions. "Of course I did, Nicolette. He was expecting it." Her father gave a very European shrug. "And who was I to disappoint him?"

As always when talking with her father, Nicole slipped into a mixture of Romanian, English, and Creole. "I told you, Jax was just doing his job."

"Just as I did mine." Though her father kept his gaze on her mother, Nicole knew he also focused on her. She'd never been able to duplicate her father's ability to split his attention. Must be a professor thing. "I want him to realize that we're not going to let him take advantage of you or your abilities."

Nicole stilled. "I'm not a naïve college student anymore, Papa," she said quietly. "I'm not going to make the same mistake again."

"I know you won't, Nicolette," her father said. "And I don't think you have. To Detective Jackson's credit, he appears accepting of who and what you are."

Nicole glanced up and found Jax watching her. Disconcerted, she reached for her water glass. "He doesn't know everything," she said, afraid he would overhear her. "For that matter, I don't think I know everything."

"You do not." He shifted, the leather creaking beneath him. "Part of that parent-protectiveness thing. And it is part of the reason why your mother, how do you say, freaked out when she discovered what had happened to you. She'll know when you're ready to hear the full scope of the Legacy."

"Surely there's something I can know now. Why did only women inherit the Legacy until Derek and Darien? Why do they have it and no other men in the family? Why am I the first dreamer born in three hundred years?"

Stefan Antonescu put his arm around her shoulder. "As much as your mother and I know, we don't have all the answers yet. I am doing my best to work on it. Going back through the history has been a challenge, especially since Giselle was the first to put the family history on paper some three hundred and fifty years ago. The Legacy is older than that, and it's taking some time to track the history back to Anika."

Nicole shifted on the couch, trying to keep the leather from sticking to her legs. As keyed-up as she was, she nonetheless found herself drifting while her father spoke. Her father had done so much to organize the memoirs of the Legère matriarchs, but there seemed to be much more to do, much more for her to understand. The Legacy, her family, her duties and responsibilities. When Jax's case was over, would she be able to keep her abilities and Jax? Or would she have to give up one for the other?

Her awareness of the room faded, and she dreamed.

She strolled along a trail worn smooth by time. Dark ivy and African violets edged the path shaded by large oak trees. Warmth filled the soft air, letting her know it was late spring. Ahead of her she could hear what sounded like a stream, and decided to find it.

Sun filtered through the oak branches above her, creating diamond-like prisms of color. A light breeze caught her hair and the flowing skirt of the pale blue dress she wore. She realized she walked shoeless, but the path was so smooth beneath her feet that it didn't bother her.

The path eventually opened onto a meadow. Wildflowers of every describable color dotted the verdant expanse, their color repeated in the air above them by hundreds of butterflies. The air had a misty, golden feel to it, like that in an Impressionist painting. The beauty of the scene stole her breath, and she had to stand there, eyes closed and face tilted to the sun, to absorb it in gratitude.

"Hello?"

The unfamiliar voice startled Nicole out of her pastoral reverie. She opened her eyes and turned to discover a woman sitting on a wood and wrought iron bench beneath a flowering shade tree in the middle of the clearing. A large beaver and a stack of books sat at her feet, but Nicole didn't find it strange. It was a dream, after all.

"Hello," she said, approaching the bench. "I didn't know anyone else was here."

"I'm usually the only one here," the woman said. Dark blond hair framed a kind and open face with warm, mossy eyes and a wide but thin-lipped mouth. "This is my private place. I daydream about it all the time when I'm stressed and I dream about it sometimes too."

She laughed self-consciously. "I'm sorry to rattle on like that. My name is Olivia."

Nicole took the woman's hand in hers. Energy coursed up her arm, and she realized Olivia possessed a small amount of psychic ability, probably without knowing it. "Hello, Olivia, my name is Nicole. May I?"

When the woman nodded, Nicole sat beside her. "This is a beautiful place."

"It is," Olivia agreed, her eyes sliding shut as she inhaled deeply. "I call it my happy place. I daydream about it all the time, especially when the kids get to be too much. But I haven't seen you here before."

"I haven't been here before," Nicole admitted.

"Maybe I'm just imagining you." Olivia folded her hands in her lap. "Someone up there must have known I needed someone to talk to."

"Why do you need someone to talk to?"

Olivia turned to face her, a sad smile curving her lips. "Because I know I'm going to die soon."

A cold hand seemed to form a fist around Nicole's heart, yet she managed to ask, "How do you know you're going to die soon? Are you sick?"

"Oh, no, I'm not sick," Olivia said, her green eyes earnest. "It's just a feeling I have, that's it's going to happen soon. Sometimes, sometimes I feel like someone is watching me, even here in this place. I feel him, like this cold, dark presence on the back of my neck, pressing down on me, wanting something from me. I don't know who he is or what he wants, but he won't stop until he gets it."

"You think someone is trying to kill you?" Nicole couldn't keep the horror from her voice.

Olivia shuddered. "He's evil, and he's coming after me," she said, her voice hushed. Tears spiked her lashes. "I'm going to miss my kids, my own and the ones I teach. And Paul, sweet Paul. He won't be able to take it."

A variety of images paraded behind the other woman as she spoke. Olivia in front of a green blackboard, interacting with a group of eight year olds. At a dinner table with a thin, brown-haired bespectacled man, a girl of about twelve and a ten-year-old boy, both with the same dark blond hair.

Tears stinging her own eyes, Nicole wrapped her fingers around the other woman's wrist. "Tell me how to help you," she urged. "That's why I'm here. What's your last name? Where do you live? Where do you teach?"

Before Olivia could answer the breeze was transformed from a whisper to a howl. Nicole glanced around her and saw that the golden day was now a dirty, grayish brown. The air around them seemed to harden with dread and menace.

The other woman's hand trembled. "He's coming."

Still gripping Olivia's hand, Nicole rose to her feet, determined to protect her, determined to see the killer's face and somehow stop him before he struck again. *You can do this,* a voice whispered in her mind. *You're a dreamer and this is a dream. This is your territory.*

"I don't know who you are, but I'm going to stop you," she declared over the rising wind. Her free hand tightened around the smooth wood staff of her spear. She didn't bother wondering why she'd conjured a spear instead of a machine gun, or a bazooka. "I won't let you harm this woman!"

Wind screamed in response, flattening the field of flowers. Dark clouds coalesced into a faintly human shape. Then she sensed it, the moment the shape became a being, became *him.*

"Two? How is this possible?"

The voice, one of cold culture, crawled across her skin. Nicole swallowed against the fear that spiked through her. "Who are you?"

"One who will take her power, and yours." The shadow moved closer, leaving dying things in its wake. "Especially yours. You are ripe with it."

Vines, thick and scaly, sprang up from the ground and rushed towards them. Before Nicole could even form a scream the spidery greenery coiled about her legs. Behind her, Olivia screamed. Nicole turned to see vines snaking up the woman's body and around her neck, eager to squeeze the life from her.

"No!" Terror filled Nicole's stomach with bile as she sliced at the vines with the tip of her spear.

"Wake up, Olivia. You need to wake up, now!"

Survival instinct beat back the terror as she turned from Olivia to focus her will on the shadowy form in front of them.

"I have this for a reason," she murmured, raising the spear before the vines could trap her arms at her sides. A part of her noticed the darkening of her skin, the bracelets on her arms, the gathering of power as she aimed for the center of the being.

"You won't take her!" she screamed, then threw.

The spear, blazing with light, struck the center of the shadowy form. A shriek split the boiling air as the shadow cracked, then shattered, throwing Nicole to the ground.

Nicole opened her eyes to find herself stretched out on the carpet, her upper body cradled against Jax. When she looked up at him, he said, "I saw you going and tried to catch you before you hit the floor. I almost missed."

Her parents knelt over them, concern limning their faces. She took a breath, a sweet, blessedly deep breath. "I'm fine, I think. I need my journal."

She struggled to sit up but her father easily pushed her back down, back into Jax's arms. "You're going to stay right there until we're certain that you're okay."

Nicole rubbed her forehead. "Since the room's spinning, I'm not going to argue."

"You had a waking dream." Her mother made it a statement instead of a question.

She nodded anyway. "Yes. I thought I felt someone interacting with me."

"We all were," her father answered. "We tried anyway. Is it always like this?"

"The other night when I tried to interact with her, it didn't work," Jax answered. "It probably worked this time because she's used to listening to you. And she doesn't have bruises this time, either."

"I don't." The fact surprised her. "Everything about this dream was different though. I had more control. And I was separate from Olivia."

Jax's arms tightened around her. "Olivia?"

Nicole gave a brief description. "She teaches second or third grade, I think. The school either has beaver in the name or the mascot is a beaver. She has a daughter about twelve and a younger son. Her husband's name is Paul."

She gripped Jax's jacket. "I know what she looks like, what her family looks like. And I think I know why he's been going after these women."

Chapter Sixteen

Do you believe this?" Bear asked as he and Jax watched Nicole work at the computer with the composite artist. It was seven-thirty A.M., and Jax was still working on his first cup of coffee.

"Hey, I told you to come along last night. You could have seen it for yourself."

"No, thanks. What I saw in the interrogation room the other day was enough." He smacked his gum. "Her explanation for why this creep picks his targets is hard to swallow, know what I'm saying?"

"I know." Hearing Nicole declare that each of the victims possessed some sort of psychic ability that the killer wanted to harvest sounded farfetched to him, even after everything he'd seen. Just farfetched enough to be believable.

"She believes it," Jax reminded him softly. "Enough to call me at five A.M. to meet her here. Besides, you read the profiler's report. We're looking for a white male, late twenties to mid-thirties, educated. He said the eyes were more than a trophy, but he didn't know what, other than taking them suggests some sort of ritual. Nicole doesn't know what the profiler said, but she nailed it."

"I don't know if it's a stretch for a psychology doctoral candidate to come up with the same profile, but given everything else, I guess we can count it as validation." Bear shook his head in disgust. "Just what we need, ritualistic killings,"

Jax had to agree. It made it more difficult to track and predict a killer.

Bear kept his gaze on Nicole as he spoke. "The eyes are the window to the soul, or something like that. But this guy doesn't want their souls—or at least, not just their souls. What he really wants is their psychic powers."

"He thinks he can get stronger by taking their power from them. And the way to do that is to hunt and kill them, taking their eyes. The eyes are necessary for the ritual."

Bear's face grew hard. "We finally got a break."

"With the clock running," Jax agreed. "Two more dreams. Two more chances to find this woman, whether that's two days or two weeks."

"Yeah. No pressure there." Bear jerked his head toward Nicole. "What's her sense?"

Jax studied the intensity of Nicole's expression as she corrected the artist. "She's feeling some urgency, so my money's on two days if the guy sticks to his pattern. She's afraid, but she's also eager to dream again, since she managed to stop the guy the last time."

Bear turned to face him, his expression serious. "You know what this means, don't you?" he asked, his voice neutral.

"Yeah." He knew what it meant. If he accepted everything Nicole had told him, and they managed to prevent the teacher's death, there was a good chance Nicole would be the next target. If he accepted what she'd dreamt, the killer was already aware of her presence and her ability to stop him.

Nicole had unwittingly made herself a target.

Identifying Nicole as a potential victim might make his job easier, but that didn't mean he had to like it.

"Should we tell her?"

Jax shook his head. "Nicole's a smart woman. If she hasn't figured it out yet, she will soon. And if she doesn't, those parents of hers will."

"So, as distasteful as it is, we know the identity of a possible victim. We can—or rather, you can—baby-sit twenty-four/seven. I'd still like to nail this guy before he goes after the teacher."

"So would I. The question is, how did he find these women? It can't be random. Something has to connect them." Jax flipped through the pile of notes on his desk, struggling to control his rising concern for Nicole. He remembered how she'd described the man who stalked the teacher. Cold, confident, and cunning. The horror in her voice as she'd described the way he'd manipulated the combined dream made his palms itch with the need to do something, anything, to keep her from becoming possible victim four.

"Did you get the notes from my conversation with Nicki's mother?"

Bear freed a folder from his desktop pile. "Yeah. Something about a class or meeting of some sort, within the last six months. Eight other women and one guy, besides our two victims. So maybe we need to go back and interview people again, tracking the victims' movements for the last six months."

"Ask if there were any classes or workshops." Jax rubbed his head at the thought of the legwork to come. "We're probably going to have to call every New Age shop in the area, see if they offered any classes that might fit our profile of dreams or psychic abilities. If you want to take Gutierrez's family, I'll try to track down Connie Reid's acquaintances."

"Good luck." Bear snorted, handing over the interview list for the second victim. "They weren't exactly talkative."

"Understatement of the year. We'll probably have better luck with the shops. So how do we find out who Olivia is before it's too late?"

"I say we try the subtle approach before we move on to alerting the media or anything," Bear advised. "I'll take on the board of education, see if they can cross reference schools with Beaver in the name or as mascot. And I'm sure they have a database of teachers in the area. With luck I can uncover the identity of teacher Olivia, wife of Paul, with two kids before the end of the day."

"I sure as hell hope so," Jax said. "Otherwise, we're going to have to plaster the woman's face all over the six o'clock news."

"We might have to do that anyway, if the captain thinks we're coming up against the clock. As it is, he wants every uniform with a beat near a school to have a copy of the composite."

The sketch artist looked up. "We're done, detectives." She handed over a printout.

Jax perused it, then passed it over to Bear. He focused on Nicole, noting the tightness around her eyes. "Are you okay?" he asked as she stood.

"A little tired, but otherwise fine," she answered, rubbing at her forehead. "I'm sorry it took so long, but I wanted to make sure I had it right."

"We'd rather you get it right than get it fast," Bear said. "Thanks for your help, Ms. Legère. I'll take this to the captain."

Jax leaned closer to her as Bear left. "Are you sure you're okay?"

Nicole managed a smile. "I didn't sleep much, trying to make sure I had Olivia's image firmly in my mind. Thanks for letting me come in so early."

"The earlier we can get started on tracking her down, the sooner we can find her," Jax said, steering her toward the exit with a hand to the small of her back. He enjoyed touching her, and he enjoyed the sway of her hips even more. "Did you dream at all last night?"

"No. I can't tell you how relieved I was not to wake up all bruised and battered."

Jax slowed his step, his hand tightening on her waist. "Being the hard-assed detective that I am, I'm not supposed to feel guilty for pushing you like this, but I do."

She smiled at him. "I don't think you're a hard-ass. Besides, I'm pushing myself just as hard."

"And don't think I don't respect that." He lightly ran his knuckles down her cheek. "When this is over, I'll make it up to you."

Her eyes sparkled. "Breakfast in bed and a massage would be nice."

Something welled inside him. "I think we can handle that. What are you doing today?"

Her smiled dimmed slightly. "I'm going to see my mother. There are some things I need to talk to her about before I go to school."

She dipped her head. "It doesn't really feel right to be worried about school and stuff with everything that's going on, but—"

"Hey." He stroked her cheek again, wanting to follow the gesture with his lips. "You still have to live your life, take care of your daughter. Like my daddy used to say, you do what you need to do so you can do what you need to do."

Then, because he couldn't just let her leave, he kissed her. A soft press of lips that made him forget, just for a moment, where they were and what they were supposed to be doing.

"Jax," she whispered when he pulled away.

The yearning in her voice made him tighten. "I'll catch up with you later," he promised, wanting nothing more than to take her somewhere, anywhere where they could be alone and forget about the case. "You'd better go while I can still let you."

Nicole's buoyant mood slipped as she rode the elevator up to her parents' suite. The feeling of being two people—one a woman with normal issues and needs, the other locked in a supernatural dream—had increased over the last few days. After writing down her dream of the previous night, she had more questions than ever. Questions, she knew, that could only be answered by one person.

She wasted no time when her mother opened the door. "We need to talk."

Arielle Legère's eyes darkened. "Yes, I suppose it is time."

They settled in the sitting area before the spectacular city view. "I know there's a lot about the Legacy that I don't know," Nicole began. "And truthfully, I didn't want to know for the longest time. But there's something going on, something more than coincidence and your motherly concern. My talent has gone from misfires to a steady current of power. There's a reason for it, besides the fact that you completely removed the block. That power is going to draw this man to me, and I want to be prepared for his arrival."

Nicole's mother folded her hands together. "You're right, Nicolette," she said after a long pause. "There is much more to the Legacy than psychic ability."

"I thought so. I got that much yesterday when I had that waking dream about Olivia." She leaned forward. "But other things happened.

When that spear appeared in my hand, I felt this huge enveloping energy. It felt ancient, I guess, but also nurturing."

"What do you think it means?"

Nicole drew her brows together. "At first, I thought it was just symbolism, but I'm not so sure. I got a sense of something or someone else with me, facing down that man. It reminded me of the woman I saw in my meditation, the one who offered me the glowing box."

Arielle Legère rose to her feet. "I've thought about this moment for years, practicing what I would say to you. Now that the moment is here, I have no idea what to say."

"What are you talking about?" Nicole's stomach clenched in anticipation. "Do you know what my vision was about?"

"It's about the Legacy. The true meaning of what it is, and why we have it." Arielle turned around, her expression solemn. "You know our tradition is to use our abilities to do good works, as much as we can wherever we can. But the Legacy is more than that. Our family, in particular the daughters of our family, has been in service to the Universal Good for generations, helping in its eternal struggle to maintain Balance."

Nicole could hear the capitalization in her mother's voice, but she couldn't make sense of it. "Universal Good? Balance? None of this makes sense, Mom."

"A Guardian came to our ancestor Anika on the plains of Africa, choosing her and her descendants to stand in the breach between Light and Dark."

Arielle sank into the couch beside her. "Light and Dark, Heaven and Hell, Good and Evil, Order and Chaos—whatever you call them—are true forces in the universe. We've given them other names, wrapped them in a hundred different religions, but the ultimate source is the same. Every myth has a basis in reality, Nicolette."

"Wait." Nicole put her hands to her head, struggling to make sense of her mother's words. "Are you trying to tell me that *Buffy* is real?"

"To put it simply, yes. But it is more complicated than that, and I've spent my adult life trying to understand it all. As far as being a slayer is concerned, only a few of us have been called to direct conflict. Other than Mala, I think only a handful of others in our family have been chosen. I do know that those who trained Mala have trained others, and that they've been doing this for centuries, even longer than our family."

"Mala?" Nicole thought of the older of her twin sisters, harder than she should have been, more solitary than she should have been. She'd abruptly gone overseas to college at sixteen. Nicole had been finishing college herself then, married to Randall and hiding her troubles, but she'd wondered at the suddenness of Mala's departure that had left Malita behind alone. Mala never really discussed what she did for a living besides calling herself a paranormal investigator, and now Nicole knew why.

"So when Mala went to Europe for school—"

"She learned more than one would from a traditional college," her mother said. "You could call her a ghost-hunter, but basically Mala tracks down and captures some of the worst things that go bump in the night."

Nicole rose, needing to walk her swirling thoughts into some order. She felt as if she'd just learned that a spaceship had deposited her on her parents' doorsteps, the news was that hard to grapple with. "This can't be happening."

"It is. I wouldn't lie to you about something like this."

"You've never lied to me, Mom. I know that. Kept things from me, yes, but never lied."

Nicole turned to face her mother. "Am I the only one in the family who doesn't know?" she asked. "I mean, I know I left home as soon as I could, but surely I wasn't so wrapped up in my problems not to see this."

"No," Arielle answered. "I haven't shared the full duties of the Legacy with anyone but your father, when he proposed to me. Mala knows of course, but not Malita or your brothers. I wanted each of you to live your lives as fully and completely as possible. Especially you, Nicolette."

"Me. Because I'm supposed to take your place. I don't even know what that means anymore. Fight demons and vampires and black magic?"

"You're supposed to do what you are doing now," her mother said firmly. "Help people, keep others from destroying innocent lives. Follow your dreams."

A sudden flash of intuition had Nicole widening her eyes. "Oh God," she whispered. "You think the man who strangled these women, you think he's one of these dark things, don't you? That's why you flipped when I told you what had happened at the precinct. You thought he was attacking me!"

"Yes," her mother admitted. "It wouldn't have been the first time that someone in the family has been attacked. It wouldn't be the last. I've done all I can to protect everyone in the family over the years, and everyone that my gifts have guided me to. Every Legère, male or female, is a target for anyone who strives to upset the Balance. Members of the family have slipped away, either by their own choosing or by temptation. Your great-aunt Sybelle was led astray. That's why the Legacy passed to my grandmother instead. Even now I'm dealing with the fallout of that."

"Lord, I was such a brat," Nicole said, her throat clogging. She sat next to her mother, gathering those slender, strong hands in her own. "Wallowing in self-pity and a desire to live a normal life, while you were dealing with—with this huge, amazing thing. I can't believe I put that crap on you. I'm so sorry."

"Don't apologize, Nicolette," her mother said, giving her hands a gentle squeeze. "Believe me, I totally understand that need to have a normal life in a world that is anything but normal. I'm glad you've had the chance I didn't, even though I wouldn't change my life for anything."

Arielle extracted her hands. "I don't want you to think that it's all doom and gloom. It's not. The results of doing good things for people either through the foundation or through the Legacy, have been the most rewarding experiences of my life after my family. I enjoy heading our family, chairing our business interests, and even organizing the family reunions."

Nicole knew her mother meant to reassure her, but she felt far from reassured. "Light versus Darkness. You realize that this completely changes my life?"

"Yes. That's why I've waited so long to tell you."

Nicole looked away, her mind reeling as she struggled to accept her mother's words. Yet how could she not? She knew enough of the family history to know that many inexplicable and miraculous events happened around Legère women, particularly Keepers. Why have such a lofty name as Keeper of the Legacy if it didn't pertain to some lofty purpose?

Could she do it? The thought whispered through her mind. She'd spent most of her life running away from everything the Legacy meant, while blissfully unaware of everything the Legacy meant.

She was already using her gifts to help the police. Trying to, anyway. Could she spend the rest of her life doing this? Her mother had offered her a choice before. Could she leave behind the life she'd begun here?

Did she still have a choice?

Bitterness welled in Nicole, acrid and dark. "I wasted four years of my life with the wrong man," she said, close to tears. "And now that I've found the right one, I'm going to have to let him go."

"You don't know that," her mother said. "He's accepted everything about you so far."

"Because he doesn't know everything!" Nicole dug her hands into her palms. "It took a lot for him to believe my dreams. I don't think he truly believed what I told him about our abilities until I flipped out at the precinct. There's a big difference in him believing what I can do and accepting what I'm going to need to do with the Legacy."

"I don't think you're giving him enough credit."

Nicole shook her head. "Mom, how did you feel when it was your turn? How did you feel when you knew you wanted to be with Dad?"

"It was different for us. Your father already knew our family had paranormal abilities, though he didn't know everything. He specifically came to America to enlist my help in breaking the curse that killed the males in his family before their thirtieth birthday. By the time we'd arrived in Hungary to break the curse, I was wholly in love with him. I couldn't imagine not having him in my life, but I couldn't imagine him accepting the full scope of the Legacy either. I was terrified of asking him to return to America with me, and terrified that he'd leave. I would have done anything to keep him with me—except turn away from the Legacy. Luckily for me, he wanted to share my work and my life."

She grasped Nicole's hand. "You do have a choice. I wouldn't be a mother if I didn't let you know that. You have free will. You can choose to stay away from the Legacy and live your life without your gifts. Or you can choose to fully embrace all aspects of the Legacy and your role as future Keeper, knowing that you'll eventually have to leave your life here."

Nicole extracted her hand from her mother's, then rose, walking over to the window. The city spread before her like a gray and green blanket, alive and oblivious.

"There's no guarantee with Jax if I stay or leave," Nicole said. "The only thing that's really certain is that if I turn my back and lose my abilities, I won't be able to help Jax find this man and more women could die. I can't do that."

She touched her fingertips to the window, then turned away. "I've had seven years here. Seven years of trying to be normal, trying to be ordinary. But that's not who I am. And now that my strength's returned and growing, I realize how much I missed it. I miss Beau-Rêve. I miss the family."

Tears sprang to her eyes. "I missed you and Dad. I don't want Danielle to miss all of that because of me. But I have to see this through with Jax, wherever it goes. After that, we'll talk about going home."

She didn't know what scared her most—trying to explain the turn in her life to Jax or what he would do once he knew everything.

Chapter Seventeen

Nine hours after parting from Nicole, Jax returned to his small frame house in East Atlanta, frustrated in more ways than one. There were a dozen public schools in the five-county area with "beaver" as part of their name or address, five more with the animal as school mascot. Adding three private schools to the mix had only increased his headache. Bear had been stonewalled at each county's educational board, leaving them with no alternative but watch-dogging the schools and visiting New Age shops around town. Both had agreed to leave Ananda Gutierrez's family alone unless they absolutely had to speak to them.

He tossed his sack dinner on the coffee table before going into the kitchen to retrieve a beer. Returning, he snagged one of his car kits from the utilitarian display shelf in the corner. Putting together a model would help him think. Lord knew he had a lot to think about.

He twisted the cap off the dark brown bottle, the hiss loud to his ears. The small two-bedroom house sat around him like the crowd at a Masters tournament, silent and expectant.

Expecting what, he didn't know. How had he not realized how quiet the house was?

Because he'd been ignoring it. Jax took a deep swallow of his beer before turning on the television. He'd been ignoring the silence for three years and instead of going away, the silence had spread like a cancer, overtaking everything but his dedication to his career.

He thought about the picture in his nightstand drawer. The picture of Felecia in her dress uniform, Old Glory behind her. The only picture he could bear holding on to. He remembered the ambulance ride, the panic and hurt that had filled his chest so full he couldn't breathe. Remembered the last word his beautiful wife had whispered: *Don't.*

That single word had meant so many things over the past three years. Don't let her slaying go unpunished. He hadn't. Don't give up his career. He'd stayed. Don't forget. He'd remembered. Don't give in to the urge to drink and rage. He'd resisted.

Now he thought he could hear something new, something different. Don't shut away the world. Don't forget but don't drown in memories. Don't stop living. Don't let silence become the only thing remaining.

It was time to move forward, to look beyond the present. He had to make the decision to move on with his life. He had to do it for Felecia, and he had to do it for himself.

His thoughts strayed, as they did with increasing frequency, to Nicole. What did meeting Nicole Legère mean? He had never been one to look for signs and symbolism in everyday life, but he'd been a detective long enough to know that clues were everywhere.

Of all the people Nicole could have met, she'd run into him—the biggest cynic in the department. His need for proof had stretched her abilities and boundaries. She'd given what she hadn't offered since her husband's death and he'd taken what he hadn't wanted, hadn't missed, for three years.

It would be easy to think that God or Fate had thrown them together, but Jax found that difficult to accept. He and Nicole were too different, blue collar versus blue blood, paranormal versus very normal. Legère women inherited their mother's name, money, and abilities; he'd inherited his parents' mortgage. The only thing he and Nicole had in common was the loss of their spouses.

And passion. Something happened to him when he stood within feet of Nicole; something hard and hot and primitive clawed through him whenever she touched him. They'd had sex two nights—even she didn't call it making love—and he'd transformed into a junkie in desperate search for his next fix.

A relationship needed more than sex. Even he realized that. As much as he and Felecia had enjoyed each other's bodies, they'd also enjoyed each other's company. He and his wife had been friends and lovers.

He took another swallow of beer, then set it down. He doubted he could be Nicole's friend. What in the hell could he talk to her about? High society? The benefits of trust funds? Jax shook his head. He wouldn't know where to begin. Each time he and Nicole talked, it had been about the case. When the case ended, what would they have?

No answer came to him, and perhaps that was answer enough. Nicole hadn't mentioned wanting anything more—she'd assumed he just wanted sex. Yet he'd meant it when he'd told her he wasn't a one-night-stand type of guy. Problem was, he didn't see them being together after this case ended.

You didn't have to be psychic to see there was no future for him and Nicole Legère.

His cell phone rang. He waited for the second ring before answering. "Detective Jackson."

"Hello, Detective Jackson." Nicole's voice flowed over him. "Have you had dinner yet?"

Jax looked down at his cheesesteak hoagie. "That depends."

"On whether or not you have to eat with my parents again?" He could hear her smile through the phone. "Don't worry, I'll spare you another inquisition."

He relaxed. "Then no, I haven't had dinner yet. What did you have in mind? Someplace we can take Danielle?"

"No, but thank you for asking. Dani is currently being spoiled by my parents in their suite, and this is after they took her on a shopping spree. Anyway, I found myself cooking more than I need and thought you might like to join me for dinner."

She paused, then added, "And maybe for breakfast?"

His earlier soul-searching burned away on a flame of need. "I'll be there in twenty," he said, then hung up.

He made it in fifteen, gripping the steering wheel like a vise all the way. Nicole opened the front door as he grabbed his bag from the back seat. He shut the car door quickly and moved up the pathway even quicker, needing to touch her. The porch light bathed her face in a warm glow not nearly as bright as her smile or her arms held out in welcome.

Bounding up the steps, he closed the distance between them, throwing his bag through the doorway behind her before taking her in his arms. He buried his face in the crook of her neck and held on, held on for sweet dear life. Her arms circled his shoulders as she settled willingly into him, soft curves to hard planes, heartbeat to heartbeat.

Her cheek rested on his shoulder. After several moments she spoke, a whisper of breath against his ear. "Hi."

"Hi yourself." Since she didn't seem to mind, he didn't move, just breathed her in. Then, because he couldn't seem to do anything else, he pulled away just enough to kiss her. Once, twice, then a lingering taste that swam through his blood and eased his soul.

Another long moment of just holding and feeling. Then she turned her head. "My neighbor's watching. She's giving me the thumb's up sign."

"God bless Miss Gertie." Jax walked her backwards into the house, taking care to avoid his bag while maintaining his hold on her. He closed the door with his foot. "How ya doing?"

"Much better now." She actually snuggled closer to him with a hum of contentment. "I guess you had a day."

"Yeah. I had a day." He relaxed his hold enough to kiss her once, twice, again. "How 'bout you?"

"The same." She sighed with what sounded like appreciation. "I like this."

"Me too." He drew her close again, focusing on the feel of her in his arms, cashmere comfort.

"I'm glad you came over."

"Me too." *The fullness of her breasts, the soft roundness of her belly.*

"I hope you're not allergic to seafood."

"Me too." *The sinful slope of her behind, those luscious thighs . . .* ."What?"

She laughed. "I didn't think you were listening. But I'm flattered."

"You should be." Realizing he was going overboard, he released her. "Did you say something about food?"

"Seafood gumbo. Homemade. And pecan pie for dessert, also homemade." She headed for the kitchen.

He grabbed his bag, depositing it in the living room before joining her in the kitchen. "I think I need to be pinched. What can I do to help?"

"Stop drooling, for one." She handed him a napkin. "You can set the table after you decide whether you want to eat at the dinette set here or in the formal dining room."

She lifted the lid off a pot, sending tendrils of steam into the air. "I'm not the formal type," he said, inhaling deeply. He hadn't had home-cooked food since his grandmother's passing. "Could you hand me another napkin?"

Dinner was just as delicious as it smelled: hot buttered bread, salad, and gumbo. He'd never been a fan of pecan pie, but Nicole's dessert changed his mind. Twice.

When he couldn't take another bite without being transported into nirvana, he leaned back in his chair. "Woman, you almost got me speaking in tongues. Can I just tell you that this was the best food I've had in a long time?"

"You don't have to tell me; I saw for myself." Nicole began gathering dishes. "Three bowls of gumbo and two slices of pie? That's thanks enough."

"Let me get that." Because his parents had taught him manners, he took the dishes from her and carried them to the sink. When she protested, he said, "You cooked, I'll clean. If it'll make you feel better, you can supervise."

She joined him at the counter with leftovers. "I realize I'm a little meticulous about things."

"A little?" He let himself smile. "If cleanliness is next to godliness, you could be an angel."

"I'm sorry." Her smile collapsed. "It's not something I can change."

"Hey." He stopped scraping food into the disposal to face her. "I don't recall asking you to change."

"That's right." She immediately brightened. "You haven't."

"In fact, if I were going to ask you to change, it would be into something a little more comfortable." He wiggled his eyebrows. "Like nothing."

He was rewarded with a laugh. "You're impossible, but I like it."

He liked it too. He liked it a lot, so much so that he had to concentrate on cleaning the dishes before he could speak again. "How did you have time to fix a meal like this? Doesn't gumbo take a while?"

"It does." She stoppered the second sink basin, then squeezed dish detergent in before commandeering the faucet. "I took a leave from work."

"Didn't I say I was doing this and you're just supervising?" He dumped his dishes into the soapy water as she rinsed one and put it in the dishwasher. Of course she'd wash dishes before washing dishes. "And what do you mean, you took leave?"

"Just what I said." She moved away, returning with plastic containers and foil. "I told my boss I needed an indefinite amount of time off. I just didn't have the heart to quit right out, but I think he knew. Anyway, after that I withdrew from school."

"You did what?"

Nicole began storing leftovers, trying not to focus on the surprise she'd heard in Jax's voice. "I wasn't having such an impact on his workload that he can't easily replace me. And withdrawing from school, well, I can just re-up next semester. Besides, what we're doing is more important."

"But getting your degree is important to you."

"Yeah." She paused, grateful for his acknowledgement. She couldn't tell him the truth she'd discovered that afternoon. The revelation still rang through her, still new, still foreign. Still incredible. No, she couldn't tell him. Not yet, not after sharing a wonderful, normal dinner without any talk of dreams or crimes. "I've already got two degrees, though. Do I really need another?"

"Nicki."

She turned from the refrigerator as he put the last of the cleaned dishes into the dishwasher. "Hhm?"

"Does this have anything to do with your talk with your mother earlier today?"

Darn. Of course he'd make the right guess. He was a detective after all. "Partly," she hedged. "But I really want to be able to help you as much as possible."

"Thank you." He washed and dried his hands. "But I don't want you rearranging your life because of my case."

"I'm not, really." It was more than his case. Much more.

He stared at her as if attempting to divine her secrets. Nicole held her ground, barely. Jax had the ability to make her want to confide in him, but she couldn't. If he knew everything, he would leave. She wasn't ready for that, not yet.

"How about we go out to the living room, watch TV?" She gathered his hands in hers, enjoying the strength and even the calluses. "I've only seen the Disney Channel and Nickelodeon for the last seven years."

They adjourned to the living room, settling on the sofa. Nicole gave Jax the remote, content to curl up beside him. He flipped to a drama, then put the remote down, turning his back against the sofa's arm before pulling her closer. His hands settled on her shoulders, massaging tension away.

Under his expert touch, Nicole found herself melting. Her conversation with her mother and decisions she'd made floated away as she relaxed more than she had in weeks. She focused on the man behind her, a mystery but not. "Will you tell me more about your family?"

He complied, his voice low and comforting. He told her about growing up with his grandmother after his parents had died within months of each other. Hearing him describe how he, his brother, and sister had all been bullies in school made her smile. He hadn't given up his bullying; he just used it now to protect people.

At his request she stretched out on the couch so that his fingers could work down her back. "You know, it still amazes me how much of your history you can document."

"More than what I told you," she murmured, her voice coming slowly. "Before the family settled in New Orleans as free people, they worked a sugar plantation on Martinique. The stories go back to an ultimate grandmother named Anika in West Africa."

"Is she the one who started your Legacy?"

"Yes." Relaxed now, Nicole let her guard down completely. "I haven't read most of the histories, and my dad is still cataloging the bulk of them into a computer archive. Most of what I know I learned as bedtime stories."

"So when did your family pick up the name Legère?"

She shifted beneath his fingers as he worked a particularly resistant muscle. "Slavers took one of Anika's descendants to Martinique, where she was purchased by Henri Legère. Eventually Giselle came along, and when Jean-Paul Legère lost his wife to childbirth, Giselle became the children's nanny—and Jean-Paul's mistress."

"She didn't have much choice, I bet."

"Probably not," Nicole agreed, "but she worked it to her advantage. Apparently Jean-Paul fell in love with Giselle. He taught her how to read and write in French, English, and Latin. In return, she used her gifts to protect him, his family, and their holdings. They had one child together, a daughter. When Jean-Paul died, his son honored his request and freed Giselle and her daughter, settled a sum of money on them, and sent them to New Orleans, where they thrived.

"Giselle was the first to write our histories down, the first to have the title of Keeper of the Legacy. From her came the structure that the family currently lives by, that every daughter born to the family would keep the family name. I think it came from being owned, subject to the whims of a man, and not having control of her own life.

"Giselle quietly made money in New Orleans, finding trustworthy people to conduct and teach her business. After the Civil War, Giselle bought Beau-Rêve from a widow who lost her husband and sons to the war, and our family has called it home ever since."

"So your family's never made money using their abilities?"

Nicole sighed as Jax massaged her legs. "Not directly, not by accepting money from others," she explained. "That goes against what the Legacy's all about."

"But indirectly is okay?"

"Yes, as in someone gifted in healing becoming a doctor. Malita is an empath who uses her gifts to create harmonious environments as an interior designer. I have a cousin who designs clothing promoting peace and harmony. The only exception might be my brothers, who use a portion of their gifts in some parts of their magic show. Yet even they give back to each of the communities they visit.

"The family has used intuition and knowledge as much as psychic ability to make money. That money takes care of the family, but it also funds the Legacy Foundation, which donates to a lot of charities around the world. Our mission is about helping people, whenever we can, however we can."

"And that's what your mother does now? Heads the foundation?" He took one foot in his hands.

His fingers along the sensitive arch of her foot made her giggle and sigh simultaneously. "Yes, among other things."

"And you're going to have to take her place, aren't you?"

Nicole froze, then turned over to search Jax's eyes. "You're good," she whispered softly, not nearly as bothered by his use of massage to distract her as she could have been. "Too bad you can't use this technique to question other people."

"Wouldn't want to. Besides, we're both enjoying it, and you looked like you needed to talk."

He was right. Again. "Yes, eventually I'll have to take over from my mother. Hopefully that's years down the road."

"I figured it was something like that," Jax said, his fingers still moving surely over her instep. He didn't appear to be the least bit guilty at being caught, or disturbed that she'd have to leave one day.

Before she could decide if that bothered her, he said, "There's something in your eyes that wasn't there this morning when you left the precinct. I don't like it. And even though you clearly didn't want to talk about it or the fact that you've put your life on hold for my case, I had to do something to make that look go away."

His simple declaration touched her deeply. "Thank you."

His hands skimmed up her legs as he moved up beside her. "I hope you know you can talk to me about anything."

"I know." It was true. She probably could talk to him about the true nature of the Legacy, but could she deal with whatever came after that conversation? She leaned forward to kiss him, thankful for his concern, his offer, his touch and his presence. "Do you think we can go upstairs now?"

He stood, eyes sparking with instant heat. "Absolutely." He held his hand out to her.

"Don't forget your bag," she reminded him, placing her hand in his.

"Later." He drew her to her feet. "Right now, I want to continue your massage. Skin to skin."

Much later, Jax lay on his back in the comfort of Nicole's bed, her warm, pliant body pressed close as they drifted between paradise and slumber. "Jax."

"Hhm?"

"Do you think we're moving too fast?"

Damn. He dragged himself back from the edge of sleep. He knew enough about women to know that he needed to be alert for this conversation. "Depends on who you ask, I suppose. Does it matter?"

"No." She tucked her head under his chin. "I just don't want you to think I'm loose."

He knew what she meant. "I know you're not. You're the soul of propriety, relatively speaking. You've had seven years alone, and I've had three. We're adult enough to decide what speed works best for us."

"You're right. I was just wondering if I'm being selfish."

"Are you thinking about your daughter?"

"Partly." Her voice flowed over his chest, a warm breath. "Dani's the most important person in my life, but now there's more. There are so many things that I have to do. Trying to carve some time out for myself feels wrong and necessary at the same time."

Jax smoothed his hand down her back. He knew exactly how she felt. Fate's clock was standing somewhere, ticking away the hours and minutes. Awareness of the passage of time struck him keenly, causing him to feel like a willful child wanting more of it for himself. Wanting more of her, before she left for good.

"Nicki, I want as much time with you as I can get, but I know for a fact that neither one of us is going to compromise our duty. We're both going to do what we have to do because that's who we are. If you want to slow down, we'll slow down." Even if it killed him.

"You always know what to say." She turned into him. "But I don't want to slow down. I need this. Dammit, I deserve this. Right or wrong, I want to have every moment with you that I can."

Before he could form a reply, she slid down his body, and he forgot everything but her.

Chapter Eighteen

The following morning Jax and Bear sat in their unmarked car, Nicole in the back seat. All had large cups of Starbucks in their hands, courtesy of Bear.

Bear took a delicate sip of his toffee nut latte. "Are you sure this is the right school?"

"I'm sure." Nicole's voice rang with conviction. The dream had come to her without the terror of previous nights, allowing her the objectivity to employ some of the techniques her father and mother had taught her.

As for Olivia, she'd walked out of her school and turned to look up at the name: Beaver Creek Elementary. On to her car, a bronze-colored Honda with four doors, and she'd paused to stare at her license plate as if she'd never seen it before. Just like the school's name, the lettering and numbers on the tag had been difficult to make out, reversed and flipped since the mind's eye sees things differently.

No stalker came this time, no sky turning black as vines crawled with a life of their own. She'd awakened to tell Jax, only to find him leaning over her, staring down at her with a thoughtful, unguarded expression that made her heart thump harder. Before she could ask him what had happened, he'd leaned over and kissed her. He'd made love to her with a gentle, thorough intensity that left her breathless and close to tears, wanting to give back to him everything he'd given to her.

Her gaze drifted to him. Jax had accepted her dream-related information calmly, then called his partner to meet them before pulling Nicole into her first shower with another human being. They'd barely made it downstairs before Marshall arrived.

It amazed her, how she could think of the case while remembering how he'd felt sliding through her soapy hand. Trying to keep it all compartmentalized should have made her head hurt.

"Got the DMV report," Jax said, his voice matter-of-fact. "The car's registered to Olivia Davenport of 1413 Madison Avenue." He glanced briefly at Nicole before turning to his partner. "How should we play this?"

Bear gave a loud, thoughtful smack of his gum. Nicole suppressed a shudder. How in the world could someone chew gum and drink coffee at the same time? "I say we go to the principal's office, request to see her. Hopefully they'll send someone to get her without causing a big deal, and we'll talk to her."

"I want to be there," Nicole said.

Both men turned to face her. It should have intimidated her, but if she didn't cave when they'd dragged her down to the police station, she certainly wasn't going to cave because they frowned at her.

Marshall looked from Jax back to her. "Why?"

Prepared for a heated argument, Nicole was caught off guard. "I'm pretty sure you both realize how intimidating you can be."

"To some people anyway," Jax murmured.

Nicole refrained from sticking out her tongue at him. "She sees two massive detectives waiting for her, and she's going to immediately think that something's happened to a family member. I'm hoping that she'll see me and recognize me. Besides, I think I can better explain why we're here better than you can."

Marshall turned back to Jax. "She's got a point."

Jax shifted. "Yeah, she does." He looked at her, and Nicole could actually feel his gaze sliding over her skin. Heat swept through her.

Bear groaned. "Can you guys save the googly-eyes for later? You're making me sick."

They parked in a visitor's spot, then went in to see the principal. Soon enough, someone was dispatched to find Olivia Davenport.

Nicole sat in the outer office, half-aware of Jax and his partner flanking her. She retreated inside her mind, reviewing her dream-encounters with Olivia. Searching for something, anything that would put the woman at ease. If she actually was Olivia.

Doubt clenched Nicole's stomach. What if she was wrong? What if her abilities were false?

"Oh my God."

Nicole looked up into the startled blue eyes of a blonde-haired woman. Recognition burned through her doubts as she got to her feet. "Olivia."

The teacher cupped her hands over her mouth. "Oh my God," she said again, her voice trembling. "It's you. It's really you." She burst into tears.

Minutes later, they'd all moved into the principal's office. Nicole sat in one of the guest chairs, Olivia Davenport beside her. The other woman held Nicole's hand as if it were her only link to reality.

"I thought I was dreaming," Olivia said, wiping at her eyes with a wadded tissue. "I honestly thought I was going insane. I'm so glad you're real."

Nicole gave her hand a gentle squeeze. "Believe me, I'm glad you're real too."

Olivia's hands fluttered at her throat. "I've been having this overwhelming sense that something was going to happen. Then two nights ago I had a dream, the dream with you in it." She turned to Nicole. "I had another this morning, and it was so real. Something's going to happen, I just know it."

"That's why we're here, Mrs. Davenport," Jax said. He and Bear stood on the other side of the desk. Even with the principal out of the room, the office felt cramped.

"Police detectives." Olivia leaned closer to Nicole. "How did you get the police to believe you? I've never heard of Atlanta police working with psychics before."

Nicole looked at Jax, who gave her a nod. "It wasn't easy, and I didn't have a lot of information to give them. Unfortunately, two other women were attacked and killed before I got a clear impression of you and enough information so that they could find you."

Olivia looked at each of them in turn. "I'll do whatever I can to help you, but I'm pretty sure I'm nowhere near your ability, Ms. Legère."

"I think we're at the point where you can call me Nicole."

The teacher gave her a tremulous smile. "All right. Nicole it is then."

Nicole gave her a reassuring smile, though she felt far from reassured herself. Olivia Davenport looked at her with such relief that Nicole felt weighted down. She didn't want to fail this woman, not now when she had a true opportunity to protect her.

"How long have you been aware of your psychic ability?"

Fern-green eyes widened in surprise. "I-I'm not sure really. I mean, I always had little feelings. I just thought it was strong women's intuition. I didn't think about trying to hone them until I saw a flyer for a psychic development class."

Nicole felt the tension in the room ratchet up a notch as Jax and his partner stepped closer to them. "What class?"

"It was a workshop, like a continuing education class, that I took about six months ago." She told them the location, and Bear scribbled it down in his notepad. "I can't remember the name of the guy who taught it though."

Jax leaned over them. "A man taught it?"

"Yes." Nicole patted Olivia's hand as the woman turned to her in uncertainty. Encouraged, the teacher continued, "I remember because I thought it was unusual for a man to be teaching a class like that. Actually, I don't even remember any other men being there."

"Can you describe this man, Mrs. Davenport?"

Nicole felt her insides grow cold as she listened to Olivia describe the man. She felt Jax's eyes on her. She looked up to see a silent question in his eyes. She nodded. It was him, Nicole knew it. This was the same man who'd strangled the nurse and the prostitute.

Jax pulled a photo from a file folder. "Do you recognize this woman?"

"She's a nurse," Olivia said, surprising them. "She took the same class I did. Oh God, she's the one who was killed a couple of weeks ago? You think this man killed her?"

This time Nicole looked to Jax in silent question. His voice was careful when he answered. "Mrs. Davenport, we have reason to believe that this man was involved in two murders. We also believe that he poses an immediate threat to you."

"Oh God." She began to tremble. "I paid for that class with a check. It had my home address on it."

"We're going to do everything we can to keep you safe," Bear informed her. "You should discuss this with your family of course, but we'd like to put you all under surveillance for the next several days."

Jax spoke up. "We'd like for you to come down to the precinct. We'll have you work with a composite artist and answer a few more questions."

"All right. I'll do whatever you need me to do. Just keep my family safe."

"Good work."

Jax watched Nicole flush at the praise as she took the chair beside his desk. "It wasn't just me," she said modestly. "Olivia's information has got to be invaluable to you."

"And we wouldn't have Olivia if it weren't for you," he reminded her. "You handled yourself well back there. The owner of that shop wouldn't have given us the time of day without a court order. She nearly bent over backwards after you talked to her. So thank you for stepping in."

Excitement pulled at him. Things were falling into place. Their suspect now had a name: James William Corcoran. All they needed was the judge's signature on the search warrant for his home, and their case would be one step closer to being solved.

"Detective Jackson?"

They both turned in the voice's direction. A bright light shone in their faces. "Peter Schilling, Channel Three News. May I have a word with you?"

Jax immediately rose, blocking Nicole from view of the camera man. "This area is off-limits to media."

The red-headed man splattered a plastic smile across his face. "Actually I just completed an interview with your captain and Assistant District Attorney Walsh on progressive ways the force is fighting crime. Is this your psychic?"

"What?" Behind him, Nicole gasped and rose to her feet. Jax saw red.

"No comment." Steaming, he grabbed Nicole's forearm to lead her to one of the conference rooms. He fully intended to toss the reporter out on his ass, then kick ADA Walsh in hers.

"Ms. Legère? Would you mind answering a few questions? Are you really a psychic? Are you helping the police find a serial killer?"

Bear took that moment to reappear. Jax jerked his head at the reporter. Bear took the hint, smoothly stepping between Nicole and the reporter, blocking his advance. Jax had no doubt that Bear would tackle the man if necessary.

He led Nicole back to a conference room, closed the door, then leaned against it. "Are you okay?"

She nodded. "Just a little shaky. How did that reporter find out that I'm helping you?"

"I get the feeling Washboard Walsh saw an opportunity for free publicity." He curled his hands into fists. "I've got some free publicity for her all right."

"Jax." She crossed to him, covering his hands with her own. The cool touch immediately dampened his temper. "Come on, don't get riled up over this."

"Oh, this ain't even half as riled up as I'm going to be," he said, feeling his blood pressure rise. "I know how your family is about being in the spotlight. I fully intended to keep you and your name out of this as much as possible. We asked for your help; the least we could do is respect your wishes for privacy." He kicked the table. "I could shoot her for this!"

"I appreciate you trying to protect me," she said, her expression soft. "I'd like to return the favor by pointing out that you can't go talk to your boss or the ADA while you're mad. You might say or do something that you'll regret later."

She was right. He blew out an exasperated breath. "I can't believe you're not screaming at me right now."

"Trust me, I'm surprising myself. But I know you had nothing to do with this."

"You do?" She was right, but he hadn't thought she'd believe him.

"Of course. I know how to be logical, and logic tells me that you didn't have time to set this up. We've been together night and day, remember?"

As if he could forget. Memories took his mind off the current situation, but only for a moment. "I appreciate you having faith in me," he said, meaning every word of it. "But I have the feeling your parents aren't going to be so accepting. This just gives your father one more reason to dislike me."

"I'll make sure he knows that you had nothing to do with this," she assured him. "But it will help to know the worst-case scenario."

Jax unclenched his fists, gathering her hands in his. "Nicki, it's going to depend. The story might not even get approval to air. If it does, it could range from no more than a blip on the TV to a full exposé, especially if someone told that reporter about the incident in the conference room."

"Oh God." She sank into a chair. "I forgot about that. I'll need to take Dani out of school, just to be safe."

"There's more." He didn't want to scare her, but she needed to be prepared.

"What could be worse than that?"

Jax took the seat across from her. "If this breaks big enough, you'll probably become Corcoran's primary target."

He watched her eyes widen, then shutter as she absorbed the information. Her hand went to her throat and his gut clenched with a mixture of emotions—anger, guilt, and fierce protectiveness. He didn't like the idea of her being put in harm's way, but the damage was done. All he could do now was make sure she didn't get hurt in the fallout.

She looked up at him. "You know, we're thinking the same thing."

"Are you sure about that?" he asked, a wry smile twisting his lips. "Because I'm still thinking about shooting Walsh in the ass."

"This could be a blessing in disguise."

He stared at her. She stared back, her expression serious. "That's definitely not what I was thinking. And here I thought you were a psychic."

"Very funny." She stuck her tongue out at him, and desire came crashing in on all the other emotions roaring through his body. "Think about it. If this goes the way you say it will, then this guy will leave Olivia and her family alone. He's all about gaining power, and he had to feel some of mine when I was in Olivia's vision two days ago. He already knows I exist, he just doesn't know who I am yet. I'd be an irresistible catch."

"You *are* an irresistible catch," he said. "But I'm not about to let you become bait."

"Well, it may not come to that, right? If everything works out with the search warrant, then my luring Corcoran is not an issue. And if it doesn't, then I'd rather it be me he's targeting instead of Olivia and her family."

"I'm sure your parents won't think so, and I know I sure as hell don't want anybody in this guy's sights. Especially you." The thought of deliberately putting Nicole in harm's way made him break out in chills. What other choice did they have but to capitalize on a bad situation?

Utter faith lit her eyes as she reached across the short expanse of the conference table. "I know you don't, but I also know you won't let anything happen to me."

The simple statement raised him up and knocked him low. Not caring who might look in, he gathered her hand in his to press a kiss to her palm. "Nicki. You amaze me."

"Yeah well, I amaze myself sometimes." She tried to extract her hand, but he wouldn't let her. "So what's the plan, Stan?"

"Can I take you home, wrap you in bubble wrap and ship you someplace safe?"

She laughed. "No to the shipping part, but rolling around in bubble wrap might be fun. Loud, but fun. Seriously, though, what do I need to do?"

He shouldn't have been amazed by her ability to calmly accept the situation and make jokes, but he was. "Just so you know, I'm going to hold you to the bubble wrap thing. But first things first, I need to get you out of here. Your parents are picking Dani up, right?"

At her nod, he continued. "As a precaution against our intrepid reporter friend, we'll go out the back way and hook up with Bear. We'll drop you off at your house so we can both get our cars. After that I want you to head for your parents' hotel. You'll be relatively safe there until I get done here. You sure your parents won't mind looking after Dani for a day or two?"

"They won't," she said. "Besides, I don't want Dani exposed to this in anyway."

He leaned forward, torn inside. "Nicki, I'm going to do everything I can to keep you and your daughter safe. I promise you that."

She looked at their entwined hands, then up at him. For just a moment he could see uncertainty, and more than a little fear. "Just be here, at least for a little while."

Rising, he came around the table to pull her to her feet, then wrapped her in the dubious safety of his arms. Knowing how she'd struggled for her own space, her own place, he knew how much the request cost her. "As long as you need me to," he vowed, knowing he'd move heaven and hell to keep that promise.

Chapter Nineteen

Nicole was relieved not to see the reporter as she and Jax left the precinct to meet up with his partner for the drive to her house. Her parents would be less than enthusiastic when she told them about it, but she had to believe that things would be all right, that Jax and his partner would be able to find James William Corcoran before he hurt someone else.

That could take some time. Before they'd left, Jax and Marshall had a quick consultation with their boss and the assistant district attorney in the neutral territory of the center of the squad room. He'd come away disgusted, but still intact. He'd told her that Walsh's probable cause presentation hadn't won the judge over. With only her dreams and Olivia's visions paired with the tenuous connection of the New Age shop, the judge hadn't been willing to sign off on the warrant.

Neither man looked happy, and Nicole understood their frustration. This was the downside to working with police. Despite the detail of the psychic information, the law needed more. What more it would take? Another body?

Fine. If the police needed more, she'd given them more. She curled her hands into fists, making plans. Check in with her parents, who should have picked Dani up from school by now. Tomorrow she'd see about withdrawing Dani from school and hiring a tutor. She didn't like the thought of taking Dani out of school so close to the end of the school year, but she had to make sure her daughter was protected. Then she'd have to step up her training. She needed to have a better handle on her abilities, and she needed it fast.

If she had to be a target, she'd be a damned difficult target.

"Nicki?"

"Hhm?" She looked up, surprised to find that they'd pulled into her drive. "Oh, we're here."

"Yeah, we're here. Where were you? Talking to your mother?"

"You're joking." She got out of the car as he held the back door open. "I can't believe you just made a joke about my abilities."

"That makes two of us," Marshall said, leaving the passenger side. "Whatever you're doing, keep it up. You're obviously having a good effect on him."

"Shut up," Jax said pleasantly. He came around the car. "I'll have you both know that I have an excellent sense of humor. Being hard-nosed hasn't burned everything out of me."

"I'm glad." She stepped onto her porch, wondering briefly what Jax would have been like if he'd chosen another profession, but couldn't imagine it. Besides, she really liked the Jax she knew, hard nose and all.

As she inserted her key into the lock, she distinctly heard Miss Gertie's voice say, "Don't go in there, child." Out of nowhere a wave of disorientation slammed into her, causing her to scream as her vision darkened and her stomach churned.

Jax's arms came around her, hard, and she realized she'd staggered backwards. "Nicole, are you all right?"

Struggling for breath, she pressed one hand to her forehead, another to her stomach. "Something's wrong," she gasped. "The h-house."

"Go back to the car and lock the doors." His hands were gentle as he hustled her to the edge of the porch. "We'll check it out."

His gun appeared in his hand as if drawn from thin air. She grabbed his wrist. "No!" It came out as a shriek. "Don't leave me alone. Please, Jax."

"You'll be safe in the car. You see anybody but me or Bear come out of the house, call 9-1-1 and drive away."

"But—"

"Go." He all but hauled her off her feet and towards the car. "Bear, you take the back."

Then he was gone, and silence began to press in on her. It took every ounce of willpower she possessed not to retch into her azaleas. Someone had been in her house, someone she didn't invite.

Someone evil.

Her legs felt like rubber as she stumbled towards the car. A shiver crawled through her veins, and she wrapped her arms about herself in an effort to combat the psychic drop in temperature. The urge to flee, to put as much distance between herself and her house as she could, rippled over her and she bit her lip against the urge to scream again.

Somehow she was able to open the driver's door and all but fall sideways into the seat, her feet on the ground. Lights danced before her eyes as pain, mind-numbing, breath-stealing pain, twisted her insides. She gripped the steering wheel, closing her eyes and pressing her forehead against it in an effort to hang on to reality. What was happening to her?

Something tapped the window. Startled, Nicole shrieked, throwing up her hands defensively as she stumbled out the open door and to her feet. The bulky shadow staggered backwards with a groan. She recognized Detective Marshall a split second before Jax charged out of the house. "Police! Hands in the air. Now!"

Marshall threw up his hands. "Hey Jax, it's me, Bear."

Jax stepped between them, pulling Nicole close. "You frightened her."

"Yeah well, she didn't exactly calm my nerves either," Bear muttered, rubbing his hands over his face. "Believe me, I won't surprise her again. I'm gonna get on the horn."

He stepped away, pulling his phone out of his pocket. Nicole leaned against Jax. Having him beside her forced some of the blackness away, but she still felt as if she danced on the razor's edge of full terror. "I think I need some water."

His arm tightened around her as he led her to his car. "I can't let you into the house right now, Nicki," he said, his voice heavy. "It's a crime scene."

"Crime scene?" Her thoughts sloshed through her fear-soaked brain as she struggled to make sense of his words.

Jax hesitated, causing Nicole to look up at him. He blanked his expression. Fear leapt inside her, because she knew he only did that with bad news. "There's something else, isn't there?"

"Hey, you bit your lip. It's bleeding."

Surprised, she lifted a hand to her lips, coming away with blood. In the midst of combating panic, she hadn't felt a thing. "You're trying to distract me."

"Yeah." Jax opened his passenger door, settling her on the seat before opening his glove box.

"No." She gripped his forearms. "I want to know what happened. Tell me."

Jax bent his head, concentrating on opening his first aid kit and tearing into a pack of gauze. He gently dabbed at her lip, avoiding eye contact. "Bear's calling for an M. E."

"M. E.?" Nicole repeated. "That stands for Medical Examiner, right? I thought you only asked for a medical examiner if someone's, if someone's—oh God."

Dizziness slammed into her again. "Someone's dead, in my house?" She heard her voice climb, but she couldn't control it. She had enough trying to control the urge to scream. "W-who is it?"

"I don't know."

"What do you mean you don't know?" As she looked at him for answers, fear gave way to terror. A simple death wouldn't have caused her reaction, the impression of something evil. No, whoever was in her house had died violently. "You don't know or you don't want to tell me?"

"Nicki, please." He gripped her shoulders tightly, preventing her from jumping up and racing inside, as if she actually could make it through her door without passing out. "I'm trying to spare you what I can," he said, his voice without inflection. "Why don't you call your family, make sure they're all right?"

On cue, her cell phone began to ring. She fumbled in her pocket for her cell phone, flipped it open. "Mom." The word came out helpless, broken. She couldn't say more.

"Oh bébé, thank God." Her mother sounded close to tears. "What happened? Were you attacked?"

"T-the house. Something's wrong with the house. S-somebody—there's somebody dead in there."

"Are you safe?"

"Yes. I didn't go inside yet. Jax and his partner just brought me home."

Her mother offered a short prayer in French. "Mala's on her way to you and Malita's on her way here to sit with Dani. Your father and I will be there soon."

Nicole swallowed a relieved mouthful of tears. "Everyone's all right," she managed to tell Jax. To her mother she said, "I need to talk to Dani."

A tense silence followed before Nicole heard her daughter's voice. "Mamma?"

Tears spiked Nicole's lashes. "Hey, baby, I'm here. I-I just called to check in on you."

"Nanna's trying not to cry. She said something bad had happened. That must be why Miss Gertie came to see me."

"What?" Miss Gertie didn't know where her parents were, Nicole was sure of it. "Are you sure, sweetie?"

"Yeah. Nanna didn't see her. She said she had to go away."

"Oh my God." It was suddenly hard to breathe. Miss Gertie. Miss Gertie had died in her house. But why had she come over? What horrible thing had happened to her there?

Nicole forced air into her lungs. She wanted to crawl through the phone, hug her daughter, and never let her go. "Dani, baby, I'll see you later tonight. M-make sure you mind your Aunt Malita, okay? That's my good girl."

Jax took the phone from her before she dropped it. Slowly she turned towards him. "It's Miss Gertie. Dani said she saw her, which means she-she's gone. Why didn't you say it was Miss Gertie?"

"Nicki."

She felt his hand wrap around hers, a solid, comforting touch. *Yes, think about that. Don't think about anything else.*

He pulled her to her feet. "If you can do this, I'm going to take you inside, just inside the door, so I can keep an eye on you. You have to be careful not to touch anything."

"Okay." She took a deep breath, searching for calm. Having Jax beside her soothed her nerves, and she was able to step onto the porch. But halfway to the door the darkness clawed at her again, and she had to stop, fighting the urge to vomit.

Jax stayed with her, supporting her. "How did you know about the break-in?"

"As soon as I stepped onto the porch, I could feel it," she managed to say. *Think of something else. Think of something else.* "We—all of our houses are protected, to keep positive energy in and negative out. Some-something broke the protection and I could feel darkness and dizziness, and just plain wrongness. I can still feel it sucking at me." She waited for him to shake his head in disbelief.

He didn't. Instead, his voice softened. "I have to tell you, it's not a pretty sight. It gets worse the deeper in we go. Can you do this?"

She swallowed, tried for a smile. "I have to try. Just catch me if I embarrass myself by fainting."

"You know I will. And there's nothing embarrassing about it."

It seemed to take forever to make it to the door. Light beckoned from the foyer, and that helped. She alternated between fighting to move, fighting her surging stomach, and fighting the scream that threatened to tear loose. By the time she crossed the threshold, sweat beaded on her forehead, and she felt as boneless as Jell-O.

Jax hadn't exaggerated when he said the house was trashed. The path from the door to the main living room was littered with broken glass and flowers from her vases and candleholders. Pictures were ripped from the walls; the drapes were in shreds. Pillows that had once covered her couch and loveseat lay on the floor, disemboweled.

It wasn't theft. It was desecration.

Tears sprang to her eyes and once there, flowed freely. Her home had been her solace, a cocoon she'd created with Malita's expertise to shield herself and Dani from the madness of the outside world. No matter how terrible things became, she and her daughter had been able to retreat here. It had been like stepping into the lush shade at Beau-Rêve, or the cooling surf in Martinique. Now it had been stripped from her.

Her chin was cradled, lifted. Rough thumbs brushed away the tears that collected on her cheeks. She looked up, and the tender commiseration in Jax's molasses eyes made her weep anew. "S-someone raped my house, Jax. My sanctuary, they destroyed my sanctuary."

"I know, sweetheart," he answered, his voice rough. "I know."

He stepped closer, and Nicole could see the variegated shades of brown in his eyes. She didn't resist as he tilted her chin, lowered his lips to hers. There was magic in the light touch and she opened herself to it eagerly, craving it the way a flower craves sunshine. Soft and hard, freezing and scorching, his lips demanded and she capitulated. Oh, the joy in surrendering.

The sounds of sirens had Jax ending the kiss and breaking away from Nicole like a suspect with something to hide. It was wrong and inappropriate to kiss her like that when he should have been doing his job. He'd only meant to offer a small token of comfort, not maul her. He consoled himself with the observation that some of the destroyed look had left her eyes.

"You can't go in there." Bear's voice cut through Jax's start at an apology. "This is a police investigation."

"This is my sister's home, and if she's in there I'm going in there too," a female voice retorted.

Nicole gasped. "Mala?"

She turned to the door, Jax on her heels. The sirens had brought the neighbors out and Nicole's family as well. Squad cars pulled up, blocked from the drive by a land yacht of a Bentley and a wicked-looking motorcycle. Nicole's parents were exiting the car, but it was the woman standing toe-to-toe with Bear that drew Jax's attention.

She had the same lightning-strike beauty that Malita did, but somehow Jax didn't think Nicole's interior designer sister would wear blood-red bike leather and a trenchcoat right out of *The Matrix.* Bear probably had a good hundred pounds on her, but she obviously wasn't the least bit intimidated. If anything, she looked ready to take Bear down.

As much as he would have liked to see the attempt, Jax knew Nicole didn't need the spectacle. "It's all right, Bear. Let 'em by."

Bear stepped back slowly, and Mala Legère advanced just as deliberately. Jax only had to watch her move to realize that this wasn't Malita. This woman reeked of deadly intent. He couldn't think of any other way to put it. He felt as if someone had let a lioness out of her cage. And the lioness was hungry.

Nicole took a small step forward. "Mala?" Even she seemed hesitant, and this was her sister.

The younger woman smiled. Jax wondered if it hurt to move her facial muscles that way. "Hey, Sis. Heard you been having some Dark trouble."

Jax had no idea what that meant, and decided not to ask. Instead, he directed Murphy and his crime scene unit up to Nicole's bedroom as Nicole ran straight into her father's open arms.

"Tell me what happened, Nicolette."

"Jax and Detective Marshall brought me home from the precinct. I-I stepped onto the porch and I just-I just knew someone had been in the house." Tears sprang to her eyes again as she gestured to the police carefully dusting the front door and frame for evidence. "All I saw was the foyer, but it was enough."

Mala stepped forward. "Jax?"

"Detective Carter Jackson." Nicole turned, including him in the circle. Mala looked at him, and Jax felt the full weight of her stare. It was much worse than being regarded by Arielle Legère, more distrustful than Stefan Antonescu's glares. He'd felt that look before, facing down a man who'd shot two strangers for the hell of it. He'd had the same detached look in his eyes, calmly debating whether he'd be able to shoot Jax before Jax shot him. A well-placed shot had disarmed the man before he could fire. Jax figured Mala wouldn't take that long to make up her mind.

"Jax, this is my other sister, Mala Legère. Mala, this is Detective Carter Jackson."

Mala did not extend her hand, which Jax was now used to with this family. She wore a distrustful look, which Jax was also getting used to.

"Detective Jackson." Mala's voice was icy. "My parents have told me quite a bit about you."

And not all to the good, Jax was sure. "It will take us some time to process the house, and we'll probably have to do Miss Gertie's too," he said to Nicole. "Maybe you'd prefer to go to a neighbor's?"

He watched her gaze turn to the street, where several of her neighbors gathered, gawking. To his utter disgust, he saw a news crew turn onto the street. Any hope of Nicole's story being a non-event faded. Guilt clawed at him, because her wounded expression was entirely his fault.

"Can't we come inside?"

He'd get chewed out for contaminating a crime scene, but he didn't care. Stefan stepped forward. "Surely that's not too much to ask, Detective?" He said the word 'detective' like an epithet. "My daughter has been abused enough by this without having her face splashed across the evening news."

He deserved that one, but he was still getting tired of Antonescu's attitude. It wasn't as if Jax didn't already know he wasn't good enough for Nicole.

Before he could speak, she stepped out of her father's hold and closer to him. "Dad."

"It's all right, Nicki," Jax said, warmed that she would come to his defense. He'd need that once her parents learned the press already knew about her. "If you could stand right inside the door, and give me a minute, we'll find a place for you to stay."

Chapter Twenty

Nicole didn't want to go into her own house. She didn't want to do this, didn't want to see the police rummaging through the shreds of her house, her private life exposed to the world. She felt naked, vulnerable. The need to curl into a ball in a corner was almost overwhelming.

Caught between the proverbial rock and a hard place, however, she knew she had no choice. She'd much rather face another psychic deluge than gawking neighbors and news cameras.

Her parents led the way. Nicole's mother gagged as she stepped over the threshold. "Oh Nicole, I knew it was bad, but I didn't realize it was this bad."

She wasn't talking about the mess in the foyer, Nicole knew. Even her father looked green about the edges. The impression of wrongness was stronger here in the foyer than on the porch, even with the police scattered about to muddy the sensation.

Mala moved to each of them, touching the back of her left hand to their foreheads. Nicole felt a tingle pass through her, and the toxic feelings of panic abated. "Thanks, Mala."

Her sister smiled thinly. Siphoning off some of the psychic pollution had obviously drained her. "See, I'm more than a killing machine."

"As long as you remember that," their mother said, pushing a little apart from their father. She looked a little better, leaving Nicole to wonder how much her mother was shielding.

"Do you think you can open up and sense anything, maybe just a little?"

Arielle closed her eyes. "Dark, twisted thoughts," her mother said, her brows knitted together in concentration. "This wasn't random. It was deliberately meant to disrupt your peace."

She sagged against Nicole's father. "He was here. This man knows, somehow he knows you're connected to him and he wants to stop you, to hurt you. But your neighbor—oh God, what did he do?"

"Mom?" Had Miss Gertie, poor inquisitive Miss Gertie, come over to investigate the strange man in her house instead of calling the police? What had he done to her when he caught her?

She spun away from her family, heading for the stairs as if pulled by a string. Several officers tried to stop her but she evaded them, driven by the need to know. Jax caught up with her just as she reached the second stair.

Blackness engulfed her as the room started to spin. She felt the truth of Gertie's violent death slam into her, changing her. Weakening her. A scream rose like bile in her throat, struggling to break free.

She dropped to her knees and vomited.

Dimly she was aware of her father's voice calling her mother. Something wrapped around her waist like an elephant's trunk as the floor buckled, lifting her to her feet and half-carrying, half-dragging her across the floor.

Mala's voice pealed, demanding answers. Jax's answering rumble sounded close, and she realized that he held her, pressed a cool damp cloth into her hands. She tried to lift it to her face, she really did, but she couldn't make her hands obey, couldn't figure out why it was so dark, why it was so cold, why she was so scared.

Miss Gertie. Oh, God, Miss Gertie.

Images and sensations ricocheted in her brain with relentless intensity. Images of Miss Gertie's broken body sprawled across her bed, her face a shattered mess. Old Perseus at the foot of the bed, bludgeoned. Blood, so much blood staining the walls, soaking the mattress. The anger and the hatred and the unholy joy of causing pain and death. Too much information that threatened to overload her psychic senses, her soul.

"Breathe, Nicki," Jax ordered, the slap of command in his voice bringing her back to reality. "You are stronger than this. You know it, and I know it. Don't let this beat you down." The cloth slid over her face. "Come on, come back to me. Open your eyes, Nicki."

She clutched at his hands, struggling to find her way out of the darkness. Forcing her eyes open, she discovered that she sat in a chair at her kitchen table, Jax on one knee in front of her. Her father sat in the chair across from her with her mother cradled in his lap, looking as distraught as Nicole felt.

Seeing her mother's distress was enough to hold her own at bay, just barely. "Mom? Are you okay?"

Arielle Legère opened her eyes. "I didn't want you to see that, Nicolette," she said, her voice shaking. "I would have shielded you if I could, but I couldn't get through the darkness."

"Detective?" An officer appeared in the doorway, interrupting them and scattering Nicole's thoughts. "Do you need me to get a paramedic?"

Nicole shook her head the same time as every other member of her family. "No, they'll be fine," he called over his shoulder before returning his gaze to hers. She saw for the first time the regret that tinged the dark molasses of his eyes. They both doubted his words.

"He-he wanted me, didn't he?" she whispered. "It was supposed to be me, but she came over and surprised him."

"Yeah." He pressed a glass of water into her hand. "I suppose I should get the tequila for you?"

She grimaced, trying to move through the shock and pain, trying not to feel, to think. "Yeah. And for Mom."

Mala moved towards the cabinets. "Where do you keep it?"

"Above the fridge," Jax said. Mala looked at them both for a heartbeat before retrieving the bottle of Don Julio and a couple of shot glasses. It probably surprised her that a police detective knew where Nicole kept her tequila, but Nicole couldn't worry about what her sister thought of Jax. She was just glad he was there, his hands on her thighs anchoring her to reality.

Her father took the bottle of Don Julio from Mala, pouring two generous portions for Nicole and Arielle. "Drink up, chèrie," he told his wife. "You need some color to your cheeks."

"I still have more than you," she retorted lightly, but obediently lifted the glass. "Come on, Nicolette. It's impolite to make your mother drink alone."

Nicole lifted her glass. The clear liquid sloshed over her fingers, and she had to put the glass back down. "Are you all right, Mom?" she asked. "You're stronger than I am, you had to have a worse reaction."

"I'll be okay, bébé," she said, reaching over to briefly clasp Nicole's hand. "And you will be too. Now drink."

Noting Nicole's difficulty holding the glass, Jax wrapped his hands around hers, guiding the small glass to her lips. What a weird family, he thought, watching mother and daughter down the liquor like frat boys in a contest. Yet he couldn't deny the therapeutic effects of the premium tequila as both women regained pieces of their composure. He withdrew slightly, just holding her free hand, resisting the urge to wrap Nicole in his arms again. This time Mala stepped forward to pour a round and Jax caught the glint of something beneath her leather trenchcoat, something that looked disturbingly like a blade. A very wicked, very long blade.

"He made her suffer." Nicole's voice was barely audible after the second drink. "He was angry that she wasn't me."

The hand in his trembled, a bird wanting to break free. "She was an old woman with an old dog. They couldn't hurt him, they couldn't fight back. Why did he have to torture them? Why would Miss Gertie come over like that, when she knew I wasn't here?"

"I don't know," Jax said, his heart shredding for her.

She raised her eyes to his, and the despair he saw in them made him want to really, really hurt someone.

The phone rang and she jumped to answer it, grateful for the interruption. "Hello?"

"Hello, Ms. Legère. Or may I call you Nicole?"

The voice on the other end was male, pleasant, and somehow familiar. Maybe it was someone from school to discuss her withdrawal. Any distraction was welcome at that moment. "How may I help you?"

"I understand that you've had some extensive redecorating done today."

Her stomach gave a sickening lurch. *Please God.* "How did you know that?" she managed to ask.

Laughter answered her. High-pitched, insane-sounding laughter. "Come on, you're a smart psychic lady. Surely you can figure that out without having to dream it. Of course, you won't be able to do much dreaming in your bedroom now, will you?"

"Oh God." Ice-cold horror slashed through her veins. It was him, the man in her dreams. Fear and anger clashed inside her like two opposing armies. "You bastard—you killed Miss Gertie!"

People sprang into action around her, reaching for phone extensions, trying to take the phone away from her. Despite the tremor in her hands, her grip remained locked as fear gave ground to anger.

"There's no point in denying it," the pleasant voice continued, as if they discussed the weather. "Just as you can't deny that you've been dreaming about me."

The sick twist he put on the words made her want to vomit again. Anxiety and anger stretched her nerves to the snapping point. Around her, the cabinet doors began to tremble. "I'm going to find you, you sick son of a bitch," she swore, her vision going red. "You're going to pay for what you did to Miss Gertie!"

"Really?" The voice on the other end of the line remained calm, even amused. "Does that mean that you're going to pay, too? After all, you're in my head. You're the one making me do these terrible things."

Her heart froze in mid-beat. "What?"

"I suppose the police are listening now," he said, the thought apparently not bothering him in the least. "Good. They should know about you and your kind. If I'm damned, it's because of you, getting into my head, showing me things, making me do things I would never do—"

"That's not true!" she screamed into the phone. Cabinet doors banged open and shut of their own volition behind her. "I'm not making you do anything!"

"Are you sure?" he said, his voice soft. Then he began to laugh. "Here's a riddle for you, Nicole Legère: Do you dream because I kill or do I kill because you dream? Your neighbor wondered the same thing."

"No!" Blood pounded in her ears, muffling sound as her sight darkened. Rage and fear rose inside her like the explosion of splitting atoms, awesome energy demanding to be released. The handset slipped from her hand, dropping to the floor before the cord contracted.

Then all hell broke loose.

Cabinets began to disgorge their contents like missiles: foodstuffs, dishes, glasses. Her hands curled into fists as she turned to the wall, slumping to her knees. She could actually feel something ripping inside her, the severing of her control. Rocking back and forth, holding her arms over her head, she fought a silent battle to regain some semblance of control. *Stop it, stop it, stop it.*

"What is this? What's happening?"

"Nicole? Stop it, you're going to hurt yourself."

"What's going on? Was that the guy?"

"Son-of-a-bitch. Son-of-a-fucking-bitch."

"I've never seen incompetence like this. I'm going to sue the pants off your department—"

"Give her some air, for chrissakes."

"Stop it!"

Her mind finally got her voice to work again. All other noise in the room stopped, including that of the cabinets. It was as if all action, all life had been sucked from the room.

She felt Jax kneel beside her. "Don't touch me."

"Nicki—"

"Don't." She lowered her hands, refusing to look at any of them. If she didn't look at them she'd be able to make it out of the room without screaming or causing any more destruction, without inadvertently hurting someone. "I have to go outside now."

How she made it to her feet, she had no idea. She was surprised further by her ability to place one foot in front of the other, make it to the kitchen door, then the patio beyond.

Chapter Twenty-one

Jax watched the uniformed officers wrap up, fighting to control his seething emotions. In all his years on the force he had never felt so powerless.

He paced through the living room, feeling very much like a beast in a cage. The wreckage of Nicole's home was violent and deliberate, but it didn't begin to compare with the damage done to Nicole herself.

He had no idea what he could offer her. The one phone in her home with caller ID had been ripped out of the wall. Murdoch had already taken the victim—he couldn't think of her as a person, as Miss Gertie—away, but it would still take some time for Forensics to go through the destruction in Nicole's bedroom. He had a sick feeling the place would yield nothing. The fingerprints would have to be matched, but he was sure they would only find hers, her daughter's. And his.

He didn't want to see Nicole's tear-streaked face, the hazel eyes dulled with shock and dismay. He didn't want her to look at him for answers, only to be disappointed.

He didn't want to fail her.

A heavy sigh lifted his shoulders, and he pinched the bridge of his nose in a futile attempt to stem his headache. It was a bitch to fail. He didn't like it.

Useless wonderings hammered at him. What if Nicole had been home? Or her daughter? The pitiful black bag taking away Miss Gertie's ravaged remains clearly demonstrated what the answer would have been.

Brutal in its punishment, Jax's imagination conjured an image of Nicole's broken body lying in her hallway, neck shattered, body bruised and violated. Dead because he'd failed her.

Just as he'd failed his wife.

A dangerous mood settled on him. It would not happen again. He would not allow Nicole Legère to be harmed.

A hand touched his shoulder. He spun around, snarling, prepared to rip a head off. "Hey man, calm down," Bear said, his walnut features frowning.

"How the hell can I calm down when this is our fault?" Several officers looked at them in curiosity. Jax took a deep breath and forced his voice lower. "Walsh gave her up to the media with the captain's buy-in. We made it easy for the son-of-a-bitch to track her down."

"Jax—"

"Did you see her bedroom?" he demanded. "Did you see what that sick bastard did to her neighbor up there? And then had the nerve to call and gloat about it?"

"Yeah, I saw it. Every goddamn cop in this house saw it." Bear grimaced. "But you still need to calm the fuck down."

Jax forced a deep breath into his lungs. Bear was right. Flying off the handle wouldn't solve this case, wouldn't protect Nicole. "If they're done, clear 'em out. We need 'em to start canvassing the neighborhood, even those houses on the back side. Somebody had to see this creep and Miss Gertie come in here. You hear from Walsh or the captain yet?"

Bear's eyes glinted. "Yeah. Captain's personally escorting Walsh to the judge. Says he's gonna bring the warrant over himself."

"Good. We can get someone to sit on Corcoran's house until we're done here." It was the first piece of good news they'd had in hours. They had a couple of hours at most before the early news broke the story, and Corcoran wouldn't have called if he'd thought they were on to him. Typical serial killer M.O, daring the cops to catch him. A mistake, a very normal mistake in a case that was anything but normal. Jax smiled. He looked forward to breaking Corcoran's door down and searching his house, legally.

As Bear hustled the other cops out of the house, Jax headed for the kitchen to tell Nicole the news. He stopped, clenching his fists as anger, shame and a great deal of worry clawed at his gut. He knew Nicole was probably still out on the deck, her family waiting for her in the kitchen.

He wanted to go to her, to hold her, to apologize. He wanted to take her and her daughter somewhere, some beautiful place far away where the worst thing that happened was rain.

"Jax."

He forced his fists to uncurl as Bear reentered the room. When Bear took that tone of voice, it wasn't going to be good. "Just say it, Bear."

"You know this is fucked up, right?"

He turned around. "What do you mean?"

"You know damn well this guy couldn't have tagged her through the media, seeing as how nothing's aired yet. So how did he find out about her? How did she know the house was ransacked before you even opened the door? She's got a sister looking like a hot female version of Wesley Snipes in *Blade*, and she supposedly saw what happened to the neighbor without going upstairs. And what the hell was that in the kitchen?"

"She's got a name," Jax said through clenched teeth. "You've used it before."

"Come on, man, cut the shit. What the fuck's going on here?"

Jax had never seen the former linebacker look unnerved, no matter how gruesome the scene. Right now, Bear looked like he was on the fifth day of a four-day binge. Sort of the way he felt himself.

"When it happened in the interrogation room, Nicole called it a psychic temper tantrum, like a psychic power surge. I guess if she gets really upset, she loses control and things start happening."

"Things start happening." Bear looked at him as if he'd lost his mind. "Crap flew around in there like Dorothy on her way to Oz, and you say things start happening. Like it's no big deal. Like it doesn't bother you."

"It does bother me," Jax said, throwing a look in the direction of the kitchen. It more than bothered him, it freaked him out. One psychic episode he could rationalize away, maybe even convince himself that it hadn't gone down the way he remembered it. But two?

"I didn't sign on for this shit."

Jax felt a spike of anger, and he latched onto it, fed it. Anything was better than thinking about what Nicole had done.

"Neither did I," he shot back, his tone clipped. "For that matter, neither did Nicole. All I know is, we wanted this guy to focus on Nicole, and we got our wish. In spades."

"You heard what that guy said, about her. What if—"

"Don't say it," Jax cut in. "Don't even think it."

"Don't get pissed at me, partner," Bear said, stressing the last word. "I'm doing my job."

"Meaning that I'm not?" If Bear wanted to make him mad, he was doing a damned good job of it.

"I didn't say that. But I think you're too close to this case. I think that Nicole Legère has gotten under your skin big time." Bear folded his arms across his chest. "Can you see this through?"

"You're damn right I can." Determination hardened his voice. It pissed him off that Bear felt the need to pose the question, that whatever was going on inside him was obvious on the outside. It pissed him off even more that the bastard had struck it tok Nicole and felt confident enough about it to call and gloat.

"We need to nail this bastard."

Bear paused in righting a ficus tree. "We will. In the meantime, the chief wants your lady friend in protective custody."

Jax shook his head. "She won't agree to that. I won't either. I'll just convince her to stay with me."

Bear stared at him as if he'd just had a psychic tempter tantrum. "Are you hearing what you're saying? I think you need to knock it back a notch."

"Like hell I will." Jax curled his hands into fists. "Report me if you want. Then you'll be in the clear, 'cause I don't want you to get into trouble if this goes down wrong. But if it comes to it, I've got some time off coming to me."

"Son-of-a-bitch, you're serious, aren't you?"

"Damn right I am. I'm not going to let anything else happen to her."

"Dammit, Jax." Bear's voice grew concerned. "She's not Felecia."

His gut clenched at the mention of his late wife. "I know that," he replied, his voice tight. Why everyone tried to connect everything he did to that one failure, he had no idea. "We pushed her at this guy and now he's pushing back. I'm not about to let what happened to her neighbor happen to her. I gotta do this."

"Then I got your back." Bear stuck his fist out.

Jax tapped it with his own. "Thanks, man."

"Yeah, just make sure we don't end up with our asses in a sling."

Do you dream because I kill or do I kill because you dream?

Nicole faced the approaching darkness of her backyard, fighting the urge to crumble. She stared up at the twilight sky, asking herself the question millions of others had asked over the course of their lives: *Why me?*

Had she brought it on because she'd asked for something that would allow her to prove herself worthy of her name, worthy of becoming the next Keeper? She didn't have the following and success of her magician brothers, the exciting life Mala led, or the serene happiness Malita had in her relationship and career. Her one moment of brilliance had been giving birth to Danielle.

Her life brimmed with activity, yet she'd still felt restless for months, felt that as the supposed next Keeper of the Legacy she was woefully inexperienced in the wielding of her gift. She'd asked for some excitement, for the chance to exercise her abilities.

And the Legacy had complied with a vengeance.

Do you dream because I kill or do I kill because you dream?

The words still haunted her, even now. As illogical as they seemed, she couldn't help asking herself what if. What if he was right? What if she was somehow controlling him through her dreams? And because she was doing wrong, because she was being evil, she was forced to feel the pain and deaths of her victims.

"No," she whispered to herself, not wanting to believe it. But all she could hear was that small voice asking again, "What if?"

There had been Legère women who couldn't stand the strain of their gifts and the requirements of wielding the Legacy, she knew. She'd heard it as she'd heard the whispers about her abilities, heard the tales about the ones who'd been lost, who'd had their minds and souls broken.

Was she next? The thought slithered through her mind, unbidden and uncontrolled. Were the episodes she'd had harbingers of her losing control, losing her sanity?

She was going to be strong. Dammit, she was a Legère. More than four hundred years of determined women had guided the family through slavery, witch-hunts, revolutions and dissension within the family. Their blood flowed through her veins. She would not falter.

Miss Gertie.

Bending beneath the weight of her grief, Nicole gripped the wood rail, struggling to leash her emotions before she destroyed anything else. "Miss Gertie," she whispered. "Miss Gertie, I am so sorry."

"Why, child?"

Gasping, Nicole took a step backwards as the shadows in her backyard coalesced into a familiar form. "Miss Gertie?"

Her neighbor—or her neighbor's spirit—moved onto the deck, though Nicole couldn't hear footsteps. Another shadow hovered near the old woman, a decidedly dog-shaped shadow. "I must be dreaming."

"Perhaps you are," Miss Gertie said, nodding. "It is your gift, though you didn't fully accept it when it was offered, did you?"

"Oh God." Nicole covered her mouth with a shaking hand. She remembered the day she sat on Miss Gertie's porch, and the old woman's advice. She remembered, and believed.

She must have stepped forward, because Miss Gertie stopped her with a raised hand. "Don't shed tears for me, Nicolette," she said, the first time the old woman had ever used Nicole's full name. "Perseus and I, we've done what we were sent to do."

Despite the admonition, harsh tears clogged Nicole's throat. "Were you sent here to die? To be brutally murdered?"

"To watch over you, and to guide you." Gertie's voice rang strong. "And even to protect you. I waited a long time for you, child. To guide you into accepting who and what you are."

Nicole felt her very foundation rock, causing her to wonder if she'd suffered a psychotic break. "You knew? Everything?"

"Your family isn't alone. It's important for you to know that. You're not alone. In the end, though, when you stand against your greatest fear, you'll feel as if everything and everyone has abandoned you. You have to remember what I've said, and you have to believe it. Promise me that you'll remember."

Wanting to promise Miss Gertie, her family, and herself, Nicole drew a deep breath, feeling far from reassured. "What if I can't do this? What if I can't stop him?"

"There you go again." Gertie gave her a stern look. "Anika didn't think she was strong enough to protect her people. Giselle didn't think she was strong enough to protect her children and endure slavery. Mala doesn't think she's strong enough to survive her battles. Yet each of you is strong. Like all of my daughters, those who are strongest doubt themselves the most. No one can believe in you the way you can believe in yourself."

"Your daughters?" Nicole's thoughts raced as she wondered how much she was imagining as opposed to how much of the conversation was actually occurring. She'd never told Miss Gertie about Mala, and she certainly had never mentioned anything about the Legère history to anyone other than Jax.

The old woman smiled at her, her expression seeming to soften into youth. "We have to go, Perseus and I. Remember my words, child. Freedom starts within, by accepting yourself. That's the only way you'll be able to beat him. By the way, I hope you kick his ass, but good."

Nicole choked on startled tears and laughter as the vision that was and wasn't Miss Gertie transformed into a younger woman with short dark hair encircled by a gleaming band. Gold encircled her neck and wrists. She looked exactly like the warrior woman Nicole had seen while meditating, the woman who had offered her gifts back to her.

"Oh my God," she breathed, as Perseus morphed into a lioness. Both of them looked at her, then Gertie—whomever—gave a regal nod and pleased smile before fading into the night.

"Nicole?"

At the sound of Mala's voice, she opened her eyes, surprised that she'd closed them. Had she dreamt the entire episode, a side effect from the wilding? Was that why she didn't feel tired as before?

The deck lights came on, illuminating the backyard. She turned to see her sister standing a few feet behind her, clearly on guard. Seeing the hard glint in Mala's gaze, Nicole couldn't believe that Mala could ever doubt herself. What kind of things did Mala face, and how did she keep going?

"Mala, did you . . . ?" She paused, unsure of how to phrase the question. Had she seen Miss Gertie's ghost? Or something more improbable?

"Yeah, I saw." Mala moved up beside her, leaving space between them. Probably so Nicole wouldn't accidentally touch her. Probably so she could pull a weapon quickly if need be. "It's nice to have validation, isn't it? To know that they're there, that there's a reason for what we do, what our family does."

"Yes." Nicole looked out into the yard for a moment longer, then drew a deep breath. "I need to talk to Mom and Dad."

Mala stayed at her back. "You've decided how to solve your problem?"

Just thinking about her "problem" sent the heat of anger and the chill of fear careening through her again. She dug her fingernails into the wood, gathering herself. "More or less. They're probably not going to like what I came up with."

"Probably not," Mala agreed. "They think we're still twelve. Not that that's a bad thing sometimes. I've got your back, whatever you've decided."

Nicole looked at her sister in surprise. She needed Mala's help, but she'd thought she'd have to argue with her first. It touched her that Mala would agree to help and support, no questions asked.

"You're the only one who doubted you," Mala said then. "I know we weren't all that close when we were kids, but I'm sorry that the rest of us kids didn't make it easy on you, about the talent thing."

"It's all right, Mala," she said softly, grateful for the apology and the vote of confidence.

"No, it isn't. Yeah, we were young, and stupid, and you kept to yourself, but those are just excuses. We're family. As lone wolf as I am sometimes, even I need family of one type or another. We should have told you we believed in you, even if the cousins didn't. For what it's worth, Derek and I beat up a couple of them on your behalf."

Warmed anew, Nicole smiled. "I guess that shouldn't surprise me. Thanks for this, even though you've got no idea what I'm planning."

Mala just looked at her. "I don't need to be psychic to know what you're planning, Nicki. I know you're going after this man, or whatever he is. If he's human, you and your detective can take care of him. If he's not, then he's my problem. Either way, I'll stand with you like I said."

Bolstered, Nicki turned to the kitchen. "Mom, Dad."

Her parents appeared as if waiting for her call. "Nicolette, I'm so sorry about your neighbor," her mother said, pulling her into a hug.

"Thanks, Mom." Nicole squeezed her mother's shoulders quickly before stepping away. It would be too easy to give in to tears again, and she didn't have the time for grief. She took a deep breath. "Is someone in the family able to practice law here in Georgia? Miss Gertie doesn't have any family left, but I want to make sure she has a proper funeral and everything. I also need someone to take care of the houses, hers and mine. When I leave tonight, I'm not coming back."

"Come back to the hotel with us," her mother urged. "I'll make calls in the morning, and then you and Danielle are coming home with us."

"Dani will, but I can't," Nicole said, even as Mala shook her head.

"Why not?"

"Because I promised Jax that I would help him. More than that, I promised Miss Gertie and Dani that I would help, however I could, so that no one else will get hurt by this man. His name is James Corcoran, and I intend to stop him. He's hurt too many people already. Jax and I had already decided to make me his next target, but he's apparently ahead of us."

Her father tensed. "What do you mean, make you a target?"

"Corcoran's targeting women who went to a psychic workshop he taught. At least he did, until today." Nicole swallowed. "Until I stopped him from getting Olivia Davenport. Now he's targeting me."

Nicole quickly explained everything that had happened earlier, though it seemed like days ago. "It's done, Dad," she added when her father began swearing in Romanian. "Besides, Corcoran must have tapped into me just like I tapped into him when I walked through Olivia Davenport's dream. That means he had two days to find out who I am and where I live. He couldn't have known about me from a news broadcast that hasn't happened yet."

"All the more reason to return to New Orleans." Her father pulled his cell phone free of his belt. "Better yet, we should go to Beau-Rêve. I'll call the pilot and tell him to prepare to leave first thing in the morning."

"Dad." Nicole crossed her arms, wishing she could hold her daughter at that moment. "I'm not going, but you have to take Mom and Dani to Beau-Rêve."

"I am not about to leave and let you face whatever this is alone!" her mother exclaimed.

"I won't be alone," Nicole corrected, her voice even. She'd found a reserve of strength after her encounter with Miss Gertie. That determination was the only reason she was still upright and dry-eyed. "Malita's here, and Mala's volunteered to stay. Besides, I can't leave."

"Of course you can leave," her father said, his accent thickening. "You have done more than enough for the police, more than anyone can ask. It has placed you in danger. Every moment you stay here gives this man more time to find you."

"Which is exactly why I need you to take Mom and Dani and go home." She swallowed the tremble in her voice with effort. "Please, Papa."

"Don't think using endearments with your father is going to get me to agree to this!" Her mother balled her hands. "Do you even realize what you're asking of us?"

Nicole thought about her daughter, wondering if she'd see her again after putting her on a plane in the morning. "Yes, Mama, I know exactly what I'm asking. Today was a close call. Corcoran came to my house, waited in my house, but got a sweet old lady instead. If this man can focus on me, he can track me. I can't take a chance that tomorrow it will be you, or Dani. The Legacy can't take that chance. You have to go back to Beau-Rêve."

"No." Power surged through the deepening night, warming the air around them. Mala shifted and her father frowned, though he didn't know which of them had opened the current.

Instinctively Nicole reached out, tapping into the psychic current with her will, feeling the power swim through her veins, her cells, her spirit. The joy of feeling the gift so strongly and easily almost overshadowed the hurt of realizing her mother had called it against her.

Mala stepped forward, clearly torn. Nicole shook her head once, then focused on her mother. "Are you trying to block me again? Because I'm not willing to turn away this time."

"Ari, that's enough." Her father pulled her mother back against his chest, wrapping his arms around her. "Nicolette is doing the right thing."

Nicole watched hurt betrayal cross her mother's face as she turned to Stefan. "How can you agree to this?"

"With a great deal of worry," her father said, trepidation clear in his eyes. "Also with a great deal of faith. This is Nicole's task, and we can't put the current and future Keepers in harm's way because of our fear for her. Nicolette is thinking like the Keeper you want her to become. Accept this, because she'll do it anyway."

Wanting to diffuse the tension, Nicole smiled. "I've got my sisters with me, Mom, and Jax. A witch, a warrior, and a wild card. Who could worry with that kind of backup?"

"I could." Her mother's voice shook, but the power in the air eased, then dissipated. "I will always be your mother first. I can't help it that I wanted to ship you all off to a convent, but no, your father wanted independent, strong-willed daughters."

Stefan looped an arm around his wife's shoulders. "I think it was the other way around, love," he said, dropping a kiss to her forehead. "Either way, we must let Nicole do this. We have to protect Danielle. Beau-Rêve is the best place for that."

Nicole watched her mother reach up, tangling her fingers with Stefan's. She realized then that although her father didn't have the gifts of the Legacy, he had a different sort of gift, one that was essential to all of them.

"I know. Of course I know," her mother said then, ending with a heavy sigh. "We'll take Danielle home, and we'll watch over her as we watched over you. But that doesn't mean that I'll be content to do nothing." She reached up, unclasped the necklace that held the family pendant.

Panic filled Nicole's lungs, and she took a step back. "What are you doing, Mom? I can't take that!"

She'd never once seen her mother not wearing the Legère necklace, the large black tourmaline stone that reportedly housed the collective wisdom of all the Keepers who'd gone before. Family lore said that only true Keepers could even touch it; anyone else would have their talent scorched. Neither Nicole nor her siblings had ever dared test the theory growing up, and she didn't want to test it now.

"You can take this, and you will," her mother said, the iron in her voice unmistakably that of the Keeper of the Legacy. "Come stand in front of me, First Daughter."

Nicole's feet propelled her forward before she realized it. Her father stepped back, joining Mala.

Arielle drew a deep breath, then spoke. "On a hot night in west Africa, Mawu spoke to our mother, Anika, calling her to service. In return, she and her daughters were given gifts to stand between Light and Dark, and thus maintain the Balance of the universe. Mawu gifted our mother with the Legacy and this stone, to be passed from Keeper to

Keeper, mother to First Daughter. Although Anika's daughters walk different paths now, those paths all lead to the same source "

The Legère matriarch, Keeper of the Legacy, held the black gemstone aloft. Even with night surrounding them, Nicole could see fire burning in the depths of the jewel. "I do what has been done for centuries. I pass the charge to you. Walk in the Light always, search your heart to know what is right, and always do the best that you can."

Nicole held her breath as her mother fastened the pendant around her neck. The black stone settled against her chest, cold and heavy. Then her mother lifted her hands away and stepped back.

Warmth spread through Nicole. An unbelievable feeling coursed through her, similar to what she found in Jax's arms, but different. She wondered if being high felt the same way.

"Mom." She looked at her mother, smiled her first true smile in hours. "Wow."

"You see, you truly are meant to be the next Keeper," her mother said as she returned the smile. "Don't worry though. This just means you are officially the Keeper in waiting. There's a lot you need to learn before I pass on the mantle."

Nicole's hand fluttered close to her heart as she fought the urge to clutch the pendant in her hands. The current of magic she'd felt from her mother seemed stronger, like a constant though gentle breeze. *I really am meant for this*, she thought, tears crystallizing her vision.

She blinked them away. "We should get back to the hotel. Once I explain everything to Dani, I'll need to leave."

Her parents protested, as she knew they would. Mala stepped forward. "What about your detective?"

"What about him?"

"I have the feeling he's not going to take too kindly to you going after this guy. What if your plan doesn't jive with his?"

"I'll cross that bridge when I come to it," Nicole said, hoping she wouldn't have to come to it for a long time, if at all.

Her mother quickly dashed that notion. "You're going to have to decide soon. Detective Jackson is walking through your house like an emotional tornado, wanting to rip someone to pieces over this. He's not about to let you out of his sight without a good reason."

Her mother was right, but Nicole didn't like it. She knew in her bones that she had to stop Corcoran. She had to, not the police, not Jax. Yet Jax had become such a part of her life that she doubted she could do this without him finding out.

She turned to her father. "Daddy, do you—do you think I should tell him about all of this?"

"I can't make that decision for you, Nicolette," her father said softly. "All I can say is that it's not an easy thing to ask of anyone, to believe in the things our family does."

"Mom?"

Arielle Legère stepped closer. "I don't know how he'll react. He's accepted your abilities surprisingly well so far. But there's a reason why no one outside of the four of us knows more about our family duty. Besides, if you told him, do you really think he'd still let you do this alone?"

"No." If she told Jax and he believed her, he would be adamant about keeping her close. If he didn't believe her, he'd still stick to her to make sure she didn't go off on her own. When the dust settled, he'd drop her like a hot potato, knowing her to be as crazy as he'd first thought.

Jax appeared in the doorway. "Nicole? May I speak with you a moment?"

"Sure." She looked at her family. "Will you guys wait in the kitchen for me? I'll come inside in a minute."

Jax stepped out onto the deck as her family passed him, meeting their eyes in an unflinching way she had to admire. Once they were gone, he turned towards her.

His hands settled on her shoulders, drawing her close. She buried her face against his shoulder, concentrating only on breathing in his scent and his warmth. Arms wrapped around her, pulling her close, keeping her grounded. Cocooning her in the illusion of peace and safety.

"Nicki." His arms tightened. "We need to talk. Police business."

Against her will she shuddered. She didn't want to talk. She'd made some hard decisions, decisions she couldn't yet share with him despite every desire to. She didn't want to think, because thinking would bring the images and the fear and the vulnerability screaming back. And the rage, the destruction that followed.

"I don't suppose it could wait until morning?" She knew it couldn't, but she had to ask anyway.

"Timing's everything," he said, his tone apologetic. "We need to get your statement about the phone call. Then Bear and I are going to search Corcoran's place."

He sighed. "Besides, after the last time, I know you're going to drop any moment now. I've already packed a few things for you and Dani. I'll have a couple of officers escort you and your family back to the hotel."

His consideration touched her. "Thanks, but I don't think I want anything, especially if he's touched them."

Jax pulled back, cupped her cheek. "I don't think he did. There were some clean things in the laundry room, which you didn't put away for some reason."

She'd left laundry out? Nicole shook her head. She really was falling apart.

"It won't take long, will it?" she wondered. "I really need to get to Dani. I have to explain to my baby why I won't be seeing her for a while."

He stepped away from her, she supposed so that he could see her face. "How 'bout you explain it to me first?"

"I'm having Mom and Dad take Dani back to Beau-Rêve." She explained, being as brief and unemotional as possible. "So let's get the statement over with, then give me time with my daughter. I promise I'll be completely available afterwards. I'll call you and let you know what hotel I check into."

"You can stay with me."

The offer surprised her. "I can't do that."

"Yeah, you can." The planes of his face hardened with determination as he wrapped his fingers around her forearms. "I'm not going to let anything happen to you," he told her. "I messed up once, by not protecting your neighbor. I need to protect you. So if you want to check into a hotel, fine. I'll check in with you or bunk down outside the door, but I'm staying with you."

"Because you need my help?"

His grip tightened. "Because I need to know that you're safe. I have to do whatever I can to not fail you again."

Nicole felt her resolve weakening. She didn't want to put anyone else in danger by being around her, but she didn't want to be alone either. Still, she had to ask, "Aren't there rules against this sort of thing? I don't want you to get into trouble because of me."

"Trust me, after what happened today, I won't get into trouble. Just think of it as an extreme form of protective custody. If you want, I'll make a call and officially get you into a safe house and protective custody tomorrow. Let me do this, Nicole."

There weren't any other options, and she knew it. Knew also, that with Jax was exactly where she wanted to be. "All right. I'll stay with you."

Chapter Twenty-two

Nicole sat on the stuffed chocolate brown leather couch, struggling to relax as she waited for Jax to arrive. It felt strange to be sitting in his house, especially without him. She'd already straightened the sofa pillows, the African knick-knacks scattered throughout the room, and the model car collection on a wooden shelf system in the corner.

Although she liked the tribal but cozy feel of the living room, she hadn't dared to explore further into the house. Of course Mala had, in the name of security. Mala had told her there were two bathrooms, a designer kitchen, and an office that included weight lifting equipment, a guest bedroom, and the master bedroom. Which didn't look as if it had been slept in, Mala had gleefully reported.

Her sister now stood in front of the fireplace, facing the entryway. "Your boyfriend's got a nice place, for a cop."

"He's not my boyfriend," Nicole said, pushing her fingers against her forehead. Whatever supernatural high she'd had from wearing the Legère pendant had dissipated in the attempt to convince a teary-eyed Danielle that she wasn't being abandoned. Her heart still ached from the memory of Danielle pulling away from her in tearful anger, only to run into Arielle's arms.

The fact that her mother knew and understood the pain Nicole felt only deepened the hurt. It took everything in Nicole to believe that her daughter wouldn't hate her forever for leaving her, to believe that she'd made the right choice. She took comfort in the knowledge that her mother and her daughter would be safe as far away from Atlanta as possible, but it was cold comfort at best.

"Your bed buddy's almost as much of a neat freak as you are," Mala said. "I wonder if he's going to notice you messed with his car collection?"

"Would you please sit down?" Nicole complained. "I'm stressed enough as it is. And did you really just call Jax my 'bed buddy,' of all things?"

Mala took the armchair facing the door, spreading her leather coat open. "What would you like for me to call him? Future brother-in-law?"

"Were you always such a smart ass?" Nicole asked, wondering why she'd agreed to her parents' request that Mala accompany her to Jax's house. Probably because they wouldn't have let her leave the hotel otherwise.

Mala reached into her jacket, extracted a pocket knife. Nicole's breath caught as she watched Mala flick it open. She doubted that anything that long or sharp could be called a pocket knife. Folding dagger was more like it.

"Hey, you know what they say," Mala said, balancing the polished hilt on her index finger. "Sarcasm is so much better than sorrow. Besides, if I could hold a man like that, I wouldn't care what people called him."

Guilt hit Nicole, launching a fresh salvo on her precarious emotional state. Here she was stressing about her life when her sister had it worse than she did. "Aw, crap, Mala, I'm sorry."

"Hey, no worries." Mala waved her dagger in dismissal. "Just wanted you to know that I know exactly what you're going through right now, now that Mom's told you everything, or just about everything, about the Legacy. Sucks to have your whole world turned upside down, doesn't it?"

"Yeah." She turned to her sister, glad for her sarcasm, glad to talk about anything but Miss Gertie and the destruction of her house. "How did you handle it?"

"A lot worse than you did," Mala answered. She flipped her dagger in the air, catching it by the hilt with a deft movement that bubbled Nicole's stomach. If Mala had missed, they'd be on their way to an emergency room. "I knew I wasn't Keeper material, but Mom thought some arcane training would be a good direction for me. Needless to say, I wasn't excited at the prospect of being shut away in some isolated university in Budapest. But I actually enjoyed it."

"But you really didn't have a choice."

"Not much of one, no. You were already out of the house by then, so you may not remember how hard it was for me. I was already living outside of the world, no matter how much I denied it. Accidentally brushing against someone opens up a window to their soul, exposing me to all their thoughts and emotions and karma. By the time I left, I could barely hug you guys. Kissing a boy, forget about it. The one time I tried . . . .

"Anyway, at sixteen I already knew that I didn't have a chance at a normal life. So going overseas probably saved my life."

"You seem comfortable with it now," Nicole said. Comfortable, but not happy.

"It took a while," Mala said. "Years, while I learned and trained at a brutal pace. Earned a couple of degrees and discovered a knack for detective work. I actually like my day job as an paranormal investigator, and I'm good at it. Then I had my first conflict."

"What happened?"

"I survived it," Mala said, her tone clearly indicating she wouldn't go into details. She held up her dagger, eyeing the blade. "That, I suppose, was graduation day. They sent me out into the world after that."

"Oh Mala, I'm so sorry."

"Don't be." She put the wicked looking blade away. "We protect people so they can live their lives as they choose, in blissful ignorance that we've sacrificed our rights to the same thing. Ironic, isn't it?"

Nicole slumped down on the couch, not knowing what to say. Mala's path meant that she'd have to walk alone and possibly die young. Would Nicole's fate be the same? Would she have to face her enemy alone, only to fail?

"Maybe it'll be different for you," Mala said then. "It worked for Mom and Dad. It can work for you too."

"Anything's possible, right?" Nicole asked, not expecting an answer. Sure, Jax would walk through the door, and she'd tell him everything. He wouldn't blink an eye at tales of universal Balance and guardians and African deities walking the world. He'd be perfectly all right with abandoning his life and career in Atlanta to set up shop on a Louisiana plantation as consort to a Keeper. Jax would wrap his arms around her and swear undying love, and they'd live happily ever after.

Right. Even she couldn't dream of stuff that good.

Mala leapt to her feet seconds before Nicole heard the sound of someone attempting to open the front door. Motioning her to silence, Mala stalked to the front door, some sort of gun in her left hand and the dagger in her right. Nicole hadn't seen her draw either weapon. Nerves stretched tight, she wrapped icy fingers about the black pendant, willing herself to be calm. It had to be Jax. Corcoran couldn't have found her so soon, could he?

"Nicki?" Jax called through the door. "It's me."

Relief launched her to her feet. Mala slashed the air in a silent order to remain where she was. Nicole reluctantly obeyed, praying that her sister wouldn't kill her lover inside his own house.

Jax pushed open the door, then stopped. He wasn't surprised to see Mala guarding the entrance, even though it wasn't every day that a leather-clad woman pointed a gun and a blade at him. She was breaking a litany of laws and ordinances, but she was protecting Nicole, and he appreciated that. Didn't mean he couldn't tease her, though.

"Well now, there's a sight," he drawled, stepping inside before closing and locking the door. "Maybe I should give you Bear's address. I think a welcome like that would turn him on."

"He couldn't handle me," Mala retorted, sheathing her weapons before stepping aside.

"You might be right," Jax agreed, idly wondering what man could handle her. Taking stock of the room, he noticed that his car collection and African figurines had been rearranged. Nicole. He caught sight of her standing in front of his couch, looking tired and worried. She still wore the necklace he'd seen on her mother before. He wondered what it meant, and if she'd tell him if he asked.

Jax crossed to her, taking her by her elbows. "Nicki, what are you doing up? You should be resting."

"Maybe she didn't want to sleep in your wife's bed," Mala interjected before she could answer.

"My wife never slept in either bed." Jax frowned as Nicole avoided his gaze. "You think I'd do that to you?"

Nicole lowered her head. "I didn't know which room to take," she answered, embarrassment softening her tone. "I couldn't sleep anyway."

In Jax's opinion, she looked as if she'd drop at any moment. He bit back an exasperated sigh before letting her go. "Mala, do you have a place to stay or do you want to stay here tonight?"

"You'd let me stay here?"

Nicole looked at him, apparently as surprised as Mala sounded. He made an effort to keep his temper holstered. Why the hell did they think he'd kick Mala out, or that he'd bring Nicole home to a memorial to his late wife?

"If you're too tired to ride that moving violation of a street bike, or if Nicole wanted you to, then yeah, I'd let you stay. But it would be your own fault if you heard something you didn't want to hear."

Mala actually shuddered. "Like I needed that picture in my head."

Jax felt his temper slip. "You staying or not?"

"Maybe I should, just to be contrary."

"Mala, please." Nicole stepped between them, and Jax couldn't really blame her. He was spoiling for a fight, and he knew he had maybe five good minutes before he became shit for company. He'd wanted to come home with reassurances, something concrete to give Nicole, but he had nothing. Not getting a bead on Corcoran had pissed him off.

"Don't worry, I've got a place to crash." Mala stepped up beside them. "You're all right, Detective. Too bad we had to meet the way we did." She extended her hand.

Surprised at the gesture, even as he realized it was some kind of test, Jax wrapped his fingers around Mala's. Shock traveled up his arm, less than a Taser, worse than static electricity.

He hurriedly extracted his hand, shaking it to relieve the sting. "So you think I'm good enough for your sister?"

"I didn't say that," she replied, rubbing her bare palm against the lapel of her coat before slipping her glove back on. He hadn't noticed her remove it. "But I think you'll do. What time should I be here tomorrow? Nicole's going to want to go to the airport to say goodbye, and the pilot said they were cleared for a ten-thirty flight tomorrow morning."

"Eight," Jax answered even as Nicole switched her gaze between them.

"I can just meet you at the hotel," Nicole suggested to her sister.

Jax shook his head as Mala answered. "Nicki, don't take this the wrong way, but you're not leaving this house without me or your detective. I'll see you in the morning. Lock up tight." She undid the locks, opened the door cautiously, then stepped out into the night.

Jax wasted little time closing and locking the door behind Mala. "Your sister's a piece of work," he said into the awkward quiet, slipping off his jacket to hang on the oak coat rack beside the door. "I mean that in a good way."

"So are you. A piece of work, I mean, and not in a good way." She settled her hands on her hips, the gesture warning him that she was getting her back up. "I can take care of myself."

"No one's denying that." Jax removed his gun, feeling a headache starting like a bass beat behind his eyes. He was going to get that fight, whether he wanted it or not.

"Good. Then you'll understand why I don't require your baby-sitting services."

"I'm not baby-sitting you," he said, barely keeping his voice civil as he advanced on her.

She folded her arms across her chest. "I refuse to be trapped here. I have stuff I need to do!"

"Yeah, starting with staying alive." He dropped his holster on the couch, then took her by the shoulders, struggling against the urge to shake some sense into her. The last thing he needed was to be thrown across the room because Nicole got pissed.

"Look, I'm trying to do right by you. I'll even give you a choice."

"Really." She cocked her head at him. "What are my choices?"

"You stay here, but go nowhere without Mala or me."

Her expression told him how thrilled she was with that choice. "Or?"

"Or I go by the book and have you placed in protective custody, which puts you and a uniformed officer in a low-budget hotel room eating bad takeout food until the captain decides otherwise."

She looked surprised. "You'd do that to me?"

"Damn right I would." His gut clenched as he punished himself with images of Nicole lying bloodied and broken in her home. "Today was too close, Nicki. I am not about to let anything happen to you. I'll do whatever it takes to protect you, no matter how much it pisses you off. Go along with me on this, for both our sakes, all right?"

For the longest time she stared up at him, and he wondered what she read in his eyes. Finally she stepped back from him, picked up the overnight bag he'd packed for her earlier. "If Mala's going to be here at eight, we should get some sleep."

"Okay." Not giving her a chance to change her mind, he grabbed his holster in one hand and her fingers in the other, leading her back to the master bedroom. He put his gun in the nightstand, then stripped down to his boxers while she went, without a word, into the master bath to change.

After turning down the bedcovers, Jax sat on the side of the bed, rubbing his hands over his hair. He hadn't meant to take his frustrations out on Nicole. The search warrant had been too little too late; Corcoran obviously hadn't been in the tidy townhouse for a couple of days, and clues were few and far between.

The image of Miss Gertie's broken body was burned into his soul. Every victim represented failure, his failure to uphold his vow to protect, to provide justice. That failure, even more personal now, pressed down on him, making him doubt his ability to hunt down Corcoran, doubt his ability to keep Nicole safe. He was the closest he'd come to knowing fear in years, and he didn't know what to do about it.

"Jax?"

At her soft call, he shifted on the bed, twisting to face her. Nicole hesitated in the doorway, her pale nightgown hugging her curves and just skimming the tops of her thighs. Something shifted inside him, something deep and fundamental.

"It didn't go well, did it?" she asked. "Going to Corcoran's."

"No, it didn't. He was long gone." He sighed, pushing away the anger and frustration. "I'm sorry, Nicki."

"For what?"

"For yelling at you." He sighed, looking away. "For turning your life upside down. For making you a target. For not protecting your neighbor. Basically, for everything."

The mattress dipped as she knelt on the bed behind him. "I came to you with this," she said softly, resting a hand on his shoulder. "You didn't have to try to help me, or offer to protect me, or even believe me, but you did—after a while. You're doing more than most people in your position would."

She was letting him off too easy. "Yeah but—"

"But nothing." Her hand lifted, hesitated, then cupped his cheek. "We're in this together, aren't we?"

He covered her hand with his own, raising his gaze to hers. She stared back, eyes dark and uncertain. So much had happened to her that day, so much had been taken from her, and yet there she was, still trusting him. Somehow he'd find a way to deserve it.

"You bet," he assured her, pressing a kiss into her palm. He stretched out on the bed, pulling her down beside him. She pulled the covers up, then curled against him, tucking his hand against her chest. "Thank you," she whispered, her eyes drifting shut.

He remained awake long after she slid into sleep, holding her close and listening to her breathe. He'd bluffed about putting her into protective custody. Not only was he reluctant to let her out of his sight, he simply didn't trust anyone to protect her as well as he or Mala could.

He had a feeling that he didn't know even half the reasons why Nicole was so important to her family's Legacy, or why Corcoran had it in for her, but it didn't matter. She'd become important to Jax, and everything in him burned with the need to protect her. He vowed to keep her safe, or die trying.

Satisfied that no dreams haunted her, he spooned her body against his and fell asleep, knowing his rest would prove to be far less peaceful than hers.

Chapter Twenty-three

Nicole stumbled into a landscape wracked by a violent storm. Strange purple-gray clouds contorted overhead; sometimes it seemed as if faces leered at her from the seething mass. Raindrops the size of pebbles pelted her, leaving her skin smarting and bruised.

Barefoot, she ran over rocks and sharp grass towards the dubious shelter of a large, twisted tree, skidding to a stop when she saw a man standing beneath it. He wore a suit as stormy gray as the clouds above them. His hands and face were a tan contrast. Nothing remotely friendly showed in his features, not the thin slash of a mouth, the unforgiving slope of his nose, the hard glimmer of his dark eyes set too close together. His short hair was neither black nor brown, but some dirty color in between.

"You've kept me waiting, Nicole. That doesn't make me happy."

She took an involuntary step backward. "Who are you?"

"You don't recognize me? How disappointing." His smile sharpened. "And we've been so close lately. You could say that we've been as close as your dreams."

Horror slid down her back like an icy hand. "Corcoran!"

"At your service." He had the nerve to bow. "So wonderful to meet face to face at last. Sort of. I thought I'd dress up for the occasion, especially considering that you now know who I am."

A dream. She knew it was a dream, but it felt different. Not like a dream at all, and she apparently had the starring role this time. "What do you want?"

"Straight to the point, eh? I like that in a woman."

Anguish throbbed through her as she curled her hands into fists. "You killed Miss Gertie and two other women, all for what? To supposedly become a stronger psychic? You can't get psychic power that way."

"That's where you're wrong." Corcoran gestured to the sky, and a bolt of lightning slashed down, frying the ground between them.

He could control the dream.

Bile rose in Nicole's throat. Nothing like this had ever happened before. Nothing like Corcoran had ever happened to her before. "I don't know what you're up to, and I don't care," she declared with more confidence than she felt. "But whatever it is, I'm going to make sure that you don't get it!"

"Don't be rude, Nicole. It doesn't become you. But then, you've let your power resurrection go to your head. Maybe it's time to give you a lesson in humility."

He gestured again, and vines exploded out of the dark ground, wrapping around her arms and legs. She shrieked in anger and fear, struggling to break free. Without warning, the vines jerked her off her feet, dragging her across the rocky ground before slamming her against the trunk of the tree.

Pain exploded across her back and stars danced before her eyes. For one heart-stopping moment the world went black. Then her vision cleared. She had to force herself to speak over the agony. "H-How did you do this?"

Corcoran stood in front of her, hands behind his back. She hadn't even seen him move—he was just suddenly there, staring down at her with cold, dark eyes. "Stupid, stupid woman. All that power and you don't even know how to use it. You don't deserve your Legacy. None of you do."

Shock spiraled some of the pain away. How could he know about the Legacy? No one outside of the family gave it that name. "Who are you? *What* are you?"

"Who I am doesn't matter. All that matters is that you do as I say."

"You must be out of your mind! I'll never do what you say!"

"You may want to rethink that." He gestured again. Another vine slithered obscenely up her legs, across her stomach and up to her neck, wrapping itself around her throat. The spiky tendril curled tighter and tighter, digging into her skin and cutting off her air despite her attempts to fight it.

He served the Dark. How else could he know what he knew, do what he'd done? Fear, true, blinding fear, settled like a stone in her stomach. He could kill her here. He could snuff her life out in this dreamscape, and she'd die in the real world, with no one knowing how she'd really died.

"Ah, I see you recognize the depth of your predicament." Corcoran studied her, much the way a leopard studies its prey before attacking. "This is your dream, but I'm master here. You don't understand the power that could have been yours. You're content to let yourself be a vessel for whatever wants to fill you. Instead of taking control, you let yourself be controlled—you and every other female of your line. That power should be mine. That power *will* be mine."

"No." The word was barely a breath. Her lungs burned with the need for air.

"No?" he echoed, and she saw real anger in his eyes. "You think you have the right to tell me no?"

He backhanded her, hard, the force of the blow splitting her lip. Before she could even gasp in agony he gripped her chin, his eyes fierce with anger, hatred, and pure evil.

"You are nothing." His voice cracked over her like a whip. "In the scheme of things you're less than a blip on a radar screen. You're only a battery to me, and I will take that power from you." His fingers eased, his grip softening to a caress as he stroked her throat. "I'll enjoy every moment of it, too."

"Get away from me!"

The sky above them pulsed as the wind rose to a scream. She screamed with it as electricity skittered along her arms, the wilding of her power. She instinctively lashed out, desperate to get Corcoran away from her, desperate to escape. Lightning blistered the air around them and suddenly Corcoran went flying, landing on his back a few yards away.

Gasping with shock and relief, Nicole could think of only one thing: escape. Knowing every second counted, she focused her mind on the living ropes, willing the vines to loosen. Some of them obeyed, but fear and panic drained the power surge away, leaving her still bound and helpless.

"Bitch!" Corcoran crouched, his eyes glowing red with anger. "That was the wrong thing to do."

One of the vines pushed between her thighs in horrifying suggestion. She screamed, only to have it cut off when the tendril wrapped around her waist began to tighten, squeezing off her ability to breathe. The razor-sharp vines hardened to barbed wire, clawing into her skin through her dress, shredding fabric and skin and muscle.

Corcoran stalked towards her, hand outstretched. "I'm going to take your power," he informed her, his voice freakishly pleasant as the vines he controlled ripped at her. "Then I'm going to kill you and your sisters. That will give me enough power to take on the Keeper herself."

Nicole screamed wordlessly as blood poured from a multitude of scrapes and tears. Her only hope, her only escape, lay in waking up. She had to leave the dream or she'd die.

Jax. Struggling against the pain, against the ripping and tearing of her skin, Nicole focused her entire being on the one person who could immediately help her. *Jax, wake up!*

Agony broke her concentration as vines slashed into her stomach, cutting her deep and causing her to scream. To her horror, the vine lifted away, taking a part of her intestines with it. Pain overwhelmed her, calling up the darkness while her attacker laughed and laughed.

She woke up to Jax shaking her. A high-pitched noise bounced off the walls, and it took her a heartbeat to realize the sound came from her. She forced her mouth closed but only long enough to scramble off the bed and into the bathroom. Falling to her knees beside the toilet, she just managed to aim as she lost the contents of her stomach.

Jax came after her, running water in the sink, then pressing a cool, damp cloth to her face after she stopped heaving.

"I'll be all right," she gasped, gripping the lid as a method to stay connected to reality. Her voice, low and raspy, sounded foreign to her, worse than after the other dreams. "You can go."

"Like hell I will." He squatted beside her, tilting her chin to gently wipe her face and mouth with the washcloth. "And I know you're not all right. Your lip's busted."

She shuddered despite every attempt not to. She'd been on the losing side of a battle, and it felt like it; even breathing was a torment. Pain rolled through her, threatening to send her under. She breathed through it, refusing to surrender. She didn't think she'd ever want to sleep again.

She closed the toilet lid and flushed, pleased that she could make her muscles obey. "No, really, I-I'm f-fine."

"Sweet Jesus." The washcloth stopped moving; he sucked in a breath. He sounded as if something had lodged itself in his throat. "There's blood soaking through your nightgown."

Blood? Her heart pounded. She gathered her courage to look. Her pale gown resembled the dress she'd worn in her dream. Where the fabric covered her stomach and most of the pain originated, streaks of blood stretched like furious claws.

The violent streaks triggered her pain receptors, causing tears to prick her eyes. Somehow she made it to her feet, to the large mirror over the sink. Somehow she peeled the gown away from her skin, over her head.

Jax made a sound, a sound as horrified as she felt. She couldn't blame him, couldn't tear her gaze from her image in the mirror. Throbbing red indentations wrapped her wrists as if they'd been bound by thin straps. Angry bruises slashed across her skin from her thighs to her chest. The skin across her abdomen was broken and bloody. Bruises ringed her throat like an angry tattoo.

Much worse than a nightmare, a true dream.

A broken, mewling sound escaped her as something deep inside fractured. Her first dream about herself, about her death. Corcoran was coming for her, and he wanted her to know it. Her pitiful power couldn't handle something this evil, this powerful. Couldn't defeat someone who could invade her dreams, assault her, and leave her bruised and battered.

Jax stepped close to her. "Your back . . . ." He stopped, swallowed, tried again. "It looks like you were beaten."

She grabbed a large towel off the bar beside the shower stall. "Don't look," she begged, barely managing to get the words out. "Please don't look. I don't want you to see this."

"Screw that." His arms curved around her, causing her to gasp in pain. "I'm taking you to the hospital."

"No." She gripped his forearms. "You can't. You know I can't go. What would we say?"

"I don't give a damn about that! You could have cracked ribs or internal bleeding!"

"Please." She still couldn't look at him, couldn't stare into his eyes and see pity, or worse yet, revulsion. "I don't want anyone else to know about this. Don't make me go."

Jax closed his eyes, praying for strength, for calm, for guidance. He couldn't erase the horror that had slammed into him when he'd first seen Nicole's bruises and wounds. She looked like someone on the bad end of a domestic violence call. How could he subject her to the rigors of a hospital exam, all the questions that would come, after everything else that had happened? He couldn't.

"Okay, Nicki," he managed to say. "We don't have to go to the hospital. I've got some first aid stuff here. I'll take care of it, ice those bruises. I'll take care of you, all right? Stay here."

He hurried into the kitchen, grabbing a stockpot to fill with ice, and the bottle of tequila he'd purchased the day before when they'd gone shopping for her. Despite his assurances to Nicole, he felt far from able to take care of anything. What the hell could he do? He couldn't go into Nicole's dreams. Jax had to hope he'd find the bastard—soon—and make sure he never had the chance to hurt anyone again.

Pausing long enough to grab his first aid kit and extra towels out of the guest bathroom, Jax returned to the bedroom. He found Nicole sitting on the edge of the bed, huddled in his blue plaid robe. The sight of her in his house, in his robe, still threw him, even two nights later.

Having Nicole spend the night would have been complicated under normal circumstances. Having her there, trying to protect her, lying beside her and inside her, had begun to strip his veneer of logic away. His career, his belief in his ability as a cop, had saved him after Felecia's death. Now he wondered if he'd be able to do the right thing if—when—he caught Corcoran.

He handed her the bottle of tequila. "Take a good swallow," he suggested, kneeling before her. Scooping up a handful of ice, he made an icepack for her. "Use that on your lip, and any other bruises you can reach."

When he opened the robe, intending to clean the wounds on her stomach, her hands clamped down on his wrists. "I already took care it." Her breath hitched, and a tremble went through her.

"I just want to help you, Nicki," he said softly, understanding her hesitation.

"You did. You saved my life," she whispered, her voice bare as she pulled the robe closed. "You woke me up. If you hadn't done that, if I'd stayed in the dream—"

"This was directed at you personally, wasn't it?" he asked, already knowing the answer. "He came at you through your dream because he couldn't get you in your house."

She shuddered again. "Yes."

Jax fisted his hands, feeling his frustration mount as helplessness gripped him. Nicole hurt, and he couldn't stop it. For the second time in his life, he felt the urge to kill, to harm the person who'd harmed him and his.

"I'm going to kill him." His words were soft but resolved. "I'm going to hunt the son of a bitch down and then I'm going to kill him, slow."

Nicole gasped in reaction, uncontrollable shudders sweeping through her. Her hands unfisted from the robe, wrapped around his. Lifted his hands to her swollen lips. "You can't," she whispered. "You know you can't. You can't be like him."

He had his doubts. Every boundary he had had begun to shatter the day Nicole walked into the precinct. He wouldn't have thought himself capable of accepting a dreaming psychic. Now, looking at Nicole's bruised and tear-streaked face, he didn't think himself capable of being satisfied with the law bringing Corcoran to justice.

A chiming sounded. "That's my cell phone," Nicole said dully. "It's probably Mala."

Jax didn't bother to ask her how she knew. He found the phone on the nightstand, flipped it open. "Yes?"

"Open the door right now," Mala said, "or I'm driving my bike through your front window."

"It's Mala," he explained. "I'm going to let her in."

He climbed to his feet, then paused, torn. He didn't want to leave her, but he didn't want Mala waking up his neighbors either.

Nicole managed a warbly curve of her bottom lip. "Go, before Mala beats down the door," she urged gently. "I'll be in as soon as I put on a fresh nightgown."

He did as she said, not wanting to upset her. He barely made it to the living room before the pounding began. Good, someone to take his frustration out on.

"Where is she?" Mala asked, pushing her way past him.

"Hello to you, too," Jax answered, shutting and locking the door. "She's all right."

Mala eyed him. "Forgive me if I don't take your word for it."

"How'd you know she was hurt?"

"Duh." Mala rolled her eyes. "What part of 'psychic family' don't you understand?"

Jax felt his temper snap. "If you're all that, why don't you tell me where the hell this scumbag is?"

The leather-clad woman refused to give ground. "Because if I knew, he'd no longer be a problem, even if he is human."

What the hell was that supposed to mean? Before he could ask her, Nicole entered the living room. She held the bottle of tequila in one hand, and with the other held the ice pack against her bruised cheek. She'd put the necklace back on, Jax noted, quickly moving to her side.

"I'm all right, Mala."

"You don't look all right," Mala said, jerking off her gloves. "You look like you've been beaten."

Her gaze sharpened on Jax as she flexed her hands. "I think you need to step away from my sister, Detective."

Jax tensed. Mala taking the gloves off—literally and metaphorically—wasn't a good thing. Remembering how bad a shock he'd gotten from a brief handshake, he wondered what would happen if she tried to choke him. He'd make damn sure he didn't find out.

He helped Nicole fold herself onto the couch, then pulled a throw off the back to cover her. "Nicki, tell your sister what happened before one of us ends up dead."

"It was a dream, Mala. The worst I've ever had." She shifted on the couch, stretched a hand out toward him, the bruises on her wrists painful to see. "Jax, will you make us some coffee?"

"Yours is better," he pointed out. He wrapped his fingers around hers, appreciating the show of support even as he hated the necessity. He was getting damn tired of proving himself to her family.

He caught Mala staring at their entwined hands. Something raw and vulnerable charged her expression before she looked away, and Jax recalled that aside from their handshake, he'd never seen her touch someone without her gloves.

Nicole squeezed his hand, distracting him. "Your coffee is stronger," she replied, giving him a meaningful glance. "I think I'm going to need it."

He looked down at her, saw uncertainty, fear, and a small flare of anger. Everything he felt every time he saw her bruises and remembered how she'd gotten them. Of the two of them, he supposed Mala was better equipped to help Nicole, but he resented being kept out of the loop.

"All right," he agreed reluctantly, knowing he was being excluded and not liking it. "Holler if you need anything before I come back."

Nicole took a generous swallow from the tequila bottle while she waited for Jax to disappear down the hall. "Stop pushing him, Mala," she said, touching the ice pack gingerly to her stinging cheek. "He doesn't need to prove himself to you or anyone else."

"You're right," Mala surprised her by saying, settling into the recliner beside her. "I'm amazed at how well he's handling this."

"Years of police training," Nicole answered, feeling the tequila beginning to take effect. "I'm pretty sure he's freaking out on the inside, and doesn't want me to know. Can't say that I blame him."

"He's pushing it aside, because the need to protect you is stronger than the need to run from the magic," Mala said, her tone almost apologetic. "He's not about to let what happened to his wife happen to you."

"I know." Nicole's heart sank. Knowing what happened to his late wife, Nicole understood why Jax would feel a driving need to protect her. A need that had nothing to do with her personally, but everything to do with who and what he was, what he'd lost.

Her dreams had brought them together. Her dreams had made them intimate. Her dreams would eventually drive them apart.

"Corcoran attacked me in my dream." Nicole heard the tremor in her voice, swallowed it. "And it was my dream, unless he was dreaming about me and managed to pull me into it. I didn't really think it was possible, but so much of this shouldn't be possible as it is. Do you think he's serving the Dark?"

Mala glanced towards the hallway. "Maybe," she replied, her tone careful. "Based on how he's attacking Latents, he's probably a low-level psychic vampire, siphoning whatever power he can from Latents until he's strong enough to take on a full-fledged psychic. If that's true, then it's my job to trap him."

"What do you mean, Latents?"

"Latents are humans born to the magic, they just haven't unlocked the pathway to it yet," Mala said, her expression as serious as Nicole had ever seen it. "Once they unlock it, they can study enough and dabble enough to re-wire their brains and DNA. Sometimes the power twists them, drawing any kind of dark entity looking for a host."

"God, Mala, you're making my head hurt," Nicole complained, feeling her world shift yet again. "What about our family? Malita's the closest thing I've seen to a real witch, and I wasn't so self-absorbed growing up that I didn't notice Derek and Darien doing real, unexplainable magic. We're all Naturals, aren't we?"

"Most Legères are. Dad's the researcher, he can probably say for sure. We know great-ancestress Anika was some sort of medicine woman or high priestess, but whether that makes her a Natural or a Latent, no one knows. Everything changed when she accepted that gem around your neck."

Nicole's hand crept up, but didn't touch the large pendant. Memories sifted through her mind, memories of drums and fire and glowing light, and a beautiful dark-skinned woman with ageless eyes and a lioness for a companion.

Nicole knew her gifts had been dormant, not latent. The dreams had broken through the barrier her mother had set in place. Hopefully in response to Corcoran targeting his first victim, instead of what he'd claimed—that she was somehow responsible for him and his crimes.

"It doesn't matter who or what he is," she said then. "He needs to be stopped."

"Yep. He hurt you. We need to hurt him." Mala climbed to her feet in a restless gesture. "So, how do you want to do this?"

Nicole looked up at her sister, absorbing her slim beauty, her skill, and wished she had one-tenth of Mala's talents. Too bad real life wasn't like *The Matrix*, and she could download her sister's abilities.

Or could she?

She sat up, wincing at the protest her muscles made. "I have an idea, but it requires Malita's help. Do you think she's awake?"

"She called me when I was on the way over here," Mala replied, pulling a tiny phone out of her pocket. "I'm pretty sure she's waiting for a return call." She hit a button, then passed the phone to Nicole.

Malita answered on the second ring. "Nicki!" her normally serene sister screeched into the phone. "What the hell happened to you?"

Nicole winced, loosening her grip on the phone. "Are you channeling Mala or something? 'Cause if you are, I need you to teach me how to do it."

Chapter Twenty-four

"Oh my God, Nicki! You said it was bad, but I didn't know it was this bad."

"You should have seen her two days ago," Mala cracked to her twin as Nicole hobbled into her youngest sister's house. "It wasn't pretty."

"Gee, thanks," Nicole said dryly, looking forward to the serenity she always found in Malita's house despite her sister's shocked greeting.

"I've got some tea that will help," Malita offered, stepping aside so Nicole could pass. "You weren't wearing the pendant at the time, were you?"

Nicole stopped short, her muscles twinging in protest. "No, I wasn't. I took it off before Jax and I—uhm, never mind. How did you know?"

"You have to figure that the Keeper's necklace is for protection as much as for amplification, which is probably why Mom gave it to you," Malita replied, helping Nicole off with her jacket before settling her into a plush armchair. She deftly moved a leather ottoman to prop up Nicole's feet. "I don't think I've ever seen Mom without it until she passed it to you."

"Believe me, I'm not going to take it off again." Just like she didn't think she'd ever sleep deeply again. She hadn't allowed herself to relax enough to sleep since she'd been assaulted in her dream. Each time she tried, panic would set in. It had been easier to lie in bed beside Jax until he fell asleep, then rise to walk away the small hours of the night with tea or a cup of coffee, thinking, always thinking.

"Good." Mala perched on the arm of a chaise. "You're probably going to need it for this cockamamie idea of yours."

"It's the only idea I've got. I'm open to other suggestions." Nicole looked around the unusually cluttered room. Malita was a strict proponent of everything having a place, and Nicole had never seen the Moroccan-themed living room in anything but sumptuous order.

"Here." Malita poured tea into an earthenware mug. "This should help." She pressed it into Nicole's hands. "How are you feeling?"

"Better than yesterday and the day before," she replied, sinking into the chair. The pain and bruises had receded but the memories hadn't, stretching her emotions to the breaking point. The lack of progress in the investigation wore on her and Jax both.

Feeling safe in her own skin was proving more and more difficult. She already knew she wasn't safe in her own mind. Her mind, her one true sanctuary, the one domain that she truly should have some power over. Corcoran had invaded her last bastion, punched through her defenses as easily as a bullet piercing flesh.

Deep inside, she knew it was a foolish exercise, staying awake when her body demanded sleep. Yet she couldn't deny that no one else from Corcoran's psychic workshop had been threatened or killed. Whether he killed because she dreamed, or she dreamed because he killed was beside the point. The fact was, she hadn't dreamed again, and he hadn't killed again. She had to find a way to stop Corcoran, to manipulate her dreams with the same expertise he wielded, before sleep deprivation took its toll on her.

She'd sworn that she would stop Corcoran the day Miss Gertie had died. She'd promised again just yesterday, when she'd buried her dear friend. She decided she would keep her promise, no matter what it took.

Jax was equally determined, she knew. He'd given her the space she'd desperately needed after her psychic attack, not pressing her about her dreams. Instead, he threw himself into the case with a single-mindedness she had to admire. She didn't begrudge him his duty so much as she envied his ability to do something.

She blinked, bringing her thoughts back to the present. "What did you do to the place?"

"Got it ready for you, of course," Malita responded. "It took me two days, but I think I've come up with something that will work."

Nicole took a cautious sip of the pale tea, found it mild and sweet. And energizing. "Something like what?"

Malita handed her twin a cup of tea, then poured one for herself. "A spell," she told them. "A transference spell, to be exact."

"All right." Soothing warmth spread through Nicole, and she swallowed more tea. If her youngest sister ever gave up decorating, she'd make a fortune with her herbal concoctions. "Are you ready?"

"Are you kidding?" With her hair piled haphazardly atop her head, large silver hoops, pale green kurta, and faded jeans, Malita looked more like a dancer than a prize-winning interior designer. "I'm nowhere near ready."

"Why not?" Mala wondered, idly turning her cup in her hands.

"Oh, maybe because I've never done anything like this before?" Malita wiped her free hand down her thigh. "You want me to create a safe space in your home? No problem. Create a specialty blend of tea to cure insomnia? Got you covered. Downloading some of your skills into the First Daughter?" She shook her head. "I can't believe I agreed to this!"

"You? I can't believe *I* agreed to this." Mala poured more tea for Nicole.

"Are you saying that you can't do this? Either of you?" Nicole felt her hopes plummet. This had been her best idea. Her only idea.

"I don't even know if this is possible, Nicki." Malita drained her mug. "Even if it is, I don't know if I can do it. Or should."

"I said I would help you, and I will," Mala assured Nicole. "Besides, the spell will work or it won't. What's the worst that could happen?"

Malita stared at her twin. "Oh, I don't know—both of you lapsing into comas?"

Color drained from Mala's cheeks. "Yeah, I'd say that's pretty bad."

Nicole swung her feet off the ottoman, discomfort forgotten. "You have to do this, Malita. You're the only one who can."

Malita licked her lips, nodded. "I did some research after you called," she said, staring at the black gemstone Nicole wore. "If we can tap into the magic in the pendant, I think we can get this to work."

Mala put her mug down, ready for action. "What do we need to do?"

"You've already started, by drinking the tea. It clears the mind and relaxes the body."

"So I noticed." Nicole stared down at her empty mug, not remembering drinking the second cupful. "Who needs tequila when you have this stuff?"

"It's a start," Malita said. "I've made room in the den, if you're ready. Will you guys take off your shoes? Mala, you need to take your gloves off too. It'll help both of you stay grounded."

Nicole toed off her flats, then climbed to her feet, much improved. Mala took a little longer, since she wore boots.

Malita led them into the den. The room had been sparsely furnished to begin with, Nicole remembered, since Malita used it for yoga and a design studio.

Now the dark wood floor gleamed up at them, mimicking the warm glow of the copper-colored walls. Assorted pictures, some of Malita's sketches, some family photos, graced the walls, with four additions. Centered against the wall directly opposite the door sat a copper and stone water fountain, at least two feet tall. In front of the window on the second wall hung a bamboo windchime. The third wall held a large terracotta planter filled with the dark green, spiky leaves of a snake plant. As Mala entered the room, Malita pulled a tall, butterscotch-colored candle into the doorway, then lit it. The four elements, anchoring the space.

She'd poured a semi-circle on the floor, Nicole noted, a mixture of what looked like coarse sea salt and soul food seasoning. Inside the circle sat a small kettledrum draped with several yards of intricately patterned Malinese mudcloth. A painted gourd bowl sat atop it, containing slices of dried yams, with a glass bowl of spices next to it. Flanking it, a thick stick of incense burned, along with several tall gold tapers.

Mala turned to her twin. "We doing a spell or cooking lunch?"

"Very funny," Malita retorted, gesturing each of them through the opening of the circle. "Since I've never tried anything like this before, I figured it wouldn't hurt to have some help from the family."

"Help from the family?" Mala repeated. "How is this supposed to help us contact every Legère female?"

"I'm not talking about every Legère. I don't even want to think about trying to control the magical output of that much focused intent." Malita picked up a slender remote, hit a button. Soft drumbeats permeated the air, blending with the incense and scented candles. "I'm hoping the power and collective knowledge of every Keeper since Anika will be enough."

Nicole lifted the pendant, watching the light reflect on its faceted surface. She could feel its energy seeping through her fingers, becoming a part of her. Four hundred years of challenges had been overcome, thanks to this pendant and the women who'd worm it. There was no way in heaven or earth that she'd voluntarily remove the pendant ever again.

"How are we going to call them?"

"Just follow my lead." Malita took the bowl of spices from the altar, humming to herself as she sprinkled some of the mixture into the two-foot gap on the floor to complete the circle. As soon as the circle was completed, Nicole felt a current of power spring up, thrumming around them. She reached for it eagerly, needing the rush, the comfort, the reinforcement. It felt familiar yet different, and she wondered if the difference lay in Malita's method of calling it.

Malita gestured her sisters into position around the drum. "Mala, pull your blade," she ordered, her voice just above the rhythmic beat of the drums.

Nicole watched Mala produce the same blade she'd seen her playing with days ago. "Do you offer this gift freely to your sister, the First Daughter?" Malita asked.

Mala balanced the sharp dagger on her palms. "I freely offer my blade and my gift to my sister, the First Daughter."

"Lay it across the bowl," Malita said, pausing as Mala followed her instruction. She looked to Nicole. "Does the First Daughter freely accept what has been offered?"

Nicole looked at both her sisters, then down at the blade balanced across the bowl. She licked her lips, then spoke, the words falling into place. "She who is First freely accepts the blade and the gifts of her sisters."

Malita's left hand reached out for hers. Then she offered her right hand to Mala. Mala's eyes widened as she thrust her hands into her pockets. "It's necessary, Mala," Nicole and Malita said in unison.

Holding her breath, Mala slipped her bare hand into her twin's. "After I say the spell," Malita told them, "you two will link hands and complete the inner circle. Ready?"

Nicole nodded, looked to Mala. Her warrior sister looked uneasy, but nodded.

Malita tightened her grip, then spoke:

"*Mothers present, mothers past,*
Aid the spell your daughters cast.
By your wisdom, strength, and will
The gift is shared, and stronger still."

Nicole linked hands with Mala. For a heartbeat, nothing happened. Then the room darkened as the circle on the floor began to glow. Over the thrilling rush of her blood, Nicole heard the recorded drumbeats become louder, richer, with wordless voices adding to the rich tapestry.

Energy danced along her skin, raising her hair, as the glowing circle thickened, became a curtain of energy around them. As they all watched, the dark gem lifted away from her chest, hovering parallel to the floor, as centered between them as the chain would allow. Nicole watched, breathless, as light flared deep inside the faceted depths.

Suddenly a spear of light shot from the center of the gem, into Mala's forehead. She gasped, staggered, but held on to their hands. Nicole tightened her grip as another beam of light hit Malita, then her. Flinching, expecting pain, she was surprised to feel an all-encompassing warmth instead, circulating through her entire body, pushing into every cell.

She felt the energy inside her reversing direction, flowing back into the Legère gem in a dark orange wave of strength and power, and purpose. Suddenly, like a rapidly rewinding movie, she could see them, every First Daughter, every Keeper. She didn't know all of them, but she recognized them, their all-too-human hopes and fears. Their tears and laughter. Their inner strength and their outer power.

It became too much, too much to comprehend or control. She tossed back her head and cried out. At the sound of her voice, everything stopped.

The pendant darkened, fell against her chest. The weight of it, heavier than before, caused her knees to buckle. Mala hit the floor at the same time, then Malita.

The three sisters looked at each other, dazed in the absolute silence. Then they burst into giddy laughter.

"Damn," Mala breathed, half slumped into Nicole's lap. "That was—that was—"

"Yeah," Nicole answered, still tingling from the residual magic hanging in the air like the feel of a summer night after a lightning strike. "That was better than your tea, Malita. Better than tequila."

"It most definitely was," Malita agreed from the other side of the table, sounding too pleased to be offended. "It was like the best sugar buzz ever."

"Yeah, and I just crashed," Mala said, obviously not in any hurry to get up. She looked up at Nicole. "Do you think it worked? 'Cause I gotta tell ya, I got nothing else."

"Only one way to find out." Nicole pushed her sister off her lap, then climbed to her feet. She reached across the drum, wrapped her fingers around the hilt of the dagger.

"Awesome balance," she murmured, feeling the weight of the dagger in her hand. "Oh, and something nasty built in for the poor idiot who thinks to take it. You've been a busy blade, haven't you? It's really beautiful, Mala."

Malita looked up at her. "Uhm, Nicole?"

"Yeah?"

"Would you mind watching where you're flipping that thing? It's kinda sharp, and I'd rather avoid getting holes in my floor, or me for that matter."

Nicole jerked to a halt, the dagger spinning in midair. It began a graceful, deadly downward spiral, right for Malita's leg. Before Mala could move, Nicole did, snagging the blade by the hilt. She flicked her wrist, snapping the blade closed before slipping it into her back pocket.

The twins looked at each other. "I guess it worked."

"Looks like." Nicole felt downright euphoric. "How are you feeling, Mala?"

Mala climbed to her feet, bracing her hand on the kettle drum. "I'm not getting hits off anything." She touched the vintage mudcloth, then the antique bowl. "I can't even feel the magic in these. Is it because we're in a circle?"

"We're not in the circle anymore," Malita answered. "It disappeared with the light."

Mala straightened, a mixture of expressions chasing across her face: fear, hope, even worry and anger. "My power's gone?"

"Probably not gone, so much as needing to be recharged," Malita said, standing and cracking her back. "It's the best of the bad things that could have happened. I don't have any idea when you'll be back at full strength, so you might want to lay low for a couple of days."

"Screw that." Mala threaded her hands through her hair. "I'm going hunting."

"Mala." Nicole looked at her sister, not liking the eagerness she saw. "You can't, it's too dangerous without your powers."

Mala rolled her eyes. "Not that kind of hunting, guys. Geesh. Do I look stupid?"

Malita raised an eyebrow. "Do you really want me to answer that?"

"Children," Nicole murmured, stepping between her sisters. She couldn't help smiling at replaying a scene from their childhood. "I think a night out is a great idea. In fact, Malita, I think you should go, too."

"What? Why?" Mala fairly pouted.

"Why do I have to go?" Malita's expression matched her twin's.

Nicole laughed. She couldn't help it, couldn't contain the joy, the hope, and the magic. "I love you guys. You're both going to go out and have a good time, on me. Consider it a thank you for helping me today."

"What are you going to do?"

"Come up with a plan to track down Corcoran," she said. "Have a good time tonight, because we're gonna kick butt tomorrow."

Chapter Twenty-five

Jax had to be dreaming.

There was no way that Nicole Legère—reserved, straight-laced psychic psychologist—was dancing naked in his backyard. Jax rubbed his eyes, then looked again. Most definitely Nicole, and she wore nothing but moonlight. The bruises she'd gotten two nights ago had disappeared as magically as they'd appeared. Fireflies danced around her, spinning in circles as she laughed and spun with them.

God help him, but she looked . . . beautiful was too plain a word. Seeing her there, with her skin glowing, her arms stretched heavenward, made him think of bonfires, singing, drums. He thought of heat and beats, love and lust, heavy and pulsing, of striding to her hard and ready, throwing her to the ground and joining his flesh to hers as they both cried out in triumph.

He shook his head to clear the heady image. Obviously they'd both been pushing themselves too hard, and the pressure had finally gotten to Nicole. He had to get her inside.

However, at three in the morning, no one should be out. And if they were, the wooden fencing made it hard to see into his backyard. Still, Jax decided to take no chances. It was one thing to have a psychic around. A naked dancing psychic was definitely too weird to continue.

He scooped her robe off the steps. "What do you think you're doing?"

She turned to face him, her smile warm and inviting. "Jax." She held out her arms, hips swaying, eyes promising. "Come to me."

Like he could refuse. He stepped away from the dim light of the kitchen and into the darkness that cloaked the backyard. Yet it wasn't completely dark. Moonlight sheathed Nicole's skin, and she seemed to glow.

"What's going on, Nicki?" he asked, crossing to her. "Are you dreaming?"

"No." She glided toward him like the ultimate woman, the black pendant shimmering between her breasts.

He swallowed against the desire that thrummed through him, a sudden, burning wind. "Am I?"

"No." She laughed, low and inviting. His entire body clenched.

Yet when he touched her, desire became concern. "Jesus, you're freezing!"

Jax threw her robe over her. She threw it off again. "I'm not freezing, I'm burning." She gathered his hands and placed them on her breasts. "I'm alive, magically alive. Can't you feel it?"

Amazingly, he did. Need rushed through him, pure and potent. He wondered if he felt Nicole's or his own, then decided it didn't matter. He wanted her. Bad.

"Kiss me." Her arms wrapped around his neck as she pulled him closer for a kiss. It was unlike any kiss they'd shared before. Hot, heady, open and thorough, she kissed him like a fertility goddess demanding her just tribute.

Golden light sparked around them. An inner voice warned him that he shouldn't be doing this, that there couldn't be fireflies dancing around them in early April. The larger part of him, the part about to surrender control, didn't care about anything but pulling Nicole's hips closer, pulling the hot core of her sex onto his erection.

She rubbed against him as her tongue swept into his mouth. He almost came. His fingers gripped her buttocks, molding the lush curves of her body to his. Just as he moved to take over the seduction, to tug off his boxers, then lift her the distance that would join them, she broke the kiss, stepping back from him, making him frown. "What the . . . ?"

Her smile flashed in the moonlight as her hands moved to his chest, pushing him to the ground. He fell on his back to the cold grass, and didn't give a damn. His attention focused completely on Nicole as she danced in a graceful, sensuous circle around him, the ripe fullness of her body glowing and beautiful. He hardened even more, painfully needing her.

In a liquid movement she knelt beside him, her hands reaching for his boxers. She pulled them down and off. Then her hands stroked up his legs, leaving fire in their wake.

He could feel the heat of her gaze on his skin as she leaned forward. "I'm going to taste you now," she whispered, causing him to jerk in response.

Her tongue swept over his balls, and he groaned at the mind-blowing contrast of the cool night air and the warmth of her mouth. He dug his fingers into the chill solidity of earth and gritted his teeth as she made her way up the length of his cock with absolute, perfect slowness.

"Tell me you like it," she whispered against him before reversing her motion. "Show me how much it means."

"I like it so much it's going to kill me," he managed to say. "It means everything."

"Good." He felt her tongue swirl in slow torturous circles back to the head, taking the moisture around the tip before closing her mouth around him.

The sensation had him shuddering in pure pleasure. Automatically he thrust his hips up and she took more of him, wrapping one hand around the length she couldn't fit inside her mouth, the other gently massaging his balls. She drew on him as if in search of nourishment, and it was all he could do to hold himself in check, to endure the sweet torture as long as possible.

God, he wanted her to go on, go on forever, but he couldn't last for much longer. He needed to be inside her, needed to feel her heat surround him before he lost his mind.

As if she'd read him, she lifted her head, licking her lips. Her eyes actually glittered at him, flashing deep into him. Before he could think about it, she straddled his thighs.

"Wait."

"No. Don't you want me, want this?"

"Yes, but—" He didn't have any protection.

"Say it." Her hand stroked his length, up once, then down. "Say you want me."

"God, Nicki, I want you," he ground out, his body pulled tight with longing. "It hurts, I want you so much."

She smiled, rising to her knees before guiding him into position. In slow torture she sank down, her sigh mingling with his groan as she took every inch. A chuckle shook her, sending delicious spasms through her and around him.

"Ah, how you fill me, my beautiful man," she said, her voice low and purring. She lifted up, then sank back against him with another sigh. "It's like magic, so powerful and beautiful and addictive. Let me show you what I mean."

With slow, rhythmic movements she rode him. Helpless, caught in a trance, he let her, watching her take pleasure from him. She gave in return, her inner muscles massaging him, cradling him. The pace increased slowly; just when he thought he would explode, she would ease up, slowing the pace or stopping altogether.

She was driving him out of his mind.

Moonlight silvered her skin, caught the gem swinging between her breasts. Goddess, he thought again, hearing the memory of far-off drumbeats and song. He had to touch her, one hand moving up her thigh to her belly, then to her breast. She groaned approval, leaning over far enough for him to take one puckered nipple into his mouth. Her pendant swung against his throat, sending a current through him.

Breath, thought, worry—it all left him, driven out by primal need for Nicole. Her scent, her heat, her soft sounds invaded every part of him, taking over. He surrendered without a fight, teasing her breasts with mouth and hand while his other hand moved between her legs. His thumb pressed and stroked her in rhythm to her movements. She shuddered and rocked against him, murmuring breathless words in what he supposed was French.

He felt like speaking in tongues himself.

Suddenly she pulled away from him, straightening to increase her pace. Her inner walls massaged him with moist heat so fantastic he felt his eyes roll back. "Come with me," she demanded, breathless. "Give me all, give me everything. Yes, oh, yes. Feel it, feel the magic."

He clamped his hands on her hipbones and drove into her wildly, striving to follow wherever she led, lifting off the ground with each desperate, upward stroke. She matched him stroke for stroke, rocking hard against him as he surged in and out of her. The chill and dark of the night disappeared; the ground beneath him slipped away. All he could see, all he could feel was Nicole and the rainbow of lights that swirled around them and through them.

"Nicki, I can't—oh, holy fuck." His entire body wrenched as his orgasm swept up from his toes as unstoppable as a tidal wave. With a long groan, he clamped her hips against him, frantically pouring into her again and again, drenching her insides, draining his soul.

A split second later she threw back her head and her arms, crying out as her own orgasm shook her. The light around them swirled into a maelstrom, then brightened to white-hot brilliance, shattering into a million multi-colored crystals.

She collapsed against him, all languid sensuality. Pure instinct made him wrap his arms about her; his mind refused to function. Long moments passed before he could see again, think again, speak again. When he could speak, it was only one word.

"Nicole."

Keeping her anchored to him, he sat up so that she sat astride his lap. She wrapped her legs around him, her inner walls gripping him as he continued to pulse inside her, filling her. He shifted slightly, settling her. Her breath hitched and she spasmed again, taking the last bit of him with her.

Emotion boiled inside him as he pushed curly strands away from her forehead. Something had happened; he just didn't know what. He felt different. He kissed her face, her neck, her gorgeous lips as she wrapped her arms around his neck, her hips flexing slowly against him as if she couldn't stop, had to continue the erotic friction. He could feel her heart beating against his chest, a rapid throbbing rhythm. Both of them were breathing as if they'd just finished a marathon, their breath coloring the night air.

They stayed like that for minutes, hours, days. Jax didn't know and he didn't care. Aftershocks trembled through him, and from the occasional catch in Nicole's breath, she must have felt them too. A peaceful contentment he hadn't felt in a long time swept through him. If the world were to end the next day, he'd die a happy man.

"Did you feel it, Jax?" she whispered against his ear. "Did you feel the magic?"

"God, yes," he answered, gulping in air. He didn't know what he'd felt, but he knew he'd give anything to feel it again. His hands roamed over her back. "This was the most incredible night of my life. You're amazing."

She laughed softly, nuzzling his cheek with her own. "We're amazing. They say it's like that, when a Legère woman loves the man she's with."

The world literally stopped for Jax. "Are you saying that you love me?"

Her tongue swept the curve of his neck, sending a shudder through him. "Do I love Carter Emanuel Jackson? Maybe I do, maybe I don't. I can't deny the magic I felt with you though, and I don't want to."

Panic squeezed his lungs. He'd give his life for hers in a heartbeat, but he couldn't give her the words, couldn't give her his heart. It had been buried three years ago.

"I know we don't have forever," she said, her voice a soft song in the moonlight. "So I wanted to let you know how I feel, what you've done to me and for me."

"Nicki." He could deal with flying crap, dream attacks, antagonistic relatives. This he couldn't handle. How the hell had she fallen in love with him?

Her arms tightened around his neck, "Jax, I can't seem to catch my breath."

He wrapped his arms around her, feeling the pendant pressed between them. Her heart pounded against his. The staccato beat wasn't the result of mind-blowing sex.

"Okay, full moon fever is over for you," he said, gently lifting her away so that he could climb to his feet. "We're going inside now."

Snagging their clothes, he half-pushed, half-dragged her back into the house, steering her toward one of the stools at the kitchen counter. "Are you all right?"

"Sure, why wouldn't I be all right?" She blinked up at him. "Are you playing with the lights?"

"What in the hell are you talking about? You're acting like you're . . . ." Realization stuck him cold, driving out the warm feeling of afterglow. He caught her face in his hands, staring at her eyes. "Jesus. You're high."

"No I'm not. It's the magic. Or it could be the coffee." She clutched her head in her hands. "Maybe I shouldn't have had that last pot."

"Last pot?"

"Of coffee. Not drugs. Drugs are bad. I don't do drugs. Unless you count the tequila. Or the coffee. Or the magic. That was some good shit."

Her eyes widened in shock. "Oh man, I don't think I've ever said that before."

"No, you haven't." Jax grabbed a glass, filled it with water, torn between anger and worry. Nicole definitely wasn't acting like herself, and he had no idea why. Or how hard the crash would be when she came down.

"Here, drink this."

She took the glass, drained it. Spluttered. "This is water. What the hell is water supposed to do?"

Concern took a temporary backseat to getting answers. "What do you want to do?"

"Stop Corcoran. Isn't that what we've been trying to do?" She slipped off the stool, lurched towards the coffee pot on the opposite counter. He hadn't noticed that it was on when he'd gone to find Nicole earlier. He hadn't noticed the bottle of pills beside it either, but he did now.

"Jesus H. Christ, Nicki." Jax snatched the bottle off the counter, so angry he couldn't see straight. He looked down at the bottle in his hands. It was a large one, but it was already half empty. Half empty, and she'd only been there for four full days. And she'd gone through coffee as if her name was Juan Valdez.

"Caffeine pills and pots of coffee? You don't want to go to sleep, do you? That's why you're doing this. You've geeked yourself up on coffee and No-Doze so you wouldn't sleep!"

"I had no choice—"

"There's always a choice!" he thundered, hurling the bottle against the fridge, sending little white pills flying. His hands settled on her shoulders to give her one angry shake. "How long has this been going on?"

"Let go of me."

"How fucking long, Nicki?"

"Since the last dream."

Three days. He could feel the anger pounding in his ears as his fingers inadvertently tightened on her shoulders. "You've been overdosing on caffeine for three days? Do you realize that you could have had a stroke?" Another shake had her head rolling on her shoulders. "Your goddamn heart could have exploded right out of your goddamn chest. Is that what you wanted?"

"I want the same thing you want—to stop Corcoran," she retorted, her expression fierce. "Nothing's happened. Don't you see? Nothing's happened since I haven't dreamed. If I don't dream, he can't do anything."

"You don't know that. All that means is that we get no warning of the next move he'll make." Jax peeled his hands from her shoulders, infuriated by her words, by the damage she'd done to herself. Infuriated for believing their time under the stars had been real.

"Did you know that you could die from caffeine poisoning, or did you just not give a damn? Just take yourself out, as if that's okay?"

Her shoulders dropped, as if every bit of energy had been vacuumed out of her. "Better by my hand than his." Her voice limped slowly from her throat. "If I can't stop him, I'll keep him from getting my powers."

Alarm crashed through him. "Jesus, Nicki. Do you even hear what you're saying?"

"Of course I do." She pushed away from the counter, her movements frenetic. "You see, I have to save the world. That's my responsibility, the responsibility of all the Keepers. Have a daughter, save the world. Save the world, have another daughter. Pass the Legacy on, make sure there's always a daughter waiting to be sacrificed to the greater good. Must be the Light to balance the Dark. Rise up, fall down, fight, fight, fight."

She laughed, a hysterical note leeching the humor from the sound. "It would help if I could be Mala. If I were Mala, I could be brave, I could take him. Of course, if I were Mala, I would know better than to even want to take Mom's place someday as Keeper."

She raised her hands, staring at her palms. "But borrowing her power doesn't make me Mala, does it? I'm me, not Mala. Just me."

Her hands curled into fists. "You know what? It doesn't matter." Her voice hardened with a growl as small appliances on the counter shuddered. "I'm going to stop him. Do you hear me, you son-of-a-bitch? I'll stop you. Whatever it takes, whatever it costs. No one else is going to die because of me."

She shrieked once, clutching her head. Jax sprang to her, wrapping his arms around her before she tumbled to the floor. Tears leaked from her tightly closed eyes. "Nicki, what's wrong? What's happening?"

"It hurts," she whispered, her voice breaking. She pressed the heels of her hands against her eyes. "My head—killing me . . . ."

Jax pulled her into his arms, locking her against him. She quivered like a frightened puppy. Fear and anger rippled off her in palpable waves as her heart beat a staccato rhythm against his chest.

He felt some of that fear and anger himself. Fear for her, for the unspoken things she'd endured because he couldn't do his fucking job and catch a killer. Anger because he hadn't seen what the pressure had done to her, anger because she had kept him in the dark.

Churning inside, he pushed away everything but the need to soothe her. "It's all right, Nicki. Slow that pulse down. Take a deep breath, honey. That's it, nice and easy. Slow that pulse down."

The litany of his words and the constant caress of his hands to her back finally seeped into her. She rested against him, her forehead to his chest, sucking in mouthfuls of air.

Keeping his arms locked around her, he led her to the guest bedroom and put her to bed. He left her long enough to wet a washcloth and refill her water glass. Returning, he folded the cooled cloth, placing it on her forehead. She gasped in relief.

He sat beside her, back against the headboard. "Is it that bad, that you'd deprive yourself of sleep for three days?"

"It's that bad."

Tears spiked her lashes and turned her eyes into glittering tortoise shell, causing him to silently curse himself for adding to her misery. "I'll find him, Nicki," he vowed. "I promise, this will all be over soon."

"Yes, all be over soon," she said, her voice hollow. Her eyes opened and closed in slow sweeping movements. Her words dragged with fatigue. "You'll do everything you have to, and so will I. And then this dream will end."

She slumped against him as she fell headlong into sleep.

Jax pulled her close and sighed, resting his head against the headboard, trying to sort out his roller-coaster emotions. Nicole had brought him magic, had taken him to a place he'd never been before. And just when he didn't think the night could get any better, she'd said she loved him.

But it was all a lie. Their moonlit escapade had been a caffeine-induced frenzy, nothing more. It certainly didn't mean that Nicole loved him. The passionate lovemaking, the feeling of completeness, the literal fireworks—it had all been an illusion conjured by sleep deprivation and caffeine.

He tried hard not to feel cheated. A stupid feeling. He remembered the way his heart had seized up in his chest when Nicole had said the "L" word. He could take a twelve year old pointing a gun at him, but he couldn't handle Nicole loving him.

He didn't want her to love him, just like he didn't want to love her.

If he did, if he accepted that love, his failure would be that much more intense, more unbearable. He hadn't prevented her neighbor's death, hadn't prevented the bastard from brutalizing Nicole in her dreams. Hadn't prevented her from hurting herself to escape those dreams.

He'd protect her now. Tomorrow he'd put her on a plane to New Orleans, far away from him, from murder, from Corcoran. Then he'd hunt the bastard down and bring him to justice, using old school methods . It would be the only satisfaction he'd get, and it would have to last him the rest of his life.

He wouldn't fail. Not this time.

Chapter Twenty-six

Nicole woke up to find the bed beside her empty. It took a moment to recognize the guestroom. Why wasn't she in the master bedroom with Jax?

"Oh, God." She dug her fingers into her hair as memories danced through her mind. "I can't believe I—and then I—oh, my God."

Overwhelming embarrassment made her close her eyes again. She didn't blame Jax for not wanting to be with her anymore. She'd freaked him out. Hell, she'd freaked herself out. Randall and Jax were the only two men she'd ever slept with, and yet she couldn't remember ever before seeing swirling lights while making love.

And it had been making love, not a fantasy induced by lack of sleep and too much coffee. Standing in the moonlight, her soul had been as bare as her body. Maybe being in circle with her sisters had given her clarity. Maybe embracing the magic of her heritage had not only given her the strength to do what she needed to do, but also to say what she needed to say. She loved Jax and had wanted to share that with him, wanted to give him some of the magic that he'd given her.

Too bad he didn't love her.

Sighing, she got out of bed. She knew he cared. She wouldn't be in the relative safety of his house if he didn't care. And she knew that he enjoyed her body. If they'd met some other way, if she'd been some other woman, she'd fantasize about happily-ever-after with Jax.

But they'd met the way they'd met, and she was who she was. First Daughter of the Legacy, chosen to protect people from things they didn't realize existed. No amount of wishing would change that, and she'd discovered that she didn't want to change who and what she was. Not anymore.

Besides, she wasn't even sure she wanted Jax to love her. He'd watched his wife die because of her job. He certainly wouldn't give his heart to a woman who could end up the same, and he definitely wouldn't want to love a woman who could die from supernatural means.

She debated talking to him about that, the full story of the Legacy. He deserved to know that it was about more than her dreaming about a serial killer. How could she, when she hadn't even told him about the transference spell she'd cast with her sisters, hadn't told him about staying awake?

The Legacy stood between them like an elephant they pretended wasn't there. No one could be that blasé about witnessing the wilding of her abilities. Her own family seemed off-balanced by what they'd witnessed in her kitchen the day Gertie Bruce died. Yet Jax had seemed to take it and her dream-assault in stride. Why?

His case.

Sudden wrenching had her dropping her toothbrush in the sink. Of course. He'd been angry about her staying awake not only for her benefit, but also because it kept them in the dark about Corcoran. Jax had told her early on that he would do anything to solve his cases. What if that included pretending to accept her and her gifts? What if everything they'd done together had been nothing more than a means to an end?

"No." She gripped the edge of the sink. Jax wouldn't do that to her. He'd told her that wasn't the reason. He wouldn't have brought her to his house, to his bed, just because of the case.

He would, if it meant he could keep an eye on her. She didn't leave the house without him or Mala. And she had a sneaking suspicion that someone else followed her and her sisters, reporting back to Jax their every move. She was a material witness, after all. Staying with him was nothing more than extreme protective custody. A gilded cage was still a prison to the person inside it.

He hadn't said the words. She had to remember that. She'd made love to him, had shown him and told him how she felt about him, but he hadn't given the words back. Maybe so that he wouldn't lie. In everything he'd done, he'd been honest, even if he hadn't always been forthcoming. Maybe he hadn't told her he loved her because he simply didn't.

She showered and dressed, trying to decide if she should pack her things. There were many reasons to go, only a few to stay. The latter reasons wrapped around her heart like chain links. She didn't want to leave Jax, her only tether to the sublimely normal. What she wanted, however, had to stand aside for the greater good. That lesson got branded into the mind of every Keeper and First Daughter at an early age. Their lives had always been about either, never both.

Jax sat at his kitchen table, a cup of coffee in his hands. He didn't look happy.

Automatically Nicole headed for the coffee pot, only to find it empty and the carafe sitting in the sink. She turned towards the refrigerator instead, looking for orange juice. "Good morning."

"What did you do to me?"

The bluntness of Jax's voice had her turning from the fridge. "Excuse me?"

His shoulders hunched, as if the mug was a fire warming him on a cold day. "I want to know what the hell you did to me."

Surprised by the anger in his tone, she shut the refrigerator door, facing him fully. "I don't know what you're talking about."

"Last night, when we—were outside, you did something to me." He turned, and Nicole could see the anger in him.

Her heart froze in her chest. "I didn't do anything to you, Jax. I did something *with* you."

"The hell you didn't!" He stood up so abruptly his chair fell over. "I know you did something. Something seeped into my blood and moved through my veins! I still feel it."

She probably should have been afraid. But she was too tired, too bruised, too *everything*, to deal with whatever rode Jax. She had enough on her plate already.

"You think I worked magic on you." She pushed away from the counter, her voice hardening. "What happened last night was so real, so pure, of course it had to be a trick. If it wasn't, if it was real, then you'd have to start thinking about me as a person, not as part of your goddamn case."

"I already think about you as a person!" His voice dropped to a snarl. "Every goddamn moment of every goddamn day I'm thinking about you when I should be thinking about my job. I'm thinking about how it feels to hold you, to hear you laugh, to have you beside me in my bed. I'm thinking about those soft little noises you make just before you cum. I'm thinking about you so much I can't do my fucking job. Being distracted like this could get me killed!"

"So it's my fault? I'm controlling your thoughts now?"

"How the hell am I supposed to know?" he thundered. "You don't even know everything you can do."

Anger made her ears burn. "Oh, like it couldn't be that you think about me all the time because you love me?"

"Love you?" He laughed. He actually laughed. "With all of the crazy crap you've got going on? What makes you think I'd fall in love with you?"

Pain blossomed in Nicole's stomach, as real as if he'd punched her. This couldn't be happening. Not now. Not Jax.

His hands clenched into fists. "This whole thing has been a freak show since day one. I'll put up with a whole lot to solve my case, but I'll be damned if I'll let you turn me into a freak!"

Shame burned her cheeks as despair lanced her heart. She'd known. She'd known all along that he couldn't, wouldn't accept her, and she'd given all of herself to him anyway.

Pain, real and voracious, jabbed at her and stole her breath. Leaning against the fridge, she clutched at her chest, trying to keep her heart from shattering. The dishes in the sink clattered violently, and she struggled for calm, for words. They ground out of her. "I. Am not. A freak."

"Oh yeah?" Belligerence rolled off him as he stalked towards her. "I don't know anybody else who wakes up bruised from a dream. Not anybody normal, anyway."

"I am normal!"

He laughed. "Are you kidding me? Nothing about you is normal. Once this case is over, I'm getting as far away from you and your freaky family as I can."

She clapped her hands over her ears and closed her eyes, wanting to block his betrayal with all her senses. "I. Am not. A freak!"

The words screamed from her throat. The kitchen exploded. She heard water burst from the tap, the fridge opening and disgorging its contents. Silverware rattled behind her, then whistled past her. She thought she heard Jax yelling, indistinct over the sound of blood rushing in her ears. Finally, silence.

She opened her eyes.

The kitchen lay in ruins. In the center of the floor, surrounded by broken dishes and crumpled pots, lay Jax. A butcher's knife split the center of his chest. He stared up at her, his eyes wide with horror, as the last breath left his body.

Screams ripped from her throat. She was still screaming when she woke up.

Jax rubbed wearily at his eyes. He caught himself reaching for his coffee mug, then stopped. He didn't think he'd be able to touch the stuff again without thinking about Nicole.

Nicole. Everything always came back to her. His job, his life, his future—everything he was began and ended with her.

Even his failure.

He couldn't help her. He'd realized that early in the morning, watching her sleep. If she didn't move or say anything in her sleep, how would he even know if she dreamed? How would he know in time to wake her up, to keep her from being bruised? He'd been lying right beside her, and she'd almost died. What good was he to her if he couldn't even keep her safe while she slept?

Across from him, Bear pushed away from his desk. "Let's grab something to eat."

Jax shook his head. "I need to go over the interview notes of Corcoran's neighbors. I'm sure I missed something."

"I wasn't asking." Bear rose to his feet, pointed at the exit. "Walk."

Pissed, Jax gathered his papers and pushed to his feet. "Fine. I need some air anyway."

He followed his partner out of the precinct to the parking lot. It didn't matter that they'd both been on the job since seven, acting on a tip that had them hours behind their suspect. It didn't matter that they had uniforms on Nicole and the other women who'd been in Corcoran's workshop, and that all of them had checked in. Jax felt time slipping away. Things had been quiet for two long. More than a week between victims was out of the pattern. Corcoran would act soon; it was just a matter of determining if Nicole or someone else would be the target.

Bear got behind the wheel. "Man, what is it with you today?"

"Do you really have to ask me that?"

"Hey, I know you're an ass when we're deep into a case and the clock's ticking," Bear said, starting the engine. "Been there, done that. Something else is going on."

"Nothing's going on."

"Bullshit," Bear said pleasantly, driving out of the lot, heading east. "You ready to talk, or do I have to beat it out of you?"

Jax snorted. "Like you could." The idea had its appeal. Taking his frustrations out on his partner would be better than smashing his model car collection.

"Uh-huh. So, when did you figure it out?"

"Figure what out?"

Bear shot him a look. "That you're in love with her."

Jax felt his chest tighten. "I'm not in love with her."

"You fell for her the first day she strolled into the precinct," Bear pointed out. "She's the first person you've had in your house in three years. You bite the head off anyone who says one word wrong about her. And you're treating this case like it could make or break your career."

"This case could make or break our careers," Jax pointed out. "Or did you forget the chief, the mayor, and Washboard Walsh breathing down our necks?"

Bear turned onto Moreland, heading for Little Five Points. "I didn't forget. I also haven't forgotten how you've bent every witness and suspect rule there is when it comes to Nicole Legère, how you peel out every time we're done for the day, just so you can hurry home to her."

"To touch bases about the case, see if she's come up with anything." It was a weak protest, and Jax knew it. He'd arrested people with better stories.

"Fine. Then maybe she should move in with me."

Jax folded his arms, refusing to rise to the bait. "Go ahead, ask her."

Bear scratched his jaw. "Of course, there's only one bed. Not a problem, though. Man, I bet hitting that is sweet."

Jax growled before he could stop himself. "Try it and die."

"Yep." Bear slowed at the giant skull entrance for the Vortex Bar and Grill, then pulled into the restaurant's parking lot. "You obviously don't care at all."

"She told me she loves me."

Bear jammed on the brake. "She told you what? When?"

"Last night. I don't think she meant it though. She was geeked up on caffeine pills and sleep deprivation at the time. Then I picked a fight and she flipped out so I put her in the guestroom. She was still sleeping it off when I left this morning."

"Jesus." His partner just stared at him. "Did you say anything to her, or you just let her believe you don't want her?"

"I do want her. That's the goddamn problem." Angry again, he slammed his way out of the car, but it didn't make him feel any better. He waited until Bear joined him before adding, "I can't focus on work without thinking about her. And when I get home and she's there, it feels right."

"And that makes it wrong?"

"I can't protect her." The admission burned in his throat. "She could have died from that last dream."

"So you decided to walk away?"

Jax hunched his shoulders, uncomfortable with unloading on his partner. "I have to. If I stay with her, if I can't help her because I'm just an ordinary guy . . . I couldn't deal with that, Bear."

"So you leave her with no one?" Bear shook his head. "You're right. You should walk away."

"Dammit! I'll send her home. She'll be with her family. All we've got to do is catch this creep and she'll be safe."

"Maybe. What about the next guy, and the one after that? How do you know catching Corcoran will be the end of it?"

"Dammit." He didn't know, and it tore him up inside. The bottom line was, he definitely couldn't protect Nicole if he wasn't there. God only knew what Nicole had thought when she woke up.

Jax hunched his shoulders again, but he couldn't shake his discomfort. He'd chalked it up to what had happened with Nicole, but now he had his doubts.

He pushed off the car, pulled his cell phone from his pocket. No answer at his house. No answer with Nicole's mobile. "Let's go."

Bear already had his door open. "Maybe she's just mad."

"Maybe." Jax got back into the car. He didn't think so.

Chapter Twenty-seven

Nicole paused on the sidewalk, waiting for the taxi to drive away. It had been surprisingly easy to spot the officer waiting two doors down from Jax's house, just as it had been easy to cut through the backyard and hook up with her taxi half a block away.

She supposed she should have called Mala and Malita, but she couldn't face them yet. They'd parted on such a high, she wasn't ready to tell them things were different.

Jax didn't want her. Waking from the dream had been bad enough. Waking to find herself in the guest bedroom, exactly as she'd dreamed, had sent chills through her. She'd been relieved to find that Jax had already gone. She'd found a terse note from him in the kitchen, saying he'd check in with her later. The caffeine pills that had scattered across the floor the night before had been gone. So had the percolator and anything remotely resembling caffeine.

Point taken, loud and clear.

Instead of taking the walkway to her house, she turned towards Miss Gertie's instead. Her life here was over, in this house and in this town. Whether she wanted it to or not, her life had changed. If she'd harbored any doubts, any hesitations that it was time to let go and move on, the dream was there to remind her.

Jax. It hurt to think about him, but she couldn't seem to stop. What she felt for Jax thrummed through her painfully, making her feelings for Randall seem like nothing more than a schoolgirl crush.

The night before, under the stars and moonlight, and magic, she'd given him everything within her, everything she was. The dream had showed her the stupidity of doing that, and it'd broken her heart. She'd embraced her abilities, so she couldn't discount the dream she'd had. It still horrified her. If she stayed, they would fight, he'd say those horrible things to her. If she stayed, he'd hurt her, but she'd kill him. She couldn't run the risk of seeing him again, couldn't run the risk of feeling the pain and anger so deeply that it made her lash out.

Her time with Jax had ended, just as she'd feared it would. She knew he'd cared for her, as well as he was able, but the psychologist in her believed that he'd crossed his concern for her with his failure to protect his late wife. She'd compromised once with her heart; she wouldn't do it again.

Unlocking Gertie's front door, Nicole took a deep breath, then stepped inside. No one had been in the house since the afternoon of Gertie's funeral, when neighbors and well-wishers with casseroles had attempted to blend with the police hoping that Corcoran would put in an appearance.

Nicole spent a few precious minutes watering the profusion of plants that occupied every inch of Miss Gertie's home. Given her dreams of Corcoran, it was hard to walk among the ivy and other vines, to be purposefully gentle with a large potted ficus. These were Miss Gertie's plants, though, and they'd thrived under her nurturing care. Nicole knew they wouldn't hurt her.

She blinked back sudden tears. She missed the old woman and her old dog, missed the tea and muffins, missed the nosy concern.

"I'll make sure your death wasn't in vain, Miss Gertie," she said aloud. "But I need your help."

She'd face Corcoran, and she'd stop him. She had more than the dagger and hours of practice in her arsenal. The circle she'd cast with her sisters had given her more than Mala's ability; she'd also received Malita's spellcraft. She'd spent the day before, before Jax returned home, working on managing both Mala's skills and Malita's. Even now she had several spells ready to spring, to trap Corcoran on the dream plane.

Opening her leather commuter bag, she went to work, pouring a semi-circle of salt around Miss Gertie's favorite chair. Then she extracted a white candle and incense, lighting both. She stepped into the circle, closed it, then anchored it with a large chunk of clear quartz, to boost the energy.

Settling into the armchair, Nicole closed her eyes, drawing in a deep, steadying breath. She exhaled, pushing out heartbreak and uncertainty. Then she wrapped her fingers around the Legacy pendant and reached for the magic, breathing it in until it filled every corner of her body. Focusing her will, she concentrated on separating herself from reality.

Silence descended, the absolute absence of sound. She opened her eyes to a world gone gray. No, not entirely devoid of color. Miss Gertie's plants seemed to have a pale green sheen of energy around them. A similar shield, blue-white, surrounded her.

She'd entered the dream.

She swallowed an elated laugh, overjoyed at achieving what she'd only hoped was possible. Entering the state of dreams while awake was akin to meditation, only she had more mental control. She could only hope that it would be enough to defeat Corcoran.

If it became too much, if it seemed that she'd lose, she'd make sure he didn't get her ability. As a last resort, she'd prepared another, darker spell that would take Corcoran out once and for all. Unfortunately, she'd go with him.

It was a chance she had to take. Danielle was safe with her mother and father. After Nicole had contacted them, related the attack, they'd decided to move to one of the family compounds in Seattle. Her brothers weren't threatened; since Corcoran hadn't mentioned them, Nicole assumed he didn't know they had inherited the Legacy. Mala and Malita would pick up the pieces here, then join their parents and Dani. Jax—

No. Shaking her head in denial, she pushed to her feet. She wouldn't think about him. She couldn't. She could, however, use the anger she felt. And she felt a lot of anger.

"James William Corcoran," she called, deliberately using his full name. It would get his attention. "You want me, come and get me, you rat bastard."

She sent the call out, rippling through the dream plane. If she'd guessed right in this, it would pull Corcoran into the dream, no matter where he was or what he was doing. If he was waiting for a train, his change at the store, or driving down the highway, he'd drop like a ton of bricks.

She kinda hoped it would be the latter.

He appeared faster than she'd expected, off balance and a little afraid. She was prepared, though. Focusing her will, she whipped looped vines around his body, intending to tie him up.

He recovered quickly, breaking free of the vines, spinning away. "Well done, Nicole, well done. Someone's been practicing. Thank you for getting stronger. It'll taste that much sweeter when I take your power."

She smiled at his bravado. She'd seen that moment of fear in his eyes, that moment of doubt. For a moment he'd believed that she could beat him. That belief gave her the power she needed.

"You know what? You talk too much," she retorted. "Shut up so I can kick your ass."

Gathering her will, she launched a spell, one meant to immobilize him. Black light spread like a shadow from her hands, spinning in a vortex around him. He ducked and rolled, coming to his feet faster than she'd thought possible.

He growled something she didn't understand. The dream version of Miss Gertie's house wavered, then morphed into a landscape of nightmares.

No. Ice filled Nicole's veins, distracting her. This couldn't be happening. She had to control the dream. If she didn't—

Pain slammed into her, driving her to her knees. Corcoran loomed over her. "Afraid yet? Let me help you out with that."

He dug his fingers into her hair, savagely yanking her head back. He lifted his right hand, and she watched in horror as his fingers lengthened into claws. She only had a moment to suck in a breath before those claws sank into her forehead.

She screamed, her very soul echoing a shriek of agony. Fighting nausea and growing blackness, Nicole buried her fingers into the earth. Roots burst from the ground, slamming into Corcoran. He screeched in anger and pain, staggering backward.

"You bitch!" Blood poured from his forehead. "I'll kill you for that!"

Vines, spiked with thorns thicker than her thumb, slithered across the bare ground, racing towards her.

Bear pulled up to Nicki's house just as Mala dropped the kickstand on her bike. Jax jumped out of the car as Mala swung off the motorcycle and pulled her helmet off her head in a quick fluid motion. The look in her eyes was hard as she stared at him.

"You let her leave?"

"I didn't 'let' her do anything. She skipped out of the house, avoiding surveillance. I came here to get her back." Kicking and screaming if he had to. He was not going to lose her.

Mala scanned the house. "Something's wrong," she said, her voice flat as she snatched off her gloves. "Someone's there with her."

His heart seized up. "Bear, call for back up," he said, reaching for his gun. If Corcoran was in there, if he hurt her . . . .

"Jax. Stand down."

"Like hell." Jax knew in his gut that time was slipping away, time Nicole needed. He headed up the walk.

"Not there." Mala gestured next door. "She's in the neighbor's house. And the only way you're stopping me is if you drop me."

Bear threw up his hands, then reached for his gun. "Fine. If we're going out, we might as well go out in style. I'll take the back."

Jax shadowed Mala. "Go knock on the door, get them to open up. Hopefully we can do this easy."

"And if what she's facing doesn't recognize your authority?"

Jax had no idea what that meant, but said the first thing that came to mind. "Then we distract him long enough for one of us to mow the bastard down and save your sister."

Mala's lips peeled back from her teeth. "I like you, Detective Jackson. Hopefully my sister will live long enough to make you part of the family."

Gun drawn, and with every instinct in him screaming that he kick down the door and start shooting, Jax approached the front door. Get inside, get inside, his heart yelled, while his training made him check the windows before passing in front of them. Mala moved ahead of him with deadly intent, pausing at the front door, her hand poised on the knob. She looked at him in silent question.

Holding his breath, he nodded. She tried the doorknob.

It turned. Nothing, no one. No sound. Even he could feel the wrongness, and his fragile control stretched tight. Entering the foyer, he caught a full view of the hallway, packed with growing things.

A sound came from the living room, sounds of a struggle, followed by a scream.

Nicole!

His heart in his throat, Jax sprinted down the hallway, Mala on his heels. He had a second to register Corcoran standing alone, before the man lurched towards a recliner.

Memories of her dream assault spiked through Nicole's mind. Screaming in denial, she wrapped her fingers around the dark pendant as the vine ropes clawed up her body, around her throat. Rage filled her, spilling through the magic, through her blood. The nightmare landscape shuddered, the air thickened.

In a burst of golden light, the vines fell away. Incensed, Corcoran reached for her, a spiked rope appearing in his hands. She staggered under his weight as the cord looped around her neck. Struggling to stay upright, she slipped her free hand beneath the spikes, ignoring the pain that lanced her fingers as the cord coiled tighter. She looked into his eyes, felt the hunger and the rage and the emptiness. In that moment, with blackness speckling the edges of her vision, she knew how to stop him.

You want the Legères' power? Try this.

She mentally threw open the floodgates, sending a wall of raw power into Corcoran. He screamed again, jerking away from her. She slumped into the recliner but didn't stop, kept drowning Corcoran in her power, the power of every Keeper. As she had in Malita's house, she could feel them, feel their essence as they gathered with her, lent their energy to her.

A thunderous boom filled the room. She watched Corcoran stiffen, a small hole appearing like magic in the center of his forehead just before blood blossomed. His expression froze into one of complete surprise. With a small, sad gurgle, he slumped to the floor.

Nicole's fingers fell away from the pendant. Immediately the flow of power broke, recoiling back into her as the dream world fell away. Pain exploded in her head as she opened her mouth to scream. No sound came out. The black speckles at the edge of her consciousness grew, overwhelming her as she did the only thing she could do.

She let go.

Gun steady, Jax approached and got his first look at the late James William Corcoran. Dark eyes stared sightlessly up at Jax in an expression of absolute horror. He'd died pissing himself.

"Serves you right, you son-of-a-bitch," Jax muttered in satisfaction as he got to his feet, sheathing his weapon.

"Nicki!"

The emotion in Mala's cry sent Jax spinning around, reaching for his weapon again. He saw Mala kneeling beside a recliner, blocking his view. She looked up at him, her expression stopping his heart.

He collapsed beside them. Nicole lay still in the chair, her right hand tangled in a braided, spiked rope wrapped around her neck. Her hand, throat, and face were bruised and bloodied, her eyes open and unblinking. His fingers reached past the ugly, barbaric weapon to touch the violently marred skin at her throat, hoping, praying he would find a pulse.

Nothing.

No. Oh, God, Nicki, please no.

"Help me do CPR," he ordered Mala as he carefully lifted Nicole's limp form off the chair, trying not to think, trying not to feel the anguish and the blame of being too late, minutes too late, yet again.

"I can't!" Mala wailed in anguish. "If I touch her while she's like this, I could kill her."

"Go get Bear. Have him call 9-1-1. Tell them we need paramedics out here now." He turned back to Nicole, trying to swallow his fear, his horror. Her hand had slipped, pulling the spiked rope away from her skin. Blood welled from the shallow puncture wounds. He yanked his jacket off to fold into a compress, but couldn't bring himself to press it against her throat.

Instead, he cupped his hands together to begin CPR. "Don't do this, Nicki," he said in rhythm to the compressions, pushing out everything but the need to save her. "Don't do this."

He blew air into Nicole's mouth, hoping enough of it got through the swollen tissue of her throat. Recriminations hammered him as doggedly as he pressed her chest. He should have been here. If he hadn't left her alone, if he hadn't picked a fight and refused to say the words, she wouldn't be lying broken, clinging to life.

He'd promised that he would be with her, he'd promised to protect her. Instead he'd broken both promises.

"Come on, Nicki," he begged. "Don't leave. I know it hurts, but you can't go. Not like this. Not before I can say I'm sorry. Please, baby, don't die."

No, he couldn't think like that. Nicole was a strong woman, the strongest woman he'd known besides his grandmother. She would survive. She had to survive.

"Dammit, Nicki," he said, his voice at turns demanding, coaxing, begging. "Think about your life here. Think about your family, your daughter. Don't let this bastard win by taking you with him. Come on back, Nicki."

Mala reappeared, gloves back on, with a handful of towels. "Don't stop," she ordered, her voice shaking as she draped a folded towel over Nicole's neck. "Your partner's calling for help. I called my parents. Dani doesn't know how bad it is. You know what that means, don't you? Danielle doesn't know."

He knew. If Danielle hadn't seen a vision of her mother, it meant Nicole was trying to hang on. Hope flooded his veins, giving him the energy to continue.

"I'll help you, Nicki," he swore, breathing for her. "I swear to God, I'll do whatever it takes."

A gasp had him straightening, darting a quick glance to Mala. She wasn't looking at him, but at Nicki. With his heart thudding in his chest, he leaned over Nicole, his fingers framing her face.

His eyes widened as he felt her breath, lighter than a feather, brush his cheek. For just a moment, he swore that awareness brightened her eyes. In the space of a heartbeat, she seemed to see him, and a single tear rolled down her cheek. He could swear that she'd whispered one word, "Sorry." Then her eyes slid shut.

"No!"

Paramedics burst into the entryway, thundered down the hall. He all but snarled at one who tried to push him out of the way. Irrationally he felt that his touch, his voice, was all that kept her here, kept her grounded. If he wasn't there beside her, talking to her, how could she find her way back?

A heavy hand clapped onto his shoulder. "Jax," his partner said. "They know what they're doing. Let them work."

"Don't stop," he ordered them, his voice breaking as he let his partner pull him away. "Don't you dare stop."

The paramedics worked quickly and efficiently, putting something down her throat, bracing her, doing everything they could to keep her breathing, to keep her here.

Jax stared up at Bear. "I was too late," he said fiercely, daring his partner to disagree. "I should have been here."

"Maybe," Bear said. "But maybe worse would have happened if you hadn't listened to your instincts when you did."

"Worse?" Jax balled his hands into fists, watching as the paramedics loaded Nicole onto a gurney. "What could be worse than this?"

"Watching them load her into a bodybag."

Something inside Jax shuddered, then broke. He sank to his knees, finding it difficult to catch his breath. Maybe he was having a heart attack. It would serve him right. Hurting more than he ever thought possible, he looked up at his partner. "If Nicole doesn't make it, if she d-dies—"

"Hey man." Bear caught him around the shoulders. "Don't even go there. You can't think like that. Not if you want to help her."

"Help her?" Jax staggered to his feet. "All I've done is hurt her, taken her from one dangerous situation to the next. I forced her into a collision course with this guy and didn't do a damn thing to protect her."

He made it to the doorway, watching the EMTs load the gurney into the ambulance. Mala stood beside the door, waiting to climb in beside her sister. She turned to look at him, and he wondered how he'd ever thought of her as cold and uncaring.

"Jax?" Bear reached out to touch his shoulder.

"Don't." He held up a hand, to ward off the touch, the pity, the inevitable. It was happening again, and he knew it. He'd been late, too late, again. If he'd been five minutes, ten minutes, even two minutes earlier, things might have been different. Nicole would be unhurt, not struggling for her next breath.

Bear held out his hand. "Give it to me."

Jax didn't pretend to misunderstand. "No."

His partner sighed. "Detective Jackson, you shot a suspect. You need to relinquish your weapon."

"Fine." Jax drew his gun, popped the clip out before reholstering it. He pulled the holster off his belt, handing it and the gun to his partner, then the clip.

Both knew it was only a symbolic gesture. Jax had a personal firearm at home, if it came to that.

He turned to Corcoran's body. Despite his heartache, he felt a small sense of satisfaction. Nicole had done what no one else had been able to do. She'd stopped Corcoran.

Jax knelt beside the body. "I hope you rot in hell," he whispered, "but you're not taking Nicole with you. Not if I can do anything about it."

Chapter Twenty-eight

Jax walked down the hall to the ICU waiting room, weary, worried, wrapped tight. It had been two days since Nicole had been admitted, two days since he'd found her nearly lifeless body. Two gut-wrenching long days of filing reports, closing the case, and having his actions reviewed.

It had nearly driven him crazy to be apart from Nicole, to have to put his duty as a cop ahead of his duty to her. She'd needed him, he'd known that in his soul. She'd needed him, and he wasn't with her.

He'd correct that mistake, if he got the chance. He'd taken leave, not reassignment to a desk, not vacation time, but indefinite leave. He didn't know when or if he'd go back, and at that moment he didn't care. Nicole needed him, and he'd be at her bedside every day

Malita and Mala sat just inside the door of the waiting area, Danielle stretched out asleep on a chair between them. For a moment he couldn't tell the twins apart, as they both wore identical faded jeans and bohemian blouses. Two men, slightly older and also identical, stood protectively with them.

All four turned as he drew near. None of them looked welcoming. He didn't blame them, and braced himself as he asked, "How is she doing?"

"Why should we tell you?" one of the men asked. "It's your fault she's here!"

"I know that," Jax said with an evenness he didn't feel.

"Derek, stop." The soft voice belonged to Malita. "Can't you see he's hurting as much as we are?"

"Good," he snapped. "He should hurt. He should really hurt."

"If busting my chops will make you feel better, go ahead," Jax said, allowing the need for violence to sweep over him before reining it back in. "Trust me, I've been doing this for the past three days. But it doesn't do your parents or Nicole any good."

The first man gave Jax a smile that held little in the way of humor or friendliness. "She dies, we come after you."

"Then you have to come after me too, Derek," Mala said, climbing to her stilettoed feet. Her eyes retained the bleak look Jax had seen three days ago. "Mom sent me here to protect her, and I didn't do it."

"That's enough."

The sound of their father's voice had an instant effect on the siblings. Jax had a mental image of attack dogs being brought to heel. He turned as Stefan Antonescu entered the waiting room. Lines had been carved into his face over the past few days, lines that wouldn't be there if Jax had done his job properly.

No, not his job. His duty. To her.

"Dad, is there any change?" Darien, the quiet one, asked after Dr. Antonescu performed cursory introductions.

"No," their father said heavily. "I'd like to think that you and Malita helped, Darien, but there's still no sign that she hears us."

There was more. Jax could see it in the older man's eyes. So could Malita. She took a step closer to her father. "What is it, Dad?" she asked, her voice trembling.

Stefan looked at each of them through red-rimmed eyes. "The doctors say that if— " he cleared his throat— "*when* she awakens, she may not be able to speak, and there's a possibility of brain damage and paralysis."

The words kicked Jax solidly in the gut, almost unhinging his knees. Nicole's life hung in precarious balance, and even if she recovered, her quality of life could be irrevocably changed. *Nicki, oh, God, Nicki. I'm so sorry.*

"Detective Jackson." Darien Antonescu laid a hand on his shoulder, an understanding expression on his face. Jax shook it off, not wanting or needing sympathy, or worse, pity.

"I want to see her." His voice rasped from his chest, barely making it past the pain. "I need to see her."

"Of course." Stefan turned, and Jax fell into step beside him, fighting to keep himself under control. One question burned inside him, burned so hotly he couldn't contain it.

"Why?" Jax managed to ask through pain. "Why did she think that she had to face Corcoran alone? She knew how dangerous it would be, but she did it anyway. Why would she do that? Why would she leave?"

"She probably thought she was protecting you," Antonescu said, pausing at the ICU door. "The work she's done with you is just a small part of what's expected of her. Eventually she'll have to return to Louisiana to learn from her mother, and her daughter will follow in her footsteps. That's a lot to ask anyone to accept."

"You accepted it."

"I did." Antonescu looked through the blinds covering the door. "But I'd already conducted extensive research on the paranormal before I met Arielle. So when she told me about the work her family has done through the centuries, it was an easy decision for me. I realized I wanted her cause to be my cause. I love her, and rather than asking her to share my world, I asked if I could share hers."

"I know there's more going on, stuff outside of the law. But she could have told me. She could have given me a chance to make a choice."

"Fear is a powerful thing, Carter Jackson," the professor said. "So is rejection. Nicole has already experienced that from one man because of the Legacy, and I know she didn't feel for him one tenth of what she feels for you."

She loved him. Nicole's father couldn't know what had transpired between them out under the stars, so maybe Nicole had told her parents how she felt about him. They knew and he hadn't believed. He hadn't believed and she'd left him.

With those words lingering in his mind and heart, Jax entered the private hospital room. A jungle of flowers greeted him. He could hear soft classical music overlaying the beeps and blips of hospital equipment.

Arielle Legère sat beside the hospital bed, her voice just audible. Nicole lay unmoving, bandages about her neck and face, bandages that covered bruises and a near-fatal wound that Jax knew he would see for the rest of his life.

Arielle looked up as he stepped closer. "I can't reach her," she said in a broken voice. "I know she's in a dark place, and I can feel her pain, but I can't help her. All my power and I can do nothing." A sob tore from her. "My poor baby, my poor little girl."

"Ari, come away for a little while," Stefan said, putting an arm around his wife's shoulders. "You need to rest, to get something to eat—"

"I have to stay here. I have to help her."

"You can't help her if you collapse. As a Keeper and a parent, you must be strong, chèrie."

"I'll sit with her, ma'am," Jax said.

Arielle raised her eyes to his, and Jax saw a world of pain in those dark depths. "Talk to her, Detective, please. There's a connection between you and my daughter. I know Nicolette loves you. Perhaps you can find a way to her, perhaps you can bring her back to us."

Jax felt a moment's panic at the thought of failing Arielle Legère. Of failing Nicole again. "You know I'll do anything to help Nicki," he said. "But I don't have the power that you and your family have."

"But you love her," Stefan pointed out.

"Yes sir, I do. She's—she's everything. But I didn't get the chance to tell her." He hung his head. "I didn't have the guts to tell her."

"Then you must tell her now," Arielle said. "Perhaps she will hear and come back to you. I know for a fact that nothing is more powerful than love."

She allowed her husband to pull her to her feet, her hand lingering on her daughter's. "Rest easy, chèrie," she whispered, bending to kiss Nicole's forehead. "Detective Jackson is here, and we won't be far."

She turned to him then, lifting her arms to hug him. Shocked, it took Jax a moment to reciprocate. "Thank you, Detective, for caring for our daughter and looking out for her. We're extremely grateful."

"Don't thank me," he said, his voice harsher than he intended. "If it weren't for me, Nicole wouldn't be here."

"You're right," Stefan said. "If it weren't for you, our child would be lost to us. So thank you, for everything you've done for Nicolette."

Not knowing what to say in response, Jax nodded. As Stefan led his wife out of the room, Jax took the chair Arielle had vacated.

He didn't deserve her parents' gratitude. He should have gotten condemnation, not thanks.

He lifted Nicole's hand with trembling fingers, careful of the IV patched into the smooth skin, trying hard not to stare at the tube stuck in her trachea. "I'm sorry, Nicki," he whispered, pressing his lips against her fingers. "I'm sorry I wasn't there for you. I'm sorry I couldn't stop him from hurting you."

Rage and guilt and sorrow welled within him in a volatile mix, forcing him to close his eyes against it. "I know I haven't been the best with you, Nicki. God knows there're more reasons for you to stay away from me than be with me. But I want to make up for that. Just give me a chance, baby, that's all I'm asking for. Give us a chance."

He had no idea how long he sat there with his eyes closed, holding her hand, silently willing Nicole to come back to him. But the exhaustion of the last few days caught up to him, pulling him down into the depths of sleep.

He dreamed.

Chapter Twenty-nine

Jax stood in the center of an expanse of . . . nothing. Whiteness surrounded him, so complete that he couldn't see where the walls met the ceiling or the floor. He wasn't even sure there was a ceiling or anything else.

Vertigo curled through him. He knew he stood on something solid, but he didn't dare start tap-dancing to prove the point. Silence hung thick with an undercurrent of expectancy that made the hairs on the back of his neck stand on end.

"Where the hell am I?"

"Not quite."

Jax spun, instinctively reaching for his weapon. A small dark woman stood before him. She wore a one-shouldered dress of bright yellow mixed with black and white geometric patterns that left her right breast exposed. Several bracelets graced her arms and ankles. A brightly hued beaded collar wrapped the slender column of her neck, with a smaller complementary band circling her forehead. She grasped a spear in one strong hand. Surprisingly, a lioness stood beside her.

"Who are you?"

The dark woman smiled, brilliant ivory against her dark features. "I am the First," she replied, her voice old and young simultaneously. "The one who came before."

Jax put his hands to his head, trying to clear it. This couldn't be happening, but it was. "You're Anika. You're the one who started the Legacy."

"I am she," the woman said with a short bob of her head.

Whoa. Jax felt the floor shift beneath his feet. "Wh-what is this place?"

"This is nowhere and everywhere," Anika replied. "Sometime and no time. A place that is but is not, and will never be."

Jax clutched his head again. "Can you not speak in riddles? My head hurts enough as it is."

The woman laughed. "Of course. I only spoke that way because you expected it. It gets burdensome at times."

She spread her arms wide, the gesture encompassing the area around them. "You can call this limbo, though some people might consider it heaven. Or even hell. Think of it as something like a universal waiting room, or an eternal holding cell, to put it in police terms."

A cold chill slid like melting ice down Jax's back. "Am I dead, then? Is Nicole dead?"

"No. Not yet."

"What do you mean, not yet?"

The woman narrowed her eyes at him. "Are you always this slow?"

Jax felt his hands curl into fists, a stupid gesture that wouldn't do him any good. He forced himself to be polite. "Where is she?"

"She's here and not here, on the bridge between two worlds."

Jax frowned. "You agreed to cut the bull."

Anika lifted her spear, her eyes taking on a dangerous glint. "And I suppose you think the Guardians of Light bent time and space just so you and I can talk about the weather?"

"I'm a detective," he said by way of apology. "Gathering information is what I do."

"All right, I won't skewer you for it, though I've got to wonder why she loves you so." Anika settled her spear again, and Jax wondered if he'd truly had a close call. Could you die in a place where you didn't exist?

"Nicole dragged Corcoran into the dream-world, to fight him there," Anika said, her voice direct. "Although Nicole had more power, Corcoran had more experience, and almost bested her. The only way she could hold him off long enough for you to kill him, was to funnel all her power into him."

"But that was what he wanted, wasn't it?"

"Basically, Nicole overloaded his circuits. That overload lashed back to her, and it left her scorched mentally and psychically."

"And that's why her family can't reach her." Jax nodded his understanding. "But I don't understand how this guy was able to do this."

Anika shook her head. "Nicole hasn't told you everything. I'm not sure that it's my place to."

Jax was quickly putting clues together. "Stefan Antonescu mentioned something about the work their family has done through the centuries. I'm guessing there's more to it than seeing the future."

"Yes. On a night full of stars, I dreamed. And in that dream one of the goddesses came to me. At least at the time I thought it was one of our people's gods. I learned a lot of things that night, Detective Jackson, about the importance of Balance in the universe. The messenger said that I had been chosen to serve the Ultimate Good in its eternal struggle to maintain that Balance. I and the daughters of my line would be given gifts to help us in our calling."

Anika rested her spear against her shoulder to fiddle with the bracelets on her arms. "I was told that it wouldn't be easy, that serving the Light would not be without sacrifice. But I already knew about strife. I knew pain and suffering. I'd already done what I could to relieve that among my people, but I always had a sense that there was more. So I said yes, knowing that would put me, and my daughters, on a path of hardship and heartache, where the needs of the many would always outweigh their own hopes and dreams. Knowing that I'd be pitting future generations against everything and everyone seeking to disrupt that Balance."

"Jesus." Jax felt the need to sit down. "Are you telling me that there are good and bad things out there, things not exactly human?"

"A little different from the myths and most accepted faiths, but yes, I suppose I am." She looked at him. "You've heard that saying that for every action there's an equal and opposite reaction? For everything we do to maintain the Balance, there are things trying to disrupt it."

"And Nicole and her family have been doing this—fighting these things—for centuries?"

"Yes."

Jax turned away from her, trying to assimilate everything Anika had told him. It was unbelievable, impossible. But hadn't he witnessed the unbelievable and impossible with his own eyes?

"So this guy," he began, turning back to face Anika—a woman who had been *dead* a couple hundred years. "This guy was one of these magic people? Is that how he was able to siphon off someone's psychic ability?"

"No, he was definitely human," Anika replied. "Nicole wouldn't have been able to stop him at her current strength otherwise. I think he might have made a pact with someone, who in essence made him a psychic vampire."

"So he was working for someone else," Jax said, his thoughts following the thread, coming to an obvious conclusion. "Someone who's going to miss the bastard now that he's on ice."

The look on Anika's face was answer enough. Someone would come looking for Corcoran, then for whoever had taken him out.

Someone would come looking for Nicole. Someone who made Corcoran look like a preschooler.

"I see that you understand," Anika said, her voice soft. "You now have a decision to make, Carter Jackson."

"I already made my decision," he said, his jaw tightening. "I'm not going to leave her. Whether that's in Atlanta or Louisiana or wherever here is, I'm going to be with her. Help me help her."

"Now I see why she loves you." The warrior-woman smiled, a slash of lips.

She rose to her toes, then planted a soft kiss to his forehead. Warmth spread through him, encompassing and powerful.

"My thanks and a gift to you." Anika stepped back, her features softened by golden light. "Take care of my children, Carter Jackson."

"I will."

"I believe you. You're a stubborn one. You're going to need that."

With a slight, regal nod, the matriarch of the Legère family turned and walked away, fading into the brightness.

Jax started to go after her, but something made him stop, turn around. Some sound, thought, hope.

She was here. He knew it suddenly and without doubt. Nicole was here somewhere, lost. "Nicki?"

The lightness dimmed slightly, and he could make out a slab of some kind not more than a dozen feet in front of him. Nicole lay atop it, wrapped in a white cloth embroidered with gold thread in what looked like African symbols.

"Nicki." He moved forward, wanting to be with her, wanting to wrap her in his arms and take her from this place.

Reaching her, he was surprised to find her eyes open. Cuffs circled her wrists and ankles, the attached chains embedded into the slab she lay on. The angry red marks remained around her neck, less horrifying here. The black stone her mother had given her nestled in the hollow of her throat. She neither moved nor reacted to his presence. To Jax, it didn't seem that she breathed.

Without thinking he reached for his gun, surprised to find it there and waiting. He aimed and fired, four quick, screaming shots that shattered the chains binding her. She didn't even flinch. He holstered his gun, then moved toward her, lifting her upper body into his arms.

"Come on, Nicki," he said, his voice swallowed by the stillness of the room. "Wake up. See me."

All at once she blinked, breath entering her lungs. Very slowly she turned her head, seeing him. "Jax?"

She hadn't spoken aloud, yet he heard her. He lowered his head and placed a gentle though shaky kiss to her forehead. "I'm here. I'm right here with you."

Pain filled her eyes. "No. This is still a dream."

"Then it's a dream we're both having," he told her. "I'm here to help you."

"Please." She closed her eyes, turned away. "No more."

"No more what?"

She grimaced. "I know. I know I can't have both. Please, please stop punishing me."

"Who's punishing you? Why?"

The whiteness around them flickered with shadows. Those shadows sharpened into images, fragments of Nicole's dreams.

"God, Nicki," Jax breathed. "Why are you doing this to yourself?"

She groaned. "De-deserve it."

"No, honey, no you don't. No one deserves this."

"I do," she whispered without sound. "I failed them."

"You didn't fail, Nicki. You stopped Corcoran. You saved yourself. I'm not leaving you here so that you can torture yourself!"

She turned her head away. "If I'd known more, been better at dreaming, they wouldn't be dead."

"Nicki, you don't know that for sure," Jax told her, his voice surprisingly gentle. "What if you were supposed to do exactly what you did? You received information and you passed it on to someone who was supposed to do something about it. You didn't fail those women. I did."

"No."

"Yes." His voice hardened. "Protect and serve, that's my job, remember? So if you want to blame someone, you're going to have to stop blaming yourself and blame me instead."

She shook her head, as if unable to believe him. He touched two fingers to her cheek, lightly tilting her chin so that she could see him. "You did your part, Nicki. You kept putting yourself out there, you kept trying to stretch your abilities. When push came to shove, you faced down Corcoran. I don't know how you did it, but you stopped him."

"I wanted to kill him."

"You did what you had to do," Jax said, brushing his lips against her forehead again. "Corcoran was trying to kill you. You slowed him down enough for me to kill him."

"But I lost the others. And I can't forgive myself for that."

"You aren't to blame for that. Just like you're not to blame for Randall's death. Just like I'm not to blame for Felecia. If you're going to blame yourself, you have to blame me too."

"I don't blame you for anything, Jax," she said, her voice soft. "You've already done more than any normal person would. Every time you tried to accept what I was doing, something else freaky would happen."

"You should blame me," he said, his voice brutal with recrimination. "I didn't believe you in the beginning. I kept pushing you. I pushed you to confront Corcoran. I didn't say anything when you told me you loved me. Instead I got so angry about the caffeine that I picked a fight. Is that why you left? Because I didn't tell you I love you?"

She had to swallow before she could speak. "Why would you tell me, when I know you don't love me?"

He was silent, just for a breath, for a heartbeat. Then came the words. "I do love you."

"You don't have to say that, Jax. I know you feel responsible, you feel protective. You probably even feel guilty. But you don't love me."

The white space around them darkened with images, and Jax recognized his kitchen. It took a moment to recognize himself because he couldn't believe the words he heard. They argued about the mind-blowing love they'd made, the magic they'd created. He watched himself verbally abusing Nicole, saying things that shocked him and wounded her. She denied his words, furious. Then the kitchen exploded with the force of her emotions, sending food and utensils flying. Finally, oh God, finally, he watched the butcher knife fly out of the block and into his chest.

The walls lightened again. Jax rubbed at his chest, his mind blank. She'd carried that with her as she'd left his house. That had smoldered inside her heart while she'd faced down Corcoran.

"You dreamed this."

She nodded, more tears glistening down her cheeks.

"So you thought this, this fight, was going to happen that day? That's why you left?"

Silence answered him. Undone, his body began to tremble. She'd left because she'd thought he was just using her as a means to an end. She'd left thinking he didn't care. She'd left thinking she would kill him if she stayed. She'd almost died, and *that* would have been her last memory of him.

"Nicki." He wrapped his arms around her, rocking her. "I'm sorry. I'm so sorry."

Tears bruised his eyes. How could she think anything different? She'd confessed that she loved him, and he hadn't believed it. She'd given herself to him and he'd taken without letting her know that she'd become as necessary to him as breathing.

He wanted to give her the words, but more than that, he wanted to give her the knowledge and the belief that he loved her. He wanted to show her that he didn't think she was a freak, that the dream wasn't a psychic warning, wasn't the truth.

He looked up, surprised to find that the void around them had changed, this time in tune with his thoughts. This was how he could show her. With nothing to lose, he opened himself, heart, mind, and soul.

"I love you, Nicki," he began softly. She jerked in his arms, but he cradled her and continued, sifting through memories to display as proof. "I wanted you all along, you know that. Then the want became need. I'd been living in emotional silence for more than three years, then you came along and shattered that silence."

Images of him jumping onto her porch to take her in his arms surrounded them. "That was the day it began to change. That day I found joy in the simple act of holding you, of having you welcome me with a smile and open arms . . . ." He faltered, then continued.

"You welcomed me. I still don't know why. You're smart, beautiful, sexy, and have more money than I could ever give you. I'm just a guy with a badge. I didn't want to love you because I convinced myself that it would never work. I didn't want to love you because I was afraid to lose you, because you'd leave or I'd fail to protect you. Then you gave me that night under the stars."

The walls darkened to stars, moonlight and fireflies. "You showed me true magic, the magic between a man and a woman," he told her, his voice husky. "I fell hard and fast and permanent. For you, Nicki. For your beauty, your grace, your courage and power. For everything that you are and will be."

He rocked her gently, willing her to understand, to forgive. "I didn't expect to hear the words from you. Why would you love me? All I've done is distrust you, harass you, try to arrest you, then set a serial killer after you. No wonder you thought I was using you."

He shook his head, more disgusted with himself than he'd ever been. "Then my worst fear came true. You left, and I failed to protect you. I followed you, and I was almost too late."

Fear snaked through him. He'd been so afraid of losing her that he'd lost her just the same. "Maybe I am too late, but I have to try. She said I had a choice, but it's really up to you. You can go back, or you can move on. If you go back, there's a chance that something worse than Corcoran will come after you. But you won't face it alone, Nicki. You'll have your family. And you'll have me. If you want me."

Her forehead wrinkled. "She who?"

"Anika."

She stared up at him in surprise. "Anika? You saw Anika?"

"Yeah, I think she's how I got here." He looked down at her, so happy to be holding her that he knew it couldn't be a dream. "She told me everything, everything that your family's been doing for centuries."

Her eyes widened. "You know?"

"Yeah." He looked away. "I understand why you didn't tell me. God knows I didn't give you any reason to trust me enough to tell me."

"I trust you, Jax. I was just scared to tell you."

"Don't be. I'm not going to run from this. I think it's an awesome responsibility. You need someone to watch your back, and I'm volunteering for the job. What do you say?"

For the longest time she stared up at him, searching for answers. What would he do if she didn't give him another chance?

Suddenly she smiled. "I say you're certainly qualified for the job. But it's a full-time position, and there might be overtime."

"I'm not afraid of long hours. I'm assuming there's growth potential, and a good retirement plan?"

"There are all sorts of perks. And I have it on good authority that the boss has a thing for you."

"That'll certainly help with performance reviews."

She laughed, her eyes bright. "I'd say you perform very well. You're hired. Let's go home."

"Yes, ma'am." Gathering her close, he rose, then paused. "Uhm, do you think you can dream up a door or something? I have no idea how to get out of here."

She entwined her arms around his neck. "As long as I'm with you, I can dream anything."

Epilogue

Smiling, Nicole closed her eyes, letting Martinique's warm, salty breeze bathe her face. Scarlet and purple streaked the sky as the sun sank on the horizon, but the bonfire provided plenty of light and warmth. It felt good, but not nearly as good as the arms wrapped around her.

"Hey, you're not falling asleep, are you?" Jax asked, resting his chin on her shoulder. "I ordered this sunset especially for you."

"You did, huh?" She leaned back against his chest. "You must have pulled some major strings."

"I called in a couple of favors," he said, gliding his hands up and down her arms. "You know I'd do anything for you."

"I know—you walked through my dreams, talked to my ancestor, moved to New Orleans—"

"Don't forget that I let your brothers plan my bachelor party. I figure that got me bonus points right there."

"They like you. Everyone in the family likes you. I was terrified of going back home, but you made it easy." She turned in his arms. "You gave me my life back, Jax."

"Hey, no more tears. Didn't we do enough blubbering through our vows? Derek ribbed me all the way through the reception for that."

She laughed as she remembered standing on the sweeping lawn in front of Beau-Rêve, four hundred of their friends and relatives gathered with them, as they cried and laughed their way through their nuptials. Their wedding had been two months to the day after she'd left the hospital, a month after they'd moved to Louisiana. Neither of them had wanted to wait longer than that.

It still amazed her how Jax had walked into her dream, freed her, helped her find her way back. He'd been beside her ever since, a steadying, loving influence. Jax's love and acceptance had made returning home, facing the relatives who'd doubted her so long, the celebration it was meant to be. With this man beside her, she knew she could face anything.

As the sky completed its transformation to night, she cupped his face in her hands, her heart swelling with love for him. "You don't have any regrets? Selling your house, leaving your job—everything you've done for me?"

"No." He gathered her close. "I'm looking forward to working with Mala on some of her more mundane cases while you're training with your mother. I've already heard from the chief of police in New Orleans, but joining the force there would be short term anyway. When your mother's ready to retire and you take over as Keeper, I want to be ready, too."

He pressed a soft kiss to her cheek. "In the meantime, I intend to spoil you and Dani rotten. And when our son is born, I'm going to spoil him too."

"You know?" she asked in surprise. "I was going to tell you over dessert. How did you know?"

"The night we made love under the stars was magical in more ways than one," he said. "Ever since then, I've been more, well, I guess you could say I've been more aware of things. Especially with you."

He was more than aware, she realized. She could sense the difference in him, a strong reserve of talent that could become stronger if he chose to exercise it. He seemed completely at ease with his burgeoning ability, though, accepting it the same way he'd accepted melding with her family.

"We can discuss all that back home," he said. "We've got one more night before your parents fly down with Dani. How do you want to spend it?"

She grinned, stretching out on the blanket. "It's a nice night, don't you think? We've got this private beach and moonlight and sparkling stars. It's almost magical."

He returned her grin as he covered her body with his own. "Maybe we can make some magic of our own."

"Why, Detective, I do believe you read my mind."

Group Discussion Questions:

Please explain the reasoning behind each of your answers.

1. Do you believe in psychic ability? Do you believe dreams can predict future events?

2. Do you think Nicole should have kept the true purpose of the Legacy from Jax? If so, why?

3. Should Nicole have involved her parents earlier? Why do you think she didn't?

4. If you could have a psychic power, which one would you want?

5. Would you keep your psychic ability secret or would you use it to help others?

6. Could Jax have been more accepting of Nicole's ability at first? Do you think he was too accepting?

7. Do you think someone/something else will target Nicole?

8. The villain in this story is a "psychic vampire" who steals telepathic abilities. Some psychologist use psychic vampires to describe people who emotionally drain others. Do you know anyone who could be a psychic vampire?

About the Author

Seressia Glass has always been a voracious reader, cutting her teeth on comics, cereal boxes—anything at hand. So it came as no surprise to family and teachers that she began writing stories about some of her favorite characters and her own original short stories. Her greatest achievement: winning the "Living the Dream" essay contest for the inaugural Martin Luther King, Jr. Holiday celebration in her hometown of Atlanta. Today, Seressia weaves the ideals in her winning essay into stories of diverse people realizing the universal dreams of love and acceptance.

A resident of Atlanta, Seressia works full time as an instructional designer for an international home improvement company. Visit her on the web at www.seressia.com.

About the Author